THE HOLLYWOOD HIGH CHRONICLES

book 7

Lifetimes

by **Melissa Velasco**

ISBN 978-1-960378-40-8   (paperback)
ISBN 978-1-960378-41-5   (eBook)

1st Edition

Models contracted through DMe Talent Agency:
Deidre Michelle (Agent) @dmetalentagency11

Front Cover Models: Maddie Dawn Cordero, Winslow Trullinger, Zane Barber, Blake Austin Monticello, Lillian Cordero, Riley Wooldridge, Sierra Kolb

Makeup and Hair: Nathaniel Garcia
Costume Concept: Melissa Velasco
Cover Concept: Melissa Velasco
Photography: Tino Duvick @brokenchainphotography
Front Cover Design: Tino Duvick and Anna Hall
Editor: Kyle Fager
Typeset: Anna Hall
Proofreader: Doris Nehrbass

This book is dedicated to two men who did the unthinkable with me. I've experienced nothing wilder in this lifetime than looking another human being in the eyes, and asking, "Wanna put on this flying squirrel suit, say screw it, and jump off this cliff together, with ZERO clue what we might hit?" I've done that twice, with my first husband, Robin (who I'm still friends with), and my second husband, Derek. It has been messy, dark, thrilling, terrifying, heartbreaking, and heartwarming. We failed a lot. We won even more.

So, to the two men that took a wild leap into the abyss with me, I thank you. Thank you for my children. Thank you for building something from nothing more than a fantasy of what could be. Thank you for being there through whatever life threw at us. You're both bat crap crazy, wonderful, volatile, saviors of a crazy gal, you call "Honey Badger" and "Poodle."

I love you guys. (I also hate you… Don't get too cocky!)

LIFETIMES

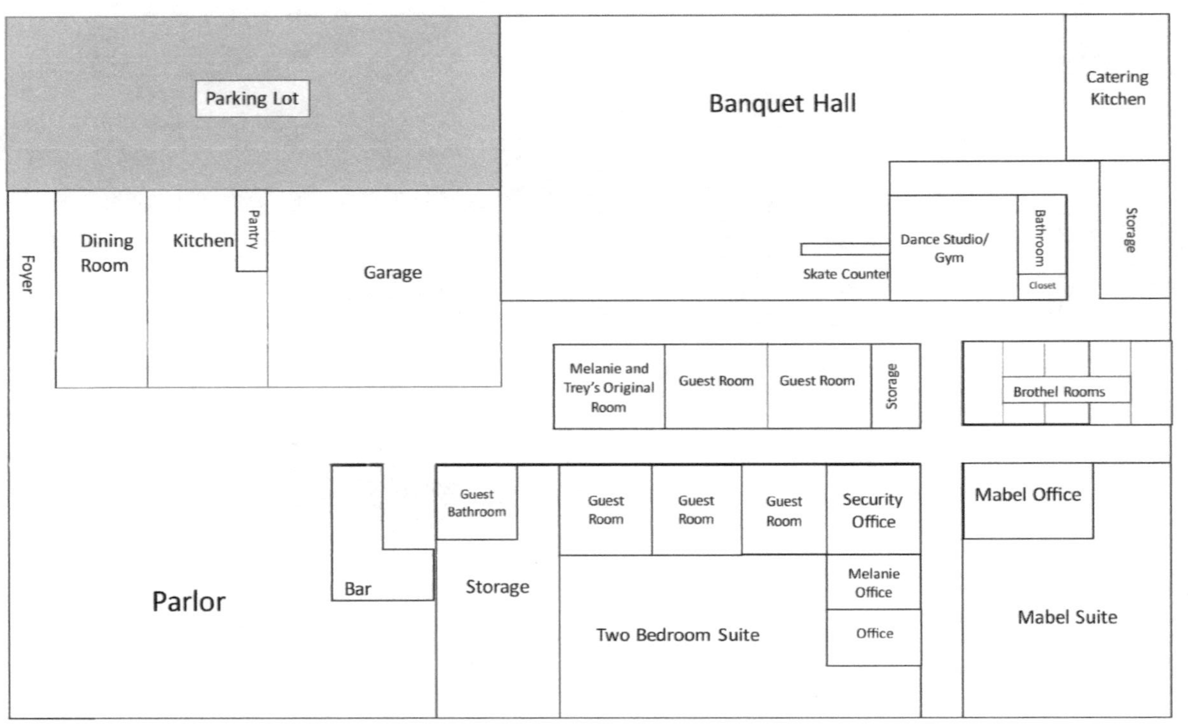

Mama Mabel's Brothel

CHAPTER 1

Now that I've parked, I'm unsure.

You need help, Melanie. Do it.

Spurred by my self-coaching, I open my car door. My flip-flop-clad feet hit the sandy pavement, and I head to the Beach Bar. I try to walk like I'm a human being instead of a pathetic heap of nothing. Stepping onto the porch reveals Rocco Rutelle.

"Melanie," Rocco breathes. He doesn't look happy to see me.

"Hi," I say hesitantly.

"Hi, honey." Awkwardly, he rubs his forehead and mutters, "Damn it. You need to know that Zane hasn't even looked at anyone."

"Neat," I reply, having no clue what to say. I haven't talked to Zane or Rocco in months, so this comes across as a bizarre icebreaker.

The story is long and tawdry. Zane Drell and I immediately had a romantic interest that wound up on ice because of our age difference. Because I had to utilize murder-and-madness tactics at my surprise handfasting to my longtime on-again, off-again boyfriend, Trey Valdez, Zane and I now fall into the "defunct best friend" category. Apparently, murder is Zane's threshold for crazy, and he bailed. Can't really blame him. Unfortunately, I currently find myself ass deep in alligators, so here I stand, ready to beg for a millionaire hero.

"Um, Melanie . . ."

"Just spill it," I blurt. "Why are you being weird?"

Rocco glances over his shoulder. I peek around him, only to spot Zane Drell, kissing a gorgeous blond.

"Ah, I see," I say, doing a solid job of hiding my dismay. "I just wanted to say hi," I quickly lie. "I'm going to head out."

"Maybe that's best," Rocco says, and it sends my stomach free-falling.

"Okay, bye," I reply awkwardly before turning to leave.

Unfortunately, there's Pepe barring my exit. "Seashellll," he foghorns.

"Fuck," I mutter. On one hand, I'm thrilled that Pepe was pleasant in his greeting. Considering how the last time he saw me, I decapitated a jackass with a katana, I wasn't sure how I'd be received. On the other hand . . .

"She was trying to covertly leave," Rocco hisses at Pepe, who winces. "Zane's eating Brandy's face."

Someone chooses this moment to crow out, "Melanie!" It's Razz, and he trots over to wrap me in a boisterous hug.

I fake a smile. Razz is just a random, but everyone here tends to receive me this way. As Razz lets go of me, I notice how Zane's head dejectedly drops. All at once, a stampede of exuberant dudes rushes to me, and they pass me around for hugs. It's one of the pitfalls of being the smallest girl in this crowd. A few of them squeeze my bruised back too hard, and I gasp.

Rocco's watching me suspiciously. "Put her down, Danny."

Finally, everyone wanders off.

"What's wrong?" Rocco asks once we're semi-alone.

"Nothing."

"You winced."

"I . . ." I take a huge breath, deciding this is it. "I need—"

"You're Melanie Strader," comes a shrill chirp. I look the chirp's way. It's Zane's date, and she's practically twittering as she scurries up to me. My eyes widen as she invades my space. *She's going to interrupt* now, *when I've FINALLY gutted up enough to ask for help?* "Yes?" I grunt.

"You were Riptide's wife!" She glances at the parking lot. "I saw you pull up in the teal car!"

"Freaking weird," I breathe. My overwhelmed brain can't quite seem to ratchet around this girl's syrupy-sweet vibe.

"I'm Brandy!"

"Of course, you are," slips from my lips disdainfully.

"You have your surfboard," she squeals, apparently noticing my board poking out of the passenger window of my car. "Me *toooooo!*" She wobbles her head about and then corrects herself. "Well, I have my boogie board, but samesies!"

"Holy crap, it's so happy," I say out of the side of my mouth to Rocco. Quickly, I cringe at my rudeness.

"Brandy, I think you should give Melanie a little space," Rocco warns.

"I HAVE to surf with Riptide's wife!" My eyes can't get any bigger as Brandy rattles me about, bubbling, "I was his BIGGEST fan!"

"Wooowww." I'm so out of sorts that I can't even fake my usual social pleasantries. I extricate my arm. "If you'll excuse me." I start to leave, but Brandy skips in step with me. I side-eye her and walk a little faster. Unfortunately, skipping is the perfect mode of quick transport, so she only has to pick up her gallop a little to keep pace.

When we get to my car, she studies my board. "So *cute*," she chirps.

"*Sooo* cute," I reply sarcastically.

"Brandy, where are you going?" Zane awkwardly questions. He and Rocco have apparently followed us.

"THIS is Melanie *STRADER*!" Brandy shrieks at a pitch that would surely make dogs howl.

Beach Bar patrons have gathered at the railing to watch. I'm known for my sarcastic humor around here. Most of these people also know that I have a history with Zane.

"I'm Melanie *Valdez*," I correct. I don't want to get into how I was Melanie Slate by birth, then Melanie Strader by a VERY brief and bizarre marriage, and now I'm Melanie Valdez by an even more bizarre handfasting.

Lucky for me, Brandy doesn't ask. Her mouth drops open like she's a cartoon bunny. "You found love again! Oooohhh!" She pounces, hugging me with awkwardly jiggly squishes courtesy of her ample girl parts.

"Fantastic," I mutter while I stand rail-rod stiff. As soon as she lets me go, I back up like I've been burned with acid happiness. I slide into my car, but Brandy kneels by the driver's side door, blocking me from closing it.

"Hang tight, girlfriend." She boings up to lean over the roof of my car. This causes her purple string-bikini-clad knockers to jostle in my face boisterously. "We brought our boards, Zannypoo!" she chortles. "Let's surf with Melanie. You'll love her. She's *sooo* nice."

"I *AM*?" I bellow through the open passenger window as I crawl across and climb out.

Rocco spurts laughter.

"I know Melanie's nice," Zane agrees. "I'm friends with her."

"You *are*?" I bluster rudely.

Zane rolls his eyes, choosing not to address our lack of communication. Instead, he informs Brandy, "Melanie isn't good being crowded, and you're currently hitting her with a sorority's worth of enthusiasm."

Cheerfully, Brandy waves a dismissive hand. "You're silly! We're girls, right, Melanie?" She cocks her head my way, so chipper it's creepy.

"I think she might be possessed, Zannypoo," I mutter.

Zane's mouth twitches with amusement. But in the next breath, he cringes.

"I see you have a type," I tell him with caged aloofness—and it's true; he does have a habit of chasing the bouncier bimbos.

"Girls, Girls, Girls" by Motley Crue comes through the patio speakers. As if the song has cranked her like a windup toy, Brandy boings about. I rattle my head in time with her bobbling boobs.

"This is the song I strip toooo," she squawks.

"Ah, yes. That makes sense," I slather. "I too am a dancer. What a kawinkydink."

"So, kawinkydinky," Brandy gushes. "Which club do you work at?"

"No, I'm the regular kind of dancer. You're smart, though. You'll make more in one week than I will my whole career." I look her up and down before cynically adding, "That's for damn sure."

Brandy flutters about. "Wanna see my routine?"

"YES, I *do*," I say with true enthusiasm. I can't think of anything better than watching Zane's girlfriend's stripper routine.

Laughter spurts from the patio crowd.

"Can I die now?" Zane mutters to Rocco, as Brandy starts jiggling and wiggling with gusto.

At Zane, I shine a look of bright amazement. "Oh, she's *goood*." I'm mesmerized as Brandy hits the pinnacle of her whole sleazy routine. When she finishes, I break into exuberant applause—to the amusement of everyone on the patio.

"You know what?" I ask her.

"What?" she crackles back happily.

"Did you know that Zaneypoo has a Tony Award for DANCE?"

She wrinkles her nose and beams. "What's that?"

"THAT is the BEST award for the *BEST* dancers," I inform, sounding so impressed.

"Zaneypoo, that's AMAAAZZZING," she exclaims like a slide whistle. She launches herself into Zane's arms.

When he looks at me like I'm insane, I give him a scrunchy shouldered sneer.

"Thanks," he mutters as she slops all over him.

"She's going to mount him like a Derby horse and ride him into the ocean," I murmur to Rocco, who sinks onto his haunches, laughing. "As I was saying . . ."

"Oh, yes, I'm sorry." Brandy floats around to face me.

My smile is surprising even to me. It feels incredible to be experiencing actual joy, even though it's at the expense of Zane. "Your boyfriend is an amazing dancer, and I'm thinking he should choreograph a new routine for you. I know a PERFECT song."

"Yeeesss!" Brandy claps and frolics.

"I have it in my car!" I say, all girly. "Would you like to hear it?" It occurs to me that this is a terrible plan, because I really do need Zane's help, but the discovery of Brandy cuts off my desire to ask for the help I came for. Maybe Zane should have done more about allowing me to leave unhindered. He knows better than to throw me to the bubble-headed wolves. But in his defense, she followed me to my car. In the end, I'll just have to be *Melanie* about this. My threshold for nonsense is very thin lately.

"I can't wait!" She's vibrating all over Zane. "Will you? Will you pleeeaaase? I'll have your name announced as my choreographer EVERY time I do my routine."

Everyone on the porch is leaning forward, absorbing every word. Zane looks like he senses the apocalypse is imminent. Rocco can't seem to stop staring at Brandy in disbelief.

"Oh, he would LOVE that," I assure. Yeah, it's catty, but I'm having trouble working through the dismay about how my hope for salvation is being hindered by a stripper called Brandy. I lean past my board, turn the key, and skip two tracks on the CD Tanner left in my stereo. "The Cars That Go Boom" by L'Trimm Valley-girls and bass-booms from the speakers. I whip around, taking in the sight of Brandy's hugely elated eyes in contrast to Zane's horror. I give him a boisterous thumbs-up. "Isn't this fun?" I lob at him. "Here I was, just trying to get help, and I'm making friends instead."

Zane's expression shifts to suspicion. He leans to Rocco, and they have a whispered conversation while I start singing the lyrics. Gracing this song with the word *lyrics* is a pretty generous stretch. This song . . . well, it's perfect for Brandy.

"I've never heard this song!" she squeals. "It's *sooo* cuuute."

"So cute!" I agree enthusiastically. "Try it."

"Will you dance with me?"

"I sure will!"

She starts wiggling about, and I wiggle with her. Try as I might to let this be her glorious moment, my dance technique shines through. Brandy stops gyrating and looks at me in sweet wonder. "You're *so* gooood. Can I introduce you to my club owner? I work at Round Up Ranch! He'll LOVE you!"

Zane rushes to say, "Brandy, I don't think Melanie's Round Up Ranch material."

"Now, Zane, don't be rude!" I scold him jokingly. I smile at Brandy. "That's so sweet of you, but I have a few jobs already."

"What jobs?" Brandy asks.

"I'm an actress. Your boyfriend is my partner at a talent agency. I'm also the event coordinator at Mama Mabel's."

"No WAY," Brandy gasps. "I hooked at Mama Mabel's for *three years!*"

"Say it ain't so!" I grin at Zane, who looks like he's in legitimate pain about this news. He loves Mabel but has always distanced himself from her working girls. His A-list celebrity status doesn't allow for dallying about at brothels. At least, that's what I'd thought before learning he's dating a hooker.

"I went by Ruby when I worked there," Brandy reveals.

My eyes widen. "Well, Brandy, your reputation precedes you. I've heard so many stories."

"Really?"

"You're a legend there." I look to Zane and add with pointed conviction, "A *legend!* You're a lucky guy."

Rocco hee-haws.

"What's your favorite story?" Brandy inquires.

"Ping-pong ball trick!" I bubble back, not actually believing the story I heard. "That's some SKILL!"

Brandy wiggles all over. "I do that routine at Round Up Ranch! Anyone who can catch one in their mouth gets a free Jell-O shot!"

A thrill ripples through me. My jaw drops. "Zane LOVES Jell-O shots. And of course, he just can't resist a talented cooter cannon."

Howling laughter, Rocco drapes himself over my car trunk.

"Oh my GOD," Zane groans as the onlookers on the porch erupt with laughter.

"I don't know how you can have such great aim," I say in a complimenting tone. "I heard that you once spread-eagle in the banquet room and hit a target clear on the other side."

"It's truuue," Brandy chortles.

"No way," I squawk in legit disbelief.

She slouches dejectedly. "I can't really claim that one though. Just before, I snorted half an eight ball, and it gave me superpowers."

Zane looks like he's having a heart attack as gasps punctuate from the porch.

"She's the one!" Razz bellows, raising his beer stein in Zane's honor.

I lean into Brandy, gossiping loudly, "My snap trap doesn't have that range. You'll have to teach me sometime."

Zane turns a shade of mottled red I've never seen before.

Brandy whips around and bellows, "Hey, Piper?"

"Yes-*sss*?" Piper, the Beach Bar waitress, replies with an amused lilt.

"Do you have any ping-pong balls?"

"I sure do!"

Brandy bounces with another little fairy clap. "I want to teach Melanie my trick. We'll need to sanitize the balls though. Don't want infections."

"That's always been my dating rule," I crow. "A good ball scrub really saves on the old penicillin bill."

Everyone cracks up while Zane covers his face and groans dramatically.

"What's the matter, Zane?" I ask. "Scared of a little ball scrub?"

People are howling at this point, while Brandy grins like a nut. "This is the best place *everrr*," she caws. "Everyone's so happy! I'm going to always be here."

Several patrons on the patio groan at the news.

"Gee, thanks, Zane," Miranda Lowell snarks. She's a high-powered professional surf chick who apparently likes her sanctuary to be bimbo-free. I don't know her well, but I suspect I'd like her.

I manage to calm my cackles, but no one else can claim the same. Piper gasps, "I'm going to die—I can't breathe," while she holds onto Pepe, who's not doing much better.

"Scurry up those ping-pong balls, Piper," I remind. "I'm gonna fire off a shot. Bet I can crack Zane in the forehead from across the patio."

Still hiding behind his hands, Zane busts up.

"Gotta tell ya, Zane, your new girlfriend sure turned my frown upside down." I jut a thumbs-up in the direction of the patrons. "I can always count on the Beach Bar."

An exuberant, "cheers," sounds from the crowded patio.

"On that note, I better skedaddle before those ping-pong balls materialize. Zane, so good to see you again. I sure am enamored with your new prize. Brandy, you're a doll. Rocco . . . Well, I see you're falling short on your best-friend duties." I sweep around to the Beach Bar crowd. "So good to almost catch up with you all. Now, if you'll excuse me, I must find a boy with a car that goes boom!"

My reference to the song lyrics brings snorts from the patio.

"Melanie, wait," Zane calls out, but his attempt to snag my arm is thwarted as Brandy melts against him and starts sucking on his neck.

"Hickeys," I say judgmentally. "Classy."

Zane gets distracted trying to wrestle her off him, leaving me an opening to get back in my car. I give a toot-toot to get Brandy to move her wiggly-jiggle to the side while she dances like no one's watching, and Zane wipes slobber from his neck. I pull out and hightail it to Surfrider Beach.

CHAPTER 2

"**W**here were you?" my husband, Trey Valdez, rages.

My eyes widen. "I went surfing and said hi to the Beach Bar crowd."

His eyes, meanwhile, narrow. "Is there a reason you didn't tell me where you were going?"

"I . . ." My head drops. "You were working. You hate when I disturb you. I wasn't gone that long."

"You got sand everywhere," Trey accuses.

I study the sand scattered on the hardwood floor. The crime doesn't fit the punishment, but it's always like that with him lately.

When Trey suddenly smirks, my heart pounds. He strides to me and picks me up before tossing me onto the bed. My shoulder slams into the headboard.

"I love you in that swimsuit," he growls.

Oh God, here we go.

Trey crawls like a panther onto the bed.

He shoves away from me, and I roll to my side as the bathroom door closes behind him. When I hear the shower start, an audible exhale escapes me. He's going to be occupied for a few minutes. I get up, quickly put on a hoodie and sweatpants, then slump into a chair at our little two-seater dining table and close my eyes, calming my panic. Trey used to be fueled by passion. Now it's anger that drives him.

Internally, I kick myself. I'd agreed to the handfasting mostly because our deceased daughter had to be avenged. But I could have taken advantage of an out from this damn situation right after she was avenged. Arrogantly, I decided to teach Trey a lesson by sticking with the marriage. Little did I know I was the one who was going to learn a lesson the hard way.

Shower over, Trey strides out from the bathroom and grabs some clothes from the dresser. He swiftly gets dressed before sitting at the end of the bed and putting on socks and tennis shoes. "I'm working late," he informs. "Don't wait up."

"Okay," I reply with as little inflection as possible to avoid making him mad.

"Have a good night," he says curtly before closing the door behind him.

As soon as I'm sure he isn't coming back, I rush to the bookshelf and grab the notebook tucked in the middle of a stack. I open it to where I left off.

> Take care of Finley. Always be nice to her,
> no matter how hard things get.
> Love,
> Melanie

It's late that night when Trey's distinct footsteps start sounding in the hall. I rush to yank open my nightstand drawer and slide the envelopes inside before lying back and grabbing my book.

The door opens, and Trey huffs as he looks my way. "You're still up?"

"I'm reading. How was work?"

"Perfect," he snarls as if to himself.

"I'm glad."

"Turn off the damn light. I hate trying to sleep while you read."

My reading habit never used to bother him, but now it seems to be a never-ending source of irritation.

"Cut me some slack. I could be doing a lot worse than reading."

All I get in return is a disgusted glare as he slides off his watch. He heads into the bathroom, and I listen while he brushes his teeth. He comes back and flops down while I turn off the light. I roll on my side, facing away from Trey, and my heart hammers as I silently cry.

CHAPTER 3

I turn from the intercom and find Mabel, Trey, and my parents staring at me. I jump. "Don't sneak up on me! Scaring me like that could level the damn building."

"Shouldn't your soulmate connection mean you're never able to sneak up on her?" Mabel ponders to Trey.

"Sorry, Mel," Trey says before explaining to Mabel, "I still have my end of our connection fuzzed out from when you and I were talking." He unfuzzes it. Trey almost always has me blocked off. No clue why he's trying to pretend he doesn't.

I take my usual seat at the conference table. "And what was that clandestine meeting about?"

The mood is serious as they all take their seats. I sigh. Whatever this is, it feels heavy.

Trey checks his watch. "We have ten minutes until Tori and Demitri arrive."

"All right, here it is," my stepfather, Rich Fairtrade, says. "The production company is sending me to Japan for six months to train a new team of animators." He glances my mom's way.

"We want to give you a choice, Melanie," Mom says hesitantly. "I can either stay behind, and you can keep your usual schedule . . . or . . ."

I work to keep my expression neutral. "Or . . . ?"

My mom sighs. "Or I can go with Rich to Japan." She rushes to add, "It's not that I want to abandon you here, and I'm worried you'll think that. Realistically though, you have a home here at Mabel's, and you have Trey, so we thought it would be nice if I could—"

I cut her off calmly, even though my heart's about to beat out of my chest. "Japan is a once-in-a-lifetime opportunity."

Mom and Rich beam.

"You won't be upset if we both go?" Rich asks.

"Not at all," I casually respond even as fear rips through me. Emotionally, I always cling to my days at my parents' house, but with them gone, I'll be stuck here. I can't be alone, without security measures, four days a week.

Rich turns a satisfied expression on my mom. "Well, Carol, we have packing to do. I'll call the studio and let the coordinator know to purchase your ticket."

My parents stand, and Trey and I hug them and wish them a safe trip. They say their goodbyes before rushing out. They're as excited as a couple of teenagers.

SIX MONTHS' living together uninterrupted?

Mabel grins. "I'm moving the two of you into the two-bedroom suite at the far end of the hall. It'll give you more room."

In the next moment, Victoria Garcia and Demitri Cantrell breeze through the door. Victoria is all things curvy and gorgeous, with her raven hair and sultry way. Demitri is a stunning brunet with an effortless ease about him. He's also my best friend . . . or was, until things got really complicated.

Constance is on their heels, with our breakfast. They take a seat, and Constance serves us efficiently before taking her leave.

When Mabel glances at my day planner, her eyebrows furrow. "Melanie, your schedule is terribly full. Did you leave any time for work?"

I laugh. "What you're seeing are all the events I've booked FOR work."

Her eyes widen. "You're kidding!"

"I know we've got a performance review scheduled," Trey explains to Mabel. "But we thought we'd have you sit in on our meeting so you can get an idea of how we're operating. Particularly now that our team has expanded to include Demitri and Victoria."

He gestures my way, and I take over the meeting. "We've got eleven banquet hall events in January. All are booked, all deposits collected."

"ELEVEN?" Mabel squawks.

I nod. "This coming Friday, we've got a *Havana Nights* bachelorette party, complete with male strippers, in the banquet hall."

"If you don't mind, I'd like to assist you with the actual party and not just the theme design," Victoria offers in an overly professional tone.

I nod enthusiastically. "Yes, indeed. I'm planning to personally oversee everything." I turn to Trey. "Also, you need to contact Deb and Presley. They'd like to be your bouncers for the event. We're thinking female bouncers would be good, given the female crowd." Victoria and I can't keep up our professional ruse, breaking into enthusiastic grins as Demitri and Trey raise eyebrows our way. Demitri is Victoria's boyfriend, but luckily, he tends to have a sense of humor.

"Uh-huh," Trey says, deadpan.

I wave a hand his way as if to clear his speculative mood. "I'll confirm with Deb and Presley. You don't need to worry about a thing. Anyhow, the following night is a beach-theme birthday party. So there's no need to change the decorations."

We continue our meeting, coordinating all the themes for the month. When we're done, Mabel scoffs. "You managed to book a wedding reception and a children's birthday party at a brothel?"

I nod and slide a flyer across to her. "I'm marketing the banquet hall as a separate event space."

Mabel takes the flyer and reads, "Moonlight Magic Event Center. Your full-service planners for every event, big and small." She looks at me. "This is working?"

"Like a charm. Besides, you keep the outside of the brothel so lowkey that most people don't know what it is." I slide another flyer her way. "I've marketed the brothel parties separately. We've got three bachelor parties scheduled."

Demitri and Victoria finish making their lists for the month and head to their shared office to get rentals lined up for the different themes. Mabel turns to me and Trey after they leave. "I can't believe the job you two are doing. There's no need for a review."

We nod our appreciation.

"If someone had told me a year ago that Melanie Slate and Victoria Garcia would be working together, I would have died of shock," Trey jokes.

I laugh. Victoria used to date Trey, and until very recently, she and I were mortal enemies.

"Demitri and Victoria should move into the room the two of you are being moved out of," Mabel suggests. "With so many events booked, they'll need a place to crash."

Trey shrugs. "You'll want to run that past Demitri first. Last I heard, there's trouble in paradise."

On hearing the news, I intentionally remain neutral. There was interest between Demitri and me. *Not anymore,* I think. He's spent the past four months ghosting me.

Mama Mabel takes her leave, and Trey and I head to our desks to get to work.

CHAPTER 4

Trey opens the door, and we quickly discover that all personal items have already been moved out, and the room has been restored to a guest bedroom.

"I guess the housekeeping staff moved quickly," I say, covering my nervousness. "Let's go see where we're living now."

We walk down the long hallway, past the rooms belonging to the girls who work for Mama Mabel, and turn right. We find our *Trey and Melanie Valdez* gold metal plaque already relocated to one of the doors toward the end of the hall. Our new keys have been left in the lock. Trey glances at me curiously as he opens the door and flips on the lights.

Our mouths drop open. This plan must have been in the works for a while. Mabel's decorator has mimicked the gray, red, and black décor from our previous room, but this space is like a whole new world. We find ourselves in an entryway with our handfasting wedding picture displayed on the foyer wall above an antique entry table with a crystal vase full of red roses.

We walk into the gorgeous living room with black velvet chairs and couch. We have full bookshelves and two squishy reading chairs with lamps next to them. There's an ornate four-top dining table set back in a little nook by another door.

Trey crosses and turns on the light to that room before announcing, "We have a kitchen."

"No way!" I rush over and am greeted with a little white kitchen that appears to be fully equipped. I open drawers to confirm, and everything we could need is here.

We head back through the living room and discover our bedroom and a huge bathroom. I glance at Trey, and he seems pleasantly surprised. Hope swells that with more space and a fresh start, Trey and I might actually repair our relationship.

We continue down the little hall. Trey opens another door. His face falls slack. It's a smaller bedroom decorated with a teddy bear theme. It houses a baby crib, a changing table, and a little dresser. Tears brim as heartbreak seers through me. Trey slams the door closed. He takes a shuddering breath before storming into the living room. I follow him, wrestling with tantamount emotion. That moment of hope that things might improve between Trey and me dissolves.

He slowly turns to face me, and his vibe shifts furious. "I'm not okay with that!" he bellows. "Did you tell her to put in a nursery?"

"I didn't even know we were being moved!" I say defensively. "Trey, we need to work through losing the baby."

"It was months ago," he reminds coldly. "Get over it, Melanie."

"The trauma of my miscarriage was monumental." I shake my head, pleading, "Please, Trey! We have to work through this."

He snorts, caging down like he always does. "You're so unhinged," he bellows.

Now for the deflection, I think, anticipating his next tactic. I know his patterns. They scare the hell out of me.

"Wanna explain that whole male-stripper-review elation of yours?" He demands as he storms my way.

I rush back against the wall, terrified. He's right on the edge of losing control, and I can empathically feel it.

"I was just joking around with friends," I gasp.

"Be professional, Melanie," he roars, looming over me.

"We work at a brothel. I don't think strippers is quite as *aghast* a topic here as it would be on Wall Street."

His fists clench, and I'm rattling scared. "You work at an *event* center," he snarls.

"I'll apologize to Mabel," I whimper.

Trey glares at me with narrowed eyes, the air so stifling, it's hard to breathe.

"I'm going to be working late again," he says as if in challenge.

When I nod frantically, he takes three steps back, but even creating the distance is just part of his dominance tactics. He's feigning giving me breathing room, but his energy surges maniacal. He smirks defiantly as he checks his back pocket for his wallet. My heart hammers. Every time he grabs his wallet, it means he'll be working extra late.

He stalks out the suite door.

My knees give out, and I sit frozen on the floor for a long stretch. All my usual badassery is gone. While I'm no stranger to tearing someone apart, literally and figuratively, I have a standing rule that I don't physically harm my soulmates. It's been engrained into me over the course of all my lifetimes. They've certainly harmed me though—even killed me in past lives—and I've been petrified for several months that Trey is going to murder me.

I'm terrified to go to Mabel, because she thinks Trey hung the moon. She wouldn't be able to be my secret confidante who helps me. Instead, she'd likely drag me to Trey, reveal my fear, and then wander off to obliviously do something else. I'm positive he'd kill me if that happened.

Of course, I've considered going to my parents, but I never went through with it because I didn't want to put them in danger. Trey is the head of security around here for a reason. He's ruthless, conniving, and very pragmatic. Connected to my work, school, and social group, he's entrenched in every part of my life. I'm thoroughly trapped with a monster who regales in the power he holds over me.

It wasn't long after the surprise marriage he forced on me that his hatred of me began to escalate. I distinctly remember the night everything shifted. Two days after our wedding, he left, claiming he needed some "me time." He came home the next morning with a black eye and has been raging mad at me ever since. I made the mistake of asking who gave him the shiner, and he was so catastrophically angry that I haven't mentioned it again. I tried to search his memory, but he's been all Fort Knoxed. The shield he keeps over his memories doesn't even weaken when he sleeps. So I don't know who hit him. I only know he's hiding something, and it's bad.

I can't do this anymore. Zane's the only one who had a shot of getting me out of here.

My hands shake as I start to feel the onset of an asthma attack. I pull my trusty inhaler from my pocket, and it takes three doses before I can get a solid breath. Tears roll, puddling on the floor. I shake my head, finally giving up.

This is it. Now that it's time, I survey my feelings. *There it is. Relief. That's what I was waiting for.*

Slowly, I rise on shaky legs. A ritualized feeling thrums as I make my way through an apartment suite I have no connection with, selecting candles as I go. I head into the bathroom connected to our new bedroom and set them on the counter, lighting them. Satisfied that I've achieved the right glow, I flip off the light.

Suddenly worried, I scurry into the bedroom and look in the nightstand drawer. All my stuff from my old nightstand has been moved into this one, and I exhale hard. I grab the envelopes from the drawer, along with my framed wedding photo, and rush back to the bathroom.

I study the picture. Our hands are tied together, arms above our heads while we flash devil horns at a crowd of friends and loved ones you can't see in the picture. I was so uncomfortable. Everything about the moment was wrong, and you can see it in my eyes, even though I'm smiling in the picture.

I take the frame apart and leave it, along with the photo, on the counter before starting the water in the bathtub. As it fills, I undress.

Realization that I have a route I haven't tried yet gives me pause. *Demitri* . . . I shake my head. Demitri barely speaks to me. He so thoroughly wrote me off that I don't dare try him. Besides, since the wedding, he has only answered *one* of my calls.

I swallow hard and try another option, dialing Adam's number. Adam Stone was my original soulmate. While he can be a flippant jackass, he might still be able to help me. When a vision of what Adam might do flashes in my mind, I hang up the call on the second ring. If he kills Trey, he goes to jail. Considering that he and his wife have infant twin girls, that's a no-go. In truth, that's what's been holding me back from going to him this whole time.

My heart hammers as I decide to try Zane one more time. I dial his number. It rings four times before his outgoing message comes on. My head hangs. The message beeps, and I say, "I love you . . ." It comes out a whimper. "I tried," whispers from me before I hang up.

Clarity fills me. I know how my life works. If I was meant to be saved, Zane would have answered. He didn't. So I'm resigned to my fate.

A quick smack against the counter, and the glass rectangle from my picture frame breaks. The glass on the floor cuts my feet, but I ignore the pain and the blood as I step into the tub. I grip one of the jagged shards of glass, then sink neck-deep into the water.

Eyes open or closed? My gaze shifts to my wrist, and my eyes close.

CHAPTER 5

It's lunchtime as I approach Actors' Alley with Presley and Victoria. As soon as we get there, I hear a gorgeous redhead partway through a flirtatious, ". . . help but notice you."

Trey looks amused as he glances up at the pretty girl's face from his spot sitting on the ground by our group's lunch table. "Is that so?" he flirts back.

Our friends are grinning as they realize I just overheard someone hitting on my husband. I couldn't care less. I'm dead inside.

"Let the games begin," Marcus Vinsky jokes.

Victoria cracks her knuckles and jokingly hisses, "Do we kill her now, or toy with her first?"

"Hey, babe," Trey calls out.

My mood bristles deep under the dull hum I've been experiencing for several days since Trey found me in the tub. He's totally different in public than behind closed doors. I now know that the public *loving-husband* routine is an act, and I feel like an idiot for clinging to it.

The girl who was hitting on him whips her head my way. She's standing with her back to our group, oblivious that they're Trey's friends. Awareness seems to dawn, because she moves slowly away from them and puts her back to the bungalow wall.

Interesting. She's got fight training.

"I just hit on Shivers, didn't I?" she asks my friends.

My group is known as the Hellcats. Long story short, we were taken in by a biker gang called the Hellhounds that run the Hollywood underground. Big Joe, the leader of the Hounds, gave us all handles to go by. Trey's is Shivers, and the fact that this girl knows this information might just be troublesome.

"You did," Arch Terani answers cautiously.

"You're Anarchy," the girl says, looking and sounding in awe of Arch. This isn't surprising. True to his black trench coat with an anarchy symbol painted on the back, Arch is a force to be reckoned with. He's sporting his usual round-lens sunglasses, and his curly black hair hangs loose around his shoulders.

The girl looks at Trey. He takes his hand out of his denim jacket pocket and wiggles his ring finger, displaying his black wedding band.

She sighs. "Damn it. I apologize. The last thing my dad said when I was on my way out the door was, 'Don't piss off the Hellcats.'" She glances my way. "You're La Diabla?" She winces. "I mean Firebird."

I raise an eyebrow. "Depends. What's your handle?"

"Dragonfly," the girl responds hesitantly.

"Who's your dad?"

"He runs the Raptors."

"George? He's awesome!"

Dragonfly's eyes soften. "Everyone's glad you're okay. I'm sorry, Melanie."

Long story short: The biker clubs all know each other, and Dragonfly's being the daughter of George, who leads the Raptors, gives her an immediate in with the Hellcats by association. A guy named Mack and his biker club, the Reapers, invoked Redemption Clause against me for leveling them when they tried to steal our supplies during a natural disaster. They didn't know that I was pregnant. I miscarried when Mack gut-punched me. Mack got his, but what I went through was horrific. That event started the downward spiral that has become my personal hell.

"Thank you," I respond quietly. "We can trust her."

Everyone's shoulders relax, the tension dissolving.

"That would make you Stella, correct?" Trey asks her.

Stella nods before focusing on me. "I sincerely apologize for hitting on Trey. I wasn't trying to stir up trouble." She tips her head Trey's way and says to me with a hint of harmless, girly gossip, "I mean . . . can you blame me?"

"He *is* a cutie-patootie," Victoria chirps.

Trey chuckles.

Marcus quips, "New nickname achieved!"

Everyone laughs.

"Don't even think about it, unless you're sick of your thirty-five-dollar-an-hour job whooping thug ass two nights a week," Trey warns Marcus.

Marcus, Demitri, and Arch, along with Tanner Devick and Javier Hernandez, all work for Trey as bouncers at Mama Mabel's.

"Sorry, boss," Marcus says, but he's trying not to laugh.

"Well, Dragonfly," Arch says, "sounds like you're one of us. Have a seat."

Her eyebrows rise. "Are you serious?"

"You're a biker club kid. We take care of our own."

Stella sits next to Susan and surveys everyone. "I'm a little starstruck. You guys are legendary among the biker kids." She turns to me. "Thank you for not incinerating me."

"I don't burn people to ash for talking to Trey."

Stella narrows her eyes. "Can you really control fire?"

The memory of expanding the fire in Jet's car from a minor flame to an inferno clouds my senses with a touch of posttraumatic fear.

Trey feels my emotional shift as my shield wavers. "That asshole deserved it, Mel. The number of women he murdered was staggering." Trey looks at Stella and answers on my behalf. "Yes. She can."

"The other kids aren't going to believe I'm having lunch with you," Stella says. "I'm not exactly one of the popular kids with that crowd."

"Are the biker club members' kids all connected?" Trey asks.

She shrugs. "Kind of. Some run together." She stops to think about it, then adds, "It's complicated. They don't all get along. The Jags' kids are rude and gross, so they stick to themselves. The Crushers', Dragons', and Raptors' kids all run together."

"Why haven't we met them before?" Tanner asks. "We know all their parents."

"We've been instructed to avoid you guys. I'm one of the calm, quiet ones. The others can be rowdy and immature . . ." Stella pauses, and her eyes widen. "The parents don't want one of the hotheads to challenge you."

"Interesting," Trey mumbles.

"The bikers won't even tell us the stories. We piece stuff together from rumors, and whatever we overhear." She tips her head toward Trey and me. "How serious does it really get if someone pisses them off?"

"Catastrophic," answers Bear, one of the spiritual gurus of our group.

"Welcome to Hollywood High," I mutter to Stella before walking away alone.

Exhausted and covered in sweat, I exhale.

"Damn it, Melanie!" Mr. Isley barks. "Get it together."

I tip my head back, beyond frustrated.

Unrelenting, Mr. Isley bellows, "Earth to MELANIE!"

I look at him with dead eyes. "What?"

"What is wrong with you today?" Mr. Isley says, exasperated. "You're two counts behind. Do you want to do this piece, or not? I can give the lead to Jayla."

"Yes, sir. I want to do the piece. Give me a second, please." I cross to my dance bag and fitfully pull off my sweatpants, revealing little black shorts. I twist my wedding ring off and toss it onto the sweatpants. On the verge of a meltdown, I swallow hard.

"Are you ready now?" Mr. Isley asks sarcastically.

I notice Demitri starting at the back of my leg. "We need a minute," he says. "Drill hell out of everyone else."

When I turn and look at my leg in the mirror, I see the massive bruise revealed when I pulled off my sweatpants. I internally wince at my disrobing shortsightedness.

Mr. Isley looks at the bruise and gestures toward his office. "Head in and close the door."

Demitri struts into the office, then turns in the doorway to look at me. My heart racing, I wonder where Demitri and I stand. He's been so damn distant. Losing him has been very difficult, and I desperately need him back. I realize he can't handle me being married to Trey, but there's so much he doesn't know. I cross the dance studio and join Demitri in the office before he closes the door. I squeeze my eyes shut, feeling feel like I'm going to pass out.

"Why are you bruised?" Demitri asks.

I begin to sob, and tears roll down my cheeks.

"Melanie," Demitri says softly.

That one word holds the weight of everything I've needed to hear. I dive into his arms, holding on to him so hard that I shake.

"Talk to me, Meley," he murmurs in my ear.

I make a keening sound, high-pitched and desperate. Demitri sets me on the edge of the desk and puts his hands flat on my back, sending a calming wave of energy through his hands. As my head falls to his shoulder, and I finally breathe, we inhale and exhale together, taking a moment.

"I've missed you," Demitri says quietly.

Unable to make a coherent thought as my mind races, I stare up at Demitri, my eyes pleading for help.

"Why do you have that bruise on your leg?"

My expression mangles. *Where do I even start?*

"You never wear long sleeves in the dance studio," Demitri says suspiciously. "I didn't realize it until now. Take off the flannel, Melanie."

I try to leave, but Demitri grabs my hand. "What has he done to you?"

"Nothing."

Demitri unbuttons my flannel and attempts to pull my sleeve off, but the cuffs are buttoned. "Melanie, what are you hiding?" he asks, dread on his face. He pulls my flannel off my shoulders and surveys my sports-bra-clad back. "Your back is bruised." He tips his head warily. He grabs the cuff and unbuttons it, pulling the flannel off.

I can barely breathe. I expect Demitri to scream at me, but he doesn't. He gasps, and his thumb rubs my wrist.

CHAPTER 7

A sobbing wreck, Demitri turns off his Jeep. He flies out, slams his door, and races to my side to get me out of the car. He's on a mission, and I'm not in charge. I'm caught between terror and hope. I need help so badly, but I'm afraid. There's no going back now that someone knows. I'm facing a complete overhaul of my life, and I'm terrified of how messy it's about to get.

Demitri wraps his arm around my waist and starts to drag me up the walkway. When I don't run fast enough, he scoops me up and runs the rest of the way to the front door. He manages to turn the knob with his hand that's holding my back. As he frantically hip bumps it open, it slams against the wall, and we skid through.

"HELP!" Demitri bellows in desperation.

Mr. Cantrell hops up from the couch, stunned. "What's wrong?"

I start to inform him. "I have an issue . . ."

Demitri interrupts me as he plunks me on my feet. "She *must* stay here tonight!" he screeches.

"Done." Mr. Cantrell grabs Demitri by the arms. "I know whatever this is, is serious, but I need you to calm down and talk to me."

Frantic, Demitri grabs my hand and unbuttons the cuff of my flannel. I yank my hand back, spiraling into a panic because this is all moving so fast. Demitri's eyes are wild. Panting, he doubles over, his hands on his knees.

"Everyone, slow down," Mr. Cantrell implores. "Demitri, I can empathically feel that her emotions are cyclonic. Her primary emotion is fear that this will unravel everything." He looks to Demitri. "You're making her panic worse. We're going to fix whatever this is, but we can do so calmly."

"You aren't safe with me here!" I wail. I rush to the window and look out, surveying the street like a nut.

Mr. Cantrell crosses to the door and locks the bolt. I point to the chain lock, and he slides it into place.

I exhale hard.

Mr. Cantrell gives the little security chain a comically unsure glance. "See, Mel, we're safe now," he says, like it's preposterous.

Demitri takes a huge breath. "I need to set a few ground rules."

"Okay," Mr. Cantrell replies, supportive, but seemingly confused.

"No panicking. No calling an ambulance."

Mr. Cantrell nods. "I think I can agree to those terms. If I can't, we'll discuss it before I do anything. Now, tell me what's happening."

Demitri turns to me. "I need you to give me your hand."

I close my eyes and put the back of my hand in Demitri's. He pulls up my sleeve to my elbow, revealing the two-day old cut marks.

"Shit!" Mr. Cantrell exclaims. "I'm pulling every set of blinds down and freezing time."

Confused, I look to Demitri.

He exhales hard and explains, "My dad used to freeze time when things became too much for me. We'd be in our own world, without anything from the outside interfering. Phones silenced, blinds pulled, nothing but a safe space where we made rules that we needed to get through it."

A wave of relief so strong that it nearly drops me reverberates through the house. It's not audible, but the resounding energy wave is enough to make everyone's head spin.

"There it is." Mr. Cantrell puts his hands around my face. "Do you need time to stop?"

I nod desperately.

"You need to call your parents for permission to stay here," Mr. Cantrell guides.

I shake my head. "My parents are in Japan. I need to let Trey know that I'm not coming home."

"Oh boy," Mr. Cantrell mutters.

"I'll call the staff line."

"The moment the call ends, time stops," Mr. Cantrell says.

I dig my cell phone out of the front pouch of my backpack and dial the kitchen line at Mabel's. Constance answers, and I inform her, "It's Melanie. I need to handle a few things. Can you let Trey know that I'll see him at school on Thursday?"

"You aren't coming home?" Constance asks, concern in her voice. "Is everything all right?"

"No. I'm fine. Something unexpected came up, and my parents aren't here to handle it. Family business. I don't want to disturb Trey during class. I won't have cell phone coverage."

"No problem. I'll let Mama Mabel and Trey know. Talk to you soon."

I hang up and turn off my phone, tossing it in my backpack.

"Ground rules. There's only one. When time stops, none of the normal rules apply." Mr. Cantrell looks at me pointedly. "Where do you want to start?"

I look at Demitri. "I can't have you gone. That distant look you give me every day is gut-wrenching."

Demitri shakes his head. "I won't be gone. The second I saw your wrist, all gone was gone."

I manage a little smile. I love that Demitri riddles like I do when he's flustered.

His dad looks at Demitri pointedly. "She refills energy reserves when she sleeps, correct?"

Demitri nods.

I put my hands flat on Demitri's chest. His reserves are so bottomed out that his usually vibrant energy only faintly hums. "That's why you emotionally cratered. Anarchy could reign, and you'd stand there, calm and stoic. I'm sorry, Demitri. I didn't notice because I was so out of sorts."

"I don't reach a meditation state anymore, and I haven't slept well in months."

I narrow my eyes. "You needed to tell me, D."

Demitri rubs his face, and his dad says, "He was convinced you were okay, and he didn't want to screw your life up."

"I've definitely not been okay," I scoff. My head sags.

"Are you comfortable sleeping in Demitri's room?" Mr. Cantrell asks.

It may be unorthodox, but so are we. As energy workers, we can stabilize each other while we sleep. Sure, it creates some boundary challenges, but desperate conditions like we're in require unconventional options.

I nod. "I need to sleep without night terrors."

"Do you want to discuss your wrist now, or sleep and talk about it later?" Demitri asks.

"Later. I'm exhausted."

"You need to promise me you aren't going to hurt yourself if

I let you sleep without discussing this first," Mr. Cantrell says in an authoritative voice.

"I promise."

He looks to Demitri. "Pull down all the blinds, and double-check that your windows are locked."

"Thank you for helping me," I say to Mr. Cantrell. "I had no intention of piling up in your son's bed when I got up this morning."

"I know. I wouldn't usually allow it, but you are a special case. Where is your car?"

"In the school student parking lot," I reply.

Mr. Cantrell looks at Demitri. "I'm going to have my brother drive me to get Melanie's car now so that Trey doesn't camp out by it when he realizes Melanie is missing. I'll park it in the garage, so no one knows she's here. I'll be back. Will you two be okay?"

We nod, and I give him my car key. "Thank you."

"You're welcome, kiddo," Mr. Cantrell says while he dials a number on his cell phone and heads out the door.

Demitri locks the front door and guides me to his room. It's perfectly neat like it always was when I used to come over. He closes the bedroom door, checks the window lock, and pulls the blinds down. He pulls back the comforter, and we climb in. When he turns his back like he used to when we'd fall asleep together, I curl up against him, my mind a whirlwind of a million thoughts and emotions.

We lie there for a long moment before he says, "Nope." He scootches about.

I chuckle as the covers dance while Demitri disappears. He settles in, all his tension melting away as he laces his hand with mine and pulls it under his chin. He wiggles again before exhaling hard. Within moments, I feel his energy shift to a sleep state.

I lie there for a long while, wrapped in Demitri's warbling energy. He's dangerously exhausted.

The door cracks open, and Mr. Cantrell peeks in.

I smile at him and whisper, "Can you come here?"

Mr. Cantrell looks quizzically at the mound under the covers.

I giggle. "I love it when Demitri's a toddler. I'm burning up, though. He's a furnace when his energy reserves fill. Can you pull the bedspread off us? I don't want to move. He's happy."

Mr. Cantrell carefully pulls down the bedspread and sheet, revealing Demitri wrapped around me, gripping my hand under his chin, still with his cheek on my stomach. His leg is tangled in both of mine.

Mr. Cantrell's expression softens almost painfully. "Are you okay with this?"

I nod and rub Demitri's hair. He sighs in his sleep.

"He's not usually this snuggly, but I love it."

Mr. Cantrell sits on the edge of the bed while he surveys his son contemplatively. "That's exactly how he used to sleep with his favorite stuffed bear when he was a baby."

I quirk my mouth. "I like being a stuffed bear."

"I know he's supposed to be helping *you*," Mr. Cantrell says, "but I think you both are going to need help. You have no idea how bad things have been around here. I've never dealt with anything like Demitri the past four months. He got home the day after your handfasting, and sobbed until he threw up. I've hardly slept since, unless Demitri was at school. I'm ready every day when he pulls into the driveway. When he gets inside the house, he melts down." Mr. Cantrell rubs his face hard.

"I had no idea that was happening."

"I figured. There's zero way you would let him live like that had you known."

"He's been so distant," I say dejectedly. "It's like I was a ghost to him. I started to think he hated me."

"Nope," Mr. Cantrell scoffs. "He certainly doesn't. What happened to make you two talk again?"

When I exhale hard, it makes Demitri flit about in his sleep. I rub the back of his head softly and whisper, "You're okay."

He settles down again with a big sigh.

Once we're sure he's still asleep, I answer. "I have a big bruise. He saw it when I took off my sweatpants in rehearsal. He marched me into Mr. Isley's office, closed the door, and suddenly he was Demitri again. Then he saw my wrist and collapsed emotionally in way very similar to what you described."

Mr. Cantrell takes my hand from the back of Demitri's head and looks at my wrist. I giggle when Demitri makes little snuffling noises. I rub his jaw with the thumb he's clutching under his chin. Demitri scrunches his chin tighter against my hand and settles down again.

Mr. Cantrell's penetrating gaze stares into my eyes. "Melanie, I'm scared I'm going to lose both of you. I really need you to open up while you're here."

"I'm incredibly conflicted about being here," I admit.

"Please tell me what you're thinking."

I swallow hard. "I'm terrified of what Trey will do."

Mr. Cantrell's gaze deepens. "How dangerous is he?"

"Deadly," I reply.

"How pissed will he be that you don't come home tonight?"

I shrug. "That could go two ways. He'll either be thrilled to have me out of his hair, or he'll hunt me down. If he does, I guarantee that Adam, Demitri, and Zane are where he'll start. I need to warn the other two."

"Trey won't go after Zane. He's intimidated by him." Mr.

Cantrell shakes his head, amused. "He might go after Adam, but Adam can hold his own."

"True," I reply, my breath hitching. "What about you and Demitri? Are you willing to face this?"

Mr. Cantrell smirks. "I'm meaner than I look, and that guy," he gestures to his sleeping son, "is a beast."

I look down at Demitri, unsure.

Mr. Cantrell gives me a pointed look. "Trust me. He covers it well, but Demitri is easily as vicious as Trey and Adam."

"Thank you for helping me."

Mr. Cantrell blows out a huge breath. "You're welcome. You need to sleep. I'll be in the living room, alert and watching for trouble. I've got the house shielded in case Trey comes looking for you." He gets up and heads for the door. "Holler if you need me."

CHAPTER 8

When Mr. Cantrell comes out of the kitchen, he's carrying plates. "Let's eat in the living room."

I smile nostalgically.

"What is that expression about?" he asks.

I sigh. "My parents and I always eat while we watch TV in the living room. Trey has this 'eating should be done at the table' rule."

"Why does eating have to involve a table?" Demitri asks.

I roll my eyes. "There are all these proper formalities. It's just how Trey operates. When I ask him to explain, he has this pompous 'rules are rules' lecture prepared."

As we all settle in, Mr. Cantrell assures me, "You fit in perfectly with us, Melanie."

I smile. "Thank you. I appreciate a break from my nightmare. He's unrelenting. He badgered me for fifteen minutes a week ago because I kicked off my flip-flops and sat on my feet in his car seat."

"You do that every time you get in my Jeep." Demitri informs his dad, "Her feet and hands are like ice cubes. They turn purple half the time."

"You likely have Raynaud's syndrome," Mr. Cantrell says. "It's a circulatory condition."

I hold out my hands, and my fingers are slightly purple.

He nods. "Yup. Raynaud's." He looks to Demitri. "Your mother had Raynaud's. Leave it to you to find a replica of your mother. They even look a lot alike."

"The first time I saw Meley, I thought she looked like my mom's picture," Demitri says wistfully.

"All the more reason for us to keep her alive," Mr. Cantrell insists. "You need to fill us in, Melanie."

I take a deep breath. "Trey has become so controlling and emotionally manipulative that I can't handle it. My life is already hard." I look at Mr. Cantrell. "I don't mean that as some whiny-brat complaint."

"I watched what you had to do on your wedding night," Mr. Cantrell reminds me. "I believe that your life is hard."

It takes everything I've got to ignore the memory that boils up. The handfasting was a disastrous surprise that Trey selfishly heaped on me. The night started off terrible, given that I had zero interest in getting married, and was physically torn up from healing work that Demitri was partway through to repair damage my botched miscarriage caused. Add to it that Retribution was invoked on me from an old problem I had with a biker gang called the Reapers, and I landed in a hell of a battle. It worked out, because they had a healer named Warlock who was able to repair my barren state, but it was a brutal night. I murdered several, and I'm stunned Mr. Cantrell welcomed me into his home after he watched me decapitate with a katana.

I nod. "I appreciate your understanding. Anyhow, whenever we're alone, he's erratic, dismissive, rude, harsh, and on edge. He's completely different at school."

"Does he hit you?" Mr. Cantrell asks.

My chin shakes as I put my plate on the coffee table and rub my face hard. "Trey . . ." My head drops. "He . . ."

Demitri gets up, leaving his plate on the floor, and sits next to me on the couch. He takes my hand, squeezing it.

I take a deep breath. "The bruises are caused in bed," I blurt out.

"What!" Demitri bellows.

"Calm, Demitri," Mr. Cantrell says as I wince.

"He's always had rough tendencies," I explain. "It didn't use to bother me, because I'm me, you know."

Mr. Cantrell chuckles

"Sorry," I whimper, blushing.

"Don't be," Mr. Cantrell says. "I can handle the topic. I shouldn't have laughed, but you're a wild one. Keep filling us in."

"Um . . . everything shifted two nights after our wedding." I fill them in about Trey disappearing and then returning with a black eye and a rancid temper. "He's been a monster ever since."

"That was the same time that Victoria mysteriously broke her hand," Demitri contemplates.

My eyes narrow. "Interesting."

"It can't be related," Demitri says, pondering the situation. "She had just helped Trey set up your surprise wedding, and you hired her the day before she broke it. It's a weird coincidence, though." He waves his hand about. "Anyhow, back to your story."

"I'm terrified of him."

Mr. Cantrell's eyebrows rise. "I know he's a mean SOB, but from what I saw when you dealt with the Reapers, I suspect you can take him."

I shake my head. "I've done everything I can to control my dark-water temper."

"Why?" Mr. Cantrell asks.

"Because I'm a killer at my core." I slide deadly serious eyes to Mr. Cantrell. "If I lose control of my temper, my rational side slips and I become unchecked. I can't do that to Trey."

"Why didn't you try to get help?" Mr. Cantrell asks.

I groan. "I did . . ." I trail off, wincing. I don't want to tell them about going to Zane. "I didn't want to face everything I knew was coming. Trey is unhinged. Anyone I go to might get hurt. Add to it that I'd have to convince the person that Trey's different behind closed doors . . ." I shake my head. "His act in public is convincing."

"No, it's not," Demitri interjects. "I've felt the shift rolling off Trey in waves. You were the one who was convincing in public, hence why I brushed off my suspicion. I should have asked you."

"I couldn't take it anymore, and had one way out," I admit. "I was willing to face Suicide Solitary because anything is better than the trap I'm in."

"What did you use on your wrist?" Demitri asks.

"Broken glass from my wedding photo frame. I got in the bathtub, so I didn't make a mess. Trey despises a mess. He was in his office working. When he came into the bathroom, I was out cold."

"Does Mama Mabel know about your wrist?" Mr. Cantrell asks.

"No one knows. Trey didn't bother to look close enough to see it."

Demitri takes my hand. "I'm going to heal your wrist on Thursday, but not until Trey sees it. I plan to speak to him myself." I start to argue that he doesn't need to put himself out there like that, but he silences me. "Enough, Melanie. Trey's gone off the deep end."

Mr. Cantrell folds the footrest down on his recliner and sits next to Demitri on the couch. "I'm going to tell you a story that Demitri's never heard before. I knew the moment you two got here what needed to happen. It's another example of how much Melanie is like D's mom."

Demitri sits back, seemingly curious.

"Catlyn was in a horrible marriage," Mr. Cantrell says. "We were just friends, but I could never get that girl out of my head. She came to my apartment one night. Desperate and crying hysterically, she gasped, 'I need you to stop time. PLEASE!' I was past the point of caring that she was married. I looked into her eyes and knew it was now or never. She had suicide rolling off her in waves. I pulled the blinds and locked the door. Time stopped for two days, and we were handfasted three days later. We got legally married twenty-two hours after her divorce was finalized. Zero regrets."

Demitri's shock reverberates through the house. "Mom was married to someone before you?"

Mr. Cantrell nods. "Her ex-husband still hates me. We've had fistfights in bars. He confronted me at my office. Hell, he showed up here a year ago, and I flattened him on the front lawn. Fortunately, you weren't home, Demitri. I never hurt people that way, but that jackass was destroying my girl. Cat died seventeen years ago, and he and I are still at it."

"Unreal," Demitri says.

"Moral of the story, I speak from experience about this. I think it's time that you say screw it to your rules and fast-track a plan." Mr. Cantrell gestures to me. "Melanie is your Catlyn, and she needs to leave Trey."

"You had a soulmate connection with Mom," Demitri insists. "This situation is the exact opposite. You're encouraging me to drag Melanie away from her soulmate."

"I was your soulmate our first lifetime," I murmur.

Demitri side-eyes me but has no other reaction to the reminder.

Mr. Cantrell gives him a pointed look. "Remember that

premonition I had the first time Melanie walked through our door with you?" he says cryptically.

Demitri silently ponders.

Mr. Cantrell looks overwhelmed. "You've done NOTHING but sob and vomit because Melanie was out of your life! Stop with the aloof act, Demitri!"

Demitri slides caged eyes to his dad, while I sit still, feeling like I'm caught in a moment I'm not supposed to hear.

"If she was happy with Trey, I'd tell you to move on," Mr. Cantrell insists. "Demitri, she tried to kill herself because she's miserable! Do you want to lose her?"

"I'm not the kind of guy who steels a married woman," Demitri insists.

"Son, sometimes you must flex on the rules because the paradigm no longer serves you," Mr. Cantrell gently encourages him. "I've had one great love of my life. She died giving birth to you, and I've never been the same. I wish with everything in me that I hadn't let that woman be miserable for an entire year before I FINALLY got up the nerve to overstep my boundaries and do what HAD to be done. Thank God I finally got my crap together and did the right thing, because her former husband would have killed her, and you would've never been conceived. The same thing is happening to your girl, right now. I'm scared that if Melanie doesn't kill herself first, Trey will murder her. I'm telling you that it's okay to overstep your boundaries because this situation warrants it. Man up, take control of this situation, and rescue your girl!"

Demitri stares at the floor, his eyes wide. My heart pounds. This talk has become brutally honest.

Needing to steer toward something else to give Demitri some breathing room, I choose a route that might help Mr. Cantrell. I owe him, because he's going above and beyond to help me. "We just glazed over something important," I quietly say. "Mr. Cantrell, thank you for trusting me with something so personal. I'm so sorry about your wife passing. I guarantee there was a reason you may not have considered. You had something important to learn in this lifetime and had to do it without her. My educated guess is that you've been codependent on her for too many lifetimes and had to learn to stand on your own."

Mr. Cantrell appears shell-shocked.

I smile warmly. "Your soulmate gave you perfection in the form of Demitri so that you could make it through. She's waiting for you."

Mr. Cantrell and Demitri both have tears in their eyes.

"You think she's waiting?" Mr. Cantrell asks.

"I'm positive of it. I've had dreams of my time in the spirit realm, waiting for Adam. It's peaceful. Lessons are learned. The soul reunion is worth it, even though I know you hurt without her."

Mr. Cantrell's expression shifts to wonder. "You don't look sixteen right now. There's wisdom in your eyes that's both scary and incredible."

I nod. "I've had two hundred and three lifetimes. Where this is concerned, I know what I'm talking about."

Mr. Cantrell smiles softly at me. "Thank you."

My intuition rumbles in a new way. My eyes unfocus as the internal rumbling intensifies. It doesn't hurt, but the gravity of it is overwhelming.

"What's wrong, Melanie?" Demitri asks.

I slide an odd expression Demitri's way before standing up and crossing the room. I close my eyes with my back to the guys and study the intuition bubble. My heart pounds as I turn and sight on Demitri while I try to wrap my mind around a new reality. "Oh my God." I study the picture on the wall of a beautiful, delicate brunette woman. Panic rips up my spine, and I mutter to myself, "What does it mean?" I close my eyes and focus on the dark water that lives in my mind. I light the oil that makes the water shimmer in black rainbows and try to force more information up from the flames. When nothing comes, I exhale hard and open my eyes.

"Give me the memory of what just happened, Melanie," Demitri demands.

"It's a big game changer, but I don't understand the game."

"Hand it to me, first," Mr. Cantrell interjects. "I'll tell you if you need to show Demitri."

Fraught with confliction, I squeeze my eyes closed. Finally, decided, I open my eyes and take Mr. Cantrell's hand. I send the premonition of my oldest future daughter walking through a movie set in a red formal dress. She has serious eyes, a no-nonsense expression, and she's clearly an old soul in a teen body. She turns in the memory and looks at me, before glancing down at the script she's holding.

Mr. Cantrell sharply inhales. "Oh my God."

Alarmed by his father's shift of demeanor, Demitri stands up rapidly.

"Trey and I have known about her," I barely get out. "We thought she was the daughter I miscarried, but . . ." My eyes flick to Demitri.

Mr. Cantrell turns to Demitri. "We're doing anything we must to keep Melanie alive. She's leaving Trey." He demands of me, "Show him."

I take Demitri's hand and hesitantly send the memory.

Demitri takes a long moment before saying, "She has my cheek-bones. She looks like a perfect combination of my mother and Melanie." He has a thousand conflicting emotions raging behind his eyes. Panicked, he backs up to the corner of the room.

"Demitri," Mr. Cantrell cautiously says, "you've wanted a life with Melanie. All this means is that you have that coming."

Demitri turns his back, leaning his forearms on the wall.

Mr. Cantrell puts a hand on his shoulder.

My gaze drops. Fear that he's scared away mixes with shame. I expected him to be stunned, but his distraught realization of a future with me wasn't on my radar. My chin shakes as I fight dejection.

I must have gotten lost in thought, because suddenly Demitri says, "Melanie, please don't ignore me."

My gaze slides from the floor to him.

Demitri takes a deep breath, before asking, "How old are you, and the girl, in that premonition?"

I shrug timidly. "She's sixteen. I'm mid-thirties, best I can tell."

"That means this is happening within the next few years," Demitri mutters to himself. He stares at me like I'm an alien. "We're teenagers!"

"I know this is a lot," I commiserate.

"You're not stunned?" he asks.

"No," I reply. "I saw the premonition of my three kids last year."

"THREE!" Demitri bellows. "I don't want ONE!"

Mr. Cantrell winces at his son's tactless outburst.

I blink rapidly. "The other two kids are Trey's," I inform. "The youngest boy looks just like him."

"WHAT?" Mr. Cantrell barks.

"Demitri doesn't want our daughter. I must go back to Trey then . . . It's best to cut this off now. I'm going to go." I grab my backpack, but Mr. Cantrell stops me.

"No, you're not. Give me a minute to help with this. Wait in Demitri's room. I'll be in shortly."

I agree, but feel trapped both by future circumstances, and this house. I head into Demitri's room, softly closing the door. Unsure what to do, I gingerly sit on the edge of his bed and look around. There are framed pictures of him and Victoria everywhere. I hadn't noticed it earlier, and it makes me blisteringly uncomfortable.

The door opens and Mr. Cantrell slips in, closing it behind him. He hands me a joint. I take it, pulling a huge hit. I exhale, filling the room with a smoke cloud.

"You okay?" Mr. Cantrell asks. My eyes flick around, apparently answering for me, because Mr. Cantrell surveys the room. "Don't get caught up in those damn pictures," he growls. "Every time that vapid bitch comes over, she brings another one with her. They interest Demitri about as much as Victoria does, which isn't much."

"Is he okay?"

"He's seventeen," Mr. Cantrell softly says. "Having a wife and three kids wasn't on his radar twenty minutes ago."

"Good times," I mutter. "I hesitated telling him for a reason."

Mr. Cantrell scoffs. "Yeah, well, hiding it doesn't help. It's better to get it out there." His expression softens. "That girl you're supposed to have is beautiful."

"I agree," is my only feasible reply. In the grand hierarchy of awkward conversations, this one takes the prize.

The door opens, and Demitri comes in. "Give us a few hours," he requests.

"I'll run errands," Mr. Cantrell says as he leaves. Demitri and I stare at each other long enough to hear the garage door open and close.

Demitri moves with purpose around the room. Gathering the picture frames, he stacks them and drops them in the corner before crossing to his boom box and slipping in a CD. Duran Duran's "Come Undone" breezes intensely through the speakers.

"I need to leave," I say apologetically, "but thank you for helping me today."

"You aren't leaving." It's the most hypermasculine I've ever seen Demitri. As he turns to face me, I see something primally new in his eyes. I shrink, but not from dejection or fear this time. I blink rapidly, assessing my flummoxed state.

Suddenly, I feel Demitri's lips on mine. I had been so lost in confusion that I didn't see him move my way. My eyes close, and my breath catches as his arms slide around me. The kiss seems unrushed, but his energy is frantic. I feel us move, but couldn't care less, lost in the moment. My tush lands on the edge of the bed, and only then does he end the kiss.

He kneels in front of me and cups my cheeks, staring into my eyes. "I'm sorry for my reaction earlier. I wasn't ready for the direction that talk went. It took me a second to get my head on straight."

"I know it's too much," I whimper.

"Shh," Demitri says, putting a finger to my lips. "I looked at you and saw something new after witnessing that premonition. You've always been my Meley, but suddenly, you were MINE. Forget my reaction about having kids. I leaned on shallow flippancy because my brain flat couldn't work around all that I faced."

I bite my lip and really study him.

Demitri's expression shifts to adoration. "I love your big eyes."

"I'm sorry you know this," I whisper.

"I'm not." Demitri puts his forehead on mine, seemingly mesmerized, and whispers, "I got to see my daughter." Before I can say anything, he delicately kisses me again.

My mind spins in a way that's so unlike me. I give in to it because it feels exactly right, and that's been such a rarity for me lately. "This feels different from our usual weird," I say, as he ends the kiss.

He chuckles. "I love you, Melanie." Before I can say it back, he adds, "I'm all in."

"Liiiike . . ." I scrunch my face. "Like how you're all in, and then you run away to bimbo-town?"

Demitri shakes his head. "I'm all in like I should be. I want you, and three kids, or three hundred, or whatever."

I feel as if I can't breathe.

He gives me a pointed look. "You're not having two kids with Trey, and he sure as hell isn't raising my daughter, though." He runs his hands down my arms. "I'm moving you out of there."

"Because of a premonition that's a big confusing mess?"

Demitri cups my cheeks. "It didn't confuse me. It cleared things up." He smiles. "Melanie Slate, will you be my girlfriend?"

A gross girly sound bubbles from me.

It's so out of character that Demitri cracks up. "I'll take that as a yes," he says, before kissing me again.

The feel of energetic satin and fur slides up my spine. Demitri moans and gets an arm around my waist, scooting us onto the bed.

I break off the kiss with a gasp, ready to ask what direction this is headed. Demitri makes the mistake of kissing my neck. My vanilla pheromone is on overdrive, and he inhales. His eyes roll into the back of his head before he collapses on me and everything blasts into the atmosphere.

Knowing he's been so hesitant with me in the past, I assess his vibe with the very little that's left of my rational side. There's zero hesitancy from Demitri, and I give in to my desire to just let go. I've wanted Demitri for so long, and this insanity feels right.

CHAPTER 9

My teeth chatter, which is both weird and new for me in this situation. Demitri's hands are shaking on my back. I make a strange sound that's something between a croak and a "gah."

He barks a laugh. "I second that."

"I think I'm going to throw up," I manage to get out.

"Go for it."

I crack up. "That's the way to win over Demitri Cantrell. Barf on him in bed." I roll off him.

He covers his face with his shaking hands. "Give me a second. I think my soul left my body. Holy shit. I know Adam gave me a heads-up, but *damn*, that tantric side of yours is a wild ride."

"Are you okay? I know you've feared that side of me."

"Are *you* okay?" Demitri asks bashfully. "I apologize for what I yammered out."

My tantric side amplifies emotions in my lover, and they generally blurt their innermost desires out . . . enthusiastically . . . during the more extreme moments. "It was charming." I absently trace his abs. "Yes. I'm okay."

Demitri grips my ribs and pulls me to him.

Terror suddenly courses through me, and I shove away and scuttle backward. I end up on my feet, with my back against the wall.

"Hey, hold on," Demitri says, concern in his voice. "Melanie, talk to me."

"Um . . ." My brain jolts through emotions that are entirely irrational. I swallow hard, squeezing my eyes closed. "I need a minute."

"What did I do?"

"It's not you." Fighting to breathe as the fear refuses to fade, I whisper, "I'm scared."

"Hey, hey, hey," Demitri says.

I open my eyes and see he's on his knees at the edge of the bed. Humiliation and fear roll from me in waves that are very noticeable to Demitri's empathy.

"Are you scared of me?" he asks.

I shake my head rapidly. "It was the way you pulled me up, but you aren't . . ."

"I'm not what, Meley?"

I stare at him, petrified, before my expression collapses. "He's going to kill me!" I ugly cry, completely out of control.

"I won't let him kill you," Demitri rumbles through a clenched jaw.

CHAPTER 10

"**H**ey, D. What's wrong?" I vaguely hear in my light-sleep state.

"Roll her mind." I feel a touch on my forehead, and my mind flip-flops. It's like being plunged into a warm pool of calm. I can still hear, but none of it makes linear sense.

"What happened?" Mr. Cantrell asks.

"I . . . we're officially together. Um . . ." Demitri sounds like he's struggling. "I'm not scared of the future possibility anymore, and I appreciate you working me through that. I'm sorry I cratered. I apologized to Melanie for it."

"Why are you so flustered?"

"Things went past discussion. There are several problems I discovered in that moment. They're personal, though."

"Tell me."

"My sheets are covered in blood," Demitri informs, but I can't wrap my warbling mind around it.

"Poorly timed normal stuff?" Mr. Cantrell asks.

Demitri clears his throat awkwardly. "Nope. She's got really intense scar tissue."

"You sure it isn't from the surgery to repair the miscarriage damage?" Mr. Cantrell asks.

"She didn't have this scar tissue then," Demitri snarls. "I would have noticed when I healed her. She told us Trey beats hell out of her in the sack. The amount of pain he must have caused for her to be in this condition makes me sick."

"Oh no," Mr. Cantrell dejectedly says. "Demitri, she can't go back to Mabel's."

"I agree. She told me her parents are going to be gone for six months. Can she please move in here?"

"How serious are you about her?"

"I'm all in." Demitri sounds like he's fighting tears as he adds, "You were right. She's my Catlyn."

"Yes, she can stay here," Mr. Cantrell says. "Do you want her to move into the guest room, or your room?"

"My room," Demitri pleads. "I need to know she's okay. I want her with me in case Trey breaks in and attacks her."

"Done," Mr. Cantrell says. "This situation is grave enough that I can justify overlooking your ages, and how this looks." He pauses. "Besides, she's Melanie. She's been through so much that it's really unfair to even treat her like a normal teenager."

"Thank you for understanding, Dad."

"Can you fix the damage Trey did?" Mr. Cantrell asks.

"I don't know yet, but I'm going to try," Demitri says. He clears his throat awkwardly, a personality staple of his I recognize. "She had a panic attack when I tried to pull her up to me. I don't know what Trey's been doing to her, but it may be a long road getting her back."

Demitri's hand lands gently on my stomach, and I sigh as healing energy wafts through my gut.

"She was desperate enough to attempt suicide," Mr. Cantrell

says. "Considering that she rescued Zane from Suicide Solitary, and knows the punishment that awaits, it must have been unlivable with Trey."

Ugh. The mention of Suicide Solitary spirals my confused brain. Zane committed suicide. Demitri was able to heal Zane's body, and I got his heart started again, but his soul didn't return. I had to astral project and make a trade with these strange gray blobs in the spirit realm. They're called Gatekeepers, and their prime mission in the afterlife is holding suicide souls until they learn penance for the infraction of taking life for granted. The trade I made in exchange for his soul wasn't clear at the time. It became clear shortly after, and I'll never be right again. The price I paid, in the form of miscarrying my daughter, was horrific.

"The way she reacted when I grabbed her . . ." Demitri sounds like he's in tears. "I wasn't trying to scare her. I just wanted to snuggle with her."

"Your and Trey's intentions are vastly different, but she instinctively panicked." Mr. Cantrell sighs. "I think she has a lot of emotional healing to do, D. You need to go easier on her in amorous moments."

"My healing ability wouldn't allow me to hurt her like that," Demitri mutters dejectedly. "Nothing was even remotely aggressive. She's so damaged, it seems to just happen when she . . . is compromised." He pauses. "I'm sorry to hit you with all of this."

"Don't be," his dad replies. "Did you have to fight not to be aggressive with her when her tantric side revved?"

"No," Demitri replies. "It had the opposite effect. I was far more delicate with her. I think that side brings out the foundation of her lover. Trey is aggressive, so it makes him violent. I'm the opposite."

"Do you think she's in pain?"

Demitri sighs. "I know she is. Sometimes, when she twists, she complains that something feels like it's pulling. I never overstep and scan people without permission, but I should have with her. You know what's weird, though?"

"What's that?" Mr. Cantrell asks.

"Trey and Victoria have an intimate past, and Vic doesn't have any of these scar-tissue issues."

"Maybe Trey couldn't handle the level of intimacy that comes with a soulmate bond. It's intense."

"So is her tantric side," Demitri says. "One of the side effects is this uncontrollable need to tell her the very deepest heart of how you feel. It's wild. I flat couldn't stop it. She told us she thinks Trey's hiding something, and he's been really shielded off. I think violence is the only way he could gain enough control against that tantric dark-water ability of hers not to spill his guts in the sack."

"What did you spill?" Mr. Cantrell asks.

Demitri coughs. "I apparently want to whisk her away and hide her forever in our very own hump hut on some remote island."

Mr. Cantrell chuckles. "That's better than beating the shit out of her as some kinky means not to reveal dirty secrets." His tone sobers. "She's going to have a hard time trusting. If she moves in, you have to stick it out while she heals. Keep your head on straight about leaving Victoria."

"I will. I hate Victoria, and I must be strong enough to fight the draw to her that the soulmate connection forces."

I feel the trance state lift, and I suddenly can't remember what I heard, but I know it was important. "I'm okay?" I mumble.

"Go back to sleep. I promise everything's fine."

I slap lightly at his chest. "Scatchies."

Demitri scratches my back, and I wiggle happily before my eyes close, and I drift away to the sound of the guys chuckling.

CHAPTER 11

"Melanie, wake up," Demitri says.

I blink sleepy eyes and prop myself up on my elbow. I'm lying on the couch, and Demitri's kneeling by me. "What time is it?"

"It's midnight," he says softly, before speaking into the phone. "Hang on, Cindy. Melanie's here."

He pushes the speaker button, just as Cindy Drell says, "Thank God."

"Cindy?" I try to wrap my lethargic mind around Zane's mom calling Demitri's house phone.

"Melanie, I've tried your cell phone so many times," she says, sounding panicked. "When's the last time you talked to Zane?"

"A little over a week ago. Why?" I rub my face hard, trying to get my head together.

"Cindy," Demitri says as he watches me struggle to deal with this call, "Melanie's not in a good place. Is there any chance this can wait until morning?"

"Please," she gasps. "I promise it's important. I haven't heard from him in over a week either. I usually talk to him every day." She sounds on the verge of tears.

Another voice comes over the phone. "Melanie, it's Rocco. I haven't seen or heard from him since he left the beach the day we saw you. Cindy called, and I'm at her house. Brian and Zane's stepdad are out of town."

"Hey, Roc." I wobble my head, pondering. "Zane might just be caught up in the whole new relationship vibe."

"What new relationship?" Cindy asks.

Rocco sighs. "He had a date that day we saw Melanie. I can't imagine he's nine days caught up in her. She doesn't offer more than a couple hours' worth of infatuation."

I snort. "He delights in shallow women."

"No, he doesn't," Cindy counters, sounding offended.

"He used to, before Melanie," Rocco says, and I cringe. Unfortunately, Rocco continues. "Melanie, he was so upset after you left. He regretted that date. He freaking hyperventilated in the Beach Bar bathroom."

"Good Lord," I mutter. "Moving on. This isn't a good time for that discussion."

"There's something else," Cindy says. "Zane's landlord called right before I finally found you. The same song has been playing in his apartment for two days, and he didn't get his rent in on time."

My intuition, sparked by that intel, blazes to life. When Rocco starts to speak, I dark-water gravel, "Hush," around the pain in my chest. Silence descends as I close my eyes and spin the intuition bubble in my mind. After carefully searching, I open my eyes. "What's his address?"

Demitri reaches for a pad and pen, and I write down the address Rocco gives me.

"I'm on my way," I growl.

"You think it's a bad sign?" Cindy asks.

"I know it is."

"I can meet you," Rocco says. "I have a key."

"I don't need a fucking key," I snarl. "I need my flip-flops."

"You plan to kick in a luxury apartment door wearing flip-flops?" Rocco asks.

"No. I plan to blast the door open, and incinerate everyone inside."

"Okayyyy," Rocco says. "We're headed to Zane's."

"Is he alive, Melanie?" Cindy tearfully asks.

"The people with him better hope he is. I'm headed to my car." Demitri hands me my shoes, and I slide them on and hang up.

"No way, Melanie," he says. "You aren't driving like this."

Mr. Cantrell gets his keys from a hook by the door. "Come on, kids. I'm driving."

I snag a CD from my backpack and head through the kitchen and into the garage. We get into Mr. Cantrell's Buick, and as soon as Demitri closes his door, he reverses out of the garage.

Mr. Cantrell glances at me in the rearview mirror. "You look different, Melanie."

"Just get me there." I hand the CD to Demitri.

"Where are we going?"

Demitri gives him the address while he pops the CD into the car stereo. L7's "Shitlist" blares, and I glare at nothing while my dark-water energy thrums in malignant waves through the car.

"Holy crap," Mr. Cantrell breathes.

"Looks like we're driving La Diabla, instead of Melanie," Demitri says.

"Melanie," Mr. Cantrell says cautiously, like he might spook me, "you can't kill anyone when we get there."

"That's not up to me."

"Who's it up to?" Demitri asks.

"Brandy."

"Who's Brandy?" Mr. Cantrell asks.

"A whore."

"I think you need to fill us in on what happened the last time you saw Zane," Mr. Cantrell prompts.

I slide my maniacal gaze Demitri's way. "Hooker. Date. Zane. Brandy. Drug addict. Stupid. Boobs."

"Descriptive story," Demitri retorts, seemingly caught between concern and humor.

"Bullet points," I clarify as the song ends and the guitar squeals. "Repeat."

Demitri and Mr. Cantrell exchange a look as Demitri starts the song over.

CHAPTER 12

Cindy fidgets as the elevator arrives at the fifth floor. A quick jog down a VERY fancy hall, and Rocco stops at a door. I listen with my eyes narrowed.

"Do you know it?" Demitri asks, as Rocco inserts the key.

I nod. "It's Mozart's *Lacrimosa.*"

Rocco opens the door, and we pour through. A glance around stops everyone short but me. I knew what was coming. One lone floor lamp reveals the disastrous apartment, the air permeated by a dank chemical smell. Zane is slumped on the couch in a pair of boxers. Draped over his lap is Brandy, naked. Another naked girl, a redhead, reclines, passed out, in a leather lounge chair.

Brandy looks our way through what appears to be an extraordinary drug state, and moans, "Make it stop."

"What in fucking drug dens is going on?" Rocco breathes.

"This isn't a shocker," I bark. "Brandy informed the entire Beach Bar that she has quite the drug habit."

Cindy starts to rush to Zane, but Rocco grabs her and pulls her back, as I yank a needle out of Zane's arm and chuck it on the coffee table. The song ends, and then immediately restarts, loud enough to be beyond irritating if listened to for long.

"What's happening, Melanie?" Cindy gasps as she gapes in disbelief at drug paraphernalia on the coffee table.

"Zane's date," I gesture to a very out-of-it Brandy, "is a reformed hooker, turned stripper." I glare at the girl in the leather chair. "Brandy apparently has friends." Brandy's moans earn my attention. "Up, Brandy."

She stares at me blankly.

I yank her limp arm, forcing her to sit up.

Zane's eyes flutter, and I smirk Demitri's way. "He's alive. I don't have to retrieve him from the spirit realm again."

"Hooray," Demitri mutters. "Don't touch that girl, Melanie. I can feel from here that she's a giant STD."

"Sorry, D, but . . ." I backhand Brandy with everything I've got before leaning into her menacingly. "What the fuck are you on?"

Seemingly unaffected by my tirade, Brandy looks around. "A couch."

I shake my head. "You're the stupidest creature the universe has ever made."

Rocco glances at the coffee table. "We can count on heroin, cocaine, and crack from the looks of it."

"Oh my God," Cindy moans, doubling over.

"Quite the trifecta," I sarcastically compliment. My face drops deadpan at Rocco.

"I had no idea about this," he insists.

"What do we do?" Cindy asks, looking panic-stricken. "We can't call ambulances. This will be all over the news!"

Given Zane's A-list celebrity status, she's right. "We aren't calling ambulances," I reply.

Brandy slumps over the arm of the couch and vomits onto the polished concrete floor.

"Holy shit!" Mr. Cantrell exclaims while he yanks Demitri out of the splash zone. "Please tell me this isn't what you kids do!"

Demitri shakes his head in mortification. "We never have, and we never will. Melanie, you're done with Zane!"

"You think?" I bark back.

My bellow raises the red-haired girl from the dead. She takes one look at me and starts screaming.

"Shut up," I snarl.

Her screams turn to whimpers as she gasps, "You're a demon."

I cock my head, playing along with her bad drug trip. *"Indeed, I am,"* I send into the room on an audibly menacing thought.

"No, please," the girl says, panicking.

"Mr. Cantrell, any chance your abilities include making someone forget what they've seen?" I ask.

"Yes, I can do that," he replies.

"Please do the nifty trance thing," I request, "but I need to insert a subconscious message that sticks."

Mr. Cantrell crosses to the girl and winces when he touches her forehead and her eyes glaze over. Disgusted, he says, "Now I'm going to have to cut off my hand, burn it, and scatter the ashes over seven rivers to dissipate the evil."

I survey the lightly tranced girl and send out, on an audible wave, the exaggerated mental thought, *"I'm Zane's demon. If you ever speak of, or to him again, I'll hunt you down. You were never here. You don't know Zane."*

The girl gasps.

I start walking slowly her way while she shakes. My mental voice slinks through the room. *"What are you never to do?"*

"See, or talk about, Zane," zombies from her.

I nod and gesture to Brandy. "Her turn."

Mr. Cantrell touches Brandy's forehead. Her expression doesn't shift, likely because she's such a bubblehead that the trance doesn't change her personality.

I roll my eyes. "Brandy, I *will* kill you if you ever speak of, or see, Zane again. Do you understand?"

"My boyfriend?" Brandy baby-talks like a ditz.

I hit her with an energy blast. The invisible attack sends her careening up the wall of the towering room. I pin her there, dangling seven feet above the ground. Even covered in barf and track marks, her assets are still impressive.

"He's not your boyfriend," I snarl. "You don't even know him." I hope what I say sticks in her subconscious.

"Not my boyfriend," Brandy states as a fact.

"Correct," I say. "La Diabla *will* kill you if you ever speak of or see Zane again. Do you understand?"

"Yes," she whimpers, fear boiling up through her tranced state.

"Good." I tip my head. "Who supplied the drugs?"

"Lucky Charms." Her blank eyes drift to her friend.

"Of course," I mutter. "That bimbo goes by Lucky Charms."

Furious, because today has been IMPOSSIBLE and I need an outlet for my rage, I send Brandy careening across the room with an invisible energy whip. She smacks into the opposing wall, and we hear a bone crack. "Ouchie," I whimper, mocking her as she hits the floor. I get an energetic grip, yank her to me, and snap my hands around her head. "If you EVER create another problem for Zane, I'll melt your fucking brain."

Even in her tranced state, Brandy completely loses it, screaming wildly.

I slap her hard. "Shut up!"

She quiets down.

"Get dressed," I order.

She slowly gets to her feet and stumbles into another room, returning in what she was wearing at the Beach Bar.

I gesture to the coffee table. "They've been here *nine* days doing THIS?" I bellow at Rocco.

He just shakes his head in disbelief.

"Up, Lucky Charms," I order, getting back on task.

The other girl zombie rises, unsteady in her lime-green platform stripper heels.

"Dressed, now," I demand.

She stumbles into the other room and emerges in a neon-green see-through fishnet "dress" that matches her six-inch heels.

"Holy shit," Mr. Cantrell mutters, while Cindy gasps, and Demitri gawks, horrified.

"Damn, Zane really does like nasty girls," I mutter. "Will the trance wear off on its own?"

Mr. Cantrell nods.

"Rocco, please take out the trash," I say.

"Yes, dear," Rocco replies. He escorts the girls out, closing the door behind him.

"Someone, turn off this music," I snarl. "Leave it to Zane to ruin Mozart." I head to the kitchen as the music shuts off.

"What are you doing?" Demitri bellows.

"I desperately need to rub my face in disbelief, but I have crack-whore on my hands," I bellow back. "Unfortunately, this room is also covered in vomit, broken glass, blood, and dirty needles."

"Damn it, Melanie!" Demitri barks. "I need to get you out of here. I've never been so repulsed in my life."

Washed to my elbows, I make my way back into the living room. I rub my face hard, and tears brim. My rage slides away now that I've kicked the girls out. I wrap my arms around my stomach and double over in shock. "Oh my God, what is *happening*?"

Demitri starts to walk my way.

"Stop, Demitri." I swallow hard. "You can't heal yourself. You touch nothing."

Rocco comes back in. "They're in a cab," he announces.

I nod, gutting up to tackle part two of this nightmare. Gathered, I cross to Zane and touch his cheek. "Zaney, honey, I need you to open your eyes."

He startles, his eyes snapping wide. He stares at me, but it takes a long moment before reality dawns. "Melanie?"

"Hi, Zane. I'm here."

He whimpers the most pitiful, "Nooo," I've ever heard. Clarity slides in as the shock of seeing me seems to sober him up a little.

"You're okay," I say softly. "I need you to come with me."

"Where?"

"You need a shower," I delicately say. It's not lost on me that it's his turn to experience humiliation like I did when he took care of me in the hospital after I broke my neck.

"Not you," Zane pleads.

"Shh. I know." I smile softly. "I got rid of Brandy and Lucky Charms."

"They're gone?" Zane whimpers.

"They'll never come back," I promise. "I broke up with Brandy on your behalf."

"Thank you. They wouldn't leave."

"Come on." I help him up and ask, "Where is your bathroom?"

He gestures, and I wave off the others. "Wait in the bedroom. He doesn't realize you're here."

His legs don't quite work, but I manage to get him through the bedroom and into the bathroom. I close the bathroom door. Still out of it, Zane leans against the wall.

I start the shower and take off my hoodie. "Undress, Zaney."

"I'm so confused," he whispers.

"I know." I turn, giving him a moment.

Undressed, Zane falls against the glass shower wall. I steady him. The moment he's under the hot water, he melts down. He sobs and shakes as I soap a loofah and get busy cleaning him up from outside the open shower door.

He grabs me, pulling me in and hugging me like I'm the last thread of sanity in his crumbling universe. My clothes now soaked, I struggle to keep him upright. I whisper pretty things while his drug-addled brain fights to clear.

Steadier on his feet, he finally lets me go, and I snag a towel. Drying off is pointless. I resort to taking off my sweats and wringing them out in the sink, while Zane stares at me with such dejected horror that it breaks my heart.

"Stay in the shower and sober up, love." I open the bathroom door enough to look through. "Demitri, don't get pissed. Zane pulled me into the shower when he was melting down. Is there a dryer someone can put these in?" I hand through the soaked sweatpants.

"I'll handle it," Rocco offers. "What about your tank top?"

"It's bad enough that I'm about to clean up a crack cave in my underwear. I ain't doing it naked. I'll just tolerate the wet top."

Cindy opens a drawer and pulls out a T-shirt.

When I step out, Zane whimpers, "Melanieeee."

I have a childish little flip-flop foot-stomping fit while I grumble, "I just want to go to sleeeeeep." Finally, I pull it together and say with a pleasant lilt, "I'll be right there. You're okay, Zaney." I close the door and blister, "Turkeys and tacos, this is madness!" I change shirts, while the others look away, and give Rocco my sopping-wet tank top.

Cindy stares at my wrist. "Oh my God," she whispers. "I had no idea you were dealing with that when I called you."

"Holy crap, Melanie," Rocco breathes.

My head drops. "I just need to get through this. One miracle coming right up."

"You need a miracle too," Cindy insists with compassion.

I gesture to Demitri. "I present to you the miracle."

Cindy and Rocco stare at Demitri.

I sigh. "Someone give me something for Zane to wear that isn't covered in hooker slime."

Cindy pulls clothes from the dresser. "Melanie, I'm so sorry. You deserved uninterrupted time to take care of yourself."

"That never happens." A fit builds, and I cock a hip while flourishing luxuriously in a rainbow arch over my head. I chortle sarcastically, "Welcome to Melanie's world."

"Melanie tantrums are the best," Demitri caws.

Despite the situation, everyone seems amused.

I gesture to my massive T-shirt and flip-flops. "Only *I* end up dressed like a ten-year-old at a summer camp jamboree, while tromping through a luxury drug hovel, smacking crap out of hookers, and rescuing a gargantuan millionaire A-lister who won't give me the time of day while I'm attempting to escape abuse." I gesture about wildly. "I HATE my life, but here I stand, the last hope in the fucking universe. My goal is to get out of this hellhole without getting STDs in my SUICIDE WOUND. So, if you don't mind, there's a wet toddler who just spent nine days dumping passionate loads into blow-up dolls, and shooting up happy juice, who needs me. Melanie to the *rescue!*"

Demitri cracks up, saying to his dad, "I'm so in love with that quirky chipmunk that I can't even be mad that she was just in a shower with Zane."

"You two are TOGETHER together?" Rocco asks.

I roll my eyes. "Who knows at this point? I'd already put Demitri through a real wingding good time. Now *this*?" I quirk my mouth at Demitri. "Run D. Fast and hard. My life is one big fart in a stuck elevator!"

"Melanie, HOW can you manage to find humor in this situation?" Mr. Cantrell asks through chuckles.

I frantically flap about. "This is *hilarious*! I'm thrilled I didn't die, because we're standing in Zane DRELL'S apartment while he enjoys a crack bender. He likely impregnated Lucky Charms and contracted gut rot, but thank all the gods that the Hercules Healer," I gesture to Demitri, "is here to save the day AND Zane can afford child support!" I nod vibrantly. "It's just another Tuesday night. This," I flap about again, "is my freaking life."

"She really knows how to take the sting out of a nightmare," Mr. Cantrell crows at Demitri.

Demitri nods adoringly. "It's my favorite survival quality of hers."

I give Demitri an exasperated look and stomp my foot. "Fuck this lifetime. I'm DONE." My spectators spurt laughter, while I peel off one more healthy, "DONE, I tell ya!"

Mr. Cantrell clears his throat. "The blow-up doll-loving heroin toddler is waiting for super-Melanie in that bathroom."

"Back to reality!" I take Zane's clothes, inhale deeply, and tell myself, "You can do this. You're a badass sixteen-year-old shit show who has it all together." As ready as I'm going to be, I plaster a pleasant smile on my face and sweep into the bathroom. "How's that sobering up going, Zaney?" I close the door on the laughter in the bedroom.

Zane is a sobbing wreck. "I never wanted you to see this."

"It's okay," I reply softly as I dry Zane off efficiently, like he did for me so many times after I broke my neck and suffered a brain injury. He gets dressed, and I offer my hand. "You ready to heal this mess?"

"With us?" Zane asks, and my heart squeezes tight.

"The drug addiction and hooker damage, Zane."

Zane's face contorts. "Can we talk about us?"

"There is no us," I inform him. "I'm living with Demitri as of this morning."

Zane's eyes widen. "What?" he barks. "That's why you came to me?" It seems realization dawns.

I nod. "I went to the Beach Bar to tell you I needed help leaving Trey."

"I'll help you!" he insists.

"Too late. Demitri figured out I was in serious trouble, took me away, and hid me."

"Hid?"

My expression mangles. "Things got bad."

Zane slumps, sobbing. Waves of tragic regret roll from him.

The door opens and Rocco comes in, closing it behind him. He's intuitive and likely felt Zane's blasting heartbreak. He sinks to his knees, putting a hand on Zane's shoulder. "Hey, bud," he says softly. "Let's sober you up."

Zane looks at Rocco like his world is ending. "She's with Demitri."

"What happened, Melanie?" Rocco asks.

"I tried to call Zane so many times, but he never answered. I finally got up the nerve to go to the Beach Bar because I was desperate for help." I shake my head. "You saw how that went. I went home when I left the beach, and things got worse. I couldn't take it."

"What was Trey doing to you?" Rocco asks.

I sigh. "Latch on." I present my arm.

"Oh my God, Melanie," Zane moans as he sees my wrist.

"Yeah, yeah," I mutter. "Whatever. Latch on so we can get show-and-tell over with."

Both guys grab me, and I send the memory of what happened the night I got back home after the beach. They witness Trey's raging fit, and then the painful aftermath. They come out of the memory and seethe.

"I'm going to kill Trey," Zane says to Rocco.

"I'll help you," Rocco replies.

"No, you won't. Demitri is handling this. The last thing you need is some pathetic teenager begging you for dinner and piling up in your apartment."

"That's exactly what I want!" Zane insists. "I'll move you in with me."

"Your apartment is covered in vomit, heroin, and sex sludge," I say as kindly as I can muster.

Zane's head drops, humiliated. "Please, Seashell. I'll figure out how to fix this."

I squeeze his hand. "Right now, I'd like to focus on the tasks that need to get done. It's been a rough day."

I open the door and guide Zane into his bedroom. When he realizes that Mr. Cantrell, Demitri, and his mom are here, he melts down again. Humiliation and tears are a hard thing to witness from Zane Drell.

"How about we talk for a minute?" Mr. Cantrell asks in his fatherly way, guiding Zane into the other room.

Demitri grimaces as he surveys the bedroom. "It looks like a rock band squatted in here for two years. HOW did two hoes and a movie star manage this in nine days?"

"Zane keeps a perfect home," Cindy insists.

"It's okay. No judgment." I smile softly her way. "I've got this."

They leave at my insistence, closing the door behind them. I wince after turning on the overhead light and revealing a biohazard disaster that's stomach-turning. The single nightstand lamp that previously lit the room hid a great deal of the reality. I grab the wastebasket from the bathroom and start scooping trash with a towel from the cabinet. Used needles are everywhere, and I don't want to touch anything with my hands.

As I come into the living room, Demitri is walking my way. "The bedroom is ready for you to work on Zane," I inform him.

Everyone emerges from the kitchen, listening.

"This whole situation . . ." Demitri trails off, lost in thought, before his demeanor shifts. "Why did you go to the Beach Bar?"

"To talk to Zane." My heart races. *Here we go.*

"You made your suicide attempt how long after that?"

"The next day," I reply neutrally.

"You chose to go to Zane," Demitri says as an accusation instead of a question.

I gesture toward the others. "We have an audience."

"I don't give a damn. Why didn't you come to me first?"

I shake my head, not having the emotional bandwidth to deal with this right now.

"If you want Zane, then be with him," Demitri bellows.

"Oh yes," I bark back. "This is my fucking fantasy!" My eyes fill with tears as I lose steam, overwhelmed by Zane being a drug addict, my life turning upside down, and Demitri launching this jealous fight my way. My head drops, and I plunk the wastebasket down that I was carrying and begin to cry. "I can't take any more."

"Demitri, you need to give her grace on picking Zane first," Mr.

Cantrell guides. "Her choice makes sense. Zane could have financially handled helping her, she trusted him, and there wouldn't have been parents involved because of his age. The universe put Brandy in the way, steering Melanie to you. Be grateful."

Zane winces grandly, while Cindy appears at a loss.

"I'm sorry," Demitri says to me, softer now. "It's been a rough day, and I'm rattled."

"I know," I whimper, working to curb the tears.

"I need to get her out of here," Demitri says to his dad.

"Then get on with it," Mr. Cantrell replies.

Demitri sweeps an arm. "After you, Zane."

Zane slogs to the bedroom with Rocco following.

After he leaves, Cindy pleads, "You have no idea what losing this chance with you is going to do to my son."

I stare at her in deadpan shock. "This situation is a hard NO."

"This isn't who Zane is!" she insists.

"You said the same thing about the Rachelle situation," I gently remind her. "I think Zane has a side that you don't have a handle on."

"I'm not letting Melanie get bullied into believing this is okay." Mr. Cantrell stabs a furious finger my direction. "SHE has been through enough, and I won't allow any more. She's right where she needs to be, with people who care."

"*We* care about Melanie too," Cindy insists.

"You can't even keep your own child from THIS!" Mr. Cantrell rages back. "Thank GOD Melanie didn't end up here with your son! What we walked into an hour ago . . ." He shakes his head. "I'm sorry, but your son's dirty secrets are filthy."

Cindy turns a bright shade of red, and tears fill her eyes.

"I think Cindy's humiliated enough without this disgrace being pointed out," I say. "She's a good mom, and this can't be easy for her."

Mr. Cantrell swallows hard. "I apologize."

Cindy stares into my eyes. "This one decision changed Zane's entire life, because being with you was his dream."

"He hasn't even spoken to me since the wedding debacle," I mutter, "yet he can entertain Brandy."

"You're so much better than Brandy," Cindy rushes to assure me.

"I agree. Her lure was irresistible for him, though. I won't compete with hookers and blow." I look to Mr. Cantrell. "Demitri's left me in the dust for a girl just as bad as Brandy more than once. If he goes back to Victoria, I'm done."

"It won't happen," Mr. Cantrell insists with certainty.

"Time will tell," I reply, before heading into the kitchen to continue cleaning up another round of Zane's fantasy disaster.

— —

"Melanie, I'm ready for you," Demitri says while he surveys the spotless living room.

I resorted to putting my hands in bags as makeshift gloves, because the living room was truly disastrous. I had never seen so much dried vomit and blood splatter in one place before. Considering my kill count, that's saying something. Cindy tried to help me, but the reality of what we found when I turned on the overhead light in the living room sent her into a sobbing tailspin.

I pull the bags off and drop them in the full wastebasket. "Please start with the others. I need to put stuff away."

Demitri calls over Cindy, checking her with a hand to her shoulder. He follows up with his dad.

I put the last garbage sack next to the others, and instruct, "Rocco, these need to go to the dumpster, but be careful. They're full of uncapped needles."

"Are you positive you didn't get stuck with any of them?" Demitri asks me.

"I'm sure." I smile at Rocco. "Thank you for taking them out. We'll wait to leave until you return in case you accidently get tagged with one."

Rocco takes the bags and makes his way out.

Demitri strides to me, and I hold up a hand to stop him. I scrub up again before changing into my clothes that I retrieve from the dryer. I liberally spray down with a disinfectant can I've used in every room. A cloud of disinfectant causes a coughing spasm, and I flap my hands.

Demitri laughs. "I think you're thoroughly decontaminated," he says.

Damp, I shudder.

Demitri puts a hand on my shoulder and closes his eyes. I feel his scan and wait long enough that Rocco returns. I finally ask, "What are you finding, Demitri?"

He drops his hand. "Nothing, but I was thorough. I'd hate for you to have super-ninja cooties that hid from me." He glances at Zane. "Some of the cooties are stealthy and have been around awhile."

I grimace. "Stealth cooties . . . nifty." Offended when I realize what he was insinuating, I snap a glare at Demitri. "Hey!"

"Sorry, but I had to make sure he didn't give you party favors," Demitri says.

"I've never slept with Zane," I condescend back.

"That's a good thing, because I can't heal myself, and I don't want what he had." Demitri gives Zane a look. "You need to be more careful when you entertain randoms. I knocked it out for you, but you could have died. Some of what you were harboring isn't a long-term good time." Demitri shakes his head with a sigh.

"I need to check your brother and Rachelle. Call me and get it scheduled."

Zane puts his hands over the mortification alive on his now-sober face, while Cindy looks stunned.

"Given Rachelle and Zane's affair, it's a good idea," Demitri bluntly tells her.

"What did he have?" Cindy asks.

Demitri shakes his head. "Just trust me. I need to check the others." He checks Rocco, while Cindy glares daggers into Zane. Demitri sighs, giving Rocco a pointed look. "Looks like you and Zane have the same taste in women."

Rocco winces. "We've run in the same circle for a long time."

Demitri snorts. "Find a new circle, and a box of rubbers, Rocco." He closes his eyes with his hand on Rocco's lower back. His forehead instantly beads with sweat, that quickly pours, while Rocco looks like he wants to die of embarrassment.

Finished, Demitri wraps his arm around me.

"You ready to go home?" Mr. Cantrell asks me.

"Yes, please."

"I want to get Melanie to bed and then talk to you," Demitri says to his dad. "We've got a tough day on Thursday, and I need to be ready. Trey's going to be livid."

I swallow hard.

Demitri tips my chin up so he can look into my eyes. "Trey isn't getting through me. Victoria isn't going to lure me back. It's you and me."

"You and me" was my mantra with Zane, and it makes him tear up. I can't deal with any more about Zane right now, though.

An idea comes to me, and I chirp in Mr. Cantrell's direction, "Can we get burgers?" My teen excitement dies on a wave of embarrassment as I realize I can't afford burgers, and he already served dinner. "I'm sorry," I bashfully say. "That was rude."

Mr. Cantrell's eyebrows rise. "It wasn't rude. It was cute. You can ask for burgers without acting like you just begged me to pay off your Vegas gambling debt with the mob."

I quirk my mouth. "As soon as my funds are released from Trey, I'll pay you back. If he doesn't release them, I have a paycheck coming on Friday. I need to make sure Mabel doesn't give Trey my money anymore."

"You just got paid for *Glamour*," Zane reminds.

"Unfortunately, by union legality, I can't touch any of it until I'm twenty-one. My parents abandoned me here for a six-month work trip to Japan." I smile sarcastically. "Once I became scared Trey was going to kill me, and I failed at suicide, I had no choice but to run. I lost access to my money that's in the account Trey insisted on controlling. The food at my parents' house was only going to stretch for so long, and I had a quarter tank of gas."

Zane rubs his face hard. "I'll set up an account for you, Melanie."

"Absolutely not," Demitri counters. "I've got her covered."

"I have twenty grand in the silverware drawer." Zane opens the drawer, and his eyebrows rise. "I *had* twenty grand in the silverware drawer."

"Hookers be hookering," Demitri jokes, and we all laugh, alleviating some of the tension.

"Ugh," Zane groans. "I apologize to all of you."

"You and I are about to have a talk," Cindy says sternly.

Zane winces at her mom tone. "I already know."

"Do you?" Cindy squawks. "Do you really? You KNOW? You don't *know*! You haven't even BEGUN TO *KNOOW*!"

Watching huge Zane cower as tiny Cindy rages is bizarre. My eyebrows rise. "I think Cindy has a lecture prepared. We should let them get to that."

"Good luck to you," Demitri says to Zane.

I say a kind, "Goodbye."

"Melanie, please," Zane whimpers.

"You have my word that none of what we saw will ever be revealed." I give him a pointed look. "*I* actually mean it."

Zane dished my dirt to his brother's girlfriend that he was having an affair with. What he helped me through while I was in the hospital is easily as rancid as what I just did for him. That betrayal should have told me everything I needed to know, but I gave him another chance and ended up neck-deep in used needles.

Zane winces. "I'm so incredibly sorry, Melanie."

"I'll leave you to your mom and Rocco now," I politely reply.

Demitri drapes an arm over my shoulders and says to our spectators, "One more miracle, brought to you live and in concert by Melanie Slate. Not only that, but Zane Drell is out of my competition picture." He exhales hard. "I never thought I'd be grateful for hookers and blow. Let's roll."

We head out the door.

"He's got nice digs," Demitri compliments as we get in the elevator.

"Show business is WEIRD," I reply. "He's got it all, but resorts to Lucky Charms."

"I feel bad for Zane," Demitri admits.

Mr. Cantrell winces. "Zane asked how serious you two are while we talked. When I was honest with him, he sobbed." The elevator doors open, and we stride out while Mr. Cantrell adds, "Full disclosure, that man is thoroughly in love with Melanie."

Demitri winces.

"Actions," explodes from me. "Sorry," I say, apologizing to a couple in the fancy lobby. I soften my tone. "Actions speak louder than words. I'm not going to be shoved aside for BRANDY."

When we get to the car, I flop over in the back seat and curl into a ball. "Those boobs deserve a freaking medal of valor! Holy crap."

Mr. Cantrell chuckles as he closes his car door. "She needs a new boob job. The right one has encapsulated."

"It's what?"

Demitri smiles at my cartoon expression. "Capsular contracture. It's caused by scar tissue around breast implants that the body rejects as foreign objects."

"She has breast implants?"

Both guys look at me like I'm crazy. "You're kidding, right?" Demitri asks.

I shrug. "Never seen a pair of bought ones. I just thought hers popped out perfect."

"She's adorable," Demitri says to his dad.

I quirk my mouth, uncomfortable as I glance at Demitri. "I'm really unsettled that you saw Brandy."

Demitri chuckles. "I'm really unsettled that you got in a shower with Zane."

"He had dried vomit all over him. I think you win."

"So did Brandy." Demitri smolders. "So sexy."

"So freaking sexy."

"Zane would have OD'd had you not insisted on going there," Demitri says. "He shot up enough heroin to put down an elephant."

"Was there anything you couldn't fix?"

Demitri shakes his head. "I knocked it out for him."

"Thank you for doing that."

Demitri smiles. "Thank you for recognizing that Zane Drell isn't your dream guy."

"This scared me," I admit. "You think you know someone . . ."

"I know, love," Demitri says compassionately. "You don't trust many people, and you've been burned a lot lately."

I nod. "The circle gets a little smaller."

"He's still the guy that got you a gummy bear hoodie and helicoptered you out of a moving vehicle," Demitri says.

Mr. Cantrell hisses, "Are you crazy? Why would you remind her of that?"

"Because I know Melanie. She's going to blame herself for not realizing he had this side. Not even Rocco knew." Demitri shrugs.

I teasingly smirk. "He's really daring and has amazing connections. Lucky Charms seemed like a real bowlful of cherries."

Demitri shakes his head. "Her bowl was full of herpes."

"Now I want you to check me for cooties again."

Demitri gives me a look. "You didn't screw Zane in the shower, did you?"

"You caught me red-handed! 'Zane Drell,' I said, 'you better shake off that heroin hangover and pony up because a secret shower romp in your junkie jamboree is hot stuff.'"

Demitri howls laughter. "I *knew* it!" He winces with one eye closed. "Were you sneaking peeks?"

"No, D. Full disclosure, I've taken a lot of showers with Zane. I've seen the show. We averaged three to four a day while I was in the hospital, and I was covered in worse than vomit. He was usually in underwear, but laundry becomes an issue when you're soaked every four hours."

"I owe him so big for everything he did for you then," Demitri says with conviction.

"I do also," I reply. "That's why I dragged us here. We paid our debt tonight."

"I'm sorry, Melanie," Demitri says. "Losing Zane is hard, I know."

"I'm good, D." I scrunch my face up. "Crack's kinda whack, you know?"

"That it is." Demitri grins at me.

Mr. Cantrell chuckles. "Let's get burgers."

I scamper up in my seat to rest my chin on Demitri's shoulder. "I get to be alive, with you," I softly say with a hint of wonder.

Demitri reaches for me and wraps his hand around the back of my head, rubbing my hair fondly. "It's going to be magic, Meley."

CHAPTER 13

"**S**eriously? Are you four?" I squeal, as Demitri splashes me.

His dad walks into the kitchen and smiles at us as Demitri coats my face with dish soap bubbles. I toss a grape, pegging him between the eyes. He tips his head back and catches the grape.

"Show off!"

Demitri grins as he hands me a dish towel to de-bubble my face.

"Well, it looks like you two are back to normal. Thank God."

I smile at Mr. Cantrell. "I need to get my makeup, and an outfit for tomorrow."

"I don't want the two of you leaving today," Mr. Cantrell says. "Give me your keys, and I'll swing by your parents' house while I run errands."

I retrieve my house keys and hand them over. "Any outfit will work."

"I'll grab several for you," Mr. Cantrell says.

"My makeup bag is on my dresser." I pause, needing to gather my thoughts. "Thank you for everything," I softly express. "I . . ." I look down. "Um, I feel so much better."

Mr. Cantrell smiles compassionately. "I know. I can feel it

empathically." He squeezes my hand. "You deserve to be happy, and *I* deserve to *sleep*!" He tips his head back, groaning contently. "I slept like the dead last night now that Demitri's energy has stabilized."

"I'm glad," I say, before gazing up at Demitri. "You're doing better, right?"

"Hell yes," Demitri crows. He wraps his arms around me. "I've never been happier!"

"I wish time could stop forever," I say.

"Don't you start worrying about that now. We've still got a whole day before time starts again," Demitri says before he tickles me.

I squeal and shimmy away from him. I twist the dish towel in both hands before snapping it and popping him in the leg.

"You brat," he squawks. He snags the towel from me, and I send out a playful little energy pop, cracking him on his tush.

"I don't need the towel," I tease.

"Naughty," he jokes, and I laugh, gazing up at him with big eyes. He wobbles his head with a quirky eyebrow raised at his dad. "I love her."

Mr. Cantrell chuckles. "I'm aware." He grins at me. "I'm thrilled that you two have FINALLY decided to give a relationship a shot. It's about damn time. The first time Demitri walked through the door with you, a premonition nearly knocked me over. He and I discussed it late that night. I knew that day that he was going to marry you."

"Well, I am," Demitri says.

"I have a fabulous track record with marriage and kids," I say cynically. I wince. "Best to avoid that route."

"Pierre was murdered," Demitri says. "You lost the baby because of Zane and Trey. Your current marriage is shit because of Trey. Don't place judgment on yourself for it."

I just shake my head, my mood shifting seriously.

"Hey now," Demitri scolds gently. "We were having fun. No getting down in the dumps."

"D, I've been down this road," I say. "It isn't all it's cracked up to be. I love you too, but . . ."

"But nothing," Demitri says. "We started out building a solid friendship. We've experienced ups and downs, but we've made it through. We also know that life apart is terrible. I hated the past four months when I made the mistake of putting our friendship on ice. It brought clarity about exactly what I want," he squeezes me, "which is you."

"Are we really discussing this?" I ask, needing to pump the brakes. "I've got big problems to worry about, like currently being married while I shack up with you." I shake my head. "I need to run to the drugstore for some stuff." I wince when I realize I don't have cash.

Mr. Cantrell focuses on me contemplatively. "I never in a million years thought you'd be this down-to-earth. I should have, I guess, because simple things like a soda make you so happy. What do you need from the drugstore?"

"I can live without the stuff for a few days."

Mr. Cantrell makes a comical face. "Sounds fancy."

I laugh. "Hair ties."

Mr. Cantrell's eyebrows shoot up. "Hair ties?"

I nod. My expression shifts with worry. "I can't even afford hair ties," mutters from me. "Hopefully, Trey releases my money from our checking account, or I'm going to have much bigger problems than hair ties."

"Like what?" Mr. Cantrell ponders.

"Electricity bills and rent."

Mr. Cantrell's eyebrows rise. "You're sixteen, Melanie. I'm not going to charge you rent! You're worried about bills?"

I nod. "My parents didn't leave me any money when they bailed for a romantic journey to Japan. I know they figured that I have a job, and a home at Mabel's, but they completely missed the part where I desperately needed out of there." I scoff. "Rich knows things with Trey are going to fall apart because he TOLD us that at my wedding! He forgot, though, because those two are acting like a couple of teenagers while I'm busy being the adult. The only time that I'm reminded I'm sixteen is when someone wants to put me in my place to control me for their own gain." I tip my head to Demitri and Mr. Cantrell. "Present company excluded. Otherwise, I'm expected to magically win against evil, feed myself, work, get stellar grades, and have it together."

Mr. Cantrell and Demitri shift to their most serious versions. "Melanie, I'll be your parent while your parents are gone," Mr. Cantrell assures me.

My chin shakes the slightest bit while emotion swells in my chest. I try to tamp it down. "I'd like that. I know I'm an old-soul warrior, but I'm also a kid who lives in a huge city and has everyday worries and problems. Sometimes I feel really lost." I swallow hard. "I pumped the brakes because I don't want to cling to Demitri out of fear because I have abandonment issues."

Demitri seems surprised.

"Tell us about that," Mr. Cantrell encourages me.

"I never see my father, who I miss so much," I inform. "I hear from him maybe once a month. My mom and Rich started acting like I was a married adult. While that was a relief, because they quit harping on me so much, I still need parents, and food, and somewhere to sleep." I shrug timidly. "They didn't even notice my desperate plight when Trey turned on me. Abandonment is my biggest fear, along with suffocation, and heights."

"Damn," Demitri murmurs.

"I'm terrified of tight spaces, in my physical and financial reality, along with my past-life experiences of actual suffocation and imprisonment," I reveal. "It's all tied together." I take a cleansing breath. "That's why I cling to a strong male figure, often to my detriment." I tip my head pointedly. "Trey, Zane, and Adam all fall into that category. I don't want to do that anymore, because I've learned that it suffocates the guy, who crumbles under the pressure, morphing into an abusive, dismissive, drug-addicted mess." I look to Demitri. "I'm working on my bad habits so I can stand on my own two feet and be more than some pathetic, needy, shivering waste."

"Melanie," Demitri breathes. He wraps me up in a hug.

"That was well put, Mel," Mr. Cantrell says. "If it helps, I think you're doing really well. You balance what you face far better than you should."

"Thank you. I'm trying." I let Demitri go and smile a little. "I recognize that my flaws are part of how I was trapped by Trey. I didn't gain security or contentment by clinging to him. All I did was back myself into a cage with a monster. I can do better than that, and I plan to. I bring out the worst in people who I depend on. The pressure of everything that I bring to the table is unfathomable, and I know that."

"How about we work to remove some of the pressure where we can, and not add any more?" Mr. Cantrell asks.

"That sounds good," I timidly reply.

"Perfect," Mr. Cantrell says. "I'm the *dad*, and I'm going to stop at the drugstore while I'm out. I'll get you whatever you need if you make a list, Melanie."

Demitri hands me a piece of paper and a pen.

"D, hate to ask you this," Mr. Cantrell says, "but are you being careful?"

My eyebrows rise. I stare at the short list I've written, but I'm not about to move a muscle while this particular topic is being broached. I'm not sure how Demitri is going to handle it.

"Seriously, Dad?" Demitri says. "You had that talk with me when I was thirteen."

"Yeah, well, you weren't living in the same room with a gorgeous girl when you were thirteen. I need to be a parent. Much like Melanie's parents, I forget that I still have a kid. You look like an adult, but you aren't. I spend as much time out of town and obliviously doing my own thing as Melanie's parents do, and after what she just said, I need to be more mindful. I'm currently condoning two teenagers shacking up in my house, so I'm asking the question."

"Melanie, can you add what he's worried about to the list, even though I've already got that covered?" Demitri requests, handling the embarrassing topic maturely.

"Sure," I reply, blushing slightly as I add condoms to the list, fold the paper, and hand it to Mr. Cantrell. "Thank you," I say. I decide to address the matter head on out of respect for how open Mr. Cantrell has been to everything we've hit him with the past few days. "To put your concern to rest, I've got my pills in my purse and my prescription was changed to a supersonic, personality-bending, hormone-raging, strongest birth control known to man, after my nightmare pregnancy debacle happened."

Mr. Cantrell chuckles at my candor.

Demitri snorts. "Good to know."

I look to Demitri. "I'm supposed to take it every morning when I brush my teeth."

"Did you take it this morning?" he asks.

I nod.

"Will you be offended if I set an alarm on my watch, so I remember to remind you every morning?"

"No," I say bashfully. "I'd like that."

"Done," Demitri says.

I quirk my mouth and look to Mr. Cantrell. "Pills aside, your son is very reliable about his end of that responsibility." I look up at Demitri. "Thank you for that. I didn't have to fight you, beg, or worry myself sick about it."

Demitri nods. "You're welcome. For the record, if there ever is a mishap, I'll put an energy block to prevent a problem."

"Perhaps you could just never have a mishap," Mr. Cantrell coaches.

"My dark-water side makes it incredibly difficult to think clearly," I explain to Mr. Cantrell.

"Damn, does it ever," Demitri mutters.

"What does it do?" Mr. Cantrell asks.

I sigh, needing to carefully choose my words. "It removes my lover's control over what they say and do, forcing them into a subservient willingness to sacrifice anything, including their hidden thoughts."

"Damn," Mr. Cantrell says. He looks to Demitri. "How do you feel about that?"

Demitri shrugs. "I don't have a problem with it, but I could see how it would be an issue for Trey."

I nod. "He battles it to the death, buckling emotionally under the extreme pressure, hence the violence in the bedroom."

Demitri gives me a pointed look. "I'm not going to let my girl go through the kind of heartbreak and pain that you experienced during your miscarriage again. Your dark-water side doesn't make me violent. Regarding the other issue, if I ever can't think through your dark-water side, then we've got a backup safeguard with an energy blockage."

I hug Demitri, burying my face in his chest. I cower for

a moment, trying to wrap my mind around this new reality. "Promise?" I whimper.

He tips up my chin. "I promise. I'm incredibly empathetic. I don't think like a jackass teenager. I'm seventeen, but I'm also as old a soul as you are."

"I'm impressed," Mr. Cantrell says. "Thank you for discussing this matter in front of me. It's alleviated my concern about a lot."

Demitri gives me a squeeze. "Melanie, my dad and I are really open with each other. I'm rarely embarrassed by these topics with him."

"I was raised similarly, but my personal experience with intimacy has been both good and bad," I inform.

"Bad with Trey, obviously," Mr. Cantrell says.

"Recently, in particular," I agree. "He wasn't responsible or receptive like Demitri is. His flippant disregard of the potential consequences has been a source of extreme anxiety for me."

"You never have to worry about me attacking you without your consent, or me being unconcerned that you might end up accidently pregnant," Demitri assures.

"Any other bad experiences that you want to get out on the table?" Mr. Cantrell asks, leaning against the counter, seeming totally relaxed about the subject.

I shake my head before looking up at Demitri. "Do I need to ask about your past?"

Mr. Cantrell smiles softly, seeming pleased with how this exchange is going.

"I have more of a past than I should," Demitri admits. "With that said, I haven't taken chances." At my askant look, he explains, "I'm a healer, but I can't heal myself. I've experienced healing things like what Zane was unknowingly harboring, and it gives me perspective. So, there's nothing that you need to worry about regarding disease from my past." He wobbles his head. "However, I'll admit that now that I've begun a romantic relationship with you, I wish I hadn't given in to such flippant connections in my past."

I ponder what he's said. "Well, we can't change that. All we can do is be mindful of the future."

"Agreed," Demitri says.

"Well done, you two," Mr. Cantrell says. "Do either of you have any other concerns you want to get out on the table?"

"Not yet, but I likely will once I face moving out of Mabel's," I say.

"I'm here to help," Mr. Cantrell says. He looks to his son. "Demitri? Anything else you want to discuss?"

Demitri hesitates before saying, "Not yet."

I look up at him suspiciously. "I don't like that tone you just used."

He sighs. "I know." He tweaks my nose. "You tend toward deeply rooted heart connections, hence why your list of partners is so selectively small. I can't claim the same, and I have evaluation to do about my choices. I'm learning a lot being with you."

"That was succinct," I say, before wincing, "and vague enough that I'm going to wonder about every girl at school."

Demitri barks laughter. "I don't cat around with the cheerleaders," he teases. I wince, and he grimaces to match. "Tactless example, given Trey's history with Tiffany. I apologize. I picked the gaggle of girls least likely to interest me as a sarcastic example. The choice was rudely ironic, but that wasn't intended."

"Forgiven," I reply. "So, I'm not supposed to overanalyze every side-eye some random girl gives you?"

"Definitely not," Demitri says. "I get a lot of side-eyes, and I don't want to have that constant fight with you."

"Understood."

"I'm going to head out," Mr. Cantrell says, satisfied with our talk. He opens the paper and scans the list I wrote. "What color nail polish do you prefer?"

My eyebrows rise at the oddity. "I didn't put nail polish on the list."

"I'm aware of that," Mr. Cantrell says. He rattles the paper. "Tylenol? You didn't put anything fun on the list!"

I clear my throat awkwardly. "The last item I wrote is kind of fun," I retort, my quirky sense of humor getting the best of me as I allude to the condoms.

Mr. Cantrell cracks up before giving Demitri an exasperated look. "I'm getting her *nail polish*. I never get to girl shop, and I'm excited about it!"

"Black," I say. "I prefer black nail polish. If that isn't available, then the darkest burgundy or vampire red they've got."

"Perfect." He tweaks my ponytail. "I'll be back. Love you, kids."

I hug him. "Thank you."

Mr. Cantrell squeezes my waist. "You're welcome."

I wait until the garage door closes before I ask, "How do you feel about that talk?"

Demitri shrugs. "It was pretty standard stuff for me and Dad, but I'm thrilled he's extended that operating procedure to you. We're living together, and he's truly brought you into the fold now. Besides, his little shopping trip saves me fifteen bucks on condoms."

I laugh. "I suppose that's true."

"And you get nail polish out of the deal," Demitri jokes. "Seems like we're making out like bandits. What did you put on that list?"

"Tylenol, a razor, and hair ties."

Demitri chuckles. "He's going to come home with four bags full of goodness only knows what."

I giggle. "It was really sweet of him to run errands for me so that we can enjoy lockdown."

He smolders at me. "We've got at least two hours." He grabs my wrist, and I squeak as he yanks me out of the kitchen and down the hall to our bedroom. "Let's go be responsible about our choices."

I crack up as he closes and locks his bedroom door.

CHAPTER 14

Trey storms across Actors' Alley just as we round the corner. "Where the hell have you been?"

Demitri stops next to me and informs him, "With me." Arch and Presley Verelle join our tight circle as I feel like I'm going to pass out from fear.

"You better have a damn good reason for keeping my wife away for two nights!" Trey snarls furiously.

Demitri grabs my hand and turns it over, revealing my wrist.

I guess we're just getting right to it.

Everyone gasps, and Presley says, "Oh my God! Melanie, what did you do?"

Trey balls up his fist. "She tried to kill herself at your house?"

"NO, dickhead!" Demitri snarls. "She tried to kill herself at *your* house. You walked in and yelled at her for being in a bathtub full of blood."

Shock reverberates through our connection. "Damn it! I didn't realize that was what was happening." Trey collects himself and says to Demitri, "Thank you for helping her."

"You're welcome." Demitri's jaw tightens. "Why did you leave your WIFE in a bathtub full of blood?"

Trey clears his throat awkwardly. "I figured if was her monthly visitor, given her bitchy mood."

Mouths plummet all around the circle. "Periods don't do that to bathwater!" Presley says, like Trey has shit for brains.

Trey makes a dumb face and mutters, "Oh . . ." He snaps a glare my way in that rapid mood-shifting way that terrifies me. I shrink back as he bellows, "What were you doing with Demitri?" I can't even gather a coherent thought before Trey snarls, "We're going to discuss this later."

"No, you aren't." Arch looks at me. "We're discussing this now! Why did you try to kill yourself?"

"Looks like your grand plan worked," Trey snaps at me sarcastically.

Presley narrows her eyes at Trey. "What grand plan?"

Trey hits Demitri with a devious glare. "She found a way to force you to put up with her again, didn't she?"

Arch steps between the guys and stops Trey from lunging at Demitri. "What the hell, Trey? You're being a dick."

I give Arch a petrified look, and everyone is clearly concerned as they glance from me to Trey.

Demitri calmly puts his hand over my wrist. His forehead beads with sweat as my wrist heats up. After much longer than I expect, he says, "There. It's fixed." He tips up my chin. "I worked longer on it, so it won't scar. Don't ever do that again."

"What else happened at your house, Demitri?" Trey demands.

Demitri morphs with blistering arrogance. "Fuck you, Trey."

"I'll find out!" Trey threatens.

"And then you'll do what? You're already neglecting and abusing her when no one's around!"

"What!" Arch screeches.

"I'm trying to keep your soulmate alive while you're destroying her." Demitri points a finger Trey's way.

"Stay the hell away from my wife," Trey threatens.

"I gave you every opportunity to make it work with Melanie. She tried to kill herself, and you can bet your ass I'm back. We'll let Melanie decide what she wants." Demitri smirks. "I'll tell you this much, I don't *buckle* under the pressure of extreme emotions."

Presley looks at me with an expression that's so mind-blowing it would be hilarious if I wasn't suddenly terrified that Demitri just announced that we've been together.

Trey slides demonic eyes my way. "We're leaving." He starts to grab my arm.

I press against Demitri. "I'm not going with him," I whimper.

"No, you're not," Demitri growls, wrapping a protective arm around my chest.

"Clearly a lot has been happening," Arch says. "What's Trey been doing to you?"

I try to answer but can't.

Arch turns to Trey and demands, "What have you done to Melanie?"

Trey stares at me, dumbfounded. "All I do is work my ass off. I keep a roof over her head and buy her whatever she wants."

Anger bubbles up. "I have a job as Mama Mabel's event coordinator. It comes with room and board, Trey. I earn my own paychecks and roof. Don't pull that 'ball and chain' bullshit about me."

The bell rings, and Demitri looks down at me. "I'll walk you to class, Meley."

He pivots me around, and we stride through the school, leaving Trey and our flummoxed friends in our wake.

"Well, Trey knows."

"Yup." Demitri's jaw is set in a steely line.

"Do you think that's smart?"

"Yup."

"Victoria's going to get pissed that you're walking through the school with me like a boyfriend."

Demitri simmers back, "I don't give a shit," and puts his arm around me.

I smirk. "Yeah . . . this side of you does it for me."

"I've got a long fuse, but when I'm done, I'm done." He smolders down at me. "I'll deal with anyone I have to to keep you safe and happy."

We pass Jayla Bethel and her boyfriend, Dante Grunier. Jayla looks like she's internally wrestling a crocodile as they stare at us.

"This is going to get around quick," I murmur, while Demitri surveys our two friends as we pass.

CHAPTER 15

"**M**y Spidey sense is tingling," Tanner whispers. "What's the haps?"

I don't reply. Demitri was just pulling back after kissing me when Tanner walked into the parlor, ten minutes early.

Tanner's eyes narrow as they shift to Demitri. "Intriguing mystery afoot." Tanner looks at me suspiciously. "This is a debacle of epic proportions. We have to talk, but first . . ." His expression snaps judgmentally. "Bitch. Trey's my best friend. How dare you." His expression makes a rapid shift back to my gossipy friend. "Demitri is soooo hot," he gossips to me, as if D isn't standing right here.

"Right," I gossip back.

Tanner surveys Demitri with pursed lips before looking at me again. "Just tell me that Trey's actions warranted this."

My expression sags.

"He's been treating her like shit and beating her in the bedroom," Demitri reveals on my behalf.

"WHAT?" Tanner blisters before looking up at the security camera in the far corner of Mabel's parlor.

"It won't pick up our conversation from here as long as we're quiet," I inform. "I don't care, anyhow. Trey already knows about D and me."

"It already came to blows this morning, but Melanie and Trey have yet to privately hash it out," Demitri adds.

"I need to know everything!" Tanner checks his watch and shakes his head. "Damn it. There's no time now. Just know that I'll help where I can."

"Trey's at baseball practice," Demitri says. "I wish we didn't have to work. Now would be the perfect time to pack her up and move her out."

Tanner's eyes widen. "Shit, that serious huh?"

Demitri nods.

"Maybe they won't show up," Tanner says.

I snort. "These guys prepaid a thousand each to frolic about with the finest hookers in Southern California at a bachelor party." I give Tanner a look. "They're going to show."

Mabel's working girls saunter out from the hall, taking spots all over the parlor. Some perch on couches, others lean against the bar. It's staged to look casual.

Tanner grins at Demitri. "Showtime. Follow my lead."

They saunter to the bar.

Working at a brothel is totally different than I expected. Coming here is taboo, but I've been surprised by the depth of a lot of the reasons men visit the brothel. We've had everything from forty-year-old virgins to married guys who have a sneaky kink but don't want the affair stigma hanging over their heads. Just people being people, I guess.

While we wait, I survey Demitri, who's talking with Tanner and Sapphire at the bar. Sapphire is making drinks for our inbound guests, and I'm curious how Demitri's going to handle it. Sapphire is the curviest bunch of anime porn gorgeous I've ever seen, and her sexy little red lace nighty is leaving literally nothing to the imagination.

Demitri slides an unsure look Tanner's way. "I don't know about this. I'm fine working security for the banquet hall events, but I've avoided the brothel stuff."

"Surely the most gorgeous man on the planet isn't shy," Sapphire says flirtatiously.

Demitri cracks up. "Shy, no. Locked into a serious thing with my dream girl, yes."

Sapphire's face slides with disbelief. "*Victoria* is your dream girl?"

"No," Demitri says. "Melanie is."

Sapphire's mouth drops open, and her eyes nearly bug out of her head. She glances my way, and I glance at the foyer door, not wanting to be obvious that I'm insecurely eavesdropping. "Trey and Melanie broke up?" she gasps.

Demitri nods.

"This is going to be messy," Sapphire says, unsure. She shakes her head. "Well, congratulations."

"Thanks," Demitri replies. He never glances down at her exposed everything, or flirts with her.

"I think you and Mel are amazing," Sapphire reassures. "I just worry that Trey's going to kill one of you. He's been a disaster waiting to erupt lately."

"What do you mean?" Tanner asks.

Sapphire scoffs. "When he's not sneaking out the door late at night, he's stalking around like a panther."

Tanner and Demitri exchange a look.

We hear the foyer door open, interrupting their chat, and six guys scoot into the parlor. Looking like they're terrified instead of excited, they glance around, taking in the lingerie-clad girls. It seems to make them even more nervous.

"Gentlemen, welcome," I bubble out, while Sapphire sways to them with a silver tray loaded with whiskey on the rocks. We always greet them and get them settled quickly.

"You're just in time," Sapphire flirts. "Would you like a drink?"

The guys each snatch one and guzzle them like shots, instead of slow-sipping cocktails. I cover my amusement with a flirtatious eye bat.

Sapphire winks at me as she heads back to the bar with the tray of empty glasses. We use the drink test to assess the state of our guests. These guests are an insecure wreck, and the girls know how to shift gears to get them into a relaxed state to enjoy their visit.

"I'm Britney," I say, coyly shaking hands with each of the guys. I rarely use my real name when I host these parties full of randoms. "I'll be your host for the evening." I gesture to the ladies. "Would you like to meet my friends?"

"Su-ure," one of the guys stammers.

Gesturing to Tanner and Demitri, who are lounging with their backs against the bar, another asks, "Who are they?" They're here as bodyguards, but we don't tell our guests that.

"Jayden and Bruce, I'd like for you to meet our guests," I say conversationally, using their brothel code names.

Demitri is new to this, but Tanner's a pro at these events. There's no one better to show Demitri the ropes. Tanner joins the guys, shaking hands, while Demitri hangs back a little.

"It's nice to meet you," Tanner says. He leans in like he's got a secret.

The guests also lean in, and I stifle a grin. This tactic of Tanner's works every time with the nervous groups.

"I know these girls like the back of my hand," Tanner says, like it's a hushed secret. "What's your poison?"

The guests look confused, and Tanner gives Demitri a knowing look.

Demitri leans into the mix. He smirks at the guests, suddenly a little more in his element as he picks up on how this works. "Blond, brunette, curvy, big boobs, goth, shy?" he prompts.

A long awkward pause follows.

"Um . . . ," one guy finally says. "I just kinda like girls in general."

"Right," Tanner says, somehow pulling off the straight-guys-guy routine like it comes naturally to him.

Demitri raises an eyebrow. "Might as well go for your dream girl."

"I like short girls," a short blond guy says. Considering that he's maybe five feet three, it makes sense.

Tanner smiles at Reagan. "Come meet my friend," he coaxes.

Reagan is new around here, but she books out constantly. She's a classically pretty girl-next-door type, petite, with a sweet face and pin-straight blond hair. "I'm Reagan," she says.

"Craig," he replies shyly. "Nice to meet you."

"You too." She flirts with an easygoing air. "Would you like to chat?"

"Ye-s-s, please," he stammers, blushing a bit.

Unfazed, Reagan laces her hand in the crook of his arm, and he tightens his arm, morphing into gentlemanly manners that hint at a proper upbringing. Reagan guides him down the hall to her room.

The other guests watch how this goes, and one seems baffled. "She said yes?"

Demitri turns his back and straightens the stack of cocktail napkins on the bartop while he silently chuckles. Considering that they paid big money to receive a yes, the guy's concern is ridiculous, but this happens all the time.

"Heck yes, she did," Tanner says. "You're all handsome, and clearly nice." He gestures to the ladies who are casually hovering about. "They love nice guys."

I know the girls are amused, but they cover it well like the pros that they are.

"Not to be forward, but . . ." Sapphire slinks up to the guys and bats her eyelashes at the one who's clearly the shyest. Considering that Sapphire is built like a pornographic fantasy, he almost falls over. "I couldn't help but notice you," she says flirtatiously.

"Wow . . . ," breathes from our guest.

Demitri has to walk across the room to cover his chuckles.

"What's your name?" Sapphire asks. The guy just stares at her, and she giggles. "I'm Sapphire." She smirks coyly. "You don't have to tell me your name. I like a mystery man." She holds a perfectly manicured hand his way. When he takes it, she leads him away.

Having figured out that they need to take the initiative, because these guys have zero clue what they want, need, or prefer, the other girls stride to our guests and each snag a guy. Our guests are perfectly agreeable with how the pickings shake out.

All the guys disappear down the hall but one, who pulls back, hesitating. My eyebrows rise. Destiny chose him, and she's our most desired girl. Guys usually drag that bombshell down the hall, they're so excited to get paired with her.

Destiny heads behind the bar and takes out two glasses. She smiles at her hesitant date. "What's your name?"

"Fred," he barely whispers. He clears his throat and speaks a little louder. "Frederick."

"I'm Destiny," she informs as she pours two whiskeys. She levels Fred with serious eyes. This is her "cutting the act" act, that's really an act. Destiny's damn good at this game. "My real name is Laura, though." It's not. Her real name is Felicia, but this 'being real' act is a solid tactic. The only thing worse for an insecure guy than going to a brothel in the first place is running away from a brothel without having any fun.

"Frederick is our bachelor of honor," I inform Destiny as I pass. I had learned of this earlier when I reviewed the booking paperwork. "He's getting married tomorrow." I casually join Tanner and Demitri at the other side of the bar and position myself so I can see Fred.

"Congratulations," Destiny says. "A bachelor party is awesome. This was nice of your friends to set up."

"Um," Fred mumbles. "I'm the one who set this up." He ducks his head. "I have a reason."

Destiny hands him a whiskey glass, and sips hers before asking, "What's the reason?"

From the corner of my eye, I see Fred, unsure, glance our way.

Destiny's laugh has a clandestine feel. "Don't worry about them, Fred. They're taking a load off, because tonight is easy. You and your friends are so nice that we don't need to be on high alert. Britney hosts, Jayden is the life of the party, and Bruce is really here as Britney's bodyguard."

Fred's shoulders stiffen. "People try to hurt Britney?" he asks with chivalrous tone.

Destiny shrugs casually. "We get all types here. Most are nice guys, but the ones who aren't nice are a serious problem. We always have a bodyguard around." She leans against the bar. "Anyhow, they aren't listening to us."

We absolutely ARE listening, but Demitri has to learn how this works, and Tanner and I are voyeuristically curious jackasses.

"Why do most people come here?" Fred asks bashfully.

"Orgasms," Destiny says, without missing a beat.

Fred chokes on his whiskey as he laughs. His shoulders relax, and Destiny laughs with him.

"Spill it. Why are you here, Fred?"

"My fiancée is . . . Well, let's just say I'm marrying out of my league." Fred takes his wallet from his back pocket and pulls out a picture to show Destiny.

"She's beautiful," Destiny says sincerely.

Clearly overwhelmed, Fred nods.

Destiny gives him a knowing look. "Is there any chance that you're new to certain things, feel like the luckiest guy in the world because you're marrying your dream girl, and you want a little crash course, so your wedding night is a little more romantic, and a little less nerve-wracking?"

"Yes," Fred admits with a huge exhale.

Destiny grins. "You've got the right gal. Let's go give you a lesson so you can blow her away tomorrow night."

"I know that's weird," Fred says. "You don't mind?"

She comes around the bar and puts a light hand on his shoulder. "Happens all the time, and I have a few tricks up my sleeve." She's shifted from being a flirt to being a confidante now that she knows his motivation.

When they're gone, Demitri's mouth drops open. "Men come here for lessons before their wedding night?"

I nod.

"Why would a guy save himself for marriage, only to give up his virginity to a hooker the night before?" Demitri asks.

I shrug. "A lot of them are more worried about disappointing their girl than the whole sacred virginity status."

"Most of them don't view it as cheating," Tanner says. "Think of it more like team practice before the big game. In their minds, they're still virgins for the big game with the right person. They just happen to have done a little research."

"I bet their fiancées don't agree," Demitri says.

"Their fiancées don't know," I school them. "The guy isn't here for a girlfriend, he doesn't have any emotional ties, and he goes into his new married life a little more confident."

"Uh-huh," Demitri says, giving me a teasing look.

"Don't even think about it," I scold. "You're confident enough already."

We're thirty minutes into waiting when the music shifts to Nancy Sinatra's "Bang Bang." My intuition connects to the song, and I gasp as pain grips my chest. I study the intuitive bubble. What I'm getting is vague but bad.

Demitri whispers, "What's happening, Meley?"

"Blood and panic from the first pulse. Random couple from the second one, but it makes my heart hurt over you." I put my hand on his chest and send my memory of studying the intuitive bubble.

He watches the memory, and his eyebrows furrow.

"Who are they?"

"No clue."

"The emotional wave about you and me is a lot, but it makes absolutely no sense. The blood and panic from the other pulse is terrifying. Something's coming, Melanie." After a pause, Demitri murmurs, "I need to get you moved out of here before you end up dead."

Mabel and Trey enter the parlor with quite a few friends in tow. "Melanie, come here please," Mabel says.

We pensively join the group, but my head is spinning. Along our circle of friends, Demitri stays on the side opposite Trey.

"I'm going to wager a bet," Mabel says to me. "If you can book two more parties out of these guys, I'll treat the entire staff and their significant others to a trip during spring break for our annual staff vacation."

We all gape at Mama Mabel.

Tanner asks, "We have an annual staff trip?"

Mama nods. "Every year."

"How do I get on staff?" Stella jokes. "That sounds amazing."

It seems she's been welcomed by the Hellcats. I'm neither here nor there about it. She seems okay.

"Stella, have you met my friend Javier?" Demitri asks. "He's on staff."

Javier is a bouncer. He's also Demitri's best friend.

"Stella likes the dark and handsome type," Demitri says to Javier.

I guess it's true, given that she hit on Trey.

Stella grins at Javier. He takes her to one of the love seats, and they strike up a conversation.

"You better start booking plane flights!" I inform Mabel. I turn to Demitri. "A little post-woo-hoo-sexy-dance piece gets us bookings every time. Adds a little extra oomph so the guests don't feel like they got hosed financially when they finish in the bedroom. Our 'Fever' piece?"

Demitri smirks at me. "'Fever.' Floor or bar?"

"Bar."

Trey glowers.

"The rest of you, be ready to have fun with the guys," I coach. "They need to feel like Mabel's place is full of sex, friends, and fun."

"We need a beach vacay sooooo bad," Arch says.

As the bachelor party guys emerge, disheveled and happy,

Demitri guides me to the bar. "It's in the bag," he says over his shoulder to Arch.

— —

"We look forward to hosting you again," Mabel says cheerfully.

"Best night of my life," the short blond crows.

These guys are happily drunk, and we all adore them. They've gotten to know the Misfits, who acted like bar customers. I managed to book a birthday party, another bachelor party, and a "just for fun" party out of them. We run a special for repeat customers that spurred these guys with gusto. Our spring break trip is solidified.

Acting as Mabel's chauffeur for the night, Bear grins at the guys. "Let's take this party to the limo." He flourishes to the foyer door. These guys certainly aren't driving themselves home tonight.

"A limo!" the bachelor of honor squawks. "Yesssss!" Whiskey certainly has loosened him up.

Destiny hugs him. "You've got this. Enjoy your wedding tomorrow."

He thanks her, and all the girls say goodbye to their gentlemen callers, before Bear escorts the guys out.

"How'd he do?" Tanner asks Destiny once they're gone.

Destiny appears surprisingly impressed. "Natural talent, with a desire to please, and enough stamina that I got bored. His gal loves him, so she'll likely be mesmerized."

Tanner high-fives Destiny. "Nice job."

"All in a night's work," she replies, as she and the other girls head to their rooms now that we're closing for the evening.

My eyes meet Demitri's across the room, and my heart races. He's looking at me intensely. Apparently, it's time to do this.

"I'm glad you're home, Melanie," Trey says.

Before I can respond, not that I know what to say, Tanner says, "We haven't seen your new suite yet, Melanie." He hits me with a brightly fake grin.

"I'd like to see it," Arch says.

I catch on that the Misfits in the know don't want me alone with Trey.

"Sure," Trey says, and leads the way down the hall.

Arch, Tanner, Javier, Stella, Victoria, Demitri, Finley, and I follow. I side-eye Tanner, who squeezes my arm. I'm hoping this goes smoothly. We get into the suite, and everyone oohs and aahs. My heart hurts knowing I'm about to leave this place, but this must happen.

I head into my bedroom while everyone is busy chatting about how great the kitchen is. I rush to grab the most important stuff and cram it into a duffel bag.

The door opens. "We need to talk," Trey says. He closes the door and locks it.

As my heart thuds, I gather my will and inform him, "I'm leaving, Trey."

His eyes snap wide. "You're what?" He grabs me by the arms, and I'm reduced to being a terrified sixteen-year-old girl. "You aren't just walking out the door like this is nothing!" He unleashes an energy wave through the suite that's ferocious.

Fists pound on the door, and Arch yells, "Trey, open the damn door!"

Trey shakes me hard, and a wave of fear blasts from me on a boom. I scream, "Demitri!"

There's a sickening crack, and the locked door flies open, bouncing off the wall. Demitri stalks in and grabs Trey by his dress shirt. Trey lets me go as Demitri yanks him around and hits him. Trey's head snaps to the side, and blood trickles from his mouth.

"They're going to kill each other, boys!" Finley screams. "Get in there!"

Trey counters, kicking Demitri in the stomach and sending him flying through the door into the living room. He narrowly misses Finley, but Tanner yanks her out of the way. I scream nonsensically. Trey rushes through the door, and I follow. Demitri hits the floor, rolls over his shoulder, and jumps to his feet. Trey and Demitri square up, radiating rage.

"Please stop," I whimper.

Arch and Javier grab both guys and wrestle them back, while Tanner strides into the middle of the fight and orders, "Stop. NOW!" He points at Trey. "You're scaring Melanie."

Trey wheels around and snarls at me, "Do you have ANY idea how much I put up with from you? You're constantly needy. You never straighten this disaster up. You're always up my ass!"

"Whoa, whoa, whoa," Javier says, as he gets a hand on Demitri's shoulder. "Ease down, everyone."

"What is going ON?" Finley asks, voicing what everyone who doesn't know the latest is no doubt thinking.

Trey rubs his face. "I can't walk through the door and always have Melanie here. She constantly wants to talk and do stuff. I feel suffocated."

Humiliation blazes through me.

"She exists in her home, and that's a problem for you?" Mabel bellows at Trey. "YOU, Trey Valdez, are the one who forced a wedding! You went from demanding marriage, to being angry that she SPEAKS?"

Trey's tone softens. "I'm sorry, Melanie. The lack of space and time has me unraveling. To be honest, the last two nights that you weren't here were a relief."

"Meanwhile, I've been lost without her," Demitri says. "Trey,

I'm walking her out the door like I should have at the wedding." He turns to Victoria. "We're done. This isn't working. I'm sorry, Vic, but I'm ending things."

Victoria looks stunned.

"I'm not happy either, Trey. I'm going to leave." I scan our friends, mortified to air our dirty laundry like this but also relieved that they finally saw what I've been dealing with behind closed doors.

Arch looks at me compassionately. "Had I known he was this on edge, I would have stepped in long ago."

Trey's eyes snap wide. "Melanie, wait."

"We need to pack you up," Demitri says.

"Everyone needs to cool off first," Mabel guides. "Melanie and Trey, take the weekend to think."

"I need to speak with Melanie privately," Trey insists.

Demitri puts a hand on the back of my neck. "Not a shot in hell, Trey."

"Let her leave, Trey," Victoria says.

"Why are you doing this, Demitri?" Trey asks.

"Because I love her," Demitri says calmly as he steers me out the door.

CHAPTER *16*

I'm in the kitchen loading the dishwasher when Demitri and his dad come in from the garage. Mr. Cantrell's project is being postponed briefly due to a permit delay, and he wanted to be here with us.

"Bruised ribs. I'm fine."

"Damn, Demitri. Sounds like Trey didn't take the news well."

"Filling him in about yesterday?" I ask Demitri.

He nods and looks around. "You cleaned up the kitchen?"

"Do I smell brisket?" Mr. Cantrell asks, his expression hopeful.

I frown, unsure if I've done the right thing. "I'm hoping I didn't step on toes, but Demitri had it thawing in the fridge, already seasoned. I went ahead and put it in the oven."

Mr. Cantrell opens the oven door and inhales. "I don't mean this in a sexist way, but having a woman in the house is so nice." He smiles at me. "I haven't come home to the smell of dinner cooking since Demitri's mom was alive."

"Well, I'm happy to do it. Thank you so much for welcoming me here." I grab oven mitts and pull a bread loaf pan out of the open oven.

"That is?" Mr. Cantrell asks.

"I made bread."

Mr. Cantrell closes the oven for me and looks at Demitri. "I hear the washer and dryer running."

"I needed to burn off some nervous energy. D had rehearsal after school."

"I'm so confused," Demitri says. "Trey screamed that you never clean that disaster up. I've never seen your place a disaster and couldn't figure out what he was talking about."

I gesture to the sink. "I have stuff from cooking still in the sink. This would be your cue to overlook what I have done and be angry that I didn't finish the dishes before you saw them. I also likely didn't tie the trash bags right that I took out." I shrug. "I do what you're seeing every day, but apparently the devil is in the details."

"Mabel has a full-time housekeeping staff," Demitri reminds.

"I don't like having them clean up after me. The one thing I let them do is grocery shop." I shake my head. "I despise shopping."

Mr. Cantrell gives Demitri an enthusiastic look. "She cooks, cleans, makes homemade bread, and she hates to shop. Son, you've hit the jackpot!"

Demitri looks shell-shocked. "Apparently." He crooks his finger my way and I cross to him, wrapping my arms around his waist. "Melanie, I promise I'll do all our grocery shopping."

I grin. "That would be amazing. I also hate the mall. Wanna do my clothes shopping too?"

"That brings me to my next observation." Demitri goes into the laundry room and comes back with one of my folded leotards. He shows me the worn-out tag on the inside. "I happen to know that your leotards are a brand that went out of business at least three years ago."

I chuckle. "Oddly accurate. What are you getting at?"

"How long has it been since you've shopped for new dance clothes?"

I shrug. "I've been the same size since seventh grade and my dance clothes haven't worn out, so I don't buy more. I'm not one of those fashion-plate girls in the studio. As we've learned from witnessing Victoria, an expensive leotard collection doesn't make someone a better dancer."

Demitri gives me a pointed look. "You knew Trey would have a fit if you went shopping for dance clothes. I listened to him squall the last time you and I went to the dancewear store for jazz shoes. He took the receipt out of the bag and yelled at you."

"Shoes and tights are expensive, D."

He hands me three purple shopping bags. I instantly recognize where they're from and narrow my eyes suspiciously at him.

He chuckles, saying, "You offered the perfect segue to a surprise we got you."

I reach into the first bag and pull out a gorgeous black leotard with burgundy velvet swirls on it. It has a low back, and a heart-shaped top. I know the brand before I even look at the tag. All the rich girls at school wear Griffon brand dance clothes exclusively. I distinctly remember loving this one until I saw the price tag the last time me and D were at the dance store.

I look in the bag and mumble to myself, "No way." I pull out a stack of six more leotards, all equally fancy, with pretty designs. I look through the other bags, and they're full of Griffon brand jazz pants, shorts, sports bras, and leg warmers. Embarrassment bubbles while I stare at the expensive pile of dance clothes.

"What is that expression about, love?" Demitri asks.

"This is unbelievable, D. Thank you. You really didn't need to do this, though. I'm not this girl."

Mr. Cantrell leans against the counter. "Why not?"

"I don't know. I always find excess silly. My parents would have bought me new dance clothes if I had asked them." I look at the pile on the counter. "Not *these* dance clothes though. D, they have other brands that are a third of the price."

Demitri smiles softly at me. "You wouldn't have asked for these, though you need them."

"I don't *need* them."

Demitri rolls his eyes. "Fine. You don't need them. You do, however, admire that brand secretly. The last time we went to the dance store, you looked at every one of those things and bought none of them."

"Just because I touch something curiously doesn't mean I pine for it."

"Let's try this route. Melanie, I'm sick of hearing Victoria say, 'What are you we*aaaa*ring?'" Demitri imitates her perfectly, and I can't help but laugh.

"I don't give a damn what Victoria thinks of me." I survey the pretty leotard and give him a mischievous look. "You popped the tags so I can't take them back?"

"Yup. Sure did."

"Can we say that this is an early birthday present?"

Demitri shakes his head. "Nope. We aren't making up some excuse so you can justify it. I got them for you because I love you and you deserve them."

"Demitri, I really do appreciate this. I'm floored right now." I take a breath. "The last thing I want is you thinking I'm some gold digger."

"You aren't a gold digger. I want to take care of you." Demitri gives me a pointed look. "It's time someone did."

"Thank you. This is really thoughtful." I peek in the closest bag. "And a little crazy."

He kisses me on the forehead. "You're welcome."

"Let's eat," Mr. Cantrell says, sounding excited at the prospect.

CHAPTER 17

I squeal, so thoroughly happy as Demitri spins me around, that I think I'm going to bust. Demitri is grinning from ear to ear. We ignore a knock on the door.

Mr. Cantrell opens it and ushers in Zane, Rachelle and Rocco.

"Hi, guys," Demitri greets them happily.

He dips me low, and I beam, chirping, "Hello" at our visitors.

"Welcome to the disco." Mr. Cantrell chuckles.

Demitri pulls me to a standing position, and I giggle as "Ring My Bell" by Anita Ward ends. He checks his watch. "Time flies when you're having fun."

"Does this still work?" Zane asks.

"Yup," Demitri says. He smiles at Rachelle. "Good to see you again. Where's Brian?"

"Um . . . ," Rachelle mumbles.

"We have a problem," Zane interjects. "Brian will be here shortly. His helicopter flight from Vegas was delayed. That's convenient because we need to talk to you."

"Okay, go ahead," Demitri prompts pensively.

Zane looks to Rachelle, who takes up the thread. "Brian asked me to marry him at my birthday dinner last night."

"Congratulations," I say. I'm surprised, given the affair Zane and Rachelle had, but people do wild things, and Brian seems to have forgiven the indiscretion of his brother and girlfriend.

"Thank you," Rachelle says bashfully. "The timing wasn't great, given this meeting tonight." She ducks her head. "We told Brian you guys invited us over to play board games."

"I guess I'll whip out the old Trivial Pursuit," Mr. Cantrell says pensively as he snags the box from a bookshelf.

"Zane, Brian, and I have been in counseling regarding the affair," Rachelle says. "At our last therapy session, three weeks ago, we were encouraged to set boundaries so we can move forward and leave the affair in the past. Brian's boundary was that zero further issues arise from the affair." She tears up.

"Discovery of my STD condition reared up after that agreement, and then Brian proposed," Zane says, taking over this slog through awkward town. "If this STD issue is broached, it violates the agreement we made, and he'll retract the proposal."

Demitri's eyebrows rise. I wince, suspecting where this is headed.

"Would you check me?" Rachelle asks. "If I'm in the clear, then we play board games. If I'm not . . ." She looks to Zane.

"If Rachelle has an issue, then it means Brian does also," Zane says. "We're hoping you'll heal him without mentioning why."

"There are two problems with that," Demitri says, with a hint of frustrated disgust. "First, I think your brother will notice when I pour sweat while I secretly heal him. Second, I have a standing rule that I don't violate another with my abilities, uninvited."

"I have a solution for both of those issues," Zane says.

"What's the solution?" Demitri asks, but an answer is cut off by a knock on the door.

Mr. Cantrell opens it, while Demitri's head drops, and Zane and Rachelle appear nervous.

Brian strolls in, grinning. "Hey guys! Thanks for the invite."

"Sure thing," Mr. Cantrell says, covering well the awkward tension that Brian just interrupted. "I'll order pizza." He grabs the cordless phone and heads into the kitchen.

"Hey, D?" Zane says casually as he crosses to the dining table and opens the Trivial Pursuit box that Mr. Cantrell left there.

"Yeah?" Demitri says hesitantly.

"You have that healing ability, and Rachelle has had chronic stomach issues lately. Her doctor can't figure it out. Any chance you'd check?" He asks the question offhandedly.

"Sure," Demitri says and looks to Rachelle. "If you'd like."

"That would be amazing," she says. "Thank you."

Demitri gestures to our bedroom, and I give him a stern look. There's no way I'm fine with him and Rachelle in our room alone. He winces slightly, but Rocco saves him.

"I'll come too," Rocco says. "My . . . finger . . . hurts." At the disbelieving look Zane gives him, Rocco shrugs. "Surfing injury," he lies, doing a shit job of being casual.

Brian looks at me quizzically and I shrug. "I burped and sneezed at the same time last year and threw my back out for two days," blurts from me. I grimace at the oddity.

Mr. Cantrell, who returned from his pizza ordering call, spurts laughter.

"Weird injuries happen?" I say as a question, instead of a statement. Apparently, I'm not any better at this than Rocco.

Demitri's face squishes up. "Need me to heal that?"

"Nope," I chirp. "All better."

Demitri looks at me like I'm an idiot before leading Rocco and Rachelle to our room and closing the door. Zane abandons the game setup and rushes to me. Mr. Cantrell engages Brian in a conversation while Zane drags me out to the front porch. He closes the door and instantly tears up.

"What's wrong?" I ask, surprised by his emotional meltdown. Zane rarely falls apart, but lately, he's been a mess.

"I checked my messages this morning." Zane shakes his head mournfully. "The message you left . . ."

I scrunch my face, confused. I think back and, "Ohhh," breathes from me. "I'm sorry, Zane."

"When did you leave it in relation to your suicide attempt?"

"Right before I cut my wrist," I admit.

Zane pulls me in, engulfing me in a hug, while his heart clearly breaks. His hands are shaking on my back while he sobs.

The door opens and Mr. Cantrell slips out, closing it behind him. "Hey," he says softly, putting a hand on Zane's shoulder. "I felt you fall apart. Anything I can help with?"

Zane lets me go and scrubs at his face, trying to pull it together. "Um, I just needed to tell Melanie I was sorry I didn't help her when she came to me needing to escape Trey."

Mr. Cantrell smile is compassionate, but it's also laced with extreme worry for Zane. "I promise we're taking good care of her," he divulges. "What you walked in on, them dancing, is how it is every moment now."

Zane wipes his face hard again. "I'm glad," he whispers, sounding regretful. He takes a deep breath. "There's no excuse for me having been so whacked out that I just got that message, Melanie. Hearing it this morning was my breaking point." He fights to breathe.

I lace my hand with his, and he manages to calm down some.

"I'm not a daily drug user, but I've got a habit of going on occasional benders. The physical addiction is gone because of

Demitri's healing work, but I need to deal with the psychological reason that I do this, so I don't slip back into bad habits."

"Do you want to talk about that?" I ask gently.

"Yes, but I need more help than a chat tonight can provide. I'm going to be gone for a few months." He slides nearly dead eyes to me. "I'm going to rehab."

My eyebrows rise. "I'm really proud of you."

"I'm not proud of me," Zane admits, "but thank you."

"I think you're doing the right thing," Mr. Cantrell says supportively. "I know it's not easy."

"Thank you." Zane rubs his forehead hard with his thumb. "Can I still be friends with you, Melanie?"

"Always," I reply, meaning it. I squeeze his hand. "That never changes. You're one of my very best friends, who's tolerated so much from me. That goes both ways. It's my turn to be here for you while you slay your demons."

Zane's eyes scrunch tight.

"Hey," I say softly. "Anything that scares you has to get through me." I smirk, confident I can take on the world for him.

"Can you combat a pathetic lack of self-esteem that creates severe depression, leading to a need to escape through a heroin addiction? Also, a habit of trolling strip clubs as a form of self-flogging because I secretly think I'm worthless and being a bottom-feeding junkie who exposes himself to STD-ridden trash is what I deserve?" Zane blusters, disintegrating.

Mr. Cantrell lets out a huge exhale in response to what Zane just word-vomited.

My heart races at Zane's admission, but I keep my expression in check, grateful he isn't an energy worker who can empathically feel my emotions. "Yup," I say. "I can combat all of that. You're my

Zaney, and I believe in you, even when you don't. You're amazing, talented, hilarious, devastatingly handsome, and incredibly generous. That's not why I love you though."

Zanes head falls.

I lift his chin to look into his eyes. "I love you because you have a heart of gold. You're there for everyone, without fail or compromise. The only person you need to love a little more is yourself. I'll show you how, because I love you soul deep."

"I wasn't there for you, and you tried to kill yourself," Zane chokes out.

I shrug. "Guess we're even." I smile softly. "I wasn't there for you, and you killed yourself. I brought you back and did nothing to help you through why you did that."

"In your defense, you had a death sentence hanging over your head in exchange for my soul's return," Zane reminds me.

"So did you, but I didn't realize it." At his confused look, I explain, "Your death sentence was in the form of pressure. You've worried incessantly about me, along with masterminding my career that I owe to you, since we met. In a lot of ways, you've been more my husband than Trey or Pierre ever were."

Zane tips his head back and chokes out a desperate whimpering sound. Tears pour down his cheeks. He puts his hands over his face.

"Let it out," Mr. Cantrell encourages. "Don't fight it."

Zane kneels, and his back racks while he loses his mind. Silently supportive, Mr. Cantrell puts a hand on his back and kneels next to him.

Zane hugs my legs tight, with his cheek pressed to my stomach. "God, Melanie," he sobs out. "You have no idea how much I love you. Please!"

My face scrunches painfully while tears roll down my cheeks.

Mr. Cantrell stands, putting a hand on my back while I suffer through the idea of losing my forever with Zane. I went to him first for a reason, and I fear I'm not doing much to hide that while I lose my emotional shit on my boyfriend's front porch. Lucky for me, Mr. Cantrell seems damn good at understanding layers and offering grace. He starts to leave, and I shake my head, needing him to stay, because I don't trust myself not to run from this porch as fast and hard as I can with Zane, who's got a drug problem, a hooker hankering, and a lot of his own struggles to deal with that aren't compatible with my issues.

I wrap my arms around Zane's head and hide him while he works through his desperate need to turn back time to when I chose him, because that future is obliterated. He had his chance, and I've moved on. I've moved way too fast if I'm being honest with myself, but that's a problem for later.

Our tears finally calm, and Zane stands, taking a deep breath. "My drug addiction revved completely out of control the night of your handfasting, and I've been a disaster ever since," he admits. "It existed before that, but not like this."

I nod, relieved that we've gotten through the breakdown and we're back to talking things out. "After what happened that night, I don't blame you for running from me, cutting me out of your life, or not answering my call. I blame myself for showing up at the Beach Bar. Yes, I needed help, but I should have respected your boundaries. I violated that and I apologize." I gesture to Mr. Cantrell. "I obviously have other people I could go to."

"I'm going to get my head on straight," Zane says. "Rehab is humiliating, and it'll be all over the news, but I have no choice. You almost died because I was acting like an absolute embarrassment with two women I wouldn't normally even glance at. Knowing that my priorities got that skewed, I must fix this."

I squeeze his hand. "You call me if you need anything. I'll listen. I'll show up. I'll help you."

"You too, Melanie," Zane chokes out. "I swear I will. Please don't let me not helping you this time sway your trust in me."

I laugh, but it's supportive. "After what you did for me in the hospital TWICE? I think I know what lengths you'll go to for me." I let his hand go, and murmur to Mr. Cantrell, "I'll head inside."

He nods, and I take my leave, trusting Mr. Cantrell to help Zane.

I step into the living room and close the door behind me. Tears boil up as my throat tightens, and I panic, feeling trapped. Unable to stop the tears, I face the inevitable and head across the living room.

"Whoa," Demitri says softly, making his way to me.

"I'm okay," I gasp, not okay at all. I keep moving, and Demitri rushes to follow. I get to our room, and he slips in before I can close the door.

"Hey, hey, hey," he softly murmurs, wrapping me in a hug.

It's the opposite of what I hoped he'd do, which is leave me alone. It's also exactly what I need. I collapse against his chest, and he holds me tight while I sob.

"I've got you," Demitri murmurs, as I hear the door open and close.

"Hey," Rocco softly says. I look his way, and he smiles sadly. "I was wondering how that would go."

"Someone talk to me," Demitri says.

"Zane checked his messages this morning," Rocco explains. "He was a wreck when I arrived at his apartment. Melanie left him a message the day she tried to kill herself. Considering how long it has been, he really dropped the ball. He called the Malibu Rehab Center, and I'm driving him there tomorrow morning. He's checking himself in."

Demitri runs his fingers under my eyes attempting to dry the tears that keep falling. He tries to reassure me. "Zane's going to be better now. This is a good thing."

"I agree," I whisper. "I'm okay. I was just surprised and overwhelmed, is all."

Demitri squeezes my arm. "I'm going to go check on Brian and Rachelle. We've left them alone." He slips out, and I double over.

"The message you left was heartbreaking," Rocco murmurs now that it's just us. "Zane made the rehab decision on his own, while I sat with him. He called, crying so hard that the registration gal couldn't even understand him. I had to take the phone and give all his information."

I take a huge bubbly breath.

"While I'm sorry that it almost destroyed you when he wasn't there for you, something good came of it. You saved Zane." Rocco hugs me. "Thank you," he says, a little choked up. "That man is my ride or die. I don't make it without my best friend."

"Please take care of him," I plead. "Don't let him screw hookers or fall victim to drug tendencies."

"I won't," Rocco says. "I knew about his hooker issue, but that had greatly improved once you were in his life. When he shut you out, old habits roared back, but I figured he needed to cope. I didn't know he had a drug habit, or I would have put the hammer down. I'll have an eagle eye on him when he gets out of rehab."

I take his hands. "We'll get Zane through this."

Rocco nods. "You and me, we can do this."

I smile softly to myself. "You and me" is my mantra with Zane, and it's fitting that Rocco said it.

We make our way back out to the living room, where we find everyone eating pizza around the table.

Zane's pulled it together, and he's sitting next to Mr. Cantrell.

"Heck yes, I think Demitri can help with your chronic migraines, Brian," Zane is in the middle of saying. "He brought me back from death, after all. What's a little headache to Superman?"

Demitri's eyes widen, and I curb a desire to laugh. This happens to D all the time. Everyone thinks he's superhuman. He usually is, but it's a lot of pressure on a teenage guy.

"I have to take medical exams every time my pilot's license renews," Brian explains. "My migraines have gotten so bad that I don't think they'll renew my license." He appears worried sick. "Sometimes they hit when I'm flying, and I can't see. It's horrible and has become a safety risk I can't responsibly overlook."

"I can see how that could be a hindrance," Demitri says. "What else do they check with this physical?"

"Everything right down to a psychological exam," Brian says. "Head to toes."

Zane looks to Demitri. "Think you could give him the old full-body once-over and just fix anything that ails him?"

Demitri shrugs. "If that's okay with Brian, sure."

"Yup," Brian says, pushing his chair out, standing up. "I've got one request, though."

"What's that?" Demitri asks.

"I don't want to know about anything you find," Brian says. "I've worried myself sick that I've got some horrible brain cancer. Are you willing to just fix me and let me live in blissful ignorance?"

"Works for me," Demitri says, heading to our bedroom.

They close the door behind them, and Rachelle and Zane exhale hard.

"I can't BELIEVE that worked," Rachelle says to Zane.

"I knew it would," he replies. "Brian's been so worried about what they'd find that he refused to even go to the doctor about his headaches."

"You're a manipulative turd," I scold Zane.

"Perhaps," he replies, "but I've also learned my lesson, and there's no sense in hurting Brian now that I've cleaned up my act."

"You got lucky that everything shook out so favorably," Mr. Cantrell guides Zane. "Be grateful and move forward mindfully."

"Yes, sir," Zane replies.

I snag a piece of pizza and take a seat at the table. We chat, laughing and cutting up, until Demitri and Brian emerge, joining us. "All good?" I ask Demitri casually, but I'm positive Rachelle and Zane are dying for an answer.

"Yup," Demitri replies.

"I feel *so* much better," Brian says.

Demitri heads into the kitchen.

I follow, with Zane right on my heels. "How bad?" I ask while Demitri fills a plate.

"Same as Zane had," Demitri quietly informs us.

"What was causing the migraines?" Zane asks. "He's had them his whole life, but man, did it get bad."

"I'm surprised he didn't give in and go to the doctor," Demitri says. "His chronic pain is worse than you think. He should have known that he was full of creepy-crawlers, because what you had was mild compared to the severity of Rachelle's infections. She's definitely the one who infected you." Demitri shakes his head. "Brian was nearly as impacted because he and Rachelle have been together so long. Anyhow, the STD discomfort was masked by his raging fibromyalgia."

"Whaaaaat?" Zane breathes.

Demitri nods. "I got it knocked out."

"Thank you for helping my brother," Zane says.

"You're welcome," Demitri says. "Meley, give us a minute."

I look up at him suspiciously.

"Don't worry about it, love," he says.

"Please don't start a fight," I whimper.

"I'm not."

I leave, joining the Trivial Pursuit game that just got started. We're in a heated competition by the time Zane and Demitri come out of the kitchen. Zane has a hard jawline as he makes his way to me with purposeful strides. I stand, alarmed by his expression. He scoops me up, hugging me tight while my feet dangle.

"Zane, what's wrong?"

"I had no idea, Melanie," Zane murmurs.

"About what?" I murmur back, realizing everyone is watching this.

"Demitri will tell you." Zane sets me down with tears in his eyes.

"What's happening, Demitri?" I ask.

"Zane needed to know some stuff," Demitri replies.

Zane demands of Demitri, "Swear to me you won't let Trey kill her!" It comes out a snarl, but there's fear behind the sentiment.

"I promise," Demitri assures him. "She needs to move her stuff out of Mabel's, but I'll be there."

"I can be there also," Rocco says.

Demitri shakes his head. "While I appreciate that, she's my girl. I'm taking this seriously, but I need everyone to let me handle what I need to."

Zane snarls in frustration.

"Zane," Rocco says, "you're headed to rehab in the morning. We need you to worry about you, while Demitri takes care of Melanie."

Zane paces across the room. He turns toward us and flourishes his arms. "She needs a security team. I'd hire retired Secret Service agents. She needs a moving team to go in, overseen by me. I'd move into a different building, with a security-monitored front entrance." He glares at Demitri. "I know you're trying, but WHY hasn't this all been handled already?"

"It's only been four days since she arrived here," Mr. Cantrell informs on Demitri's behalf, because Demitri looks overwhelmed with this line of questioning from Zane.

"FOUR DAYS!" Zane bellows. He inhales sharply, dropping his tone. "I would have handled it the minute she walked through my door!" He glares at Demitri. "How did beating the shit out of Trey for what he's done to her go?"

"I confronted him," Demitri says. "We got into it, but my goal was just to get her out of there. We didn't get a chance to get her stuff. Mabel asked that we wait."

"Of course she did," Zane says in a demeaning tone. "Mabel doesn't want to lose Melanie, so she's stalling. You agreed?"

Demitri blinks rapidly, seeming unsure what to do.

"Simmer down, Zane," Rocco says. "Demitri's doing his best. Melanie is safe and seemed really happy when we arrived. We're all feeling better." Rocco gives Zane a pointed look, indicating that he needs to watch it. "Demitri healed everyone, which he didn't have to do. Cut him some slack. Not everyone is Zane Drell, but last I checked, Demitri Cantrell brings some very solid qualities to the table."

Zane puts his hands over his face and harshly inhales and exhales. "You don't understand," he finally says to Demitri. "You can't possibly get it. When Melanie was in the hospital . . ." He tears up again and snarls, "I'm so FUCKING SICK of crying." He growls again, fed up. His gaze settles on Demitri. "When Melanie was in the hospital for a month with that broken neck, it was her and me. We were rarely interrupted, and when we were, the person briefly visited and then left. Melanie was mine. I know how she likes her coffee, her favorite shows, we have more inside jokes than I can begin to list." He shakes his head, losing steam, but he got his point across.

I'm a dejected mess on the inside, but this is what it is. Knowing I'm likely the only one who can curb this meltdown, I speak up. "Zane, I'm okay. I promise. I'd tell you if I wasn't. You need to focus on rehab."

Zane stares off into space before nodding. "Okay," he says, giving up.

"I think we should head out," Rocco says.

Brian, Rachelle, and Rocco say their goodbyes before shuttling Zane out the door.

"Who needs to talk?" Mr. Cantrell asks after the front door closes.

"I do," Demitri says.

I go into the bedroom and close the door. Talking is the last thing I want to do.

CHAPTER *18*

Demitri and I are still lounging in bed. We woke up an hour ago, but it's Sunday morning and there's nothing to get ready for. We're doing okay now, because we hashed everything out last night after Mr. Cantrell gave me some time to ruminate on my own. Turns out that I do better when I openly communicate. Shocker, right? Anyhow, I was honest with Demitri about the porch talk, and he was honest with me that he doesn't like it. His father interjected, rationalizing that I made him stay during the talk with Zane, and that seemed to help Demitri believe that I'm on the up and up. So, in a better place now, I close my eyes and lay my head on Demitri's chest. He's reading and rubbing my back absently with his free hand.

My cell phone rings, and I groan. Demitri puts his book down, reaches for my phone on his nightstand, and hands it to me.

I answer, putting it on speaker. "Hello?"

"What's up, Mel?"

"Same shit, different Sunday."

Tanner laughs. "Righhhht. Nothing new. Finley and I want to hang with you two today. Wanna go to the Renaissance Faire?"

I sit up with bouncy excitement. "Renn Faire! Are you serious?" This is EXACTLY what I need.

"Yup," Tanner says, excited. "You know you want to."

Demitri contemplates my hopeful expression. "We're in."

We hear Finley squeal. "Perfect! Oh, Mel, we're going to have so much fun."

I giggle, loving Finley's enthusiasm. "What's the plan?"

"Is it okay if I pick the two of you up at ten?"

We quickly accept Tanner's offer, hang up, and hightail it to get ready.

— —

We hear a knock at the door. Mr. Cantrell answers as we get to the living room.

I squeal and rush to Finley. "You're gorgeous," I exclaim, as I survey her pink-and-teal fairy costume, complete with intricate wings that I'm positive Tanner designed for her.

Finley grins. "*We're* gorgeous." She hands me a wrapped gift.

My eyes widen. "One for me?"

Tanner cocks a hip in his tight black jeans and swashbuckling heeled boots. He's wearing a teal blousy dress shirt, along with a black corset that appears to be designed specifically for his male body. His set of fairy wings matches Finley's. "Girl, do you really think I'd let you go to the Renaissance Faire in jean shorts?"

Demitri chuckles. "How do you do that, Tanner? No other guy on the planet can pull off fairy wings and make every girl drool."

Tanner snaps a sassy look Demitri's way. "There may be one other guy on the planet who can." He smirks. "I happen to have your measurements because I've made dance costumes for you." He reaches past the doorjamb and brings another wrapped package into sight.

Mr. Cantrell chuckles, enjoying our banter.

Tanner hands the package to Demitri with a flourish.

Demitri looks at Tanner like he's insane. "We just said yes. How did you get this done so quick?"

Tanner chuckles. "I knew Mel would want to go, so I knocked out the costumes yesterday."

Tanner and Finley pose in unison, and their gorgeous wings flap.

Tanner grins. "Yours flap also."

Demitri sighs heavily.

"Give it a shot," I encourage him. "If you don't like it, you can ditch the wings."

Demitri rolls his eyes, but he's amused.

"Pleeeease, Demitri," Tanner begs. "I need a guy friend who will play. I've been shackled with Mr. Grumpapotomus."

Demitri chuckles. "All right, that did it. I'll give it a shot."

Mr. Cantrell cracks up and points at Demitri. "You're going to spend the whole day in pink fairy wings?"

Tanner snaps a haughty look Mr. Cantrell's way. "Do you really think I'd put DEMITRI in pink wings? Please!" He grins. "The pink wings are in the car. Wanna come with?"

Mr. Cantrell rolls his neck back. "Yes, but also no."

Finley and Tanner squeal, while Mr. Cantrell glances Demitri's way.

Demitri smiles at his dad. "I'd love for you to join us."

Mr. Cantrell winces. "How about I avoid the fairy costume, but come along?"

We all exclaim our excitement.

There's nowhere else in the world like Renn Faire, and I nostalgically take in the mixed aroma of turkey legs, caramel, essential oil perfumes, and happiness.

When I open my eyes, Finley is gazing at me. "I've never seen you this relaxed, Melanie."

"I've been a lot more depressed than I realized. It feels weird to be happy."

Our quiet girl talk is cut short as a red-and-black wand snakes around my side. It suddenly lights with a red glow, and bubbles shoot out the top.

"Bubbles," I squeal and grab the wand. I whip around and leap into Demitri's arms.

"I saw it and thought you needed a fairy wand."

I pose and hit the button, letting loose a cascade of bubbles. Finley poses to match, holding a purple-and-teal wand. She pushes her button, and Tanner laughs as he's coated in bubbles.

Demitri high-fives Tanner. "Bubbles create happiness. Mission accomplished."

Mr. Cantrell chuckles. "You two girls are the cutest thing I've ever seen."

Finley and I link arms, and we're off, strutting through the Faire. The guys follow us, and we come to a large crowd watching a show on a stage. The actor and actress are working through slapstick hilarity with an audience participant.

"Hi, guys," jubilantly tinkles.

I hug Jayla, while Dante claps Demitri on the shoulder. They survey us in our fairy costumes as Demitri drapes an arm around my shoulders.

"You good?" Jayla asks quizzically.

I nod absently, not wanting to discuss this. People at school have figured out there's something up, but the details have yet to be splashed about. Dante and Jayla are our good friends, but keeping the sorted details private seems better for now.

The actors freeze as the audience participant is dragged comically from the stage. The actor playing the comedic flirt points our direction. "Black wings, let's go. Let's see if you can steal my girl!"

Demitri laughs evilly, and women gasp as they watch him strut through the crowd. His custom male corset, that Tanner made for him, dramatizes the impressive V shape of his waist. His tush is spectacular in the fitted black pants as he traverses the steps before turning with a modelesque flourish. "I've arrived, per the request of a simpleton." He gives the actor who summoned him an arrogant look.

The actor's eyebrows rise, and he grins at the audience.

"Scene," the narrator prompts.

"My love, there's no one but you who could ever win my heart." The female actress coyly wafts a feather fan while she bats her eyelashes at the actor who called Demitri to the stage.

"Best never to forget that, Guenevere."

The narrator announces, "All was well, until . . ." He points Demitri's way.

Demitri rapidly pirouettes the actress's way before launching into a grand split leap. He lands, crouched on the wooden stage just behind her, while she comically pans a surprised look over her shoulder. Demitri stands dramatically, taking the fan from her and snapping it closed with the flick of a wrist.

"Smooth," the narrator says.

Demitri's wings rapidly flap as he fans the woman. "Don't bring a fan to do a fairy's job," he smolders.

The actress giggles.

Demitri flirts with her. "You make me flutter. Wanna fly away?"

The actress swoons. "Oh my."

"There's nothing solid about the constitution of a fairy," the male actor crows indignantly to his beloved.

Demitri fluffs his wings haughtily. "Once this corset is off and I regain blood flow, I'm solid indeed!"

Even the actors howl with laughter as the audience doubles over.

Demitri juts his tush comically in the girl's direction. He bats his wings and coyly asks, "How are you with a knot, gorgeous dame?"

The actress points to the back of Demitri's corset with a dramatic finger. "Knots, I can handle, but this appears to be a bow. Whatever will I do?" Feigning vapors, she sinks to her knees.

Demitri backbends over her and pulls himself into a handstand on one arm. He hits the wing button in his other hand and rapidly fans her.

"Oh, my," she repeats, but she's not acting this time.

We all howl with laughter again.

The woman snakes around to look into Demitri's upside-down eyes. "Perhaps if we find a knife, we could free the flow of passion."

Demitri gracefully flips to his feet and wraps an arm around the actress's waist. He dips her low. She squeals with girly surprise.

"I'm ripe with anticipation, but a knife . . ." He scans about comically. "Ah, a solution is afoot." He scoops the woman up and turns rapidly around the actor playing her suitor while his wings flap, then snags a ceremonial knife that's tucked into the actor's belt. "Thank you, kind sir. Your dagger will infuse my dagger." He looks to the woman in his arms. "Let's fly!"

The woman's expression is hilarious.

Cradling her, Demitri rapidly spins toward the side of the stage, before dramatically leaping out of sight with his wings batting frantically. He's brought back to the stage by the actress, and applause roars as he takes a quick bow. When he gives the actor his knife back, he gets a pat on the shoulder from the amused guy. He looks to the actress and flirtatiously flutters his wings while announcing,

"Blood flow still works. We don't need the knife."

Demitri struts down the stairs while the actress announces, "I think I need a minute," and fans her face.

The audience laughs again. I hug Demitri, all smiles, as he gets back to us.

"Go find a grassy spot," Mr. Cantrell tells us. "I'll get us turkey legs."

Demitri offers to help, and Jayla and Dante saunter away with him and Mr. Cantrell.

Tanner holds out two crooked elbows, and Finley and I lace our arms with his. Tanner doesn't stop until we're well out of the crowd. We sit in the grass.

Tanner hits me with a serious look. "You and Demitri are a thing of perfection. I'll admit that Trey asked me to feel out the situation."

I clear my throat, suddenly weighed down with reality. "How is he?"

Tanner huffs as he slips off his wings. "Furious. Irrational. Generally dickish. Pompous. Full of fear."

I scrunch my face. "I'm scared of him."

"Judging from what he was like during my talk last night, you should be."

Demitri and Mr. Cantrell join us as Tanner says that. They pass out turkey legs and drinks.

"Explain," Mr. Cantrell requests.

Tanner winces. "The way he talked about Melanie boiled my ass. He was possessive, but also dismissive. I pointed that out, and his reaction was pure entitled arrogance. Melanie, I'm stunned you didn't leave sooner."

My shoulders cave in. "I stayed out of obligation."

Tanner's expression droops. "I'm so sorry, Melanie. I'm scared of what he'll do if you walk back into that apartment without all of us there."

My thoughts tornado as fear races. "It's taken so much not to lose it and kill him." I inhale hard. "Every time he . . . I was scared my dark-water side would finally blast him. I can't always control it!" My eyes snap wide. "What the hell am I doing here?" I mutter to myself. I look around, suddenly scared to be at a festival. "I've wasted five days!" keens from me. "I should have disappeared the day I left school." Everything cyclones at once, and my chest rattles as I fail to inhale. My asthma proves to be a mean bitch today as my lungs seize.

"Damn it! Her inhaler's at the house." Demitri kneels by me as Tanner eases me to the ground. D puts his hands on my chest. I feel him scan my lungs. His forehead beads sweat, but his eyes quickly snap wide. "I can't fix it!"

"Get help," Tanner orders Finley. "Hurry."

She takes off running.

My blockage with Trey crashes down, and he roars into my psyche. He scans my condition while looking through my eyes as I watch Finley run toward the Renaissance Faire in the distance. I feel him yank the steering wheel hard. He sends, *"I'm on the way. Hang on, Melanie. I'm around the corner."* I see him pop open his glove box and pull out my inhaler he keeps in his car.

Mr. Cantrell puts his hand on my sternum and sends a calm wave of energy. I try to gasp, but to no avail. Mr. Cantrell holds my hand, and I see panic in his eyes. I hear pounding feet as medics rush to us. When Mr. Cantrell is ordered to move, he hesitantly backs away. An oxygen tank is cranked before a mask is put over my mouth and nose. I still can't get a breath, and my eyesight starbursts.

One of the medics demands, "Call an ambulance! Someone find an inhaler. There must be one here."

I see through Trey's eyes as Finley spots him. He's running, and demands, "Where is she?"

Finley grabs his arm, and they race through the crowd. Trey comes into view and orders the medics to give him space. My eyes flutter as something is shoved between my lips. I taste my inhaler mist, but it goes nowhere. Trey hits me with another puff and pinches my nose and mouth closed, keeping the mist in me. I attempt to inhale, but it doesn't work. Trey releases his grip on my face. My chest is so tight it feels like it's going to explode.

"We have to do this, Melanie. Gut up." Trey puts the inhaler in his mouth, hitting the button three times, but not inhaling. He pinches my nose, locks his lips over mine, and I know what's coming. Panic irrationally fills me, and I fight to get away from Trey. He forcibly holds me down, locking his leg over my hips. He exhales hard into my lungs, forcing the medicine further into the constriction. I wrench my face away from him.

"Damn it, Melanie, stop fighting me." Trey straddles me, trapping me under him, and hits the puffer three more times, before grabbing my hands and yanking my arms over my head, immobilizing me further. He forces his lips on mine and exhales hard into my mouth while tears run down my face. He clamps down on my mouth and nose and orders, "Hold it, Melanie. I know it hurts."

I stare into his eyes, frozen. The medicine makes me both jittery and limp.

I droop, and Trey softly says, "There it is. Relax into it, Melanie." He lets go of my mouth, and I exhale. Trey scoots off me and caps the inhaler, handing it to Demitri. "Never leave the house without that. I have them in every room in the suite, in both of our cars, and in my backpack. Melanie's asthma is panic-induced. It's nearly killed her twice. Do what I just did. She'll fight you, but you must force the albuterol into her lungs."

The medics back off a few steps, and one asks, "You're EMT trained?"

Trey nods. "She's my wife. I've got her."

"Do you want the oxygen tank?"

"She's okay now. She just needs a minute." As the medics walk away, Trey brushes my hair from my face. "You okay?"

I nod, croaking, "Thank you."

"That's what he does, isn't it?" Demitri bellows.

"Demitri," Tanner says cautiously, but it doesn't stop Demitri.

I glance around, relieved that there's no one near.

Demitri stabs his finger Trey's way. "You've severely damaged Melanie. I've started using my energy-mapping abilities to rewire her pathways. Her pain and sensuality centers are all crisscrossed and wired together in ways that are dangerously not right."

"What?" That's news to me.

Demitri takes a deep breath before telling me, "The pain you've been in for the past few months is caused by wicked scar tissue. That's what I work on when you sleep."

My mouth drops open.

Trey rubs his face hard. "Did the scar tissue show up on a scan you did?"

"I've scanned for it, but that's not how I found it, Trey."

"It's so bad that it's noticeable without a scan?" I whimper.

Demitri puts his hands on my cheeks. "Don't freak out. Yes, it is. It's going to be okay."

My self-esteem completely craters as I survey Finley, Tanner, and Mr. Cantrell. I'm humiliated that they're hearing this.

"How bad is it?" Trey asks.

"It's devastating!" Demitri bellows. "Now I'm POSITIVE that you caused it!"

"What about Zane?" Trey asks.

"She's never been with Zane," Demitri replies.

"Seriously?" Trey asks me.

"Wow," I whimper. "I've told you that."

"I didn't think you were telling me the truth," Trey admits.

"Demitri, how many people have known about this personal issue while I've been oblivious?" I shirk away from Demitri, and Finley puts an arm around me.

Demitri winces. "Zane, Adam, and my dad."

Humiliated tears brim in my eyes. "Now you've added Tanner and Finley? I don't want people to know something like this!"

"I'm sorry, Melanie. I needed help."

"I'm not saying a word to anyone," Tanner assures me.

"I would never tell anyone about this, Melanie," Finley adds.

A memory jumps into my head from Trey. I didn't search for it, but I'm apparently spun out enough that my abilities are going wonky. My eyes close, and the memory plays in my mind. I see my bunched back through Trey's eyes, with my hand tense on the headboard. My head hangs. I'm obviously in shock, but I didn't realize it at the time. I distinctly remember that harsh night. Trey shoves away from me and wipes sweat from his forehead as he thinks, *'There. Romantic night accomplished. Hopefully I wore her out. If she'll just go to sleep, I can leave.'*

I come back to reality and realize, based on the state of everyone, that I accidently projected the memory to them. Trey grips his head as he processes the memory. Demitri's hand is over his mouth with his eyes squeezed closed.

There's apparently no privacy, so I decide to make sure everyone understands. I pull my memory of that night and send it, uninvited, into all their minds. They close their eyes and witness the tail end of the pain Trey was putting me through. In the memory, Trey shoves away from me and goes into the bathroom. When he closes the door, tears roll down my cheeks.

'I asked him for a romantic night. This isn't what I meant.'

I'm shivering in pain as I hear the shower come on. Realizing that he's occupied, I jump up and grab a pair of sweatpants and a hoodie from the closet. I put them on as fast as possible. I feel safer in as much covering as I can get. I curl up in bed and pull the covers over my head. My eyes light on my wedding ring, and I'm scared.

I hear the door open and close. Certain that he's gone, I reach for the phone on the nightstand. I hesitate, knowing Demitri isn't speaking to me, but desperation wins. Demitri answers.

"Can I please come to your house?"

"What's wrong, Meley?"

I close my eyes tight and manage to say in something close to a normal tone, "Nothing. I'm just bored."

Now that I sound okay, Demitri's tone shifts to aloofness. "I've got plans with Dad."

"Sorry to disturb you, D. Good night." My breathing is labored as I hang up. I wonder who else I can call. I settle on Adam but think twice because I don't want him to kill Trey. I just want someone to hold me. I try Zane, but he doesn't answer.

'I can't be here when Trey comes back from his office.' The thought sends my blood running cold. I grab my purse and peek out my door in the direction of Trey's office. Finding the coast clear, I scurry down the hall to my car in Mabel's parking lot. Realizing that I have nowhere to go because I can't wake my parents this late, I opt to drive to the neighborhood that Demitri and Adam both live in, a few blocks from each other. I park, unsure if I'm safe, but one of them would likely get to me in time if something happened.

After shutting off the car, I climb into my back seat and spread my blanket over me, clutching the stuffed bear Zane got me. Tears fall, and I'm an insecure mess about how needy and immature I am, but I now know that it's Trey's diatribe in my mind. I've heard it so many times that I believe it in the memory. It ends with me slipping into sleep.

We all open our eyes, and Finley tearfully asks Trey, "How could you do that to her?"

In traumatized silence, Trey stares at nothing.

Demitri hits me with blistering eyes. "I had NO idea that was happening that night!"

I know he means it to defend my honor, but his tone scares me. I'm still internally rattling. I rush back unintentionally, and Tanner stops me from behind with hands on my shoulders.

"Demitri, you need to tone it down," he says.

"I'm not mad at *you*!" Demitri blisters, totally spun out. "I'm mad at *myself*! I didn't realize what you were going through."

Finley puts a hand on Demitri's arm. "I think the problem is that Melanie was in slowly boiling water. She didn't know she was in trouble because the temperature rose subtly enough that she could handle a little more each time it got more intense. It became her normal operating procedure." She looks to Tanner. "If Melanie calls, sounding off, we must help her. She usually doesn't ask for help, and things are bad when she does, even if she tries to cover it."

Realizing everyone in this counseling cluster from hell is cratering, I face Tanner and stare at his shirt. I take a sharp breath and work to rally. My eyes jostle a touch. I get a firm handle on the shock and shove it down, locking it away somewhere deep inside. I feel my expression morph normal.

Tanner's eyes are huge. He's the only one who could see my face as I got it together. He breathes, "That's what you do. I recognize what just happened, but I didn't know what causes it until now. Melanie, we need to get you to a therapist."

"Therapists don't understand me. The things I'm capable of don't make sense to most people." I whip around to take Demitri to task. "Was this," I gesture about, "really the best place for *that* conversation?"

His shoulders slump. "Shit. I'm sorry, Melanie."

"I was so excited about today!"

Mr. Cantrell clears his throat. "There's more fun to be had. Melanie, what are you up for?"

I start to answer but get interrupted when Jayla bounces up in her rose-colored maiden costume. There's something sultry about the costume's innocence, and I suddenly feel like a vampy gothic hoe in my fairy outfit.

"Hey, Dante's about to start a music set on stage three," she informs. "Do you guys want to come watch?"

"There's heavy metal at the Renn Faire?" Tanner asks doubtfully.

"No," she chirps. "He plays the dulcimer hammer also."

"Weird flex," Tanner mutters.

"Come on," Finley encourages me. "It'll be fun."

Jayla studies me. "You okay?"

"Peachy," I reply, in a clipped tone. I don't want to discuss this with her.

Jayla leads the way back through the faire to a stage. We arrive just as the pretty music starts. Presley's by the side of the stage with Marcus. Her eyes narrow as she sees me. She skirts the crowd and snags my hand, pulling me to the side. Finley joins us.

"What's the haps?" Pres asks.

My chin shakes as I fight tears.

"It's a long story," Finley says. "Demitri just confronted Trey about some very personal stuff."

Presley rolls her eyes. "During Renn Faire? This nonsense is a Melanie playground!" She gestures around at the festivities that she likely isn't enjoying. My guess is that Marcus dragged her here because he's the tech guy for Dante. "What a douche."

"Hey Presley," Jayla says, joining us.

"Oh, ew," Presley grumbles.

Finley winces a little. Presley can't stand Jayla. Those two couldn't be more different. Presley is cynical on a good day, and downright cruel on a bad one. Jayla's gumdrop vibe comes across as fake to Pres.

Jayla deflates and scuttles to Demitri. We watch as she talks to him, before he puts an arm around her shoulders and leads her to a quiet spot.

"He can have a private chat with HER, but my personal snaptrap drama gets splashed publicly at Renn Faire?" I snarl.

"Wow," Finley mutters, glaring at Demitri.

Trey snorts, and I realize he's hovering.

Presley grabs my elbow and drags me to Demitri. "Yo, Peter Pan!" When Demitri looks to Presley, she rattles her hands about. "Clearly you were in line for a second helping of looks when God was passing out tact and a brain."

"What?" Demitri asks, seemingly miffed.

Trey smirks, having followed us. "You just publicly spilled your girlfriend's dirt, but you're privately cooing at Mary Poppins. You've riled up the hornet's nest." He flicks his eyes to Presley before laughing at Demitri.

"You two are DATING?" Jayla screeches at Demitri.

"Yes," Demitri says, but the breath he holds after he admits that makes me suspicious.

Trey rubs his face, and I know he's frustrated. It's a trademark of his. "I need to talk to you," he hisses at me.

"The LAST thing I want to do is discuss our nightmare here!" boils from me.

"Heeeyyyy," Marcus draws out as he joins us. "No clue what's up, but yelling isn't conducive to a dulcimer hammer concert on a balmy Sunday."

I glance over my shoulder to see half the spectators staring at us. "Ugh," I mutter. "Considering that I rode here with Tanner, I have no escape route."

"Let's bounce," Presley says. "I'll drive. This place sucks."

My head drops.

"Melanie was so excited to come here," Finley tells Presley.

"Oh, right," Presley says, surveying me. "Costumes and *everything*."

I slip off my wings and hand them to Demitri.

"Please, Melanie, I'm sorry," he implores, trying to hand the wings back, but I shake my head.

"Our *deepest* apologies for interrupting your little chat," Presley snarks nastily to Jayla. "Come on, Mel. We're going to gander through these weird trinket shops."

"Do you have any cash on you to shop?" Trey asks.

I shake my head, feeling pathetic.

"I heard from our banking rep this morning, Melanie," Demitri says. "Our joint account is set up. My account balance is being transferred today." He takes his wallet from his back pocket and hands me cash. "Go shopping."

I hand it back.

Trey looks shell-shocked before snapping into professional mode. "I need the account information. I'll wire transfer Melanie's thirty-three thousand over today." He pulls his wallet and takes out a stack of cash, giving me a quirky half smile. "How about I advance you three hundred now?"

"Less awkward plan," Mr. Cantrell says, holding cash my way.

"So much less awkward," I mutter.

"New plan," Presley snidely says, while pulling a little silver case from her purse. She waggles it about. "We're going to go smoke pot in my car and talk shit about all of you."

I exhale hard. "Perfect."

Presley sarcastically bats her eyelashes at me. "Do you need fairy wings for that?"

"Nope."

Finley slides off her wings and hands them to Demitri. "Neither do I," she says, less than chipper. "Nice work, Demitri. We were here to have fun."

"Luckily, I always have a whole case of *fun* sticks in my purse," Presley snarks.

"I'm going with," Tanner says, snatching Finley's and my wings from Demitri.

"Will you stay and talk to me?" Jayla asks Tanner, who's frequently Jayla's confidant.

"As IF!" Presley barks. "Who do you think is going to spark the shit talking?" She smirks at Tanner, who flamboyantly wiggles his shoulders.

"We've interrupted his and Jayla's little private chat long enough," I mutter scornfully.

"How rude of us," Presley sarcastically slimes at Jayla. "Toodles."

Finley, Tanner, and I follow Presley to the parking lot, leaving a flummoxed Demitri, Mr. Cantrell, and Jayla behind. Trey follows us and gets into his car as we pile into Presley's red Volkswagen Rabbit after she puts the top up.

CHAPTER 19

While Presley's catty shit talking certainly made me feel justified in my irritation, it did nothing toward clearing my head. The car ride back to the Cantrells' house was quiet, and I'm unsure how this is going to go now that Tanner has dropped us off. Mr. Cantrell got in his car and headed out for a date the moment we got back, and I'm less than thrilled to deal with Demitri alone.

"Can we please talk about all these difficult things?" Demitri asks.

I nod yes, then no. "We'll see."

Demitri exhales hard. "I'm sorry I blew up, but Zane was right that I didn't challenge Trey like I should."

"You picked the Renn Faire?" I ask, baffled.

Demitri winces. "I'll never have a discussion like that in a public place again. I apologize."

"Thank you," I say. "That checks that off the list of issues we must discuss. Knock it out while I'm willing."

"Okay." Demitri says. "I'll never fail to dig further when I suspect there's a problem. We all heard suspicion in my voice in the memory you sent of calling me. I'm incredibly rattled that I let it go so easily."

"Thank you. That wasn't on you, though. I needed help, but to admit that meant I had to face a huge issue that would unravel my life. I didn't know how to do that at the time and intentionally hid my need for help."

Demitri raises his eyebrows. "That was succinct."

"You've chosen the easy-peasy lemon-squeezy stuff. Points for you."

Demitri laughs halfheartedly. "Get your concerns out on the table."

"What the hell do you have going on with Jayla?" I ask.

Demitri's expression snaps confused. "Nothing, why?"

His response feels preplanned, and my suspicion intensifies. "What are you hiding, D?"

"I'm not hiding anything, Melanie." Demitri swallows hard. "Are you going to crawl back to Zane now that I've pissed you off?"

I snort. "No. Especially not now that you've informed that I'm horrifically damaged."

Demitri's head drops. "I'm so sorry I discussed that there. The way Trey held you down completely spun me out, and I snapped."

"I'm sorry," whispers from me as I burn fuchsia from humiliation that's been eating me alive since Demitri revealed the severity of my issue. I squeeze my eyes closed to get through this. "The last thing you, of all people, need is unpleasant . . ." I trail off, unable to say it.

"Holy crap," Demitri gasps. "Melanie, no! It's not like that." He hugs me. "Let's go to our room and lie down to discuss this. I need to show you the memory of the healing I'm doing so we can clear this up."

"Fine," I whisper.

Demitri guides me into his room. "Lie down, love." He scoots onto the bed and lies down next to me. He sets a hand low on my stomach.

I feel him scanning. I take the memory of the scan and am mortified by the sheer magnitude of the problem.

"The reason your gut always hurts is that the scar tissue doesn't stretch like normal tissue." He puts a hand on my cheek and looks me in the eye. "It's going to take a long time for me to fix this. Scar tissue is much harder to heal than fresh injuries."

"I know it's awkward repairing injuries caused by someone else."

His cell phone rings. He reaches over and snags it from the nightstand, silencing it after a quick glance at the number. "We'll get through it," he murmurs, as he sets his phone down. He lies back down and puts a hand on my cheek. "The last thing I want is for you to feel inadequate over this."

I start to respond, but his home phone rings.

He flicks his eyes toward the living room, clearly distracted. The ringing stops, and he focuses on me again. I start to respond, and the damn phone rings AGAIN.

"Seems like there's an emergency," I say. "Maybe you should answer it."

"I'll be right back," Demitri assures me. He leaves, closing the bedroom door behind him.

I wait for what feels like forever. Finally, I get up and head to the living room. I watch from the hall door as he hangs up and his head drops. "Bad news?" I ask.

His gaze snaps my way.

"Sorry," I say. "I got worried and decided to check on you."

"I need to handle something," he says. "I won't be long."

"Okay," I reply, unsure because we were right in the middle of an important, and incredibly embarrassing, conversation. "When will you be back?"

He glances at the wall clock. "It's only four. How about I take you to El Coyote for dinner at six?"

"I need to grab an outfit from my parents' house. I'll head over there and get ready, then come back here."

Demitri agrees, and I grab my makeup bag from his bathroom and snag my purse before heading to my car out front. Today has been a lot, but I'm hoping we can salvage it. A dinner date sounds really nice.

CHAPTER 20

I pull up to Demitri's house, but his Jeep is gone. I walk up the front steps and discover the door is locked. I ring the bell, but no one's home. I check under the doormat, and there's no key. I try calling Demitri, but he doesn't answer.

Damn it. I bet his phone is still silenced from our chat earlier.

I check the time on my phone: 6:03. With no idea what to do, I sit on the front steps and wait.

This is ridiculous, I think, as I check the time on my phone again. It's 6:26, and still no Demitri. I've tried calling him three more times, with no luck. I pop my spine, in disbelief that I've been stood up and locked out. I've been a lot of things, but the pathetic girl waiting on some guy's front stoop isn't one I'm comfortable with.

I don't want to go back to my parents' empty house.

An idea sparks, and I get into my car.

Walking into the Malibu Rehab Center is nerve-wracking. I have no clue what to expect, but it doesn't feel like a hospital. Considering how I detest them, that's a good thing.

A cheerful woman with a maternal feel smiles brightly. "Welcome. How can I help you?"

"I'm Melanie Slate." I flutter a bit, unsure.

"Hi, Melanie," the lady replies encouragingly. "I'm Jennifer."

"I'm here to see Zane Drell."

"I see." She cages. "Is he expecting you?"

"No." My head drops. "I'm sorry. I'll leave."

As I turn, the woman pats my hand that's still on the check-in desk. "Hang tight." She picks up a phone and dials a number. "Yes, hello. There's a Melanie Slate here." She smiles. "Excellent. I'll see her to visitor room one." She hangs up. "He'd love to see you." She guides me down a hall, explaining, "We keep our celebrity guests under lock and key. They get fangirl visitors."

"Understandable, particularly with Zane."

"Your willingness to leave clued me in that you likely aren't a fangirl," Jennifer informs me.

I'm guided into a serviceable little room with a couch and table with two chairs. I look around politely. I don't see any surveillance cameras and relax a little.

Zane strides through the door and smiles with everything in him when he sees me. "Seashell. Yes!" He hugs me while saying, "Thank you, Jennifer. Melanie is always on my approved visitor list."

"You got it," Jennifer replies, before pulling the door closed.

Zane gestures, and we take a seat on the couch.

"How are you doing?" I ask.

He sighs. "Good. This place isn't too bad. I've already had two counseling sessions." He winces. "My therapist is a rather no-nonsense type. Apparently, I need an escape, and choose," he wobbles his head about while imitating who I assume is his therapist, "unhealthy means to avoid my deeper feelings."

"Brandy would be a good route to avoid deep," I commiserate.

Zane swallows hard. "I've been honest with him about you. The situation seemed to interest him far more than the hookers and blow nonsense."

"I'm sure he was thrilled about our ages."

Zane shakes his head. "He was surprisingly cool about it. Apparently, life in the performance industry is built a little different. My therapist wants to meet with you."

I blow out a hard exhale. "I'll meet with him, if you think it'll help you."

"I have my next appointment in thirty minutes." Zane gives me a hopeful look.

"I have literally, truly, undeniably, nowhere to go," I inform him.

"Looks like I have company for a while," he says hopefully.

"Lucky guy," I reply with dejected sarcasm.

"The luckiest ever," Zane replies. "What's wrong, Melanie?"

I side-eye him. "You know when you've got a feeling? Not an intuition magical 'holy shit, it's coming' feeling, but an old-fashioned gut feeling?"

"Yeah," Zane replies suspiciously.

"He's hiding something."

"Who?" Zane chuckles. "No offense, but you have a collection of guys that are likely to hide something."

"Demitri."

"Amen and hallelujah," he breathes, before rattling his head. "I mean, so sorry to hear that."

I snicker.

"Sorry, but Mr. Perfect fucking up would be the greatest day of my life." Zane happily sighs, before looking at me quizzically. "Last night he was Mr. I need space to superhero up a solution while I sit around doing fuck-all," he smolders. I crack up while Zane rattles his head. "What changed?"

"Catering to Jayla Bethel," I say.

"Who and what?" Zane asks.

I giggle again. "Girl from school."

Zane's eyebrows rise. "Some high school bimbo?"

"Nope. She's so sweeeet and niiiiice," I slop. "You've met her. It's Split from the Hellcats."

"You have to be KIDDING? The timid one that flutters around the edges of the group?"

"Indeed," I reply. "She fluttered over timidly, and he catered to her after spilling dirt about me publicly that was so humiliating I thought I might have to dig a hole, die, and bury *myself* in a shallow grave in the middle of Renn Faire. The distinction between how he treated me and her, in the span of ten minutes, was very concerning."

Zane opens an arm so I can curl up against his side. "There now," he says once I'm settled, and jokes, "Tell me all about my new hero, Jayla Bethel, who's the best wingman I've ever had."

I crack up. "I love you so much," slips from me.

He squeezes me. "Don't you forget it."

"Unfortunately, I must send you more than just the Jayla nonsense. Memory incoming. It's long, tawdry, and humiliating."

"Hit me with it."

Zane blinks as he comes out of the memory of what happened at Renn Faire, the phone call situation, and Demitri standing me up. "That's a lot."

"Survey says?" I ask.

"He's hiding something, Melanie." Zane shakes his head. "Knowing Demitri, it isn't going to be something small. He doesn't usually hide things."

"Fantastic. My funds just got moved to his account." I groan. "Codependent Melanie strikes again."

"Have you asked him?"

I snort. "I tried, but he went AWOL."

"Where do you think he went?"

"No clue, but it's weird." I slide off my heels and prop my ankle on Zane's knee, getting comfortable.

He smiles. "I miss that."

"What?"

"You're being casual with me in this everyday way that I love."

I tip my head, studying him. "It's been like that with us from the first day I met you."

Zane nods. "Best thing that ever happened to me was meeting the one person who doesn't watch movies. I kept staring at you the first day I met you, waiting for you to drop the 'I can't believe you're Zane Drell' bomb. You never did."

I shrug. "I still haven't seen any of your movies except the one I'm in."

"Why?"

"Meh. I'd hate to have to act impressed."

Zane's mouth flops open. "You brat. Most of them are good!"

I grin.

"I wonder why Demitri suddenly flipped the switch."

"I'm not a good time, Zane. I eat men alive." My eyes close. "Do you know what I'd give to be a sixteen-year-old girl who's excited about the latest Stone Temple Pilots' release?"

"I'm so sorry, Melanie," he says. "As if being an actress and dancer doesn't earn you enough scrutiny, you're also an energy worker that everyone needs, but no one wants." He grimaces. "I'm sorry for how that came out."

"Don't be. It's true."

"For the record, I *do* want you," Zane says. "I can see how you're a lot for a teenage guy, though. It ate Adam and Trey alive."

"It also ate Pierre to death," I dejectedly add, before sliding remorseful eyes to Zane. "Last I checked, you're in rehab because of it."

"I'm in rehab because I'm a pathetic tool who couldn't handle the pressure of fame." He gestures to me. "Meanwhile, you're hunted daily and suffer dealing with more idiots than I can count, yet you're not a junkie. I think your idiots, myself included, need to get it together."

My cell phone rings, and I groan.

"Answer and see what Demitri says."

I dig around in my purse and pull out the phone. "Hello?" I put the call on speaker, so Zane can hear the conversation.

"La Diabla?" A guy growls.

My suddenly alert gaze snaps to Zane. "Who's asking?"

"Kane."

"You're gonna need to give me a little more info, Kane."

"First, I need to know if I'm speaking to La Diabla."

"You'll speak to me," I respond sternly.

"Fine. I need to hire La Diabla to run a hit for me."

Zane's eyebrows shoot into his hairline.

Didn't expect THAT. Unsure how to respond, I go with, "La Diabla isn't an assassin. Have a good day."

Before I can hang up, Kane says, "Maybe I'll force her to do it, then."

I scoff. "What's your handle Kane? Identify yourself and your affiliation."

"I'm Goliath from the Jags."

I run through the Jags' roster in my head, and my eyes narrow. "The Jags don't have a Goliath."

"I'm one of the kids."

I snort. "Let me get this straight. You're a big, dumb teenager—"

He interrupts, defensively. "What makes you think I'm big and dumb?" he asks, sounding *exactly* like a big, dumb teenager.

I laugh. "Because your handle is Goliath."

"I got the name from a kick-ass video game."

"Uh-huh. Fine, who are you looking to take out?"

"The leader of the Machetes."

I squish up my face. "You want to take out *Juan*? Boy, you chose a hell of a target. Juan will choke you out while he polishes off a dozen donuts."

Zane silently chuckles.

"Hence why I need La Diabla and am hiring you," Goliath says in a demanding voice. "We voted, and the decision was unanimous."

"Who is 'we'?"

"The Jag kids."

I nod matter-of-factly. "I see. There's one problem with your genius plan."

"What's that?"

I roll my eyes. "You forgot to include me in your little planning committee meeting. I don't do assassination."

"If you won't do it, then we'll *make* you do it," Goliath threatens.

"You and what army?"

"Me and the Jags. Those guys hate you."

Alarm bells go off in my mind. The Jags are a massive biker gang with a brutal reputation. "Why do the Jags have a beef with me?"

"Because they lost their drug runners."

"What are you doing?" hisses from someone else.

"What's she going to do if I tell her?" Goliath comes back on the line. "The Reapers were our lackeys. They won't help now. They're all terrified of you."

I'm rattling worried. The Reapers are a biker gang that I humiliated. We're now in a hard-won alliance. "What does Juan have to do with this?"

"My father tried to get the Machetes involved," Goliath says. "Apparently, Juan isn't much of a businessman."

"So, because Juan blew you guys off, you're choosing to come to me to kill Juan?" I shake my head in disgust. "HOW does that help you? You do realize the Machetes have over two hundred members, right?"

"Why do you think we need them?" Goliath replies. I can hear him smiling as he informs, "Guess who added energy workers when the little story of what you did to the Reapers popped up on the scene? The Machetes." He sounds excited.

"I thought they ran a cocaine-running operation with the Mexican cartel?" comes pouring from my mouth.

"Woo-hoo," peels excitedly from Goliath. "La Diabla's collecting secrets. What are you planning? Blackmail? I want in!"

"I'm not planning shit," I reply while my heart pounds.

"Suuurrrre you're not."

"Scurry along now. Have a nice day." I hang up, and mutter, "Fuck."

"Who are the Jags?" Zane asks.

"A huge problem that I avoid," I reply. "I just made a monumental mistake. Rule number one, you don't dish dirt about other clubs. I just dished to the wrong person, about the WRONG people." I dial a number.

Trey answers.

"Yo, Shivers, we've got a problem."

"Talk to me," he replies, all business.

My use of his club name gets the serious reaction I was hoping for, and I fill him in.

"Are you at Demitri's house?" he barks.

"No."

"Where's Demitri?" Trey asks.

"That's an excellent question."

"Amen and hallelujah," Trey breathes, and I silently laugh. He just said exactly what Zane did earlier. "Come home," Trey says intensely.

"Which home, Trey? Mabel's, where my supposed husband doesn't give a shit about me? Demitri's, where I have no key and will sit on the front porch until he's done doing secret things? Or my parents' house that's abandoned while they flit around Japan?"

"You don't have a key to Demitri's?" Trey asks.

"Nope."

I can hear him smile as he replies, "That's the best news ever!"

"Ah, yes. Such excellent news that I'm homeless except when he's interested." I sigh. "Can we please get back to the issue? Do you think we have a legit problem with the Jags?"

"I'm more concerned about the Machetes," Trey says. "On one hand, they're apparently on edge about you, and you've now revealed that you know about their illegal operation. On the other hand, who gives a damn what Goliath says?"

"Hell, I don't know? Why would the pisspot come to me to run a hit on JUAN? Freaking *Juan*, Trey!"

"I'll call Big Joe," Trey assures me. "I want you on lockdown here."

"Gee whiz! Where would you suggest I sleep? The nursery in our suite?" I wince the moment it comes out of my mouth.

"Please, Melanie. I . . ." Trey struggles. "The nursery . . . My reaction was so wrong when you were upset about it. Your suicide attempt was right after that. I'm sorry."

"Machetes, Trey," I remind.

"Fuck Goliath. I'll just have Big Joe run a hit on him."

"Ah, yes. Let's add that war. We won't have any trouble taking out the Machetes AND the Jags."

Trey sighs. "I'm calling Demitri. You can't be alone. You need to be locked up at his house, with the security system on."

"There is no security system, Trey."

"There's no security at Demitri's?" Trey barks.

"No. Do you think I actually need to watch my back?"

"Yes." Trey groans. "We need the Hellhounds to negotiate this for us. You made a mistake, and the Machetes collecting energy workers scares me. If the Machetes come after you for dishing their dirt, it'll take every biker gang in the state to get you back. We have a battle coming our way. Get in your car." He hangs up.

I chuck my phone into my purse. "Damn it!"

"How serious is this?" Zane asks, as I nearly rattle out of my skin.

"The Machetes are the deadliest biker gang in Southern California. I just put myself on their hit list." I rub my face hard before glancing at the wall clock. "Let's go to your counseling session. It's about to start."

"You need to get to Mabel's," Zane insists.

I shake my head. "These kinds of hits take time to orchestrate. Nothing is going to happen tonight. Helping you at counseling might clear my head."

CHAPTER 21

We exit the Malibu Rehab Center, into the warm night air. I exhale now that the pressure of Zane's counseling session is done. It was intense but productive.

"It was such a pleasure to meet you, Melanie," Mr. Apadaca says. He chuckles. "I'm excited to see *Glamour*." He side-eyes me mischievously. "The trailer is wild."

My nose scrunches. "I'm nervous about the premier. I liked the movie when we went to the screening, but . . ." Insecurity bubbles in my gut.

"The adult content has her a little bunched up," Zane explains on my behalf.

"It's done now," Mr. Apadaca says. "No sense in worrying about the movie release."

My intuition rages to life as the elevator doors of the parking garage close, and the elevator starts to slowly slog us to the top floor. My chest feels like it's going to explode, and I double over. "Oh, NO!" I manage to stand upright and open my connection with Trey. "*I'm in terrible trouble.*"

"*Where are you?*"

"I'm at the Malibu Rehab Center visiting Zane. Parking garage. Top floor," I send. "Flatten against the elevator wall NOW," I order Zane and his counselor, Mr. Apadaca. "Don't exit. The second the doors close, take the elevator to the bottom floor and run."

"What's wrong, Melanie?" Zane asks.

I say aloud, "Trey, I'm in deep shit here. What I'm up against is ten times worse than what Warlock presented." I shove my discontent aside, unable to focus on Warlock, who taught Demitri how to fix my barren post-miscarriage condition. Losing Warlock to energy backlash after he healed me is something I'll never get over. I can't focus on that guilt right now, though.

Zane starts to hit the button to stop the elevator, and I order, "Don't. They'll hunt me either way."

"Who's Trey?" Mr. Apadaca asks.

"Her soulmate," Zane informs him. "She can talk to him in her head."

"Fascinating," Mr. Apadaca replies, obviously not grasping what I face.

"Find an energy source, Melanie," Trey sends.

When I close my eyes and send out a seeking line, I find a generator in the basement of the rehab center.

"What's happening, Melanie?" Zane demands again.

"Attack is waiting. Machetes."

Mr. Apadaca's eyes widen. "You're in danger?"

"Yes. An enemy has been gathering weapons against me."

"How did they find you here?" he asks.

"I believe they've been tracking me with energy workers."

"We have to run!" Zane insists.

"I can't run from this! These people will kill all the Hellcats." I growl as I open the line to the generator. Power pours, bowing my back. Zane holds me up as I fight not to scream, and my spine blisters as white-hot fire fills my reserves. My entire body feels like it's been struck by lightning. Luckily, my dark-water side blasts to the surface. I roll my neck as the power suddenly fits and my legs work again. The elevator slows. "Here goes nothing. Get the elevator door closed as soon as I step out." The elevator stops, and I add, "I love you, Zaney."

"I love you too, Melanie," Zane chokes out around fear.

The doors open, and I stride onto the top level of the parking garage, confronted by a long line of thugs. Juan steps forward and starts to go through the usual Retribution Clause formalities.

I cut him off. "Don't run. Stand your ground. Club edict. I know the drill. Why are you bringing retribution on me?"

Juan just glares, along with his officers. It looks like, other than the energy workers, there are only around twenty of Juan's Machetes.

"Count the front line," I send to Trey. *"They're the energy workers."*

"Already done. There are thirteen."

"Shit." Unfortunately, Zane and Mr. Apadaca step up to my right. "What the fuck are you doing?" I murmur to Zane.

"I'm not leaving you up here to get your ass beat," Zane murmurs back.

"Why did you threaten to kill me, La Diabla?" Juan demands.

"Pardon? Goliath from the Jags called me trying to hire an assassination hit. I laughed at him."

Juan's eyes narrow. "Trace's son?"

"Fuck," Trey gasps in my mind. Trace is the leader of the Jags.

"I don't know who Goliath's dad is," I reply to Juan. "I've never even heard of the kid."

"I don't appreciate you spreading our business around town," Juan says. "Would you like to explain that?"

"Mistake. Oversight. Unintentional. My apologies."

"Not accepted," Juan says.

The thirteen energy workers seem to respond to an unspoken command all at once. They start simultaneously blasting me with everything they've got.

Just in time, I snap up a shield over me, Mr. Apadaca, and Zane. "Here we go," I gravel.

Trey screams in my mind. Mr. Apadaca and Zane panic, hunkering down, and Zane is suddenly in my head. We've had a completely unexplainable mental connection that seems to pop up during life-and-death nightmares.

"*Zane?*" Trey sends, surprised.

"*Yeah, hi,*" he replies. "*Looks like I'm in Seashell's head again.*"

I'm being hit with the equivalent of invisible fire, lightning, sledgehammers, chainsaws, and missiles. With every new hit, I scramble to put up a reinforced layer. I'm sweating with the effort to keep up with the blistering attacks. Zane wraps his arms around me, covering my back.

"*What's the plan, Firebird?*" Trey's mental voice is strained with worry.

"*Tire them out. I'm going to let them attack for as long as I can stand it. They'll drain. I probed them and didn't find a line to a power source. They're working off of only their own reserves.*" My shield starts to buckle, and I exhaust my third reserve reinforcing it. "*I have to pull from the generator again. We're not going to make it at this rate. Thirteen of these fuck-knockers is a stretch.*" I pull power that roars through me.

Zane and I watch through Trey's eyes as he dials his phone. We hear through Trey's ears as Demitri picks up. Trey demands, "Where the fuck are you?"

"Why?" Demitri asks, put off.

"Because, you world-class fuck-up, Melanie is being attacked by thirteen energy workers! The Machetes brought retribution on her."

"WHAT?" Demitri screams.

We hear, "What's wrong?"

My eyes narrow. *"That's Jayla's voice."*

"Can we focus on the attack?" Zane sounds exasperated.

"Let them keep hitting my shield," I snarl. *"I want to know about Jayla."*

It spirals Trey into a rage. "You're with JAYLA while Melanie is about to die?"

"Jayla needed to talk to me. Why isn't Melanie at home?"

"Because, she doesn't have a GODDAMN KEY to your house!" Trey roars. "She had no choice but to visit Zane to kill time."

"Ouch," Zane sends.

"For the record, I wanted to visit you," I send. *"Let Trey be an asshole. Demitri deserves it."*

"How do you know she's being attacked?" Demitri gasps.

"What?" Jayla barks in the background. "Oh no!"

I'm hit with a blow so devastating that I barely hold together my shield. I pull another power load, my spine seething.

"Shut your hoe up! I know what's happening because I'm watching through our soulmate connection," Trey snarls back, but I can feel his panic blaze. "If Melanie dies, I'll hunt you down and KILL you and Jayla. There's a reason I never left her alone unless she was behind Mabel's security system."

I struggle to my feet, expanding my shield enough to make room now that the attacks are weakening. Zane stands next to me, and I scan the line, microscopically assessing how each of my attackers is holding up.

I usually work in metaphysical fire and steel, but with this kind of power at my disposal from the generator, I choose lightning energy. I struggle to gather the generator energy into a finely honed collection of five points and send them invisibly crashing down all at the same time. All five hit their marks and take out the most worn out of the line, the ones I'm positive I can floor. They drop to the ground, and I'm sure at least one of them is dead.

"Hit them with another round," Trey sends. *"They won't expect it."*

I create an energy wall and lace it with deadly electrification, blasting it into the lineup. Four more fall over, out cold.

I hear through Trey's ears as he says aloud, "That's my girl. Four more to go, baby."

"What's happening, Trey?" Demitri whimpers, as Jayla loses her mind in the background.

"Shut the fuck up and shut your yapping mistress up, Demitri," Trey barks back ferociously. He switches gears but continues to speak aloud so that Demitri might hush as he gets in-the-moment intel. "Zane, Melanie's burning out, and her spine can't take another generator load. I'm going to watch, and I need you to do what I would if I was there. I'll coach you."

One of my enemies steps forward, and my intuition breathes through me. I send to Trey and Zane, *"They're going to try to raptor us. He's just a distraction."*

Trey nods in my head. "Zane, you need to knock out the one headed to the right. He won't expect a physical attack. That leaves the other three. Melanie, keep them busy, and we'll regroup after. You can do this, Zane."

"Ready," Zane sends back.

"Why can Zane hear you?" Demitri asks.

"Because he has a weird connection with Melanie," Trey snarls back.

The guy in the middle starts waving his hands artfully.

"You realize you look ridiculous, right?" I can't help but scoff.

The guy appears peeved but continues his unnecessary process. Anyone with magical knowledge knows you don't have to go through all of that.

"Rush him, Zane," Trey barks, and Zane dodges forward.

I drop a bolt down on the one the farthest to the left, who plummets, unconscious, just as Zane drops the one on the right with a blistering punch.

"Yes!" Trey bellows. "Good work, Zane!"

Zane rushes backward to regroup with me, and I send, *"Mr. Handwaving is your next target. The other one is the real deal. I need to handle him."*

Trey sends confirmation, and Zane rushes the hand waver. I shift my focus to the other one, taking him off guard as I expand my energy shield and rush him. He runs back, but I change the image in my mind to a bubble made of water vapor. I get him inside it before I snap the construct to electricity. Anytime he gets too close to the edge, he'll get zapped. That should keep his attention split.

Zane and Mr. Apadaca are now out of my shield, and I get another intuition pulse. I send, *"Run. Elevator. Do it!"*

"I'm not leaving you!" Zane sends back.

"You must. He's going to attack both of you to split my resources. If he does that, I die. GO!" I distract my opponent by wrapping his shield and squeezing as hard as I can.

I shake with the effort and wait for what feels like an eternity until Zane sends, *"We're in the elevator!"*

"Here we go, my girl," Trey says. "One more, and then you face Juan and his officers. You can do this."

I give one final squeeze, and my opponent's shield collapses. I create an invisible wall and run it at him. It slams into him, and he bounces into my energetically electrified shield bubble. When he collapses to one knee, I drop an invisible lightning bolt on him. Instead of writhing in pain, he smiles evilly.

"Shit," Trey gasps.

"What?" Demitri begs.

"She just juiced the last energy worker. He steals power. He's no joke."

"Oh my God." Demitri sounds beside himself and shushes Jayla.

I snap the image from electricity to steel around my shield so I'm not fueling him, but he turns my own bolt on me, and it slams into my chest. I scream, and my eyesight blazes pure white.

"NOOOOOOOO," Trey roars, and it sends shivers up my boiling spine.

I blink, trying to work through the pain. My attacker takes my stunned condition as an opportunity and starts pounding me with blast after blast.

I barely manage to send, *"Block off Zane, Trey. I don't want him to feel this. Block yourself off. Tell everyone I love them."*

"Baby, no," Trey gasps.

"Melanieeeeeeee." Through Zane's eyes, I see Mr. Apadaca attempt to restrain him as he fights to get back in the elevator on the first floor of the parking garage.

Trey screams like his world is ending, while love for me boils in him so strongly it engulfs what's left of my mind.

"Trey, what's happening?" Demitri yells.

"She's about to die," Trey says. "Zane, don't. It's over. They'll kill you."

"I shouldn't have been here," Demitri sobs. "I should have been with Melanie."

My eyesight blasts with stars from unbearable pain. Trey drops to his knees on the parlor floor at Mabel's. I see through his eyes as

Mabel and Victoria rush to him. He throws up, but it does nothing to stop his nonsensical screaming.

Out of nowhere, I hear a gunshot. The relentless assault stops, and my eyesight clears a little. I look up from my collapsed position on the pavement and see Mr. Apadaca. He fired the shot into the pavement, and it's enough to distract my attacker. Zane hauls me to my feet. I do the only thing I can think of—raise the temperature in a bubble I snap over my attacker and me. The hotter it gets in the shield, the calmer I feel. We're both human, and when it gets hot enough to drop my adversary, I'm also going to drop, but that's not my plan.

"Come on," Zane sends. *"You can do this."*

The man hits his knees, his head hanging. I'm one breath from death, and this is pointless because Juan's just going to kill me, but I ignore common sense as I race forward just before my knees give out. I clamp my hands around my attacker's head, but I have nothing left. My reserves have never been this depleted before. If I pull another generator load, it'll kill me.

"Break his neck, baby," Trey snarls aloud, animalistically.

"Oh God," I whimper.

"Do it!" Zane screams in my head.

I wrench my hands to the side and hear a sickening crack. The man drops, and I close my eyes. *"This is a new low."*

"Fuck him," Trey growls. "He deserved it."

"I can't take on Juan and his thugs," I send while I fight to keep my knees from buckling.

"I'll kill every fucking one of them," Zane sends. He's glaring at Juan with such malice that my destroyed arms goose-bump.

"Shit," Trey says dejectedly.

"What?" Demitri begs.

"Zane is so in love with Melanie that he's prepared to kill Juan, and all his officers, barehanded," Trey informs. "I think he can take them based on what I'm feeling."

Mr. Apadaca raises his gun, sighting on Juan.

"She's alive?" Demitri gasps.

"We'll see," Trey replies. "She doesn't have the juice to kill the officers, but Zane's buddy is armed, and Zane is more than dangerous right now."

"You brought Retribution Clause on me and lost," I announce to the stunned Machetes. "I have the right to kill you all. You've now seen that I can and will." I focus on Juan. "What do you propose?" This is all bravado. I'm barely able to stand, but I must get through to them to leave me alone.

Juan's expression registers shock, before he announces, "I'd like to call a truce. You took out the thirteen strongest energy workers in this state."

I laugh and it hurts terribly, but I push the pain conveniently underneath the shock that's thrumming through me. "Wrong. Some of them may have claimed that title, but *I'm* the strongest energy worker in the state." I scan their group. "Leave and don't come after me again."

The officers scurry around gathering the unconscious. Conveniently, they also take the dead with them, loading them in a van they brought.

"They're running scared," Trey says. "You did it, baby! Zane, I need you to get her here."

"I can't leave here, Trey," Zane says aloud, as motorcycles and the van screech down the exit ramp of the parking garage, leaving only my car on the top floor.

"Like hell you can't," Mr. Apadaca bellows. "We aren't a detention center. You need to go. Come back by tomorrow night, and you're in the clear." He catches me as my knees give out.

Trey gasps as my pain blasts down our connection line. "Demitri, get to Mabel's fast!"

"I'm running to my Jeep," Demitri barks.

Trey hangs up the call to Demitri.

Zane carefully picks me up. I gasp, and Zane says aloud, "This is bad, Trey."

"Do you want me to call an ambulance?" Mr. Apadaca asks.

"No. I need to get her to a healer," Zane replies as he starts running toward my car.

I scream as pain rips through me. I can hear Trey barking orders, and through his eyes, I see the staff and Mabel rush about like ants on an anthill.

"Sweetheart, you're going to be okay," Trey says through tears. When Victoria gives him a nasty look, he screams, "Get out!"

Mr. Apadaca opens the passenger door of my car and pops the seat latch, then Zane slides me in. I moan as my skin touches the warm back seat. "Call me and tell me that she's okay!" Mr. Apadaca insists as the passenger door closes.

"I will," Zane barks. "I'll be back to finish my therapy." He mutters to himself, "I swear Melanie is a fucking garden gnome," while he tries to get in the driver's seat.

Trey laughs through his tears.

Zane scoots the seat all the way back and starts the car. "Hang on, gorgeous. I'm going to get you to Mabel's."

I'm in serious trouble.

My world goes black . . .

CHAPTER 22

The closer to consciousness I get, the worse the pain burns.

"Help her," Zane bellows as he races through the door that Arch holds open.

The jostling stops, and I moan.

"Lay her down!" I hear Trey order.

Zane slowly lowers me, and as his arms move from under me, my spine bows. I scream as white-hot fire seers through me. I panic and reach out desperately. A hand grabs mine, and I open my eyes. I exhale hard as a little of the pain edge drops off. "Don't let go," I barely whisper to Zane.

Adam leans over me. "Ground and center, Melanie. We have a plan, but I need you to climb on top of the pain until we can fix you."

I gasp, and Adam grabs my other hand.

Demitri pushes through the crowd and announces, "If you can't send energy into me, you need to back up."

Trey drops to his knees by my head. Mabel steps up behind Demitri.

Panicking, Demitri shakes his head. "Where do we start?"

"Demitri, LOOK AT ME!" Arch roars. "I know you love her, and she looks like she just got plunged into a volcano, but I need you to focus."

Demitri closes his eyes and attempts to ground and center. When he's as calm as he can be in this situation, he puts his hands on my chest and stomach. His scan sends a fresh wave of lancing pain through me. I moan, and his eyes snap open. He looks at Trey. "Pull pain. This is going to be bad. I'm starting with her spine. She has nerve damage." He turns to Mabel. "I need Destiny and Sapphire to start working on her external burns. I'm going to pass out before I get through even part of this." He looks to Darren and Adam. "I'm going to need you to boost me after I drain Mabel."

Trey grabs one of my hands from Zane as Demitri shifts and slides his hands under my spine. "Don't move Melanie," Demitri orders. "We're starting with the worst of it."

Blazing fire rips through me, and I feel every nerve in my spine twitch. I scream, and my eyes roll into the back of my head. Trey's hand shakes as he pulls pain.

I suddenly realize that I'm not Trey's problem anymore. I gasp, "Trey, let go."

"NO," Trey insists through gritted teeth.

"I have an idea that won't hurt you," I whimper.

Trey hesitantly let's go.

I shutter down my connection with him. "Demitri, stop!"

Demitri stops. "Talk to me, Meley. What's this new plan of yours?"

I take a shuddering breath. "My dark-water side is what you pull energy from. Your calm is what I pull from."

He looks blazingly unsure. "Now isn't the time to try something new."

"My life is all about trying newly insane things in moments of crisis," I plead.

"If it doesn't work, and I somehow become trapped in that dark water of yours . . ."

My eyes snap terrified.

"Let's talk through this, gorgeous," Zane says.

"I can't handle it." I whimper. "The spine healing is unbearable."

"I know. We could all see that." Zane smiles softly at me. "Demitri's not down with your plan. So, here's the deal. It's you and me, right?"

"There's nothing you can do, Zane," I whimper. "You're not an energy worker."

Zane gives me an arrogant look. "Excuse you, little miss. I'm Zane fucking Drell."

"I felt the connection close between you two when Melanie passed out in the car," Trey interjects.

Zane snorts. "We don't need it. It's unpredictable anyway."

"Do you have abilities we don't know about?" Bear asks.

"Sure do," Zane replies. "I'm the Melanie whisperer when I've got my head outta my ass." Zane lies down next to me. "Put her on my chest."

Trey, Arch, and Tanner reach for me. "We have to do this in one motion," Trey says to his helpers. "It's going to hurt Melanie. Slight lift, and roll on three. Three!"

They roll and lift me onto Zane, without the dreaded countdown.

I scream.

The moment I'm on Zane, his hand threads through the back of my hair. "Pain countdown, Seashell," he says over my desperate screaming. "Ten, nine, eight . . . It's fading . . ." He keeps it up, and it works. "Three, two, one."

Tears are still rolling, but I'm a quieter shivering disaster now. I exhale fitfully.

"Good work, Melanie," Zane says calmly. "You got through being moved. That's over now. Deep breath in and reset with me."

We inhale and exhale together.

"How are you doing that?" Trey asks, as I limply settle.

"The hospital time was rough, "Zane informs. "She worked her ass off while I coached to get her muscles to fire. It was excruciating." He addresses me. "Now, gorgeous, I have a super special memory for my favorite girl. Do you want to see it?"

"Yes," I whisper, calming down.

"Okay, take it," he invites.

I close my eyes and pull the memory he's actively thinking of. I feel hands on my back, and it heats up. I'm enchanted to find myself inside Zane's sleeping mind.

He seems enthralled in the dream, as he thinks, '*Yes! This again.*' I can feel that he anxiously hopes for these dreams, but they don't happen often.

I watch through Zane's memory eyes as I appear. I smile vibrantly in the dream when I see Zane. His heart pounds as he crosses to me. Dream Zane wraps his arms around me, and we sink slowly into dark water. He has no idea where the water comes from, but dreams are funny that way in his estimation. I know that it's the dark water in my mind, though. The liquid completely engulfs us. We stare at each other under the water, before breaking the surface. I lie on Zane's chest as he floats.

Dream me sends, *"I love you."* I feel him smile.

"I love you too." Zane is completely content.

It's odd being in his body in the dream. I feel tiny in his arms.

After another long while, dream Zane gets me under the armpits and pulls me up. He kisses me softly, which makes me gasp in reality. A shift starts. Subtle at first, it picks up rapidly in intensity. The energetic swelling builds to quaking and detonates from both our chests in the dream. It's the purest, softest vibe I've ever felt.

We hear exclamations of wonder. "I have no idea what that was, but I didn't cause it!" Demitri exclaims.

"Ugh," I mutter. "I'm trying to enjoy Zane's dream."

Zane chuckles under me. He's been watching with me and murmurs, "Almost through the memory," to the room.

I settle back into the dream, thoroughly enjoying the combined energy of Zane and me. "It's magic," I whisper aloud.

"I know," Zane whispers back. "It's my favorite moment I've ever had."

I watch as Zane and I end the dream kiss, and then, the dream pops like a bubble. That must have been when he woke up. I blink, coming back to reality.

"How's it going?" Zane asks Demitri.

"I . . ."

As Demitri falters, I chance the pain it'll take to look his way. When I turn my head, nothing hurts.

Everyone in the group looks down at me. Mouths hang open all around the ring of faces.

I joke, "This must be what goldfish in a bowl feel like."

"Something blasted from her, connected to my ability, and finished the healing," Demitri says in wonder. "I wasn't even a tenth of the way through what needed to be fixed."

Zane eases me onto my back on the floor. He looks me over and smiles.

"Not only are you healed, Melanie, but you look radiant," Mama Mabel announces.

"What caused it?" Adam asks Trey.

Trey shakes his head. "I have no clue. My access to her mind oddly blanked out when she took Zane's memory."

I smile. "I was due a miracle. Maybe that was it." I glance at Zane.

"Must have been a miracle," he says cryptically as he taps my arm.

I pull the memory of Zane thinking, *'I've always told you that we're magic.'*

I giggle before looking to the group lording it over us. "Any chance that blast healed my favorite dress?"

"The dress is screwed, and yet again, I'm seeing more of you than I prefer," Tanner sasses.

I crack up. "At this point everyone in this damn group has seen more of me than they prefer. I'm over it."

"I'm enjoying hell out of it," Adam crows.

Mama Mabel jokingly smacks his arm, and everyone laughs.

"Well, I'm enjoying that she attacked bikers in stiletto heels!" Tanner sizzles.

I hold up a hand, and Trey and Adam help me stand. A touch dizzy, I close my eyes. Zane steadies me after he stands.

"Thank goodness you're okay," comes Jayla's poorly timed exclamation.

"What is she doing here?" I ask Demitri.

"She came with me."

I slide caged eyes Jayla's way. The fear and pain of the Machetes' attack has left me incredibly pragmatic. "We aren't speaking." I look to Demitri. "Thank you for hauling ass here to help me. Until you can explain what you were doing with Jayla, while I was locked out, you can kiss my ass."

Demitri's eyes widen. "She just needed to talk to me, Melanie."

"I'm not buying it," I reply. "You got beyond weird when we were talking, and then you were gone."

"It was a hell of a day," Demitri insists.

"It turned into a hell of an evening for me," I retort.

"I know." Demitri's head drops. "I'm so sorry, Melanie."

I smile up at Zane. "You ready? I can't drive, I need a cheese-burger, and I'm scared to be alone."

Zane looks pleasantly surprised. "I would love too. Astro Burger is open twenty-four hours. Let's roll."

"Melanie, I'd like for you to stay here," Trey says. "The Machetes may not be done with you."

"Um, NO," I reply. I smile around the room. "Thank you all for helping me. If you don't mind, I'd like to go home and put on something a little less revealing."

"Your dresser is full of clothes," Destiny reminds me. "I'd love for you to stay in my room with me."

"That's so thoughtful," I smile softly at Destiny, "but I really want to go home, and after the movie we did together, a rouge boob in a lightning-struck dress ain't gonna sparkle Zane while he drives me."

Zane cups my revealed boob. "Better?"

I crack up. "Much, thank you."

"Hands off," Demitri snarls.

Zane chuckles. "If you knew how many times I've slid my hands over this girls' boobs in that movie, you wouldn't give a damn about that right now."

"What the hell is in that movie?" Demitri demands.

My mouth falls open with feigned thrill. "You're going to get to see for yourself. Guess who has a premiere on Friday?"

"We do," Zane crows, and we give each other bright looks.

"I can't wait!" I giggle and bop about while he continues shield-ing my boob with his hand.

"Bouncy," Zane says, delighted.

"Hands OFF," Demitri barks.

Zane ignores him, instead saying to me, "Cheeseburgers and milkshakes await." We stroll out the foyer door.

I exhale hard. "What a day!"

Zane stops and slides a cocky look over his shoulder. "Oh, and Demitri? Thanks for not giving her a key. Also, thanks for not giving in to her idea of you two combining energies." Zane tips his head contemplatively. "I'm not an energy worker, but I wonder what that would have done? You two combining abilities . . . No fused soulmate connection, while her guard is down because of earthshattering pain . . . Not to mention that you're in hot water, and she needs a hero." Zane happily sighs. "Mystery, mystery."

I give Demitri a cold look as his mouth drops open. "I was NOT trying to deny you a deeper connection with me," Demitri insists.

I smirk. "That blast came from me and Zane when he kissed me in the dream memory."

Surprise registers from everyone.

Zane raises an eyebrow Jayla's way. "Thank you for being a sneaky little scoundrel."

"Melanie, nothing happened," Jayla insists.

We start to stride away, and I flip her the bird over my shoulder. "He picked you, Jayla. Enjoy it. I'll be pissed soon, but it's not your turn yet. I've earned a happy night."

Zane belts the theme song to *Happy Days* while everyone gapes at us as they pour into the parking lot. I giggle as he opens my car door and flourishes grandly.

"Melanie, please," Demitri says, jogging to me. "I'd like to take you home."

"You have to drive Jayla home!"

"I need to go back to Malibu," Zane quietly says.

I sigh. "Fine. I'll get Zane back to Malibu and then head to my parents' home." I give Zane a cute look. "I get a cheeseburger still." Zane chuckles as my expression morphs with disgust when I swing it to Demitri. "What you do, Demitri, is entirely up to you."

"Are you driving, or am I?" Zane asks.

"You," I reply. "I need a minute to get it together." I slide into the passenger seat and exhale hard as he gets in on the driver's side. "Get out of this parking lot and then stop."

He pulls out of the spot and stops when we get around the corner.

I smile at him. "Wanna see something amazing?"

"I already looked at your boob earlier, if that's the amazement." He glances down. "Just did it again."

I giggle. "After Brandy's boobs, eh."

Zane shakes his head. "You win. I'm not a fan of fake."

Demitri's Jeep speeds past with Jayla in the passenger seat. "And he's off on a *magical* adventure," Zane crows.

I laugh pensively before putting my hand on his chest and sending him a memory. He closes his eyes and gasps a moment later. He watches long enough to know what it is before his eyes open.

I smile. "They're my favorite dreams also. I hope every night they'll happen."

"You were *actually* there with me?" Zane asks.

I nod. "Seeing your side of it was magic though." I curl up in my car seat and gaze at Zane. "Thank you for helping me. You fight like a demon."

Zane chuckles. "I was both terrified and thrilled. I love a bar brawl, but getting to fight for you was a new level." His eyes soften. "Thank you for showing me your side of that dream."

"I was worried you were going to miss the premiere because of rehab," I say.

He shakes his head. "I negotiated that before I checked in. I'm cleared to go."

"Good," I say. "Ready for burgers and a long drive with no drama?"

Zane chuckles. "Think the Machetes are coming for you?"

"Who knows? You willing to chance it?"

"All day, every day," Zane assures me. He puts my car in drive and pulls onto Hollywood Boulevard.

CHAPTER 23

I close the door at my parents' house and turn to Demitri, who was waiting in his Jeep when I arrived. "Cut the shit. What were you doing with Jayla?"

"She wanted to talk to me, Melanie."

"About?"

Demitri's eyes close. "I apologize for bolting. This is a lot."

"What is?"

"Us." Demitri crosses his arms over his chest.

"What does that have to do with Jayla? You're deflecting."

"No," he replies, "I'm not. I needed to talk to someone I trust, and I've known Jayla forever. The last week has been a lot. We weren't intending to be sneaky." He shakes his head. "I'm sorry you got that impression. Jayla's incredibly worried about this."

"I don't give a damn that Jayla's worried," I spew.

"I know you don't trust easily." Demitri gives me a hopeful look. "I'm sorry I brushed you off, left, didn't give you a key, and you got hurt while I was talking with Jayla." He rubs his forehead. "I recognize it sounds bad."

"Anything else?" I ask.

"I think I covered it."

My eyes narrow. "Head home. Lock the knob before you leave. I'm going to bed."

"Please, Melanie."

"I know this game, Demitri." I feel dead inside. As much as I hate it, I also don't, because I'm on familiar emotional ground. I stare at the wall, contemplating options.

"I'm not leaving you alone!" Demitri insists.

"I survived the Machete attack without you."

"I . . ." Demitri stares at me like he has no clue what to do.

"Good night, Demitri." I head down the hall and close my bedroom door. I look around, feeling like a stranger in my own room.

There's a knock on my blockage between me and Trey. I drop the blockage, and he sends, *"Are you okay?"*

"I'm fine, Trey."

"Come home, Melanie," Trey sends, before fuzzing me out just as I hear another voice through his ears. He's so quick about it that I'm not sure who interrupted him. He's gone a moment, and when he unfuzzes me, he's in tears. *"I need to admit some things to you."*

"No thanks," I reply. *"I'm done. Good night."* I block him and double-check the lock on my window. I peek past the curtains warily as guilt bubbles in me. Demitri's Jeep is still by the curb. If Demitri's not having a fling with Jayla, then I'm making a huge mistake. I swallow hard, realizing that I'm irrationally running, like I swore to myself that I wouldn't. I just need to tell him I'm furious that he stood me up while he was with Jayla. Demitri and I agreed that we'd talk instead of having a meltdown. "Change, Melanie. This is part of getting out of unhealthy patterns," I grumble to myself as I unlock my door and head down the hall. I stop short as I hear Demitri quietly talking.

"I have no clue what to do. She's barely even speaking to me."

"Did you tell her there's nothing going on?" comes Jayla's response.

"Yes, but she flat doesn't believe me." Demitri sighs. "I triggered every insecurity in Melanie when I left to see you."

"What you told me about her condition is beyond alarming, D."

I step out of the hall and stare at Demitri. "You told Jayla?"

Demitri's eyes widen.

"You promised you were done spreading my dirt around!"

"Jayla, I need to go," Demitri says.

I gesture to the phone. "Don't end your little secret lovers' chat on my account, but take it the fuck out of my house."

"I'm not having a secret lovers' chat," Demitri insists. "She asked me to let her know after I talked to you."

"How does it feel to be a Tiffany, Jayla?"

She whimpers through the phone.

"Jayla isn't a Tiffany, Melanie," Demitri says, defending her.

"Seems a whole lot like Tiffany to me," I say, disgusted. "So much for fixing us."

"Wait," Demitri pleads while he jumps up from the couch. I storm down the hall and lock myself in my bedroom.

A knock comes a moment later. "Please let me in."

"How dare you call her after everything that's already happened!"

"Damn it, Melanie, please," Demitri says.

I turn on my CD player and crank the volume as Foreigner's "Urgent" blasts. I climb into bed and curl up with the teddy bear Zane gave me. Tears fall as I realize all the sneaky bullshit Trey put me through is happening again.

CHAPTER 24

I get out of my car just as Demitri's Jeep skids into the student parking lot and pulls into the spot next to me. Our friends are smoking by Bear's Bronco, and eyebrows rise.

"Looks like there's trouble in paradise," Arch points out. "Melanie's dressed like a micromini fantasy."

Everyone surveys my black minidress and wedge heels.

"She's wearing her black cat-eye sunglassessssss," Tanner sasses.

Demitri rushes from his Jeep, slamming the door and racing around the back of my car to where I stand.

"Demitri looks like leftovers nuked in a worn-out microwave," Bear says.

"Gotta love Mondays," Presley mutters disgruntledly.

"Melanie, please."

"Melanie, please. Melanie please." I mock him while I cock a hip. "Please what, Demitri?"

"I have nothing going on with Jayla!"

"Ooh, ooh, ooh," Tanner singsongs.

"Get him, girl." Presley spurs me on.

I take my sunglasses off and chuck them furiously.

Trey catches them expertly and smirks at Demitri. "Rule number one, don't EVER mention another girl while you're reasoning with *that* girl." He points my way.

I give Trey a dangerously flirtatious side-eye.

He tosses my sunglasses back to me. "I'd hate to see those get broken," he says. "They're your favorite gift I ever gave you."

"That they are," I reply, before hitting a hip-swaying clip across the parking lot.

"Melanie, wait," Jayla pleads, making the mistake of touching my arm.

I whip around and hiss, "Who the fuck do you think you are? DON'T challenge me, Mary Poppins."

Jayla tears up. "I'm not looking for a fight."

"Step back, Jayla," Trey warns. "Melanie sees you as a threat, and she's dark-water thrumming."

Jayla whips her stunned gaze from Trey to me. "She's never attacked one of us!"

Trey chuckles. "You aren't one of us now. You're a Tiffany. She destroys her amorous competition." Trey grins at Demitri. "Of all the girls you could have picked, I applaud you for Jayla. She's so sweet and easily killed. This will only take a few minutes, and then a little counseling after."

"Thank God," Tanner snarks. "I hate when Melanie decides some catty hoe deserves weeks of banter first. Let's get straight to the big show."

Tears roll down Jayla's face as she pleads Demitri's way, "You promised you told her we weren't a thing!"

"I did tell—"

I cut him off with a sharp, "If you speak to her, it's game on." Dark-water evil thrums from me in such blistering waves that the

Normals in our group gasp. Jayla starts to back up, and I bark, "Stop her."

Deb and Presley each get a hand on Jayla's shoulders.

"You guys are my friends," Jayla whimpers.

Deb snorts, while Presley informs her, "If you're screwing Demitri, we're screwing YOU."

"You remember what we did to Tiffany during the brawl, right?" Deb asks.

Jayla's eyes blank, and she drops like a sack of potatoes.

Her boyfriend, Dante, runs to her as he sees her fall. "What happened?" he barks.

"She's apparently screwing Demitri behind Melanie's, and *your*, back," Tanner says with a no-nonsense tone that's chock *full* of his gossipy nonsense.

"You people are insane!" Dante yelps. "Jayla isn't messing around with Demitri."

Jayla comes to, and I give Dante a look as he helps her sit up.

"I'm telling you they are."

Dante glares at me. "Leave Jayla alone, Melanie."

"Melanie's never wrong about this stuff," Arch warns Dante.

"She is this time," Dante assures.

"WHY are you *this* mad about a misunderstanding?" Demitri asks me.

Trey chuckles when I fume instead of answering. "Melanie," he gestures to me, "despises an overstepping female who sets her claws into her guy more than anything. You either fix this to her satisfaction, or she'll blow your house apart."

"There's *nothing* going on," Demitri insists.

"Maybe she won't find out," Bear says, not believing him.

Trey shakes his head, amused. "I don't believe them either,

Melanie. I heard guilt in his voice during the Machete battle. All you have to do is search their memories." He studies Demitri's and Jayla's reactions.

They keep their expressions in check.

"Guilt will eat them alive. It'll come out." I walk up the alley, bypassing my usual spot that I'm positive the group will commandeer with Demitri and Jayla.

Trey jogs up next to me. "We've got twenty minutes until class starts."

"It seems our latest life-and-death Machete nightmare has made you more pleasant toward me," I say.

"You leaving caused that, but I don't want to discuss it at school." He smirks at me. "You don't like to discuss personal things in a crowd."

I laugh a little. "No, I don't. I'm doing my own thing." I thump my backpack on an empty bench and plop down, then pull out my math notebook and yank out a worksheet.

Instead of going away, Trey sits next to me.

I stare at the math problems before huffing.

"Here we go, Melanie," Trey intones with looming dread.

I scan the campus for trouble.

He pauses dramatically before graveling, "The battle of the math worksheet." I giggle, and he smiles.

He points to the first problem. "Parentheses. Always start there."

CHAPTER 25

I pull into the alley, which is lit by a full moon, and park. Mabel requested that I arrive for a party after rehearsal. I have no interest, but decided I need to talk to her, so here I am.

Mabel's parking lot houses an alarming number of motorcycles. I jump out of my car just in time to watch Trace, the leader of the Jags, flash something silver. Panic rips through me as I realize that a confrontation is mid-rage with the Jags.

Gun in hand, Trace gives me a maniacal look of finality. "My son is facing Retribution Clause!"

Time stops as I hear the BANG, see the recoil of the handgun, and watch the flash from the barrel. I follow the path of the bullet. My gaze meets Trey's as his chest explodes, and he drops. My psyche tornadoes as Trey's shield collapses over our soulmate connection. His pain doubles me over as the Hellcats rush to Trey, covering his chest with all their stacked hands, trying to stop the crimson river that's gushing from his mangled chest. I fight to put a shield up to block out his pain so that I can deal with the Jags. I scream, "DEMITRIIIIIII," but he's already running to Trey.

"That's how you deal with Super Bitch!" Trace crows proudly. "You take out her soulmate."

I empty what's left of my exhausted reserves to audibly boom the mental declaration, *"Retribution CLAUSE!"*

The Hellhounds all shift with purpose to surround the Jags, ensuring that they have no escape route. Guns are drawn and aimed at the Jags.

I'm running at full tilt across the parking lot to Trey. He tries to speak, but blood bubbles from his mouth. Demitri looks at me, distraught. I think quick, closing my eyes and reviewing the memories I pulled from Warlock. He was a healer with a lot more experience than Demitri has. I find a memory of Warlock healing a gunshot wound to the chest and hurl it into Demitri's mind. "Watch it," I insist.

Demitri's eyes close, and after only a moment, he barks, "Bear and Darren, boost me!" Bear and Darren put their hands on Demitri's shoulders, and he frantically pulses energy into Trey, trying to heal him. Trey's eyes slide from panic into understanding that this is it.

I kneel and gasp through a torrent of tears, "No, don't do this! Trey, look at me!"

Trey's gaze flattens to the finality of death. The light that's Trey flutters in my mind, and then my soulmate connection crashes down. I'm left empty, alone in my head.

I inhale and send out a resounding vocal and mental scream. "TREYYYYYY!"

Our friends sob and crater all around us.

My dark-water side slides up calmly from the churning storm in my psyche. *"It's not over yet, Melanie. Kill them all and use every resource at your disposal."* My dark-water side gives me a route, and I study the plan in my head at rapid-fire pace.

I look down at Trey, and through the hole that's blasted in his chest, see mangled exposed ribs, torn muscle, and organs. My body collapses as panic overtakes me.

"Melanie, do something!" Victoria screams.

Arch kneels next to me. "Gut up, Firebird! Do it! NOW!"

His no-nonsense tone settles into my core, reinforcing my resolve. I take a deep breath and burn through the torrent of tears with white-hot rage. "Hang on, baby. I'm going to fix this," I choke out. I gasp, realizing the number of times Trey has said those exact words to me over the course of our lifetimes. I look to Big Joe in desperation.

Big Joe snarls, "Kill them all, La Diabla, and we'll handle the cleanup." He surveys the crowd of the Cats and the Hounds. "We see and hear nothing. Club edict."

I can see the Jags panic, but they aren't getting out of this.

I close my eyes and create an individual line to each of the Jags, who are surrounded by the Hellhounds. Once I'm sure I've got the lines right, I straddle Trey, and instruct, "Put your hands on him, Demitri." He does, and I cover his hands with mine. Without warning, I pull all the life essence out of the Jags in one cataclysmic wave. My back bows, and my spine incinerates. I scream as all the Jags drop, dead before they hit the ground.

Adam steps up to Darren and Bear, saying nothing. When they drop the wall between the soulmate connection, Adam blazes to life in my mind. *"Let's do this,"* he sends, and clamps his hands on my shoulders, pulling pain. He screams behind me as the torrent of ransacked energy pain courses through him at unexpected strength.

I blast the energy into Demitri's hands. I feel Demitri channel the energy as he tries to repair Trey's lifeless body.

I hear the whiz of little wheels pull up next to me, and Mama Mabel frantically asks, "What's Trey's blood type?"

"B positive," I choke out around the pull of energy Demitri uses for the desperately complicated healing work.

"Who has B positive blood?" Mabel asks. "You MUST be sure!"

Everyone announces that they aren't sure, or that theirs is a different type.

A fearful voice says, "I'm B positive."

Goliath. Looks like I missed him when I was killing the Jags.

As Goliath approaches, my empathic gift picks up on the emotions and thoughts he's blasting. I feel his heartbreak over the death of his father, who was the leader who shot Trey. He's reeling with regret for stirring this mess up because he was just trying to get his dad's attention, who thought little of him. He lied to him about me starting the mess with the Machetes. Unfortunately for him, in my world, there are consequences for actions.

Mabel starts a line in Goliath's hand. His blood pours through a tube to a medical blood bag that Mama's holding. Thank God she keeps a full supply of medical equipment. Considering how often we find ourselves in dire situations, it's proven necessary more than once.

Demitri stops what he's doing and puts a bloody hand around the filling bag. He closes his eyes and nods, before concentrating on Trey again. "The blood type is right. Goliath's blood has no disease that I can detect."

When the first bag is full, Mabel switches the bags and hands the full one to Finley, who hangs it on one of the curled hooks on the metal IV stand. I watch, dazed from shock and energy backlash, as Goliath's knees give out.

"We have to stop," he groans.

I say with ringing clarity, "Thank you for your sacrifice."

Goliath panics and rips the needle from his body. Stealth and Mercury, the two most lethal of the Hellhounds, shove him flat on his back, and pin him down. Mabel reinserts the needle in Goliath's hand, and we watch as Goliath is drained to a lethal point. His mouth barely moves as Mama Mabel pulls the IV and hangs the second bag on the metal stand. Goliath's eyes shift to the expression of the nearly dead.

Mabel wheels the stand to the opposite side of Trey, while Stealth puts his hands around Goliath's head and wrenches it around with practiced simplicity. We hear a crack, and Goliath's life snuffs out. In the back of my mind, I realize that we've resorted to copious amounts of murder, but I can't panic about it. Trey must be saved.

Covered in blood, Demitri shifts his gaze to me. "His body is fixed, but his heart won't beat."

"I need a heartbeat to start the blood infusion," Mama Mabel says.

I straddle Trey, putting my hands on his chest. My head hangs. I'm running on empty. Bear and Darren each put a hand on my shoulders. Adam kneels next to Trey and places his hands over mine. The Hounds step over the Jags' lifeless bodies, and all the Cats and Hounds form a circle. Every face is tear-soaked. They take hands, the closest two gripping Bear's and Darren's shoulders, connecting the circle. I close my eyes and using the energy flowing through Bear and Darren from the entire circle, I send a jolt into Trey. His body spasms and drops again to the pavement.

"Three, two, one," Mabel says.

I send another jolt. I feel Trey's body tense and then collapse again.

Mabel calmly says again, "Three, two, one."

I send another jolt, but still nothing. I tip my head back as earth-shattering heartbreak rips through me. We've had a horrible run of it, but losing a soulmate is catastrophic. I scream, "COME ON, TREEEEY!"

"Focus, Melanie," Mabel snaps.

"This is it," Bear says. "We get Shivers back. Energy jolt on three."

Mabel says, "One, two, THREE!"

A bolt of collective energy seers through my hands and Trey bows, only his head and feet left on the ground. His body slams to the pavement, and there's a massive gasp. The soulmate connection with Trey roars back to life in my psyche. Everything that makes Trey, Trey rushes through me on a soul-bending wave. A hand lands on my back, keeping me from smacking my head on the pavement. Tears stream down my face, and I hear gasps and relieved exhales all around me. I don't have the guts to look at Trey and confirm it's true . . . that he's alive. I grab the nearest leg, hanging on like a terrified child. I feel the person kneel.

I reach blindly, sobbing, and Big Joe gathers me up. "I don't know how, but you did it again. You always do."

"Melanie," Trey rasps.

I meet his gaze.

He has the IV in his arm and the first blood bag is half drained, but he's gray still.

I feel sick with relief.

Trey smiles at me. "You did it. I was watching."

Everyone quiets to hear this.

"Your dark-water side held me in limbo. He points to Adam, Demitri, Bear, and Darren. "Melanie's spirit guide wants to talk to us."

"Are you up for this?" Adam asks.

Trey nods. "She's insistent."

We all sit knee to knee in a circle. We close our eyes, and I draw them into my psyche. We watch my spirit guide slide up calmly from the dark water that lives in my mind. *"I'm seeing all of you together,"* she breathes in wonder. *"You've been together from the start."*

We exchange a curious look.

"You did well, Melanie," she says with an ethereal lilt. *"I had to argue with Trey's spirit guide about letting him go. We had to follow the plan, though."*

"I met my spirit guide while I was dead." Trey scrunches his mental face. *"He's kind of a cynical dick."*

"Imagine that!" Adam scoffs.

"What is 'the plan?'" I ask.

"Your life-path plans," my spirit guide says. *"To explain, before each new lifetime, you're asked what you need to accomplish. Your spirit guides take your preferences and balance them with the larger picture that only we know. We put you into your next life with the equivalent of amnesia. Left to your own devices, you must find your way, learning and growing, facing the hindrances of rage, fear, jealousy, regret, and heartbreak, along with all the positive emotions."* She sighs. *"Bear and Darren, you've done your best to advise them, but things have hit such a confused and dire point. Melanie and Adam were the original soulmate pairing. You slowly started to derail with each lifetime. You've tortured each other, and done unbearable things, all in the name of love and hate. When you're in the spirit realm, between lifetimes, you're a match made in heaven. Unfortunately, when you're in these human bodies, you're cataclysmic together."* She shakes her head. *"Now, though, is critical, because Adam has drifted so far from the plan."*

"What is happening?" I ask suspiciously, but I'm ignored.

She shifts her gaze to Trey. *"So, around twenty lifetimes ago, we selected Trey for Melanie. He's always been a part of your group, and he wanted this."* She smiles softly at me. *"But we couldn't just eliminate your connection with Adam because it was a natural bond. You two had to decide. Before this lifetime, Adam finally decided that he couldn't take the whiplash heartbreak of how you two hurt each other during each lifetime."*

"What?" I screech.

My spirit guide glares at Trey. *"You've failed her. I don't know what direction this is going to go."*

Trey doesn't seem to know what to do. He looks to me.

"You're the one who called us in here," I remind him. *"If you don't know, what makes you think I do?"*

My spirit guide holds up a hand to halt me. *"It's time for all of you to understand a bit more about your lifetimes."* She waves her hand, and something akin to a movie montage plays on the wall of my psyche space.

We watch snippets of all of us from many lifetimes, before finally settling on one of Trey and me. The "movie" slows to real time, and we see me as a redhead and Trey as a black World War II soldier. Our eyes are both the same as they are now, mine a warm brown and Trey's a golden brown. Memory Trey kisses me.

Adam of that time stalks up behind me while Trey and I are distracted and thrusts a knife into my back. I turn, in disbelief, and past-life memory Adam snarls to Trey, "If I can't have her, neither can you."

I die in Trey's arms in the middle of a USO dance. I'm wearing a USO uniform and must have worked at a canteen.

The memory movie ends, and Trey's breathing is ragged as he relives the pain of losing me. Adam is struggling, his eyes huge with panic from what he just saw in that memory.

"Adam started failing you long ago," my spirit guide explains. *"What you just saw was fueled by passion, though. We could accept that because he still felt a draw to you. Now, though?"*

"Wait just a damn minute," Adam interjects.

She turns to Adam, her expression taut. *"You and Melanie were a force to be reckoned with for many lifetimes, but it's time."*

"Time for what?" I demand.

My spirit guide snaps her fingers and the image of Adam's

face through every lifetime we've had flashes in my mind. Every new face looks different except for those blue eyes. Every image is of my guy, who I loved more than life itself. The images halt on his face in this lifetime, and I open my eyes to Adam standing in front of me.

He crushes me to his chest. *"I'm so sorry for so much Melanie,"* he whispers. *"I'm even sorrier for how many lifetimes I've said exactly those words to you."* He puts his hands on my cheeks and gazes at me. *"Those eyes."*

I smile through tears. *"Your eyes were always how I found you."*

He nods. *"Same. I love you"*

"I love you too," I whisper.

"That'll suffice," my spirit guide says with finality.

Panic explodes through me as my spirit guide raises her hands over her head. Her gaze shifts with maniacal power just as a soul-deep boom explodes from her hands as they meet.

"NOOOOOO," I scream as I feel like my soul is being torn in half. I can't hear or see. All I can do is feel, and it's horrendous. The flash clears, and I'm left panting on the floor of my psyche.

Everyone else is still standing, and they all look like they've witnessed the apocalypse.

"What did you just do?" Adam screams.

I blink spirit eyes as I survey the empty, raw spot in my psyche where my soulmate connection with Adam has always lived. It's gone, and I can't breathe.

"Adam, you wanted a fresh start with a new soulmate," my spirit guide reveals.

"WHAT?" I screech.

She waves her hand, and the memory of a secret meeting he had in the spirit realm plays on the wall of my psyche. I apparently wasn't present for it, and I'm heartbroken by what he says. He wants a fresh start. He's bored and feels like I'm holding him back. Because we have so few lifetimes left, he wants a fresh start while there's still time to build a bond that's less turbulent.

The memory ends, and I stare at him with my mouth hanging open. *"How could you?"* whispers from me.

"I have NO recollection of that," Adam insists.

"That's because you asked not to," my spirit guide informs. *"You wanted no hindrances while you chose your new soulmate during this lifetime, but we planted the desire in your subconscious. You followed that desire and chose Valerie."*

"Oh, wowwwww," Bear breathes, his eyes the size of Jupiter.

"Note to self," Darren murmurs in horror, *"Don't make soulmate plans in the spirit realm that come to fruition during a lifetime while we can't remember."*

My spirit guide looks to Darren. *"You don't have to worry about that. You made a different choice that you've done surprisingly well by."* She gives him a pointed look. *"Bear is your soulmate, but the two of you needed to deepen your bond, because you get distracted by physical connection with each other."* She chuckles. *"Hence why you're a man this lifetime, Darren. I'll admit, I was doubtful, but the two of you have done miraculously well as best friends, who are both unwaveringly straight, per your imprinted plan this lifetime."*

"That's why we're together all the time," Bear breathes on a wave of realization.

He and Darren stare at each other quizzically.

Darren shrugs. *"Whatever. I'll take it."*

"Me too," Bear says. *"After dealing with the crazy females in our group, I have no desire for one."*

"You done yet?" I screech as tears stream down my cheeks.

"Sorry," Darren says.

*"I don't want this! Adam gasps. *Please reverse it!"*

"I can't," my spirit guide says.

"Can't, or won't?" Adam demands.

"Won't," she clarifies. *"You wanted someone else and were clear that if you chose someone else this lifetime, she would be your replacement soulmate. You chose Valerie."*

Adam starts to hyperventilate. *"Oh my GOD!"*

"You're dismissed," my spirit guide orders with finality, and Adam, Trey, Darren, and Bear are forcibly shoved out by her. She surveys Demitri, while I'm left reeling on the ground. *"I'm in the process of finalizing a lot of decisions, but I'm unsure what to do about you. I can't leave this to your spirit guide. Pierre is too new and wasn't there for two hundred and three lifetimes of watching all of this unfold. He's been shut out, and I was deemed the spearhead of the decision-making. Adam's and Trey's spirit guides have all but given up."* She shakes her head, seeming disgusted. *"Unfortunately, I don't know you as well as I know the others. So, Demitri,"* she says after a dramatic sigh, *"what can I do to move your trajectory forward?"*

Demitri stares at her intensely, and they seem to be communicating mentally because I can't hear it.

"All right," my spirit guide says, *"let's start here."* She puts a hand on Demitri, and a soft glow builds to a bright flash.

Demitri gasps before exhaling and doubling over. *"Thank you."*

"Soulmate bond with Victoria is no more," my spirit guide informs, riding a wave of unbelievable power. She stares intensely at me. *"We'll see what direction things head. I'll know what to do soon. Your job is to just wait, because you have no control over the outcome, per the plan. Control was yours, but your soulmates never respected that. They requested control, and you rather snidely agreed,"* she wobbles her head, *"more as a punishment for them than a deep decision, but you were right."* She smiles wickedly. *"It's certainly been interesting."*

"You voyeuristic BITCH," snarls from me as hatred swells.

She shrugs coyly. *"Takes one to know one,"* she cats before snapping her fingers.

When my eyes fly open, I'm lying in a heap on the parking lot pavement. I roll onto my knees, my head hanging. I feel like I've been hit by a truck. No one pays me any mind. They're all focused on Adam and Valerie.

"What is it?" Valerie asks.

"A soulmate bond," Adam informs, his tone dead.

Her eyes light. "Whaaat?"

"My soulmate bond with Melanie was shifted to you," Adam says.

Unsure looks are exchanged by everyone except the few who were there when it happened.

Valerie's expression slowly morphs, and there's an arrogant undercurrent as she pans her gaze to me. "Finally," she breathes on a wave of elation. She seems to be intensely focusing internally before her expression bunches quizzically. "How do I tap into the power?" she asks Bear.

He blinks befuddlement back at her.

"You have none," Adam says, sounding disgusted. "You're still a Normal, Valerie."

"But you said I got Melanie's power!" she snaps back.

Adam shakes his head. "I said you got her soulmate connection to me. That connection doesn't come with her abilities."

"This is going to be hell," Darren mutters to Bear.

"I deserve the power that comes with a bond!" Valerie demands.

"You got the *responsibility* that comes with a soulmate bond," Adam counters.

"What the fuck does that mean?" she snarks back, proving to be precisely the clueless Normal I've always known she was.

"What lifetime is Valerie on?" Adam asks, sounding defeated.

Darren crosses to Valerie and puts his hand on her shoulder, closing his eyes. "She's on her second lifetime," he says.

Reality hangs heavy in the air for the energy workers.

Adam's hands cover his face as he panics, while I struggle to stand, feeling dead inside. Trey gets an arm around me and scoops me into his arms.

"Melanie," Demitri says as he rushes to me, but Trey refuses to give me to him.

"Come on." Mabel rushes through the door, and Trey follows with me through the parlor. Mabel unlocks our old room and opens the door, wincing as she realizes it's a guest room now. "Damn it. Sorry."

"This works," Trey says, carrying me inside and setting me on the bed.

"What do you need?" Mabel asks us.

"I'll get her sorted," Trey assures.

Mabel closes the door, and Trey pushes the panic-room button on our old panel on the wall. We stare at each other as the locks slide into place. The moment they finish, my entire body contorts with a bout of ugly crying.

Trey lies down on the bed and holds me tight. "Let it out, Melanie," he murmurs before descending into silence while I sob hysterically.

While I howl and wail, we hear a pounding on the door, but we ignore it.

I finally calm, lying limp and thoroughly spent. I roll and rest my head on Trey's chest. "What am I going to do?" I whisper.

"The same thing you've been doing," Trey says. "Live without Adam."

"This is different."

"No, it's not," Trey softly says. "He hasn't been there for you as a soulmate this whole lifetime." My breathing calms, and Trey drapes his arm around me. "You need to work through the initial shock, but the reality is that this shift isn't going to punish you. Adam's dismissive flippancy has prepared you to handle this shift. Your spirit guide removed that destructive tendency by forcing a bond with Valerie." Trey takes a slow breath before adding, "Adam Stone is about to get what he deserves, and I've never felt sorrier for anyone in all my lifetimes. Can you IMAGINE suffering a soulmate bond with VALERIE?"

A giggle bursts from me that quickly turns into raucous laughter that Trey joins in on. We sit up, howling at Adam's predicament. When our tacky laughter at Adam's expense calms, we stare at each other.

"Why are you helping me?" I ask softly.

"Because," Trey says, "I was shown the moment that you were presented as my potential other half. I knew you were perfect for me for many lifetimes before that."

"What happened to your previous soulmate?" I ask.

"I didn't have one."

"You terrify me," I admit.

That realization drops Trey's head. He rubs his face hard. "Thank you for saving me, Melanie."

"You're welcome." I think for a moment. "The only one who my spirit guide was merciful with was Demitri. After she pushed all of you out, she removed the soulmate bond between Demitri and Victoria."

"She did?" Trey asks, seeming stunned.

"You should have seen the relief in D's eyes," I say.

"We should get back out there," Trey says. "We have a parking lot full of dead bodies."

That spurs me to my feet.

CHAPTER 26

"The parking lot issue?" Trey asks.

"Handled temporarily," Big Joe replies. "I need help on this one."

Trey nods. "Any chance it'll come back on us?"

Big Joe looks guardedly pensive. "There were a lot of them. We generally only cover up one or two. I'm not sure this time."

Officer Striker winds his way through the parlor to us, and Big Joe quietly explains, "I called him in."

Officer Striker was raised in Hollywood, and we trust him, but I'm surprised because this is a problem I don't know how he'll handle.

Trey gestures for us to follow him through the crowd and down the hallway. Mabel flows into our group. Trey unlocks his security office door, and our select few slide in.

Intel gets up from the desk chair and hands Trey a VHS tape. As Trey closes the door, Intel explains, "I didn't destroy anything yet, per Big Joe's request. This is messy, and we need to figure out our course of action first. This is a compilation tape."

"Bruce is almost here," Mabel informs. Bruce is Marcus's dad. He's a lawyer who regularly keeps us out of hot water.

"Did you physically touch any of the people who died?" Officer Striker asks.

"Only one," Mabel answers. "We drained Goliath's blood to save Trey, and his neck was snapped."

There's a knock on the door, and Trey opens it, ushering in Bruce. His eyebrows are in his hairline. "What happened now?"

"We have a serious problem." Officer Striker asks Big Joe, "How many?"

Big Joe sighs. "Thirty-three dead."

Bruce's mouth drops open. "WHAT?"

Big Joe nods.

Trey slides the tape into the monitor system VCR, and Big Joe asks Bruce, "Considering that we have law enforcement in the room," he gestures to Officer Striker, "are we safe to show this?"

"Depends."

Officer Striker shakes his head. "I'm off duty now, as far as this is concerned. I know how to handle the police report, and you know the lawyer end of this."

Big Joe nods to Trey, who presses several buttons, changing the big monitor to the VCR image. He hits *play*, and we watch the Jags come onto the screen in the parking lot. As the gun is raised, I turn my back on the monitor. I can't relive this. I put my forehead on Trey's shoulder, and he wraps an arm around me.

"Oh my GOD!" Bruce gasps. "Trey!"

Trey nods. "What's about to happen is justified."

I hear the video continue. The sounds of chaos, me screaming far more than I recall, and finally, Trey's voice as he's brought back to the land of the living punctuate the moment. Trey shifts to pause the video, and I turn to face everyone.

Bruce exhales. "Well, here's the good news. Enough of them died that we can get away with erasing the part with Goliath donating his blood for Trey to live. There's no way they can count the number of bodies that were piled up on this footage." He looks to me. "There's also zero proof that you did anything to anyone. Our biggest problem will be explaining how Trey's chest got fixed."

"All the bodies are still in Mercury's van," Big Joe explains. "We parked it in Mabel's garage and we closed the rolling door. The bodies in the van are covered with ice bags. We need to know if we should dump them in Death Valley or take them to the coroner."

Officer Striker exhales and rubs his forehead. "How many of these guys have families that are going to be looking for them?"

"A lot," Big Joe answers. "Most of the spouses are as ruthless as they are."

I roll my eyes. "Fantastic. Just what I need: a pack of pissed-off wives coming after me because their meal tickets are dead."

"I'm shocked that anyone still challenges you at this point," Officer Striker says.

I put my hands out and quip sarcastically, "Yet here we are, again and again."

"Here's what I think needs to happen," Officer Striker says. "I need to radio this in, with the understanding that Mabel called me. We need to put the bodies back in the parking lot and have the coroner come out. Make sure the one with the snapped neck is at the bottom of the pile and angle him right to account for his neck injury. The video of the collaborate footage needs to disappear."

"We have all the original footage from each camera," Intel says. "You just have to pick your poison."

"Realistically, the attempted killing of Trey is ground for self-defense," Officer Striker informs. "Now, how do we explain Trey's miraculous healing without also clueing in the powers that be about Melanie's ability to kill a parking lot full of people with a thought?"

"How about we leave the part about my getting shot out of it?" Trey suggests. "Instead, we only show the one video of the Jags suddenly falling over dead."

Bruce and Officer Striker exchange a look.

"It could work," Bruce says.

"Do you plan to take legal action against the family of the slain man who shot you?" Officer Striker asks Trey.

Trey snorts. "No. I want to keep Melanie out of jail on thirty-three murder charges."

"Anyone want to look at the tape of that one angle?" Intel asks. We nod, and he pops it into the player. He hits *play*, and we watch the footage that conveniently only shows the Jags stepping up in the parking lot. The Hellhounds that blocked the Jags from running aren't in the shot. Next thing we know, the guys just fall over mysteriously.

"That's our evidence tape," Big Joe says. "We'll explain that the system's been shorting out. It's happened before, and we have that documented. Handle it, Intel."

Intel grins. "Did y'all know that this system needs a massive overhaul? Damn thing only has one recorder that works." He pops empty tapes into each VCR and hits *play* to make sure they're blank. He takes out a little machine from his bag, puts the gadget up to each VCR one at a time, and hits a button. The lights blink out on each VCR except the one that records from the camera angle we've chosen.

"What did you just do to my equipment?" Trey asks.

"Pulse gadget." Intel turns to Mabel. "You must have bad outlets that aren't grounded in here. Hell of a shame." He flips a switch. "Trey, I'm disappointed in you. Why in the world isn't your system recording sound?"

Trey snorts. "Now I know what switch to flip to make it record sound," he replies sarcastically.

Intel takes the one videotape that we're using and pops it into the editing machine. He scrubs evidence of the Hellhounds dumping the bodies unceremoniously in the van. Next, he runs the tape back and checks his watch. "We're setting this little event to take place in ten minutes. I'll scrub and set the counter to the time we need. I'm eliminating the sound. Put the bodies out in the parking lot."

Big Joe leaves, likely to speak with Stealth and Mercury.

Trey holds up the stack of surveillance tapes that we aren't using. "What do we do with these?"

"I think all the evidence needs to be gone but fear we might need it one day," Officer Striker says.

"I have a vault in my office," Bruce offers. "Should I put them in there?"

Mama Mabel snorts. "Give them to me. You guys are silly. You think I run an illegal business and don't have secure hidey-holes?" She takes the tapes and heads out the door.

We watch as Intel does a rapid-fire job with the evidence.

Trey grins at Mabel as she comes back in without the tapes. "Thank you, Mama."

She pats his shoulder. "You're welcome, kiddo."

"I need everyone in the banquet hall, now," I announce.

Everyone except for Intel follows me out. We rush through the huge building, with the Hounds and Cats following. Mabel unlocks the banquet hall, and I flip on the switches, turning on the disco ball and starburst flashy lights.

"We're having a staff party," I instruct. "That's why we closed early. Trey wasn't shot tonight. I didn't do anything to the Jags. We were working, then we switched gears to our party. That's it. Got it?"

Everyone nods.

"Skates on," I order. "Fast."

Everyone rushes to the skate racks to pull pairs. Hiram and Dante head to the deejay booth and get music rolling. Everybody starts skating, but they look nervous.

We hear a bang on the door to the parking lot a few minutes later, and in walks Stealth and Mercury.

Stealth announces, "No clue what happened, but the parking lot is full of dead bodies."

Everyone skates over to the doors, and Mama Mabel makes a phone call from the cell phone that materializes from the pocket of her fancy swishy pants. We stare at the bodies, stacked exactly how they were before.

I lean to Intel, who just showed up in the banquet hall, and quietly ask, "How did they get it so right?"

"Stealth has a photographic memory. He looked at the paused image on the monitor. Goliath's hidden under the pile."

I smirk. *Nothing surprises me anymore.*

"I must applaud you for the design of this place," Bear says to Mabel. "Having a business parking lot that's blocked from view by the building has come in handy."

Mabel raises a sassy eyebrow. "I own a brothel. I can't have my clients ogled by tourists on Hollywood Boulevard while they come and go." She wobbles her head. "I never imagined the amount of death, battles, and fistfights that would go on, though. It's been a hell of a year."

Officer Striker pulls into the parking lot in his squad car. He gets out and puts a handkerchief to his face, loudly announcing, "Possible gas leak. Everyone, stay clear!"

"He's got to be kidding!" I send to Trey.

"The police and coroner will believe it, or something equally ridiculous. Hang tight."

Adam skates up behind me and drapes his arms over my shoulders. He murmurs in my ear, "Maybe this will be the last lifetime that we have to hide this kind of crazy shit."

"We're not that lucky," I whisper back.

He holds his hand out. I lace my fingers with his and take a memory from what looks like hundreds of years ago. We're in some European-looking town square, faced with an unruly mob hell-bent on lynching me as a witch. In the memory, I level the crowd with an energy blast, and as the authorities arrive, we *must* figure out a way to explain why we're the only ones still alive. I laugh as I come out of the memory.

"I'm suddenly recalling more moments from our lifetimes," Adam whispers.

"Are you okay?"

"Nope," Adam whispers. "I fully admit that I've screwed up with you over and over, but I'm not ready to let you go."

I sigh. "There's nothing we can do about it, Adam."

He skates away.

Trey glances my way from his spot leaning against the doorjamb and sends, *"Fill me in."*

I send the memory of what just happened with Adam. Trey's eyes unfocus as he watches the memory. He sighs. *"Fantastic. Now Adam's going to chase you."*

"Hopefully, Valerie can keep him distracted while they build their soulmate bond."

Trey scoffs. *"Highly unlikely. All they do is fight."*

"All he and I apparently did was fight to the death and drive each other insane. He likes that sort of thing."

Trey chuckles, and Demitri glances suspiciously from Trey to me.

The police chief pulls in, gets out of his car, and surveys the situation. He speaks with Officer Striker, and they cross the parking lot together to the open door where we're all standing. "It's Raining Men" is enthusiastically playing over the sound system.

"How did these people end up dead in your parking lot?" the police chief asks.

We all shrug, appearing baffled.

"We closed early tonight for a skate party," Mama Mabel explains. "Maybe they were coming to have drinks at the bar."

The police chief knows that we're really a brothel that fronts as a bar, but he has an understanding with Mabel, so he doesn't question it. He looks over his shoulder at the dead thugs. "Have you had any gas-leak issues?"

Mabel shakes her head. "Not that I know of. We've had some power-spiking issues, though."

"I'd like to see your security footage," the chief requests.

Trey kneels to unlace his skates. He winces, and Demitri puts his hand on Trey's shoulder. It looks like he's steadying him while he undoes his skates, but I know he's healing another round of sore tissue that's popped up as Trey's body tries to resolve the catastrophic injury and subsequent quick healing.

Trey stands, now skate-free. "The security system's been problematic, but I'm happy to show you. I've got to make an appointment with the repair technician."

The chief follows Trey through the doors on the far side of the banquet hall.

"Keep us apprised," Mabel whispers to me.

Big Joe, Adam, Intel, and Stealth gather around.

I watch in Trey's mind. "They're in the office."

Trey gestures to the system and explains the ungrounded outlet issue that caused some of the machines to short out. I relay the information. Trey shows the chief the footage we have.

The chief looks to the clock on the wall. When the video finishes, he says, "Well, something happened. I can confirm that they were alone in the parking lot though."

I inform our group when Trey and the chief leave the office. We wait, trying to appear casual as they come in through the hall doors.

"Anything?" the police chief asks the fire chief, who comes through the parking lot door along with the coroner.

The fire chief shrugs. "No gas leak."

"What else could it be?" the police chief asks.

"Radon? Carbon monoxide?" Officer Striker offers.

I roll my eyes in Trey's mind, and he mentally chuckles.

The coroner joins the conversation. "We found a needle mark on one of the bodies."

"Huh. A bad batch of drugs could explain it." The police chief looks to Big Joe. "Do you know if the Jags have a drug habit?"

Big Joe's expression shutters down. "No clue." Big Joe knows the answer, but he's not about to tell the police chief. Snitches get stitches in our world, as I've learned the hard way.

"I'll check the bodies for drugs, and we'll see," the coroner offers. "That's the only feasible explanation I can come up with. Bad drug batches kill groups of people all the time."

Satisfied, all the officials take their leave, and the coroner's van pulls out of the parking lot. We all exhale, relieved, as Mabel closes the doors.

"The chief may have just given us our out," Big Joe informs. "The Jags are known for their rampant drug use."

"The coroner may discover that the bodies have been dead longer than our story admits to," Trey says, worried.

Big Joe shakes his head. "The coroner's office is so overwhelmed, they won't get to that stack of bodies for a while. The report will be narrowed down to a wide enough time range that the coroner will use our security footage to determine time of death."

"Mama, can me and Tanner stay here tonight?" Finley asks. "I'm scared to go home."

Mama Mabel smiles at her endearingly. Others from the Hellcats pipe up with the same request, and Mabel offers to set up camping cots in the banquet hall that doubles as a skating rink. Trey sighs in my mind.

I rescue him, saying, "I'm going to take Trey back to the suite for a bit. He hasn't had a chance to process any of what's happened."

We hastily leave the banquet hall, and Trey exhales. "Thank you. I need a few minutes."

"I know."

When we get to the suite, Trey unlocks the door, and we head in. He sits on the couch and puts his head in his hands. I try to wrap my buckling psyche around reality. With monumental effort, I pull myself together and join him.

We sit in silence for a long while before he holds a hand out to me. I take it and pull a memory that surprises me. It's of me and Trey from many lifetimes ago. I was blond, with my trademark brown eyes, and I'm wearing a conservative red dress. I look at him from across a park and smile coyly. He smiles back. A man walks up beside me and glares Trey's way, his ocean-blue eyes flashing. I hear Trey think in the memory, *'I don't know who that jackass is, but his girl's about to be mine.'*

When the memory finishes, I laugh.

Trey smiles. "Past-life memories are popping up. It's not ideal given my current state, but I must admit they're interesting."

"We now know where your love of me in red comes from."

"Yup," Tray says, "and you were a redhead in the USO lifetime, hence why redheads spark my interest."

I smile.

After a long stretch, Trey says, "I've got something I need to talk to you about, but I can't do it in my current condition. Will you stay here with me while I work through this, and then hear me out when I can handle the discussion we need to have?"

Every ounce of my mind, body, and soul, thrum with confliction. I whimper, "What did I do wrong?"

He closes his eyes, clearly pained. "You didn't do anything wrong. *I'm* the problem."

My face falls.

"It kills me when you get that look. I'm sorry, Melanie." He looks like he's going to cry and blinks rapidly. "Tonight's been a lot. I need to sleep."

I help him to his feet and guide him into our bedroom. After he strips down to his boxers and slides under the covers, I pull the blankets up to his chin and kiss his forehead. He falls asleep in a matter of moments.

I head to the living room to fall apart but am interrupted by a knock at the door. I open it and find Valerie on the other side. She's steely-eyed and forces her way in, slamming the door closed after her. The loud bang of the door makes me jump. I'm not up for a confrontation. I was on edge and emotionally exhausted before Trey got shot.

"I want it clear that you and Adam are done," Valerie screams.

"Trey's sleeping. Get the hell out!"

Valerie narrows her eyes. "Stay away from my HUSBAND!"

Our bedroom door opens, and Trey blinks sleepily just as our front door opens and Mabel pours in, followed by Adam and most of the Hellcats.

"AM I IN THE BANQUET HALL WITH ADAM?"

She doesn't answer, and I cup my ear sarcastically. "Was that a no I just heard? Very good, bitch! I'm not!"

"STAY OUT OF MY HUSBAND'S HEAD!" Valerie screams.

"I'm not in his head," I lob back. "Those are HIS thoughts. I don't control those; he does."

Valerie starts to launch herself at me, but Arch grabs her and wrestles her carefully to the ground.

I glare at Adam. "How about you take your devil-spawn and teach her how to handle your new soulmate bond? She's clearly got a lot to learn."

"I apologize, Melanie. I realized what was happening after she left." Adam collects his raging wife from the floor. "Look at me, Valerie. I get that you're new to this soulmate situation. We need to set some ground rules."

"You were thinking about her," Valerie whimpers.

"I think about a lot of things," Adam says. "What isn't going to happen is you digging through my thoughts. You must control yourself. Based on your insane behavior, I'm seriously wondering if this was a massive mistake."

Valerie seems to deflate.

"I feel for her," I send to Trey. *"She isn't ready for everything that comes with this soulmate bond she's landed in. No one asked her if she was okay with this. It just got dumped on her."*

"Come on, Valerie," Bear says. "We're going to help you figure this out."

I'm relieved, because Bear has a chance of guiding her. He and Darren shuttle her out the door.

Adam and I look at each other across the room, and I inform him, "I'm not going to tolerate a whole Valerie shitstorm. Get her under control. She just tromped on my last nerve. The day's going to come that I blast her into next Sunday just to shut her the hell up."

"I'm going to level with you. I don't think Valerie has the

temperament to handle this soulmate mess. She's not even an energy worker." Adam gestures to Trey and me. "The three of us know how complicated it is. There's little privacy, and without boundaries that all participants follow, it doesn't work."

"This has the potential to be a nightmare." Trey levels Adam with steely eyes. "Your rogue soulmate is making critical errors. I'm not in my best mental condition right now, and Melanie's forethought is paper-thin."

"I'm asking that Valerie not come back into Melanie and Trey's suite," Mabel says to Adam. "This intrusion is very concerning. Melanie and Valerie had problems before this that we don't want to fire back up."

"Understood," Adam says.

"Come on, Adam," Arch says. "Let's go talk." He shuttles him out the door.

After the door closes, Mama Mabel crosses to me and wraps me up in a maternal hug.

"I'm sorry for all the problems, Mabel," I quietly say. "It's one thing after the other."

Mabel pulls back, gripping my arms. "I know, my girl." She turns to Trey, and the dark circles under his eyes are frightening. She calmly says, "Everyone out. These two need rest."

Everyone passes through the door, squeezing our hands or hugging us as they leave.

Victoria hangs back, asking Demitri, "What happened to that bond between us? It feels different now."

"It's gone."

"Thank God," Victoria snarks. Her eyes narrow at Demitri. "I'm over your games."

Demitri's mouth drops open. "MY games? Oh, please."

"Get out, Victoria," I order.

She gives Trey a look, and he says, "Leave, Tori." She does, and Trey heads back into the bedroom and closes the door.

With just us left, Demitri gives me a caged look. "Where do we stand?"

"Can we go in the hall?" I ask.

Demitri agrees and follows me out the door.

I swallow hard. "Trey's talking about revealing some damn secret he's harboring. Apparently, I have a chat coming."

Demitri wraps his arms around me. "You need to follow your gut."

"Is everything okay?" comes an unexpected voice. "Presley said Valerie hurt Melanie."

I inhale sharply and whip around. There stands Jayla, right behind me.

"Give me a minute, Jayla," Demitri responds. "I'll fill you in."

I glare at Demitri. "Is there a reason you didn't tell me she was listening?"

"I closed my eyes when I hugged you. I didn't know she walked up."

"Follow my gut, huh?" My expression cages as I step back.

"Melanie, please," Demitri begs.

"If you want to talk to Jayla instead of hearing what I have to say, then be my guest."

"That is NOT what I was trying to do." Demitri laces his hands on the back of his neck. "My goal was to get back to what you were about to say as fast as possible."

"The best way to do that was to promise Jayla my secrets if she could just be a patient girl for a few moments?" I sarcastically lob back. I glare at her. "He's all yours." I side-skirt Demitri, who grabs my arm.

"Please, Melanie. I need to know where you stand about us."

I yank my arm from his grasp. "I won't be interrupted by Jayla. If this mattered to you, you would have told her to go the fuck away."

"Why would I be rude when I could just ask her to give us a minute?" Demitri appears so confused.

I toss my hands up. "Her interrupting the moment that I was making the decision about us was worth demanding privacy for. It's also not her damn business!" I flip a hand toward a frozen Jayla. "She's still standing here waiting for you, Prince Charming."

Demitri's head drops back. "Jayla, please leave."

She scurries away.

"We were clearly a mistake." I head into the suite while Demitri pleads for me to talk to him. I close the door on his desperation.

I swallow hard and cross to the bedroom, where I survey a sleeping Trey. He doesn't seem as scary lately. I'm realizing that the pressure he's been under has a lot to do with his anger. I think whatever this secret is has also created a lot of these issues for Trey and me. I need to work through it, because he's finally willing to talk. That's what I was waiting for since my miscarriage. I close the bedroom door. Deciding that my soulmate deserves a chance, because losing that connection with Adam has given me perspective, I leave the suite and hurry to my car.

CHAPTER 27

I rush into the suite and lock the door behind me before tossing my backpack onto the couch. When I open the bedroom door, my jaw drops. There, asleep in my bed, are Victoria and Trey. I storm into the kitchen while dialing a number. When Bear answers, I ask, "Where are you?"

"The banquet hall. Why?"

"You might want to get to the suite before I kill someone." I end the call.

—

I point in the bedroom to where Trey still has Victoria spooned around him.

Bear and Adam appear as surprised as I was when I found them.

"I left to get stuff from my house after Trey requested another chance. He said he had something to reveal. I came back to this," I whisper while pointedly raising my eyebrows.

Bear and Adam exchange a pensive glance.

"I'm going to see what I can find." Stealthily, I make my way into the bedroom. A cursory glance around reveals nothing odd.

I go into the bathroom, and there's nothing on the surface to discover. I open the bathroom cabinet under the sink, and find a makeup bag, pink toothbrush, and hairbrush that's full of raven-black hair. I wave the guys in and point. They take in the evidence, and then I shoo them out and follow them. Adam closes the door quietly.

"What's the plan?" Bear asks.

"Wait until they wake up, and confront them," I reply.

"You could just search their memories," Bear says.

"I could search Victoria's, but ugggghhhh." I shudder. "That means I'd have to be in her mind."

Adam shivers, looking repulsed, and Bear makes a disgusted face.

I shrug. "Trey's got a shield over his memory center that's so intense I'd have to do serious damage to get in, hence why I haven't searched before."

"That's suspicious as fuck," Adam says.

"Maybe she's just consoling him," Bear says.

Adam grimaces. "Gross."

I sigh. "I've suspected those two for a long time."

"Want me to throttle him to death?" Adam offers.

"No," I reply. "I want to confront him after I clear my head."

"Don't make assumptions." Bear gestures to the couch. "We should talk."

We sit, and Bear levels us with serious eyes. "How are you two holding up about the decimation of your bond?"

"I'm not pleased with your feelings that led to the removal of our soulmate bond," I say to Adam, "but I must respect it." I shrug. "I'm going to truly learn what it means to love somebody enough to let them go."

"I don't want to let you go," Adam groans, rubbing his face

hard. "I . . ." He trails off, wrestling with this. "This is the most cataclysmic change I've ever experienced."

"You set this path for a reason, Adam," Bear says.

"I have a lot of thinking to do," Adam says. "I'm not even close to clear about how I'm going to make it without Melanie."

"You've lived without her most of this lifetime," Bear reminds.

"I hate my life," Adam admits.

Bear gives Adam a pointed look. "You now have a soulmate who's a loose cannon, but you chose Valerie after setting this course. You didn't consciously remember, but subconsciously, you knew. The only reason I can surmise is that you're about to be on the receiving end of what you dished out for many lifetimes, so you can learn balance."

Adam huffs.

I smirk. "Little old soulmate me looks pretty good in hindsight, huh?"

Bear chuckles. "Sometimes we don't know what we have until it's gone. There's a great deal to be learned from that."

"I've got a lot of past-life memories coming through," Adam says. "They're overwhelmingly about me failing Melanie."

Bear crosses to my bookshelf and grabs my tarot deck. "Why not work to get some of the fun past-life memories to surface?"

Begrudgingly, Adam follows Bear to my four-seater dining table, but I think it's as good an idea as any.

As I'm about to stand, an entire lifetime's worth of memories knocks me back on the couch, seemingly delivered by my spirit guide. I gasp while I rip through the memories at lightning speed. My psyche rattles and my heart nearly stops, just before blazing clarity fills me. *Game changer. I'm so sick of layers.* I make my way to the table while Bear expertly shuffles the cards.

I wipe laughter tears from my cheeks. Bear and Adam take my hands, and I send the memory of us in a saloon, piss drunk. I'm in a burgundy velvet, gorgeously suggestive dress. I have blond hair, curled into ringlets. I'm at a table with Adam, who has jet-black hair and his trademark blue eyes. Bear's next to Adam, but he's a wiry guy in that lifetime. They're both rough-and-tumble cowboys. A Hispanic Trey, who looks a lot like he does now, saunters up and demands, "Priscilla! Up. You have a customer."

"Screw him yourself," I slur drunkenly. "I'm having fun."

"Up, P."

Memory Adam stands and swings Trey's way, but he misjudges and stumbles, falling face first into Bear's lap.

Bear takes a revolver from his hip holster and waves it wildly. "Might as well head upstairs, Priscilla, because me and Travis are apparently busy."

Memory Bear taps Adam on the head with the butt of the revolver, and Adam pushes off Bear's lap, turning to Trey. Instead of telling him off, he passes out, hitting the wood floor.

Memory me slops clumsily from my chair and crawls to Adam, draping myself over him. I drunkenly pet Adam's head and slur, "You're okay." I dissolve into a giggling fit before throwing up all over Trey's shoes. When Bear falls out of his chair and lands with a thud on top of me and Adam, I squeal, "Wheeeeeeee."

Trey snaps his fingers in the direction of two huge men, and they drag Bear, Adam, and me out the saloon's swinging doors, dumping us unceremoniously on the wood porch.

We're all laughing, as we come back to reality. "Well, I guess we know why we're so comfortable at a brothel in this lifetime," Bear says.

Victoria and Trey are leaving the bedroom. Our laughter makes them whip around to stare at us.

"I thought you left." Trey barks. His stunned energy ricochets, unchecked, through the suite.

My heart pounds now that it's time to confront him. "I went to get some stuff from my parents' house. I came back and found you in bed with Victoria. Care to explain?"

"I . . . ," Trey falters.

Before he can get his reply together, there's a pounding at the door. Victoria heads that way and opens it like she owns the place.

Demitri struts in on a wave of challenge. "You're here? This is going to easier than I thought," he arrogantly states. "Victoria, come sit down."

Victoria crosses the room and takes a seat at the table, looking unsure.

"Treeeey," Demitri draws out. "You should join us."

It sounds more like a threat than an invitation, and Trey hesitantly hovers by the kitchen door.

"I went home, and rage cleaned my house." Demitri hits Victoria with a steely glare.

"I believe I was questioning Trey," I mutter to Adam and Bear.

Adam waves his hand in my direction. "Shh. I have a feeling Demitri has dirt to spill."

"Hear me out," Demitri says to me. He glares at Victoria. "Are you missing something?"

"What are you talking about, Demitri?" Victoria snarks.

"Anything lost? Something important?" When he doesn't get an answer, Demitri pulls up the back of his shirt and takes a velvet-covered gray book out of his waistband.

Victoria's eyes snap wide. "Give it to me!" She makes a grab for it, but Demitri skirts the edge of the table, out of her reach.

"Victoria's diary was under my bed," Demitri informs, before opening the diary and turning to a page marked with a slip of paper. He clears his throat and reads, "I hate Melanie. She's nothing but an attention hog with her 'Wah, poor me' bullshit. Trey needs to get his head out of his ass and leave her. This affair has gone on long enough. After all this time, you'd think he'd know that I'm the one. He can't stand Melanie, and I can't stand listening to him bitch about her. I can't believe he canceled with me to deal with her sniveling." Demitri snaps the book closed and looks at me. "That was written the night you and Trey figured out you were pregnant. Your affair suspicions were right."

Bear's mouth drops open, and Adam mutters, "Holyyyy shit."

Humiliation swells in me as I look at Trey. "Melanie, that's Victoria's take on things, not mine," he says, thunderstruck.

"No, it's not, Trey," Victoria defensively retorts. "You say it all the time."

"Please stop talking, Victoria," Trey breathes.

"That's the conversation you needed to have with me?" I say in disbelief.

Trey doesn't answer, but his panicked eyes speak volumes.

"The whole diary is full of everything you need to know." Demitri holds out his hand over the table. I reach, my hand shaking, and pull the memory of him reading the diary. I speed-read every word through Demitri's eyes, and my heart constricts. All the details of Victoria and Trey's affair are revealed. She quotes him all through the diary, and it seems that I irritate him to no end. At the end of the memory, Demitri closes the book and thinks, *'I'm getting my girl back.'*

I open my eyes. "Unbelievable," mutters from me.

"I appreciate this," Demitri says to Victoria, thumping the diary on the table.

My wide-eyed gaze slides Victoria's way, and I decide I have no choice but to riffle through her memories. I'm sick of not knowing and want clarity on at least one area of my life. After everything Trey has put me through, I deserve it.

I quickly get to a memory of her in my shower today. I watch through her eyes as Trey steps into the bathroom and strips down to join her. My hands shake from shock. He tells her he loves her. The sex is passionate. He isn't aggressive, and it's the opposite of him and me.

I come out of the memory and slide sad eyes Trey's way. "I just saw everything I need to. Your heart belongs to her, and I've been nothing but dead weight in your life."

Trey clears his throat. "That's absolutely not true, Melanie."

"What did you see?" Adam asks.

"While we were playing with the tarot cards, Trey and Victoria were exuberantly slopping about in my shower. He loves her. It was everything I've wanted from him."

Trey appears ill. "I woke up, and you were gone. I thought you left because you were done with me."

"I left to grab my stuff to MOVE . . . ." I rattle my head. "I'm not going to fight. There's no point in lying to me, Trey. Her makeup is in the cabinet."

Trey's eyes widen. "We need to talk alone, please."

"Don't you dare, Melanie Katherine," Demitri intensely says to me.

I hold out my hand to Demitri. "I got this an hour ago." I send the lifetime's worth of memories that flooded my mind earlier.

He closes his eyes, and his mouth drops open as he watches some of them. Apparently, fifteen lifetimes ago, I got thoroughly sick of both Adam and Trey. Demitri, who was a tall brunet with a sexy Viking-esque flare, whisked me away in the light of a full moon. We boarded a ship and were off on an adventure we never returned from. We lived that entire lifetime together. Nearly every moment was happy, calm, full of easy laughter. We never had kids in that lifetime because I had a medical condition that didn't allow it, but he stuck with me, even though it broke his heart. He truly loved me.

"We're the couple in your intuition pulse you got in the parlor," Demitri says in wonder as his eyes open.

I nod. "Yes, and the other pulse about blood and chaos was a warning about Trey being shot, but I didn't figure that out in time to prevent it." I reach out to Bear and Adam. They take my hands, and I send a few of the memories. I send Trey the memories through our soulmate connection. He closes his eyes, and an incredible strain distorts his face as he watches.

"Can I see?" Victoria asks.

"Shut up, Normal," Adam snaps.

When everyone else is done watching, clarity sits in the room. "Everything makes perfect sense now, Trey," I say. "You treated me like shit because I stood in the way of what you really wanted." I slide my wedding ring off.

"You're wearing your wedding ring?" Trey asks, shocked.

"I killed thirty-three people to save you. We saw our past lives. You asked me to give you a chance to fix it. I left to go to my house to get my ring. It was a mistake, though." I take his hand and remove his wedding ring. I place both rings in his palm, closing his fingers around the rings that still hum with our combined energy. "I'm Melanie Slate again, and our handfasting bond is severed."

Tears slip down his cheeks as he places the rings on the table, staring at them.

I rush to the bedroom and grab several duffel bags from the closet. I toss in a few things I can't live without and race into the bathroom. Victoria left it a disaster, with towels and her dirty clothes all over the floor. Open makeup compacts are strewn all over the counter.

Demitri comes in, and I wave to the mess. "Trey thought *I* was bad. Holy shit."

"I refused to spend time at Victoria's house," Demitri informs. "She's disgusting. Victoria is everything Trey accused you of being. Messy, needy, constantly buzzing around like a gnat to the point that I thought I'd never have a quiet moment again." Demitri smirks at me.

I shake my head. "I think karma is about to crawl up Trey's ass and die. He's going to go nuclear. He can't live like this."

"Trey's in for a long walk off a short sanity pier with Victoria," Demitri says. "Pop the popcorn and watch the show. It'll be a doozy."

I suddenly panic. "We have unresolved issues, Demitri."

He grabs my cheeks. "Focus on it finally being over with Trey. Once we get you past this hurdle, we'll talk about everything involving us. It's time to leave."

I look around the bathroom again and take a moment to assess my feelings. Awareness dawns. "I'm finally *free*," whispers from me.

"You feel good about that?"

I nod frantically. "It's over." I take a huge breath and relish my unhindered lungs.

"The girl is breathing," Demitri marvels.

I wince a little. "How does it smell like dirty hair in a bathroom Victoria just showered in?"

Demitri grimaces. "She's rancid. Let's go." He rushes me through the bedroom, picking up my duffel bags on the way. We enter the living room to find Adam in a full-scale meltdown.

"Are you DEMENTED?"

"I . . . ," Trey stammers, getting nowhere as his mind races.

Adam flaps a hand to Victoria. "She's a GOBLIN! Literally EVERYONE hates her!"

"I'm the most POPULAR girl in this *GROUP!*" Victoria blisters.

I halt Demitri so we can spectate. I should be heartbroken, but I mourned the loss of Trey while I was with him. It occurs to me that Adam's likely projecting his own feelings about Valerie, who he's stuck with now, but whatever. Let the man process how he will. Adam's shenanigans are welcome, and I suspect he's about to thump Victoria. I'm *so* here for it.

Adam looks to Demitri and comically scrunches his face. "Holy BALLS!" he sarcastically crows. "You lost your *soulmate.*" He flaps toward Victoria again. "How will you ever get over the LOSS?"

"That bitch is Alcatraz," Demitri barks, pointing at Victoria, "and I *escaped!*" He dances about like a happy toddler, and I double over, cackling.

"Excuse YOU!" belts from Victoria.

"*Damn,* that was honest," Bear expels, ignoring Victoria.

Adam looks at Victoria like she's the abomination I've always thought she was, before swinging his confoundment to Trey. "Hooray. You won . . ." He rattles jazz hands, his face awash with mortification.

"I love you so much, Adam." I get out around a fresh round of the hee-haws.

"Fuck you, Melanie," Victoria spits out.

I howl louder laughter, draping over the back of the couch as my knees give.

"You screwed her?" Adam asks Trey, aghast, while he points at Victoria. "ON PURPOSE?" He rattles his head. "Sober? Over and over?"

"I'm hot," Victoria bites back.

"You're a HOSEBEAST," Adam bellows.

Trey looks from Victoria to me, and self-destructive clarity fills his eyes. "What did I do?"

"We're all wondering that," Bear says to Trey.

Victoria glares at Trey. "Don't act like you give a damn about Melanie," she chastises.

"I do care," chokes from him.

Adam gives me a look. "Don't get snowed by him now. Trey manipulated you into a wedding you didn't want, then he neglected and treated you like shit after he trapped you, all in honor of VICTORIA. Your entire relationship has been a lie. The level of deception that goes into that is unbelievable."

"You feel that way?" Trey asks me desperately.

I nod. "I suspect you were giving Victoria what I needed, and there was nothing left for me."

"Damn right," Victoria interjects arrogantly.

"You *do* realize that you just got caught having an affair with La Diabla's HUSBAND, right?" Bear asks Victoria.

She rolls her eyes. "He was always *my* man!"

We collectively study Trey's dejection and Victoria's arrogance. I don't have to be offended, because Trey is so mortified that he's doing it for all of us.

"We've dealt with a lot of weird over our lifetimes," Bear marvels, "but this is truly, undeniably, the strangest abominable disaster I've ever witnessed." He looks to Adam. "Can you *imagine* choosing Victoria over Melanie?"

"It's absolutely *preposterous*," Adam bellows.

"Not even ADAM thinks you're hot," I marvel at Victoria, "and Adam's done some serious swamp-monster entertaining."

Victoria gives me a snide look before posing seductively for Adam's benefit. Adam slides confounded eyes to Trey, who's staring at Victoria like he just woke up from a nightmare.

"Looks like we've got entertainment at my surprise divorce party," I say to Adam.

"Indeed," Adam agrees as he slowly gazes from Victoria's toes all the way to her face. "Buuuuuhhhhhhhh." He shudders dramatically.

"How long has this affair gone on?" Bear asks Victoria.

"We got back together the night Adam was rescued from the Drones' dungeon," she snidely confesses.

I pan shock Trey's way. He leans on the back of the couch, seeming horrified.

Bear's mouth thuds open. "That was almost TWO YEARS ago!"

Adam blows out a gargantuan breath. "Damn, that's a hell of a tour of duty."

"You two were together when I started DATING YOU?" Demitri bellows. Victoria suddenly looks a bit ashamed.

Adam and Bear lean closer to Demitri from either side. "You're over it, and we can ask questions, right?" Bear asks.

"I've never been so over anything in my life," Demitri marvels, as the guys continue studying Victoria like she's a lab experiment gone wrong.

"Is she at least good in the sack?" Adam asks.

"Not in the *least*," Demitri says.

"Excusssse you?" breathes from Victoria.

"Good conversation?" Bear asks, earning such an unsure look from Adam that I spurt laughter.

Demitri shakes his head. "Unbearably shallow conversation skills."

Adam snaps his fingers contemplatively and tosses his hands up. "I got nothing."

Victoria's mouth flops open, aghast.

"She has a wide yapper," Adam barks, pointing at Victoria's gaping mouth. "Any skill with *that*?" Adam gives Demitri a suggestive look.

"Terrrrrible," Demitri groans, in a state of befuddlement at his own stupidity for dating her.

Victoria snaps her mouth closed, crossing her arms defensively over her chest.

"Cooking?" Bear asks.

"Nope," Demiri replies.

"She literally has *zero* redeemable qualities," marvels from me.

"You wanna *go*, bitch?!" Victoria threatens my way.

I nod frantically. "Yes, please! I want to go *now*." I pull at Demitri's arm, earning a chuckle from Bear.

"There's a mystery afoot," Adam scolds me. "You can't leave yet!"

I huff, but the mystery squad is deeply committed to this process.

"She's pretty," Bear says, desperately unsure, because in our world, that's not enough.

"There!" Demitri ticks his pointer finger at Bear. "When Victoria's asleep, she's pretty. It's the only time that her bitchy expression," he gestures to her face, "softens."

"*And* she's quiet then!" Bear adds, because he *must* find a positive.

"Victoria is SOOOOOO lazy," Adam gloms on. "I bet she sleeps a lot." He swings an enthusiastic fake smile Trey's way. "That must be the draw."

"It's been a source of conflict," Trey says, dejected.

"Trey likes to get things done efficiently." I nod with bright sarcasm. "On his time schedule, while *he* runs the show, because *he's* in charge."

Victoria gives Trey an arrogant look. "Trey's not bossing ME around."

"Ha," belts from me. I swing my amusement Trey's way. "I believe you've met your match."

"I want you out of his life!" Victoria screeches.

"You got it!" I yip. I close my eyes and focus on the connection between me and Trey, Fort Knoxing my side. I can take it down at any time, but it'll give us some distance for now. I open my eyes to the sound of Trey gasping.

"Open it back up, Melanie," Trey hoarsely pleads.

"Trey, I'm going to help you through this," Adam says, giving up his amusement for compassion.

"I can't lose Melanie," sobs from Trey as he starts to cry torrentially.

"You have to be KIDDING!" Victoria snarls.

Everyone ignores her.

"I have Trey covered," Adam tells Demitri. "Be prepared with Melanie. Leaving a soulmate seems okay at first, but the realization crashes in after a few days and it's catastrophic. She's going to crater, and we need to hope she doesn't level the Valley when she does."

"Trey will be *fine*," Victoria insists. "He hates Melanie!"

"Actually, I think *I'm* legit fine," I say.

Trey looks like he's going to throw up. "I created a whole fantasy that Victoria was what I wanted. I believed it and got caught in my own fictional mess."

"Trey! Take that BACK!"

I nod, ignoring Victoria. "You did the exact same thing with Tiffany. Our soulmate bond is too much for you, and that's how you cope."

Trey curls around his constricting lungs and gasps, "Oh my God! I felt like I was trapped, but I wasn't."

Adam nods. "I know, Trey. I've been there and done that. You've got some seriously wild shit coming your way, because the guilt is going to eat you alive. There's a deep-seated responsibility built into this soulmate bond."

"I never knew you felt that way, Adam," gasps from me.

Adam looks at me. "Losing you was horrific when I chose Valerie. I regret it." His expression morphs pained, likely because he realizes he has a worse round coming now that I'm not his soulmate anymore. I can't worry about that now, though.

"Melanie, I love you. Don't do this," Trey begs.

"*I* didn't do this," I reply. "*You* did. I'll pack the rest of my stuff in a few days."

Demitri guides me to the door, while Victoria screeches dramatically about Trey, who is saying she was a mistake. A distraught wave of heartbreak booms from Trey as I run with Demitri down the hall.

CHAPTER 28

Terror rips through me, and I scream. I feel my shield over my connection with Trey blast open. I can hear what's happening through Trey, but I can't wake up.

Trey's cell phone rings, and he answers. "Hello?"

"I'm sorry to bother you—"

Trey cuts Demitri off. "Melanie has night terrors. She gets trapped in them and can't get out. Her blockage crashed down in our connection right before you called."

"What do I do?" Demitri asks. "The foundation of the house rumbled before I called you."

Trey sighs. "I'm at a pool hall five minutes from her house."

The nightmare swarms up and overtakes me again.

After what feels like an eternity, Trey's voice softly drifts in. "Melanie. Calm down."

My scream cuts off as I blink up at Trey. He's next to me on the bed, with his hand on my back, siphoning off my night terror fear. I exhale, relieved. Once I'm leveled off emotionally, I curl my knees under me and sit up. I tip back my head and exhale hard.

"You okay?" Trey asks. "That one was rough. Burning alive this time, huh?"

"Big emotional shifts throw me." I wall off my connection with Trey. "I'm sorry you got dragged over here."

Demitri sighs. "I apologize, Meley. You were screaming, and I didn't want the neighbors to call the police."

I rub my face. "You're good. Trey's dealt with this a million times."

"Don't try to wake her up when the night terrors happen," Trey instructs Demitri. "One of your gifts is radiating calm, and you need to use it. Hands flat on her back. Works every time."

"What's happening in your head when you get like that?" Demitri asks me.

I close my eyes, and Trey answers for me. "She relives attacks from her past lives. Be glad you don't have a soulmate connection with her because the attacks are horrific. I've seen her past-life deaths repeatedly. This one was her execution by fire one of the times she was tried as a witch. It's a cycle she can't climb out from without either help, or a full-blown meltdown. You don't want her to reach meltdown. It gets bad."

Demitri looks like he's in way over his head.

"Where is ephalump?" Trey asks me.

"Epha what?" Demitri interjects.

I point to my duffel bag by my closet, and Trey slides off the bed and riffles through the contents. He pulls out my stuffed teal elephant and hands it to me. I clutch it to my chest.

"La Diabla has a stuffed elephant?" Demitri asks.

"Yup. She sleeps with it when things get bad," Trey informs him. "As much as you know about Melanie, you seem to be missing key puzzle pieces."

"Explain," Demitri requests.

"I was close by on purpose," Trey admits. "Melanie is deadly, as you know. It doesn't scare me when she decides to take out a parking lot full of fuck-sticks." He gestures to me. "*This* is the side of Melanie that terrifies me."

My eyes widen, and I feel like a toddler who can't find her mom. I hate this abandoned feeling. I look up at Trey, and his head falls.

"Melanie is plagued by her past lifetimes," he reveals. "The dreams are catastrophic when they aren't handled right, and she instinctively tries to blast her way out." He levels Demitri with serious eyes. "Considering that Melanie is capable of Final Striking, that becomes problematic when you're asleep next to her."

"Final Strike, as in booooooom?" Demitri barks.

Trey nods. "There's a side of Melanie that no one sees." He gestures to me. "She doesn't mean to fall apart. She must sleep at some point, even though she fights it when she knows she lacks control over her abilities."

"If unhappiness and big emotional shifts cause her to have less control than normal, then why did you make her so miserable that she attempted suicide?" Demitri asks.

"Because I was exhausted," Trey admits. "Selfish control over my own time is something I've always struggled with. I balanced it until the job at Mabel's almost buried me ten feet under. Between school, baseball, and work, it was a twenty-four-hour-a-day grind."

"Melanie became the schedule suck that you resented?" Demitri says.

Trey nods. "I didn't realize it at the time, but yes. I was very overwhelmed. When Melanie would have one of these episodes, or get attacked, or almost die . . ." Trey snorts. "Even when Melanie would ask to spend fun time, I'd lose it." He levels me with serious eyes. "There was nothing wrong with you wanting time or needing me. I was your husband, and that's part of a relationship. The problem is that I did such a shit job of balancing the rest of my life that the time you needed took away from the only time I had for myself."

"Why don't you say that about the time you spent with Victoria?" Demitri asks, caged.

Trey takes a slow breath. "I categorized that time as 'my time.'"

I tear up at that news.

"I already know what you're thinking," Trey says to me. "It's not that Victoria and I were such a unit that I could have 'me time' with her." Trey takes my hand while tears roll down my cheeks. "Time with her was shallow, leaving room for what I needed. I could ignore her chatter. She rarely said anything that interested me, or I had to focus on. She offered a body, and sex helped clear my mood. That was the draw."

I wince, and Trey sighs.

"Sex with a soulmate is very 'all in' emotionally," Trey explains. "It's not the same thing as a casual conquest. With you, it was a deep dive into the heart of our soulmate connection, and I didn't have anything left to deep dive like I needed to. I also had to hide what I had been doing for so long with Victoria, which is damn hard to do with that dark-water side of yours that drags truth out of me. I was floundering, hence why, when I did go there with you, I was harsh and distant."

"That's what my dad and I thought," Demitri mutters.

"Everything shifted two days after our wedding," I whimper. "Did Victoria give you the black eye?"

Trey's head drops. "Yes."

"That's how she broke her hand," Demitri says, putting the pieces together.

Trey nods. "I went to her house to end things. We landed in a raging fight. She punched me, furious that I committed to Melanie after our pregnancy was realized."

"Why did she help plan our wedding?" I ask.

Trey shakes his head. "I don't want to get into that."

"I think Melanie deserves the answer," Demitri scolds.

Trey sighs. "Victoria thought a handfasting was more like a play than real. Something about coordinating my and Melanie's wedding was oddly kinky for her and me, and we fell back into messing around, even though I left her after Melanie's pregnancy was discovered. The night she hit me, she realized I used her. I went over there because she kept threatening to tell Melanie everything. I wanted to try to reason with her."

Demitri glares at Trey. "Why did you terrify Melanie with rage and threats?"

"The guilt I feel about that makes me sick to my stomach." Trey looks at me. "You didn't deserve any of what I put you through. I cut things off with Victoria without taking the time to help her work through me ending the affair. She turned into a spiteful volcano. At that point, I was trapped. I had to protect you from her, and I resented you for it, which was entirely irrational. Obviously, none of this was your fault. Anyhow, Victoria sucked me back in and used my frustration to manipulate me into despising you. I realize all of that now, but at the time I was such a mess that I didn't get it."

I can't reply around the painful lump in my throat.

Trey tips my chin to look in my eyes. "What I should have done was talk to Adam before things got so out of control."

"You and Adam despise each other," Demitri reminds him, confused.

Trey laughs, but it's an exhausted laugh. "That's true, but also not. Think of Adam and me as siblings who had to share a room for a very long time. We fight, sometimes to the death in some unfortunate lifetimes. We also hold each other up. All of Adam's lifetimes are connected to Melanie, and he's experienced this." Trey slides a vulnerable look to the floor. "When I crash, Adam can fix it."

"Do you fix him the same way?" Demitri asks.

"I would, but he won't ask," Trey replies. "If Adam Stone asks for that, we're all screwed." Trey scoffingly chuckles. "He has better coping mechanisms than I do. Adam's excellent at saying 'screw it' and walking away when he's overloaded."

"Like he did before this lifetime?" Demitri asks. "Choosing to ditch his soulmate connection for a new conquest?"

Trey wobbles his head. "Losing Melanie permanently is proving to be very difficult for him. It may drive him to need help. We'll see." He takes a fitful breath. "Melanie, I'm so sorry. Adam is just as sorry. You don't deserve being abandoned."

"I feel for you and Adam," I inform. "While life with me is bad, at least I'm an old soul who focuses on things that matter. Victoria and Valerie are an annoying young-soul mess."

Trey squeezes one eye closed, grimacing before leveling Demitri with a pained expression. "Victoria really is horrific."

Demitri nods. "I hate her, and I never hate anyone. She's gross in every way."

"Yet both of us stuck it out with her." Trey's eyes narrow, but Demitri apparently anticipates what he'll say.

"I was incredibly different around Victoria. It was so out of character that my dad suspected something metaphysical. He checked." Demitri meets Trey's eyes. "He didn't find anything. We think it was just human nature. The most toxic person in the room always drags everyone down."

"Victoria's truly this shallow, isn't she?" Trey asks.

Demitri rolls his eyes. "Let me guess. Instead of being relieved you're alive, and helping you through dying by gunshot, she's pissed Melanie had to save you?"

Trey nods and Demitri smirks.

"Let's see what else I can guess. She's mad that Melanie straddled your dead body while she fixed your blasted chest?" At Trey's affirmative nod, Demitri plows on. "She's also mad that you revived and dealt with your soulmate instead of rushing to her?"

"All correct," Trey confirms.

Demitri nods. "Victoria'll surprise you every time with her ability to completely miss the deeper point, and side-skirt any sense of propriety and compassion. Every issue will selfishly revolve around her need to be the prettiest, most important, most powerful in the room." He gestures to me. "Hence her hatred of Melanie. She covers it well at work, but Victoria is so blazingly jealous of Meley that it consumes her. My friendship with Melanie was a constant fight when I dated Victoria."

"It's been like that through the whole affair." Trey clears his throat. "I was so overwhelmed while I was with Melanie that Victoria's hateful rhetoric offered an excuse to justify my feelings. I bought it all, hook, line, and sinker."

"I put those pieces together after I read Victoria's diary," Demitri says. "All your dismissals of Melanie suddenly made sense. It had Victoria's vibe all over it."

"I'm not going to tolerate Victoria," I warn Trey. "She can either behave or face the same treatment Valerie receives."

"I don't care," Trey groans. "Actually, I do. Please kill her."

I laugh, but it lacks heart.

Demitri shakes his head. "Deep down, Melanie and I knew you were having an affair. We speculated about it several times."

"I'm sorry that I had an affair with your girlfriend," Trey says.

Demitri shrugs. "You did me a favor."

"Just know that my friendship with you matters to me." Trey rubs his hands on the knees of his jeans before standing. "I'm going to go. Thank you for talking with me."

"Thank you for helping with my night terror," I dejectedly reply. "Have a good night, Trey."

"I'll walk you out," Demitri offers, and the guys leave my room.

Alone for a moment, I feel nothing and everything all at once. Demitri comes back in, and informs, "The front door is locked."

We stare at each other. After an uncomfortable silence, I quietly say, "You should head home. I'm okay."

Demitri's brow furrows. "You want me to leave?"

"I think I need some time to work through things on my own. If it helps, I'm feeling a lot clearer now. I won't have another night terror issue."

"After what happened with the Machetes, there's zero way I'm leaving you alone," Demitri insists. He blows out a huge breath. "I respect that you need space, though. I'm going to sleep on the couch." He grabs a pillow and my throw blanket from my reading chair. "Good night, Melanie," he softly says as he leaves my room, pulling the door closed after him.

CHAPTER 29

I gasp as I'm suddenly trapped in my psyche. Panic rises and I scream, before the trapping hold releases. I whip around in my mind, and my spirit guide is staring at me. Before I can say anything, Demitri suddenly materializes in my mental space.

"I'm proud of you, Melanie," my spirit guide says. *"I never imag—"*

"How DARE you invade my psyche!" I interrupt. *"You dragged Demitri in here without my consent?"*

"You'll be okay with it in a moment," my spirit guide assures.

It does nothing to assure me, though.

She focuses on Demitri. *"Can you handle what Melanie is? There's pragmatic evil and seething passion that makes her thrive."*

"I absolutely can," he responds. *"Everything about the evil in her is somehow okay because she has a solid moral compass. The seething passion is everything."*

After a long moment of consideration, she says, *"I see no other way."*

"What is happening?" I ask.

"I'm still working on things," my spirit guide responds. *"I need you to trust me."*

"TRUST YOU?" I bellow. *"After what you did to me and Adam? I'll never trust you AGAIN!"*

"I didn't do that," she defends. *"HE did."*

"How DARE you!"

"Enough! I must ensure that you live, Melanie." My spirit guide grasps a wafting, rippling veil of soft white energy that looks like a curtain. She rips it down, and I'm suddenly flooded with the most perfect energy. My confliction skyrockets. This isn't just a conversation. This is another life-altering moment, and I realized it too late.

Demitri groans. A relieved wave rushes from him down our new connection.

"You've been living with an unfused soulmate bond, Demitri," my spirit guide says.

"It's so much better now." He looks at her. *"Because of my calm ability, I have extreme control of my emotions, but things were getting to the point that I was going to lose my mind."*

My spirit guide smiles compassionately. *"Anyone else would have lost it within weeks."*

"What the hell just happened?" I breathe on a wave of stunned shock.

She smiles at me. *"You deserve Demitri. He's your perfect counterbalance."* She gives him a mischievous look and adds coyly, *"And damn, is he pretty!"*

"Pretty?" I blister. *"Fuck that shallow nonsense!"* I gesture angrily toward Demitri. *"You did this with the JAYLA problem looming!"*

"Jayla?" my spirit guide asks.

"Please don't spiral," Demitri rushes to say to me. He looks to my spirit guide. *"It's nothing."*

I glare at my spirit guide. *"You and me, we've got a problem!"*

"Problems are getting fixed." She snaps her fingers, and my eyes

open. I'm in my bed and look to the clock, realizing it's seven in the morning. I blink rapidly, trying to wrap my mind around what just happened.

"Melanie!" The door opens, and Demitri runs in and sits on the bed, grabbing my hands. "Are you okay?" he asks.

"I did NOT agree to this soulmate bond," I reply, my mind a whirling mess.

Demitri winces. "You're not okay with the soulmate bond?"

My mouth falls open. "What my spirit guide did to me and Adam was horrific! Then I found out Trey beat my ass on behalf of VICTORIA! NOW my spirit guide just forced *this* on me!"

"Melanie . . ." Demitri's head falls. "Shit," he mutters.

"I can't take anymore! I'm going to lose my freaking MIND!"

Demitri takes my hands again. "It's going to be okay."

My chin shakes. "I was finally getting control of my life. I needed time, and to make my own choices."

"I respect that," Demitri says.

Through our new connection, I feel his emotions spin. I touch his forehead, putting a shield between his thoughts and me, and he blinks rapidly.

"I thought you could use some privacy. I'll teach you how to shield thoughts all the time without blocking or fuzzing. Having someone in your mind constantly is daunting. and you'll get tired of second-guessing your thoughts."

"I wasn't thinking anything bad," he assures me. "Thank you." He gathers himself with a deep breath. "I'm sorry this soulmate bond was decided without your consultation. I didn't realize what was happening until it was done."

"My spirit guide manhandled me and used my psyche as her meeting room!" I bellow.

Demitri quirks his mouth. "That was certainly rude."

I can't help but laugh at his innocently polite take. "We're such opposites," murmurs from me. At Demitri's curious look, I gesture to him. "You so nicely put that. Meanwhile, I'm inclined to scream and rage about it." I make a scoffing sound. "Not to mention that this is apparently all acceptable because you're so pretty that I should be grateful to have no say."

"I don't think that's what your spirit guide was getting at," Demitri says. "If it helps, I think you're so pretty that I'm a bit blown away that you're mine."

My face Fraggles. "Didn't expect that."

"I've always thought you were the prettiest girl I've ever met." He tips his head adoringly. "The first time I saw you, I swear my brain leaked out of my ear. Then I got to know you when I took you away when Arch and Hiram's party went sideways. I learned that night that when you giggle, everything in me synchronizes. It's the first time I ever felt completely content."

"Well, damn if that isn't the most charming bunch of drivel I've ever heard," blathers from me.

Demitri cracks up. "You're so romantic," he teases.

I ponder while really looking him over.

He draws his head back, appearing a little insecure.

"You really are pretty," I mutter.

Demitri bashfully ducks his head before the sweetest smile slides up. "You're my soulmate," whispers from him.

I melt from his sweet tone. "How do you feel about that?"

"I don't know how to voice it. Can you do the thing where you feel what I'm feeling?" Demitri asks. "That's a soulmate thing, right?"

"It is. You know that, though. You've had a soulmate."

Demitri shakes his head. "I had none of the perks with Victoria. We couldn't talk mind-to-mind or feel each other's emotions.

I asked Adam why once. He said it's probably because Victoria doesn't have the capacity."

"Ohhhhh," mesmerizes from me. I get lost in thought, and Demitri gives me time to ponder. Settled, I gaze into his beautiful steel-blue eyes. "Trey and Adam lacked a lot of capacity in their ways also. Do you think this could be a fresh start for both of us? Even though we've both had soulmates?"

"I would love that." Demitri squeezes my hand. "Kind of seems like a good time for a fresh start. So much has changed so quickly. I know this new soulmate bond is hard for you, but I'm completely beside myself excited. I'm just trying to cover it because you're all freaked out."

"Demitri, I really need you to be more upfront with me," I express. "I'm so raw from everything Trey put me through. Please don't blindside me with your sneaky dealings."

"I swear to you that I was never attempting that," he says.

"Curb Jayla," I request.

Demitri nods. "No more Jayla sneak attacks. Fresh start."

"Okay, fresh start," I say, needing to try because nothing else in my life is working. "First test." I smirk knowingly. "Buckle up, because it'll be a doozy." What I'm about to do has a manipulative undercurrent, but if it solidifies his attention on our relationship, then so be it.

"What will?"

"You ready for a new first kiss?" I flirt.

Demitri curiously perks. "Different from the usual?"

"Yeah," I softly say before leaning and kissing him delicately.

There's something magical about a first kiss from a soulmate. Energy ripples up my spine, and my head spins. Demitri gasps. We get lost in the oddly calm heat. There's a slow burn with Demitri that's far more intense now.

I break off the kiss and smile at him.

"Wow," breathes from Demitri. It's the closest thing to mesmerized I've ever heard from him. He's usually the one doing the mesmerizing.

"Second test." I send, *"I love you."*

Demitri looks at me in wonder. *"I can talk to you mind-to-mind now."*

I wobble my head. *"I've got the capacity,"* I joke.

"This is wild," he sends back.

I smile. *"You've already got it down."*

He looks at me in wonder. "I can't believe this is happening."

I exhale, thinking maybe this will be okay. "Obviously we aren't going to school today. What's the plan?"

"I miss doing normal things," Demitri admits. "It's been a rough couple weeks. I haven't spent time with friends in a while. Mind if I invite a few of the guys to hang with me?"

"Perfect." I'm secretly relieved. "I need some alone time. I've got a lot to work through and need to clear my head."

CHAPTER 30

Demitri answers the front door. I can see his face instantly freeze before he fakes enthusiasm. "Hey, guys."

"Hey," I hear Dante say. "Soooooo, Stella couldn't ditch. She has a test today in fourth."

Demitri looks my way. Only he can see me in the kitchen. He taps on our shuttered soulmate connection. I drop my blockage, and he sends, *"Please don't kill me, and I'm so sorry."*

"I didn't invite Stella, so who cares? I can't wait for the guys to distract you so that I can work through my mess of a life."

"I know how much you need that," Demitri sends, oddly cautious.

"I love Dante," I send, trying to figure out Demitri's behavior. *"I'm relieved. At least you didn't invite Javier."*

Javier is Demitri's best friend, and he's always been suspicious of me. We've never gotten along, but he's faked niceties when we have to share a dance studio. I don't feel like dealing with that today.

Looking pained, Demitri closes his eyes.

"You okay, bro?" I hear.

It's not Dante's voice, and my expression slides slack. *"You didn't seriously invite Javier, did you?"* I send to Demitri.

He gives me a pleading expression.

"I'm so excited to see Melanie," overenthusiastically bubbles from the porch, and I gape at Demitri.

"You ditched school?" he asks, in legit disbelief.

"Ditching was exciting!" Jayla chirps.

In troops Jayla, Dante, and Javier.

"I thought it was a guy day?" I pan huge eyes to Demitri.

Javier and Demitri give Dante a look. Jayla blinks sweetly, oblivious, as usual.

"Jayla was with me when Demitri called," Dante says, unsure but trying to play it off.

"We stopped at the craft store on the way." Jayla holds up a bag. "I got us stuff to make dreamcatchers."

"Golly gee," I mock, coming out to where they can all see me.

"This will be fun!" Jayla enthuses.

"I haven't had a moment to catch my breath from getting my ass beat from the Machetes, dealing with Trey being shot, destroying the Jags to save him, losing my original soulmate, or losing my husband," I inform with a little sarcastic flutter of my shoulders. "But there's plenty of time for dreamcatchers." I tip my head, overly chipper. "Do you think a dreamcatcher can solve my problems? Gee whiz, I hope so."

"No," Jayla says with more savvy than I expect. She sways the bag about. "The dreamcatcher project is a distraction so you can stay busy while you aloofly spill your guts."

"*Uggghhh,*" I groan in Demitri's head. Aloud, I say, "How thoughtful."

Jayla heads down the hall to my room.

With her gone, Dante says, "I'm sorry about this, Melanie."

"Yeahhhhhhh," I say, having no clue what else to say.

"I got pizza," Demitri informs.

"Awesome!" Javier skirts me, heading into the kitchen and helping himself to paper plates that he finally finds after going through half the cupboards.

Dante joins Javier at the pizza boxes, and Demitri runs his hands down my arms while the guys are distracted. *"I had no idea she was coming,"* he sends to me.

"Sure, you didn't," I send back, very unhappy.

"I swear, I didn't invite her," he insists.

"I don't want Javier here," I send, while Javier helps himself to my fridge without asking.

The guys start tussling over the last soda. They roughhouse, banging into the stove before Javier shoves Dante into the counter by the sink.

"Yo, tone it down," Demitri orders. When the guys look at him, he tips his head toward me. "Girl house, morons. We aren't at *my* house."

"So sorry I didn't wear a *bow* tie," Javier cats back dismissively.

Dante grimaces a little, but he tends to be more polite than Javier. "Sorry, Mel."

"There's a mini-fridge full of sodas around the corner in the laundry room," I grumble. "You don't have to kill each other over a Cactus Cooler."

"These things are nasty," Javier says after taking a sip.

"Then don't drink it," I grumble.

Demitri winces. *"I shouldn't have invited Javier."* He huffs. *"Or Dante, apparently. I didn't expect him to invite Jayla, but I should have."*

"Didn't you JUST promise that there would be no more blindsiding, sneaky-Jayla nonsense?" I send.

"I swear I just wanted a guys' day," he dejectedly replies.

"YOU entertain her!"

"Then you'll just get pissed that I spent the day with her," he replies.

Unfortunately, he's right.

"Whatever, Demitri," I send as I walk down the hall, gutting up to host Jayla. Considering that Demitri and I haven't worked through our issues yet, it's a tall order.

———

"You're stuck with that succubus FOREVER!" Javier blisters as Jayla and I round the corner into the den.

My stomach drops. This isn't what I expected, but I don't know why I'm surprised. Demitri always spills his guts to Javier.

"You realize you can screw a guy without owning his soul, right?" Javier snarls at me.

"Back off, Jav," Demitri orders. "That's not how this went down."

I smirk. "You figured out my secret. I steal guys one, 'Oh my God, Melanie, destroy my soul,' moan at a time."

Javier looks at Demitri. "Her soulmates lose their ever-loving shit. Trey is a disaster. Adam *married* the first chick who said yes just to escape Melanie."

I wince. Javier doesn't know that I just lost my soulmate connection with Adam, and his comment cuts deep.

"Your assessment of the Adam situation is harsh," Demitri snaps at Javier.

"My assessment of the Adam situation is dead-on!" Javier looks to me. "Demitri's like my brother. I'm not letting him ruin his life." He looks at D like he's nuts. "HOW do you know Melanie didn't do something evil to make you agree to this?"

"Melanie didn't want this, but her preference was overlooked," Demitri informs.

"I don't suppose you could quit revealing our details?" I fire off at Demitri, who winces.

"Seriously, Javier?" Jayla interjects. "Melanie was doing better when we were talking in her room. She's your friend."

That talk went surprisingly well. I shove the thought aside so I can concentrate on this fight Javier's lobbing my way.

"A reminder that you're speaking about me this way in my house." I look from Javier to Demitri. "This is why we distance ourselves from Normals. You're asking a spiritual toddler to grasp something WELL beyond his reach."

Jayla and I grab a stack of beach towels by the back door and go outside. The pool glistens in the bright afternoon sun as the roving sweeper drifts by. This is the first day in a while that it's warm enough to swim, even though the pool is heated.

"Are you okay?" Jayla asks. "That was harsh."

I roll my eyes. "Javier's just looking out for D. I didn't trap him, for the record."

"Javier should know better than anyone that you're all Demitri's wanted for a long time."

"I'm sorry about Jav," Demitri sends.

"I get tired of hearing that I'm an evil waste."

He sighs in my head.

I fold in half, stretching my hamstrings while Jayla wades into the pool. I hear the sliding door open, and Dante walks down the pool steps and swims to her.

"Hey, Mel," Stella's voice rings out happily. "Nice ass."

I look behind me from my upside-down position. "What's up, Stella? I thought you couldn't make it."

"I finished the test and dipped during the passing period," Stella informs, as Javier comes outside with Demitri. She and Javier are still at the cute new phase, and she giggles and bounces to him.

"Oh good, a party," I cynically send to Demitri as I ease into my center splits.

"Now I get it," Javier sarcastically says.

Demitri snorts. "She doesn't do that in the sack, for the record."

"I'm best handled like an amusing sprite instead of a biker-killing sex demon," I jokingly inform Javier, trying to lighten the mood.

Apparently, Javier doesn't take my attempt to lighten things, because he says, "Demitri, you can have any girl you want. Why are you wasting your time?"

Adam unexpectedly struts into my side view. He hears Javier and flexes his hands, snarling, "What the fuck did you just say?"

"Oh shit," Demitri breathes, as Adam balls up a fist and rushes Javier.

I grin and leave the rescue to Dante and Demitri, who jump in front of a stunned-stiff Javier.

"If you think I won't level the two of you," Adam snarls, "then you haven't been paying attention. Move!"

"Melanie . . . ," Demitri pensively says.

Nonchalant, I ask, "To what do we owe the pleasure, Adam?"

Adam slowly pans a furious look my way that morphs into a smoldering eyebrow raise as he surveys my current split stretch. "I came to discuss this soulmate-losing, disastrous-ass, I-can't-live-with-this, needing-you-back, fucking-shitstorm disaster," he informs, like it's a totally normal statement. "Nice swimsuit," he adds nonchalantly.

"Thanks," I reply as I lie down flat, rocking through my pelvis to deepen my stretch.

"Yeah, I'm an idiot," Adam mutters.

"Well, you showed up at the perfect time to discuss the destruction of our connection," I inform, blasé, as Adam helps me up. "We've got so many Normals here to guide us through that." I smile tackily at Adam.

"Any of you have advice about how to resolve our soulmate connection being obliterated by Melanie's spirit guide, who I'm planning to annihilate?" Adam sarcastically asks the pensive spectators. No one says anything, and Adam gives me a hilarious look. "What a fucking shocker!" he squalls. "They're useless!"

"Now, now," I scold Adam. "They're Demitri's invited guests of honor."

Adam gives Demitri a disgusted look before his expression slides deadpan to me. "This is *your* house."

"You'd think," I reply. It's rude, but whatever. Demitri shouldn't have created this mess, and I'm doing my best.

"Why the hell is some pointless Normal talking shit about you in your yard?" Adam asks.

"Because he apparently has a death wish," I joke back.

Adam snorts. "That's for damn sure." He gestures to Javier. "Don't let me stop your assholery."

Javier doesn't speak, and I scoff. "He's got balls of steel when it's just me defending myself."

Adam sneers at Demitri. "You can't defend your girlfriend? Scared to get that pretty face mangled?"

"She's not his girlfriend," Javier bitingly informs. "She's his soulmate."

"WHAT?" Adam screams.

I internally groan. I had no intention of telling Adam that yet. I sigh, resigned to dealing with this. "I'm not any happier about it than you, and apparently Javier, if it helps."

"Melanie," Demitri whispers, aghast.

"What?" I ask. "I'm not. All your sneaky nonsense and disconnection is a treat." I flip a hand toward Jayla. "At least she's here to enjoy the show firsthand so you don't have to sneak around telling her my secrets this time."

"Why *is* she here?" Adam asks condescendingly.

I roll my eyes. "Demitri insisted on inviting Dante and Javier over for *friend* time. They took it upon themselves to invite their girls. It's gone swimmingly thus far." A slight pang of guilt twinges as everyone reacts awkwardly. What I just said isn't fair based on the really supportive convo I had with Jayla in my room, but I'm overwhelmed, and it's bringing out my catty side.

"Who the hell is *she*?" Adam asks while he looks at Stella likes she's a bug.

"That's Stella, a.k.a. Dragonfly. She's George's daughter."

"*George* George?" Adam asks.

"Yeah," I reply. "She also gets to enjoy my pool and personal nightmare."

Adam rattles his head. "A soulmate connection with HIM?" He points at Demitri, getting back on track.

I sigh luxuriously. "My spirit guide strikes again. I'd like in on her annihilation."

"Done," Adam says. "If there's a way to destroy her, I'll find it." Adam opens a cigarette pack that he produces from his leather jacket pocket. He pulls one out and lights it. He takes a drag before handing it to me.

It appears that Javier has zero survival skill, because he condescends Demitri's way, "She's a repulsive biker-killing hellspawn who smokes and hangs with thugs. She wasn't even good enough for *that* trash." He jabs a finger Adam's way.

"Oh shit," I mutter.

Adam gestures for the cigarette that I hand him. He takes a drag and hands it back. "If you'll excuse me," he politely says to me before turning on a mind-bending wave of rage that blisters through the backyard. He rushes Javier, grabs him by the front of the shirt, and snarls, "Let me tell you a few things, dickhead. That girl was my ride or die for over two hundred lifetimes. I don't give a fuck what you think about me, you rich-boy scum, but don't you *dare* insult Melanie." Adam glares at Demitri. "You don't have any clue yet what you have. You're just standing there, you spineless sack of shit!"

"I didn't expect things to go this way," Demitri says, in an attempt to defend himself.

Adam shoves Javier into Dante before pointing at Demitri. "You didn't expect . . . THAT is what you have to say?" Adam glares at me. "THIS is who you chose for your forever?" He jabs a finger Demitri's way.

"I didn't get any say in it," I inform.

Adam rubs his face hard. "Unbelievable. It's always like that." He crosses to me. "What else did Javier say about you?"

I shake my head.

Adam turns to Javier. "I'll find out. You're playing with fire. I'll rip out your fucking heart. Making her sad is my job, asshole."

Javier cowers, clearly stunned.

Adam wraps his arm around me. "Come on, Firebird."

"Where are you going?" Demitri asks.

"None of your goddamn business," Adam snarls.

"Talk to me, Melanie," Demitri pleads.

"You have a party to host, Demitri," I sarcastically snap back. "Enjoy my pool."

"Let's go, Angel Eyes," Adam says.

"You haven't called me that in a longgggg time," I gasp.

"Again," Adam says, "I'm an idiot."

We walk into the house, and everyone follows.

"They walk the same, they act the same . . . ," Jayla says. "It's like they were made for each other."

Adam rotates us to face the spectators, and we both get the same steely-eyed look. "We *were* made for each other," Adam informs arrogantly. "Our souls were created at the same time."

"Shit," Demitri murmurs. "I never realized how alike you two are until now."

"Same sense of humor, same blistering temper, same quaking libido, same sense of daring," Adam informs.

I curl against him.

He smirks down at me. "God, I miss that." He says to Demitri, "Our bodies fit perfectly like puzzle pieces from head to toe every single lifetime. Melanie is my other half, but I'm an idiot who didn't appreciate what I had." He looks at me. "Go get changed, Melanie."

I rush to my room and come back out in a heavy metal crop top, Doc Martens, and leather pants. We strut out the door. Demitri and his friends run out front just in time to watch me swing my leg over Adam's Harley. Adam fires up the bike, and we take off down my street at Mach 10.

I hear through our connection as Demitri bellows at Javier, "What the HELL did you do?"

CHAPTER 31

Windblown, we pull up to the house. We ended up not talking. Instead, we took a dangerous ride through Topanga Canyon. We don't have a soulmate connection anymore, but my empathy picked up on a lot of intense emotions from Adam. The predominant sentiment was a need to protect me at all costs.

I get off the motorcycle, and Adam cuts the engine. He swings his leg over and puts his arms around me. "Are you okay going back in there?" he asks, likely because Javier's, Dante's, and Stella's cars are still here.

"I don't know." I put my head on his chest. "This latest mess is a nightmare. The last thing I need is another soulmate." I hear running and whip around.

Demitri's there with our friends. "You came back," he expresses, seeming both relieved and surprised.

"I live here," I reply, baffled.

Demitri tosses a stern look at Javier, who rushes to say, "I apologize, Melanie. It's hard to see you as a soft girl with feelings. I know what lives in you, and I'm positive Demitri can't handle it, but I shouldn't have been dismissive of you."

"Demitri has no choice but to handle life with Melanie," Adam schools Javier.

"I *want* to be with Melanie," Demitri insists.

Javier huffs. "I think you need to pump the brakes, slow down, and give this some time."

"You're clueless, Javier, but you seem to have good intentions." Adam's anger has apparently diminished. "Do you really care about Demitri?"

Javier nods. "He's my best friend."

"Then you need to come inside and hear me out," Adam offers. I give Adam a look, but he just smiles sadly at me.

"Any chance we can all come?" Dante asks.

"Whatever," Adam mutters. He drapes his arm around my shoulders.

We walk into the house, and he leads us out to the backyard. Everyone sets up folding chairs at Adam's request, while I start a fire in the courtyard firepit.

"How do you know how to do that?" Jayla asks curiously.

"Start a fire?" Jayla nods, and I laugh a little. "I've had a lot of lifetimes where a fire was a nightly necessity."

"Jayla's question is a good opener for what I want to discuss," Adam says.

Everyone settles in their chairs, and Adam passes out tequila shots from a bottle he snagged from the bar inside. I sit with Demitri on one side and Adam on the other. I drape my leg over Adam's knee, and he laces his hand with mine.

"Is that supposed to bother me?" Demitri interrupts, gesturing to our hands.

Adam raises an eyebrow. "If you're going to be with her, you must understand Melanie and me. We aren't soulmates anymore, but this," he raises our laced hands, "doesn't go away. I understand

Melanie like no one else can."

Demitri glares at Javier for stirring up this mess.

"Buckle up," Adam says. "Melanie story number one. Rome, 81 AD."

"Wait . . . ," Dante interrupts. "Are you serious?"

"Hell yes, I'm serious. We've got some wicked history."

Jayla's eyes widen. "You plan to tell us stories?"

Adam slouches further in his chair. "Maybe if you all understand Melanie better, you'll quit disrespecting her." He gives Jayla a look. "May I continue?"

"Su-uure . . . ," she stammers, sounding intimidated.

Adam sneers at her before pulling a glug from the tequila bottle. "I was arrested and put in slave quarters. Melanie managed to get into the audience area of the Colosseum. The gates opened, and I was forced out into the arena with forty other guys to an ear-shattering roar. Gladiators came at us, and I was certain it was the end. Melanie hopped on the wall and levitated down on a shield bubble wave of rage. She blasted the gladiators with the most ferocious attack I had ever seen, before blowing a hole through the walls and allowing all of us to escape."

"You don't seriously expect us to believe that?" Javier snarks.

I snort. "Wanna see?"

Heads nod.

I take Adam's memory of the event through our laced hands. I lean forward and explain to the others, "Put your hands on my arm if you want to see it." When everyone does, I pass the memory to them.

Jaws drop as they watch it with their eyes closed.

When everyone comes out of the memory, Adam looks at Javier. "*That's* what Melanie will do when she loves a man."

"How do I keep her safe?" Demitri asks.

Adam shakes his head. "*You* don't. You punch like a demon, but it's the mindset that you're missing. You don't step into a room and already know how to kill anyone you have to if Melanie needs to be rushed through the door. She keeps *you* safe. Your job is to love her. Hold her when she cries. Make her laugh. Fix her with your healing ability when she gets destroyed in battle. Never hurt her when it's avoidable."

"You realize you're talking about teenagers, right?" Javier exclaims.

Adam pours another round of shots while he explains, "You need to quit thinking of Melanie's physical body age. She's an ancient soul. So are me, Trey, Demitri, Bear, and Darren." He gives Javier a look. "You people," he scans a finger, indicating the Normals, "are everyday teenagers." He hands a shot to Demitri. "Bottoms up."

They clink shot glasses and down them.

"I've never been a big drinker," Demitri croaks around the fiery liquid.

"Soulmate life is hard," Adam says. "You'll need to let loose on occasion."

"I feel like I can't catch up since the soulmate bond fused," Demitri admits.

"Time moves at the speed of light for a bonded pair," Adam schools. "I guarantee that what you've experienced in a few hours since your soulmate bond fused is more intense than what you've felt with every girl you've had combined."

"True," Demitri whispers, seeming overwhelmed.

"Now, the real question is, can you handle the pressure?"

"Explain," Demitri requests.

Adam looks down and contemplates. Finally, he instructs, "Demitri, you need to keep it together. I'll show you why."

Adam squeezes my hand, and I ask pensively, "Which one is this?"

"Cliff plunge."

"I don't want Demitri to see that."

"I need him to understand." Adam looks at Demitri. "This was two months after we discovered our soulmate bond that lifetime. I don't want you to judge Melanie. Much like this lifetime, I made the wrong call in the form of another woman, and that tends to get ugly."

I take the memory and hold out my arm. As everyone latches on, I send the memory with my heart squeezed tight, close my eyes, and watch with everyone. We see through Adam's eyes in the memory as he says, "I can't do this, Deidre. I'm sorry. I'm choosing her."

Memory me craters. Tears roll from my big brown eyes. I'm a curvy raven-haired beauty in that lifetime.

Adam walks away, trying to ignore his confliction. He looks back as he hears movement, and he's stunned stiff as I run toward the cliffside. I take a flying leap, and Adam screams, "DEIDRE!" He races to the cliffside and looks down, watching as I plummet toward a boiling ocean.

I hit a rock outcropping, and my body splinters. I'm still alive, blinking up at him from far down. A massive wave comes and sweeps me off the rocks and under the angry ocean.

Memory Adam hits his knees, sobbing.

We all come back to reality. Adam clears his throat, as Jayla and Stella wipe tears from their faces. Demitri takes a shuddering breath.

"This current lifetime is one of tenish where I've run from Melanie," Adam says. "It's always a disaster. Demitri, it'll be intense. Stick it out or you'll destroy both of you."

"That memory was horrible," Jayla whispers.

"We're just getting warmed up," Adam scoffs. "Here's what happened during my least favorite affair with a vapid bitch."

"You're ripping through our greatest hits tonight," I mutter.

"I've got the guts to get through this level of Demitri coaching once," Adam says. "I'll help him, but the memory shit must happen now." He takes a deep breath. "Here we go. The village priest, my mistress's father, was an evil energy worker. He spurned the locals out of spite when my mistress lost it after I tried to end my secret affair. Chaos reigned and mob mentality ensued when he accused Melanie of being a witch. Because of her abilities, it was easily believable to the Normals that dominated the village. The priest clamped down on our abilities, and Mel was ripped from my arms in our little house. She found out about my affair while she was dragged to the riverbank. Every man in the village held me back, while the priest and my mistress tied Melanie to a door that was yanked from the church-front hinges. Boulders were put on her, excruciatingly slowly, one after the other. I was forced to watch as her bones and organs were crushed one at a time. The pain was so bad that she couldn't hold together her blockage over our connection. I felt it all with her. When the last boulder was finally placed, I heard a popping sound I'll never forget. It was her skull crushing." Adam takes a deep breath. "I was locked in the village prison, and Melanie's destroyed body was hung from the tree outside my barred prison window. My mistress's brother was the prison warden, who did it with her encouragement."

"Holy crap" Dante breathes.

Adam nods. "Melanie paid dearly for my indiscretion that lifetime. The sad part is that I didn't even like my mistress. I was just bored and wanted an escape. You haven't known true torture until you've spent weeks smelling your soulmate rot in the summer heat while your ex-mistress howls with laughter outside your prison." Adam's expression crumples. He turns his head, and it takes him a second to get his emotions back in check.

I hold out my arm, and everyone latches on. They watch my side of the memory, feeling my terror and the pain of my body being broken in stages. I choose not to relive it. It regularly tortures me during my night terrors, and I'm well acquainted with the moment. When they finish the memory, everyone looks shell-shocked, and we give them a minute to collect themselves. It's not every day that someone feels crushing death.

"That was horrific," Jayla breathes.

Adam gets a far-off look. "Moments like that have destroyed me."

I duck my head. "Javier, Adam didn't run because I'm horrible."

Adam looks at me. "Is that what he thought?"

"I was trying to talk Demitri out of this, and I said you married the first chick who said yes just to escape Melanie," Javier admits.

Adam closes his eyes, pained. "You have no idea how bad your timing is. Don't use me leaving Melanie for Valerie as ammo against her. Did I propose to Valerie when I was overwhelmed? Yes. Was it a mistake? YOU HAVE NO IDEA. It wasn't a reflection on Melanie, though. My weakness and lacking caused that, not hers."

Javier looks ashamed. "I apologize."

Adam hits Demitri with a penetrating glare. "The fact that you didn't lay him out for putting that on Melanie makes me question your integrity."

Demitri closes his eyes, his expression gaunt.

"Demitri asked him to can it."

Adam gives me a sarcastic side-eye. "Phenomenal. Your soul-mates always suck, Melanie."

"Can I ask something?" Javier interjects.

"What?" Adam says, sounding exhausted.

Javier clears his throat. "We all know about Trey and Victoria. Victoria was quite the showboating bitch at school this morning. For the record, we're all backing Melanie on this, including Trey, oddly enough. He seems mortified by Victoria's braggadocious bullshit. It's obvious, based on what he screamed at Victoria in the middle of Actors' Alley, that he loves Melanie. I don't understand why Melanie keeps getting cheated on by soulmates."

Adam chuckles with no humor. "Trey cheats on Melanie because he's scared of deep commitment. Regarding me, I'm not showing you the happy lifetimes full of soulmate glee. I'm showing you select moments intentionally. The general answer to your question is that soulmate life is damn hard. The depth of soulmate love consumes your sanity, and a normal girl, who does the dishes and takes strolls, is alluring. It never works out, though. The problem that I've discovered, and Trey is learning, is that a soulmate bond drives you insane when you're not with your other half. It doesn't just go away when you break up."

"You seem okay," Javier says.

Adam shakes his head, his eyes haunted. "I'm not okay, Javier. When the kids and Valerie are asleep . . ." Adam takes a sharp breath. "That's when it gets bad. I pace the house. I hurt so bad I can't breathe."

Adam's never told me that, and my heart squeezes tight.

"Is it better now that your soulmate bond is gone?" Dante asks.

Adam shakes his head. "Once you're soulmate bonded for as long as Mel and me, you need each other."

I swallow hard, fighting tears.

"Do you experience that about Adam?" Jayla asks me.

"Yes, but I don't have the luxury of really wallowing in it, hence why I'm a basket case. I deal with Adam, Trey, and Demitri, while

I attend school five days a week, same as you. All of that, while I'm hunted by biker gangs and serial killers. I rarely sleep, and when I do, I'm plagued by night terrors full of the horrors of my past lives. Then, I get to wander to Actors' Alley at lunch and receive nasty looks from cheerleaders and Javier."

Javier's head drops in shame, while Stella gives him an aghast look.

"How does Pierre fit into this?" Dante asks.

"Who is Pierre?" Stella asks.

I scoff. "Pierre 'Riptide' Strader."

"The surfer who died?" Stella asks.

"Yes," I reply, emotionless. "Pierre was my selfish attempt at a normal life, but it worked because he wasn't a Normal. I needed freedom from soulmate pressure. I fell in love with him, we got hitched by simple handfasting conversation, and he promptly was murdered that same day on national television."

Gasps sound.

"As complicated as my life seems, it's really quite simple. Roadblocks are never-ending. Fear is my go-to emotion. Happiness isn't my privilege. My soulmates are in my life to remind me that I'm no one."

Adam scoffs. "Imagine the ultimate fairy-tale fantasy love that every girl dreams of. Now, imagine finding that *four* times by the time you're sixteen. Two of those four Prince Charmings tossed Mel away for women that weren't shit."

"You're saying that about your wife?" Dante asks, aghast.

"Yup," Adam says without hesitation. "Valerie can be a good person, but it's buried deep under a whole lot of shallow. I NEVER should have chosen Val over Melanie." Adam clears his throat. "Trey tossed Melanie out for Tiffany, got a second chance, and did it again for Victoria."

Everyone winces, while I blush a humiliated red.

"Pierre was ripped away from her because of the deadly nature of Melanie's life," Adam continues. "Then, a soulmate connection with Demitri was forced on her. Naturally she got no say in this dramatic shift."

"Do her soulmates fold to pressure because her life is so fraught with danger?" Dante asks.

Adam shrugs. "The pressure of keeping her alive, and watching her be attacked, is a damn hard thing. That's part of it, but there's something ego-driven about finding your soulmate, who's perfect for you. 'I got her. I should go for bigger air.'" Adam shakes his head in disgust. "Then you discover that the 'big air' conquest ain't shit. You must admit your mistake because your perfect little soulmate can dig around in your memories for the dirty details, and it's better to fess up and at least get a word in to explain yourself for fear that Melanie will eradicate you. If she doesn't kill you for it, you then spend every moment battling with Melanie because she's distraught and doesn't trust you anymore." He slides a smirk at Demitri. "It's not like pissing off a girlfriend who you never deal with again. Cheating on your soulmate is a life sentence because your soulmate doesn't go away, and you get to live with Melanie Slate's brand of pissed until you die. It doesn't end there though. There's no 'til death do you part' with a soulmate. You get to hear about your indiscretions *again* in your debrief in the spirit realm."

"Holy crap," Javier breathes. "Death isn't an escape for soulmates."

Adam shakes his head while he stares at Demitri. "Two hundred and three lifetimes I've been with Melanie. Every living moment, except the few years before we meet each lifetime, or the occasional lifetime that you or Trey steal her, we were together. We've also spent every soul moment together between lifetimes." He points at me. "That girl is now *your* air, food, water, sanity, comfort, best friend, and lover. Hurting her is the same as cutting off your arm and then having it reattached, but it never works again. She doesn't go away, so you better treat her right."

"She went away for you, though," Javier says.

Adam nods. "My indiscretions over our lifetimes were so immense that I couldn't live with the guilt, and I tried to run." He looks to me. "My spirit guide plunked that intel into my mind when I was distraught about why I'd ask for the soulmate connection to be removed before this lifetime. That's why I came over here." He shakes his head at Javier. "I have a wife and children at home, but look where I'm at."

"Next to Melanie," Javier says.

Adam nods. "I'd rather coach her perfect new soulmate, as painful as that is, than be away from her. She's my heart and home."

I wince from the pain of him saying that so succinctly.

Adam smiles congenially, his attempt at lightening the mood. "The other reason I came over was to fill Melanie in on a little heart-to-heart that I had with Trey."

I blanche, glancing at the others.

"Who gives a fuck if they're here?" Adam admonishes. "Maybe they need to know the sorted reality so they can understand what a nightmare you've lived with." He shifts his intense focus back to the group. "I barged in last night, finding Trey and Victoria in a squabble because he was out late."

"He came here to talk to us," Demitri divulges.

"Yeah, well, Victoria didn't take kindly to it," Adam informs.

I snort. "She better get used to it. He was always MIA when he was with me."

"That's because he was with her," Demitri reminds.

Adam grins. "She told me to get out of HER suite. So, I took him with me, to her great consternation. I explained to him that he spent his marriage, that blessedly was short, raping his wife." Gasps punctuate and Adam nods.

"That's a harsh word," I admonish.

"Trey Valdez," Adam doubles down intensely, "spent his marriage forcing himself brutally on you." He focuses on the others again. "He tore her up so severely that Demitri spends every moment that she's asleep healing severe internal scar tissue."

"Oh no," Javier whispers.

I blush, while Demitri winces. "Melanie doesn't want that splashed around."

Adam flips a hand to Javier. "Maybe it'll curb his judgment toward Melanie."

"I had no idea," Javier breathes, horrified.

"I had no idea either," Adam says, "or I would have killed him for it. I'm choosing to teach him instead because he needs to understand why he hurts so badly, and is so full of guilt that he can't function. Trey now understands that his loyalty was with Victoria, and subconsciously, he thought that if he was savage with his wife, and loving with his mistress, then he wasn't cheating on Victoria."

I take a shuddering breath as Adam puts psychological pieces together for me.

"I drove that point home," Adam continues. "Then, I reminded that he did that to his *soulmate*." Adam shifts steely eyes to Demitri. "To clarify, marriage is nothing but a formality for a bonded couple. Soulmates are married on an ethereal level the moment the soulmate bond fuses. You," he points to Demitri, "are married soul-to-soul with her," he points to me. "THAT is why I'm having this discussion. I'm hoping to educate you before you make irreversible mistakes like Trey and I did. Melanie deserves to be happy." Adam sits back in his chair. "Let's drive home my point, because the last two past-life examples I gave were of sweet, docile Melanie. She's not sweet and docile this lifetime, and that's when it gets REALLY interesting. Our forty-third lifetime . . . to put that into perspective for you, it was around 6,400 years in the past." Eyes widen and Adam nods. "Melanie's abilities weren't what they are now, but she was still wicked. How about we just show you, instead of tell you?" He touches my arm, and I pull the memory.

"I'm not proud of this one."

"You should be," Adam replies. "I deserved it. It tortures me to this day."

I sigh and hold out my arm. Everyone touches me, gaining the memory. I close my eyes and watch through Adam's memory eyes.

I walk through the door, a tall, eagle-faced woman. There was nothing delicate or pretty about me that lifetime. I was certainly striking in my harsh angularity, though. Whipcord and muscled, I'm in exceptional shape, but as I turn my head, it's apparent that my excellent condition was hard-won through battle. The left side of my face sports a sword scar. My left eye is that murky milk white from a blinding injury. "Move," I say in the memory. It comes out a guttural demand.

"What's wrong?" memory Adam asks.

Adam translates to the others as we go. I'm unsure what language we're speaking, but I understand it without the translation.

In the memory, my hand flicks, and pain blisters through his chest. We all feel it. He flies across the little room and smacks into a wall. I stalk past as terror rips through him. We feel broken ribs as he fights to stand, but he's spurred into motion because of what he fears is coming.

Memory Adam rushes into the bedroom. The moment he gets through the door, he's splattered with blood and guts. He gasps as he surveys all the walls and the bed, coated in gore. I face him, and power rolls from me in waves. The room is suffocating.

He fights to breathe through terror as I deeply gravel, "That problem is solved."

Memory Adam is overcome with the monumental understanding that this is it, but I stalk past him instead. He collapses at the waist, relieved I didn't kill him, but also heartbroken.

The sounds of screaming chaos emit from outside. He rushes through the living room and out the cottage door. His gaze pans, taking in the inferno and chaos in the little village.

I slowly turn to him in the middle of the village square and loudly announce, "Secrets are revealed."

My hands rise and the entire village goes up in a blaze of revenge so deadly in its ferocity that no one stands a chance. Bodies burn, buildings collapse, and then there's nothing but the sound of fire.

As the flames tamp, he rushes to the center of what used to be the village square. There, on the ground, is a pile of ash where I was. Panic and devastation collapse Adam's knees. He crumples and surveys all that is no more.

Our eyes open, and Adam levels Demitri with an evil glare. "I had an affair with Melanie's daughter, Antrell, that lifetime. She was the product of rape when Melanie was twelve. I met Melanie at sixteen and helped raise the girl. Melanie was twenty-eight in that memory. Her daughter was sixteen. I was twenty-nine."

"You slept with your *stepdaughter*?" Dante asks, mortified.

Adam nods, slow and steady. "Melanie found out through unsubtle village gossip. Until then, everyone knew except for Melanie. What you witnessed was the aftermath." Adam's head tips. "Melanie suspected it. She confirmed it. She handled it. She eradicated her own daughter with an energy blast. Then she felt nothing about desecrating every soul in that village, except for me.

I became a nomad the rest of that lifetime. What you just witnessed rendered me insane."

"Oh my GOD," mutters from Dante.

Adam swings slightly insane eyes to Dante. "Yeah, bud." He flips a hand toward Javier. "Yet, assholes still toy with Melanie, poking at her vulnerability and putting her down." He scans my friends. "You fucking gerbils shouldn't taunt a rattlesnake. She eats motherfuckers like you for a snack, because she's not docile this lifetime."

Uninvited, I pull Adam's cigarette pack from his jacket pocket and light two, handing one to him.

I take a drag, as Adam asks Javier, "Still want to talk shit about Melanie for trivial nonsense like smoking?"

Javier stares at me like he doesn't recognize me.

"I don't irrationally destroy people anymore," I lifelessly profess.

Adam belts a humorless, "Ha!" and slides harsh eyes my way. "You incinerated Jet. You diced Mack up with a katana. You killed how many of the Reapers while wearing a wedding dress? You sucked the lifeforce from thirty-three of the baddest bikers in the country, and they dropped dead."

"They deserved it."

"So did Antrell and me," Adam says. "You were justified." He smirks. "So does Victoria. I'm shocked you haven't killed her yet."

With nothing to say, I pull another drag from my cigarette.

"Demitri, use that adorable soulmate connection of yours to scan her vibe right now," Adam requests.

I drop my shields and feel Demitri's energetic probing.

He clears his throat nervously. "She feels dead inside. There's a neutral hum that's odd."

Adam smirks. "While I no longer have a soulmate connection with Melanie, I know that feeling well. Welcome to the third side of

Melanie. Sure, there's the side you love that's adorable and bubbly, with her giggles and big eyes. Then there's the side that gives Trey hard-on's while she cuts a fat fuck in half and says witty shit. This, though," he gestures to me with his cigarette, "this is the side that gives *my* trashy ass vapors. Welcome to the mode that allows Melanie to serial kill without discretion. *This* Melanie doesn't give a shit that you made a whoopsie. She doesn't give a shit that the other woman feels bad about the indiscretion." Adam shakes his head methodically. "She killed her own daughter for a whoopsie. Then she killed everyone that hid the whoopsie from her." He pans the group. "Demitri, I recommend you don't whoopsie, and I recommend the rest of you don't hide his indiscretions." Adam's hard stare lands on Jayla. "I especially advise that women never *be* the whoopsie daisy." Adam smiles, slow and vicious. "Good thing for all of us, Demitri's not 'that guy,' because it would be a hell of a shame for Melanie to finally snap after everything Trey and I put her through and lose it on Demitri's whoopsie." He ashes his cigarette. "To clarify, because Normals tend to be naïve, Melanie is at her breaking point, and it's best not to test her."

Heaviness hangs in the air, but I'm comfortable in it.

"Thus concludes my performance," Adam says, while he stands and takes an obnoxious bow.

I look up at him with dead eyes.

He studies me. "Don't forget who the fuck you are. They can think we're trash. We don't care what they think. Demitri used to be an exception to that rule for me, but I'm reconsidering my loyalty to him since it came out that he was with Jayla while you were attacked by the Machetes." Adam hovers over Demitri menacingly. "*That* is why I selectively chose so many of my affair stories." He slides his angry eyes to Jayla. "I've lived a lonnnnnng time through brutality you can't imagine over my lifetimes, but

I've never met anyone, or any THING, more sadistic, pragmatic, or willing to kill than that woman." He points to me while his gaze pans his audience. "You've all been warned, and my conscience will be clear if she loses it."

"Adam, please," Demitri says, stunned.

"I hope, for *everyone's* sake, that you've been everything you claim to be, Demitri." Adam smirks, his eyes flashing wickedly. "Now that you understand the consequences, you'll always be Mr. Perfect with your little serial killer, right?"

Demitri nods, but it's tentatively scared.

I stand, and Adam hugs me. "I love you, Melanie," he says softly. It holds a world of pain.

"Thank you for tonight," I whisper. "I feel understood."

"I *do* understand you," Adam promises. "I just wish I had understood before it was too late for us." Adam Stone tears up and strides away quickly.

I hear the sliding door open and close. My head drops as abandonment grips my gut.

"Melanie," Demitri says, gravely and weighted. I look his way, and he asks, "Are you okay?"

"No. Like I told you when you asked if you could invite the guys over, I have things to work through. Looks like they got worked on, publicly, like you promised wouldn't happen again."

"Shit," Demitri mutters. "I'm so sorry."

"It is what it is." I survey the others, but have no idea what to say, because who I am was so brutally revealed. I finally settle with, "Enjoy the pool."

I start to walk away, but Stella rushes to block my path. "Stop, Melanie," she implores. When I do, she smiles the slightest bit. "You've earned a breather. I'd love to swim with you. How about we go inside and chat while you get changed?"

My eyebrows rise. "You're willing to walk into my house with me after what you just heard?"

Stella smiles softly. "You're my friend." She shrugs. "I've got an iffy past also. I stole my best friend's boyfriend last year out of pure spite because I was jealous of her. The fallout was horrible. It's why I switched schools."

"Did you blow her up with an energy detonation?" I joke.

"No, but hearing that story made me realize I should be more careful who I steal ugly guys with bad haircuts from."

I crack up, the tension dissolving.

"Come on," Stella says. She guides me around the corner and inside.

CHAPTER 32

I hesitate at the sliding door. "I don't want to go back out there."

Stella gently takes me by the arms. "Remember what we just talked about."

I'm stunned by how succinctly Stella talked me through what happened with Adam. I was so relieved during that talk that I also blathered my Jayla suspicion. Stella plans to keep an ear out and let me know if Jayla spills it.

I wince. "I'm sure they all think I'm a freak. Adam wasn't tactful."

Stella shrugs. "That's okay. I guarantee he got his point across to Javier. I plan to talk to Jav also. I won't allow my boyfriend to treat you badly."

"Thank you."

She opens the door, and we head out. Javier passes me. He doesn't say anything but squeezes my arm as he walks inside. Considering how poorly he and I were communicating before Adam's little story-time extravaganza, I'll take it.

I scan the yard, finding Demitri and Jayla in a hushed conversation in the deep end of the pool. Demitri has me blocked off, so

I'm not sure what they're talking about. My eye catches Dante's, and he squints suspiciously as he watches the pair.

I leave Stella, who's going through a stack of CDs at the table, and make my way to him. "What did I miss?" I murmur.

"They just started talking," Dante murmurs back.

"What do you think?"

Dante shrugs. "Considering how guilt eats her alive if she forgets to return a borrowed pencil, I can't imagine she could hide an affair with D."

"That's an excellent point."

Dante snorts. "I don't like how secretive they are, though. The good news is that I think Adam rattled every square inch of Jayla's cage with his 'Melanie will blow you up' stories."

Demitri swims away from Jayla and ascends the pool stairs. He's even more ethereally perfect by moonlight. Instead of making my heart flutter, his perfection brings dejected fear.

I don't stand a shot of keeping Demitri's interest.

Demitri stares at me, his expression vulnerable. I avert my gaze, and it spurs Demitri to traverse the distance to me. Dante tactfully takes his leave.

"Hey," Demitri says.

"Hi."

"I just heard your thought," he says. "You've got my interest, and it won't waver. You're perfect."

I scoff. "I'm not perfect. You saw for yourself."

He smirks. "You blew your daughter's body the hell *up*!"

I quirk my mouth. "Liquifying my daughter isn't exactly charitable."

He leans into me. "Too soon for the topic?" he whispers.

I giggle, having not expected that. I whisper back, "I hate that you're effectively turning around my pensive mood so quickly. I was prepared to wallow in stoic misery and weirdness for a week."

"I'm trying some new tactics," Demitri covertly whispers. "Glad to know it's working."

"To answer your question," I whisper back, "I blew my daughter up a hundred and sixtyish lifetimes ago. It's not too soon to mention it."

"I can't believe Adam did that with her," he commiserates in a normal voice.

"He's done so much worse than that," I inform. "He picked polite memories."

"Worse?" Demitri breathes.

"Yes," I bashfully reply. "In one of the lifetimes he flat won't talk about, he had an affair with my mother of the time. He got her pregnant, she died in childbirth, he killed himself because he was so distraught, and I had to raise their love child."

That story stuns Demitri stiff. He rattles with palpable shock.

I nod. "Your reaction is correct."

He snaps into a comical smolder. "Clearly Trey and Adam have been soulmate *heaven*." Demitri melodramatically cups my cheeks. "Considering how high they set the bar, whatever will I do?"

I laugh. "It's been a real humdinger."

"Wait, wait, wait. I jumped the gun." Demitri wrestles his expression dramatically serious, and I'm amused. "Before I flirt with you, I'd like to preemptively assuage a suspicion I'm positive you're harboring."

I laugh. "Curiouser and curiouser."

He chuckles. "Jayla and I were just talking about the Antrell situation. She's terrified that she's on your bad side. I'm not thrilled that you came outside and found us talking. I was swimming laps while you were inside. She swam up to me and started flustering, literally moments before you emerged."

"I appreciate how upfront you just were," I reply, feeling a little better that he didn't make me beg for intel.

He makes a cutely surprised face. "Look at me! I'm learning. I'll store that little 'upfront and honest' tactic away in my Melanie Handbook."

I giggle again. Maybe there's a shot at turning tonight around. "You were going to flirt," I remind him.

"Ah yes, so sorry," Demitri says.

I lean in to whisper, "Store away the 'whispering amusedly to shift the mood' tactic in your Melanie Handbook also."

He chuckles. "Done." He flutters up his flirtatious act before gossiping my way, "There's this guuuuy."

"Oh yeah?" I ask, willing to play along because it's way better than wallowing in what happened earlier.

"Yup," he says. "He's never screwed your daughter, so I'm not sure if you'll like him." I jokingly smack his arm, and he grins at me. "He's kinda cute, and all insecure, but he covers it well," he teases. "Wanna hang with him?"

"If he has gorgeous eyes and wears fairy wings, then maybe," I flirt back.

He smolders at me for real this time. "Can we go inside, and you can get to know him? There's been some confusion, and I think he needs a new soulmate introduction to you."

I swallow hard, dropping the ruse. "You're still interested after what Adam dished?"

"I've got a sick side." Demitri scrunches his face attractively. "Something about your serial-killing tendencies has me hot and bothered."

I crack up. "You're bent, Demitri."

He nods. "Agreed, but so are you, so it works."

"It'll be different now because of the soulmate bond," I warn.

He leans his arm against the wall above my shoulder, and it suddenly feels like we're the only people in the backyard.

"Really?" he flirtatiously asks.

"Very different," I breathe.

Demitri grabs my hand and hauls me into the house. He practically drags me down the hall, and I giggle girlishly. He gets me to my room and discovers how incredibly different things are now.

— —

With Demitri's arm around my shoulders, we exit the sliding door. Javier claps hands with D in some bro way. I tactfully take my leave, as Javier asks, "You good?"

"You have no idea," I hear him say.

Stella bites her tongue at the girly look I give her. She and Jayla meet me by the pool. "Soooooo?" Stella murmurs.

I giggle, completely out of character, but damn, was the last hour something. "That's the first time we've . . . you know, since our soulmate bond fused," I whisper. "Freaking fireworks."

"Girl, yes," Stella says. "How is he handling the talk Adam had?"

I shrug. "We haven't had a chance to really dive in and discuss it, but he's suddenly all playful and attentive."

"Sounds like he learned a few things," Stella says.

"I heard Javier ask D how he was handling it while you and Stella were inside," Jayla says to me. "Demitri said that he's not scared of the things Adam revealed. He also said he thinks that Adam and Trey forgot how to have fun with you, and that was a big part of the problem."

"You do a lot of lurking and hearing stuff," I point out to Jayla.

She shrugs. "I'm quiet, which makes hearing stuff easy."

I briefly wonder if she's collecting secrets but brush off the thought. I deserve a happy night, and I'm determined to have one. I excuse myself and head to the waterfall, climbing up. I tip my head back and stare at the moon. My body and mind are in harmony for the first time in a long while. Connecting with a soulmate the way we just did does this, and I'm deeply relieved. I've missed that kind of bond for a long time.

I take a deep breath, and then I leap with a jackknife and torpedo to the bottom of the pool. I grip the drain and let the quiet dark water do its work. I've started doing this to balance the dark-water chaos in my mind.

Demitri forgets to shield, and I hear through him as Jayla whispers, "She seems okay."

"She is," Demitri replies.

"That stroll through past-life heck was horrific."

Demitri scoffs. "Yeah, it was. That's Adam's way though. He's brutally succinct when he wants to be."

"You did good hitting her reset button," Jayla whispers.

I'm instantly suspicious. I thought he was being genuine. It wasn't on my radar that he had some scheme cooked up with Jayla.

I hear a bellowed, "Holy crap," through Demitri's ears, and then I'm grabbed a moment later from behind. I fight my attacker, almost out of air because whoever it is chose when I was about to swim up to grab me at the bottom of the pool. The person lets go, and I kick hard to the surface.

"What the HELL?" I roar, as Dante emerges next to me with a gasp.

"You weren't drowning?" he barks.

Demitri chuckles.

"No," I reply with a quizzical look.

"Do you know how long you were down there?" Dante screeches.

I get out of the pool, needing space. "I was on a swim team."

"*Swim* team?" Dante squalls, treading water. "I thought you took dance classes."

"I did." I sigh. "I've been a regular person who does regular things before. My life-and-death nightmares didn't start until I got to Hollywood High."

"What were you before Hollywood?" Stella asks.

"A lonely no one with zero friends or excitement."

Everyone but Demitri gapes at me. He already knew this, but the reaction of the others drives home how much they aren't a part of my inner circle.

Fear blisters up my spine. *Strangers knowing deep details gets me killed.*

"You're okay, Meley," Demitri insists, seeing my flustered state. "You were so rattled that your blockage dropped. You don't need to fear the others here. They handled tonight well, and you have four closer friends now." He gives me a look. "You've referred to Jayla as your best friend before. I think you're safe."

"I didn't realize that we're . . . ," Jayla stammers. "I'm . . ."

I take a wary breath. "It's nothing, Jayla."

"I'd like to be that more than you know," she insists.

I scoff. "Riiiight." I look to Dante, caged. "Don't grab me like that. I'm on edge, it's been a difficult three months, and I'm very reactionary right now."

"I'm sorry, Melanie," he replies softly.

"I know your intentions were good," I assure him as I cross to the boom box on the porch table and hit the *skip* button. Paula Abdul's "Rush Rush" breathes from the speaker.

Demitri joins me at the porch. "Hey, you okay?"

"Wanna explain that covert convo you had with Jayla?" I ask. He appears confused.

"Hitting my reset switch?" I add.

Demitri shakes his head, befuddled. "What about it? She asked if you were okay and said I was doing good with you."

"Don't plot nefarious schemes with Jayla to manipulate me." I start to walk inside, but Demitri snags my wrist.

"Stop, Melanie. There's clearly a misunderstanding. Why are you suspicious of that?"

Feeling defensive and tricked, I flip a hand his way. "I loved how you were with me before we went inside together! It was easily my favorite moment I've *ever* had with you. I bought it hook, line, and sinker. Then I overheard you and Mary Poppins whispering about how you two plotted that scheme to manipulate me!"

"What?" Dante asks Jayla, who shrugs.

"Melanie, you've got that all wrong," Demitri says. "Jayla and I didn't plot me resetting your mood. She just happened to notice that we were doing better and complimented the shift."

"Don't whisper suspiciously about me with Jayla," I say, fed up.

"How did you hear our conversation?" Jayla asks. "You were underwater when he and I discussed that."

I bark a harsh laugh. "Righhhht. You waited until I was underwater to sneak over. Good to know." I tap my temple. "Soulmate connection. Your secret squeeze hasn't learned to Fort Knox his side of the bond yet when he has sneaky little chats." I smirk. "You might want to remember that next time you think about sidling up and whispering in his ear."

"Why are you whispering with Jayla?" Dante asks Demitri.

Demitri flips a hand to Dante. "You were whispering with Melanie when she came back outside."

"WE were whispering about how YOU TWO were whispering in the pool!" Dante lobs back.

"That's two whisperings!" I accuse, pointing from Jayla to Demitri.

Javier's eyebrows rise, and he steps away from Jayla. "Don't want to get hit by the kaboom splat," he mutters.

"Wait, wait, wait," Stella says. "What whisper started the fight between Demitri and Melanie?"

"Jayla and I talked, and Jayla said I did good with Melanie," Demitri says.

"That is NOT what happened!" I blister, frustrated. "Jayla said I seem okay, and Demitri agreed. Then she said the stories Adam told were horrific, and he agreed. Then she super covertly said, 'You did good hitting Melanie's reset switch.'" I imitate her in an obnoxious manner.

Javier scrunches his face. "That sounds bad."

"I agree!" I bluster. "You want the memory?" I hold out my arm.

Dante stomps to me and takes my arm, followed by Stella and Javier. They close their eyes, the memory only taking a moment to get through.

Their eyes open, and Javier wobbles his head. "It's borderline."

Stella huffs at him. "Pure misunderstanding." She looks to Dante. "What do you think? We need a tiebreaker."

"I think my girlfriend and I need to have a private chat, given Melanie's dislike of sneaky women!" Dante fumes.

Demitri's mouth drops open. "There was literally NO plot or sneak! Can I please see the memory?" He asks this because he didn't latch on when I sent it to Stella, Javier, and Dante. After I send it to him, he closes his eyes. When he opens them, he chuckles. "That's not how it felt or sounded on land." He gives me a cute look. "Underwater feels all isolated and weird. Our intentions came across different in that environment. Take my memory of that moment."

I do, passing it to the others. He's right. Jayla sounds supportive instead of like a sneaky sleaze. Demitri sounds like he's just casually chatting instead of having a plotted lovers' chat.

"Yup," Stella says. "Underwater made it feel secretive and private." She smiles at me. "Nothing to worry about."

"Huge worries!" Dante barks. "Big fat gargantuan worries!" He points to me, but says to Demitri, "She's incredibly on edge about Jayla, and I'm heeding the warning Adam gave. The last thing we want is an accidental deadly attack, only to discover it's a misunderstanding. Do more to protect Jayla, please. No more whispering."

"Done," Demitri says. "I apologize. It's just habit. I've always had little private chats like that with Jayla. She prefers that tactic."

My expression drops deadpan. "You used some Jayla tactic on me?"

"Melanie, don't start. It wasn't a tactic."

"YOU *called* it a tactic!" I bluster.

"I meant it wasn't a *bad* tactic." Demitri insists. "No ill intentions."

"Unbelievable! YES, it's bad. I thought that was some cute new special soulmate thing you were doing with me." I give him a stunned look. "Special, between us? Apparently not! Don't use recycled sentiment with me. Ugh." I flip a hand toward Jayla. "Especially not one that's HERS!" I glare at Jayla, disgusted. "It's always something with you."

I head inside to Demitri saying, "Damn it, Melanie. Please!"

"Let her go, Demitri," Jayla says.

Rage swells in me so fast I don't even realize what's happening. I whip around and storm back outside. "HOW DARE YOU!" screeches from me as I lunge at Jayla.

Demitri grabs me, spinning me around and hunkering over me as he sweeps my legs to drop me to my knees.

I start fighting back and manage to twist around. I grab him by his neck. "Let me go, or I'll rip your fucking throat out," snarls from me.

Everyone freezes.

"Tell me why you attacked just now," Demitri insists.

"That BITCH!" growls from me.

"Melanie, I need you to drop your blockage so I can figure out what's wrong with you," Demitri says, his tone gravely and dark.

I do and feel him digging around in my psyche.

Demitri says with aggravated calm, "Jayla just said exactly what Victoria did when you left the suite the night of that bachelor party." Tears fill my eyes, and Demitri nods. "You've got a lot of layers to unpack about how brazen we now know Victoria was during their affair, but we've discussed none of it because we just found out about their affair yesterday. I'm telling you though . . ." His voice chokes off.

"Can you let go of Demitri's neck?" Dante asks in a calmly guiding tone.

I splay my fingers, but don't remove my hand, my palm still pressed to his neck.

"You don't need your hand there," Dante says, realizing I'm still in a prime position to harm Demitri.

I slowly remove my hand, revealing Demitri's bright-red neck where I squeezed. Tears roll down my cheeks.

Javier and Dante stand on either side of us. Still on my knees, I warily stare up at them.

"Take several steps back, guys," Demitri says. "Melanie's on her knees, and you just took dominant positions. She fights instinctively when she feels threatened. Remember, she's got thousands of years of warrior training built into her."

The guys each take two steps back, and Demitri wipes under my eyes with his thumbs.

"I'm sorry," I whimper.

"I'm okay," Demitri says. "I apologize that all of this got so mixed up. I wasn't attempting some sneaky little whispered chat. Victoria and Trey did that a lot, now that I think about it. I understand why you're so on edge, but this is purely a coincidence. Yes, Trey and Victoria were being brazen. Jayla and I aren't, but we can shift gears to give you more breathing room while you work through everything that has happened."

My head drops to the pool deck.

Demitri's hands land on my back, and he sends a wave of calm energy. "Good, Melanie," he says as my energy levels out.

Calmed, I sit up and put my face in my hand. I exhale hard.

"I shouldn't have had anyone over," Demitri says. "You were a hundred percent right that you needed time to work through a lot. I apologize Melanie, and I apologize to the rest of you."

"I don't even understand what just happened," Dante says.

"I don't either," Jayla whimpers.

"Stella and I were there for what triggered this," Javier says. "Demitri and Trey got into a hell of a fistfight at Mabel's. Trey didn't want Melanie to leave, but Victoria flippantly said, 'Let her leave, Trey' at the tail end of the fight. Melanie didn't know that Victoria was Trey's mistress, at the time."

"I swear to you that my statement wasn't the same," Jayla says.

"No," Demitri says, "but it triggered Melanie, along with our habit of having whispered chats, and me lumping some cute stuff I did that Melanie liked with the mention of you. Melanie and I agreed right after our soulmate bond fused that we'd try to have a fresh start. I meant it, and still do, but I think it had a much deeper meaning to Melanie than I grasped at the time."

"I won't come second to her," I say, getting up.

"No, you won't," Demitri agrees, countering by standing.

"I'm not going through this again, Demitri."

"I agree," he replies. "The problem is that Jayla has a very unfortunate, and not at all premeditated, habit of saying and doing things that trigger rage in you. It requires a whole lot of unraveling to get to the bottom of it, but it always turns out to be nothing. It drives you insane, though."

I shake my head, radiating disgust. "After what you two did, I can't believe I gave you a second chance."

"Melanie, we've already worked through me being at Jayla's when you were attacked."

I tear up again, hating myself for it because the last thing I need is to look weak in this moment. "Sure, you addressed that, but you didn't address standing me up."

"What are you talking about?" Demitri says.

"We were supposed to go to El Coyote at six the Renn Faire day," I remind him. "I've been waiting this whole time for you to apologize. You never did."

His expression slides slack. "Shit."

"I sat on your doorstep for thirty minutes in my favorite dress, that ended up destroyed because the Machetes attacked me while you fawned all over Jayla. I refuse to be the pathetic girl who sits on some hot guy's doorstep, forgotten, because he's got a sneaky side chick. Same crap Trey put me through. I deserve better than that."

Demitri's shoulders slump. "I can't believe I forgot that date."

"Jayla's *that* captivating," I say, disgusted.

"She's not," he says. "I'm just that big a screw-up."

I slide hateful eyes to Jayla. "I'm done with you. I've had enough. After he stood me up for *you*, and didn't even have the manners to apologize, I'm left with no choice but suspicion. You refuse to be decent around him, and I'm sick and tired of this."

"Voice of reason," Dante softly says. "Pardon the intrusion.

Melanie, I don't understand. You worked through the worst part of that experience, getting attacked by the Machetes. Why is this El Coyote dinner situation not resolved as a part of that? It's just dinner."

"I don't give a damn that the Machetes nearly killed me," I reply. "I care that Demitri treated me like some waste while he put Jayla on a pedestal AGAIN. He did the same damn thing at Renn Faire, spilling my dirt publicly while privately cooing at Jayla."

Demitri holds a hand Dante's direction to stop him from replying. "She's right on this. I absolutely planned a date. I completely forgot until she just mentioned it. I was at Jayla's, and that's why I missed the date. I'm fully aware of how much that hurts Melanie. It completely destroyed her when Adam left her stranded on Hollywood Boulevard because he was buried in Valerie. She almost died that time also."

"I'm not even asking to matter to you," I say, my gaze destroyed. "I just want common decency. Considering that I'm your soulmate, I don't think that's too much to ask. After your standing me up, the fact that you even speak to Jayla anymore is abominable. I tried, but you invited her to my house without my permission, and she didn't have the decency to apologize for stealing my date." I shake my head, disgusted. "Isn't that exactly what Victoria's been doing to me? I was too stupid to realize it then, but I've learned, and some vampy hoe isn't doing that to me again."

"Melanie, I formally apologize for monopolizing your boyfriend, who missed your date," Jayla politely says.

I look to Jayla. "As Adam so eloquently enlightened, I can't leave my soulmate, but I can kick *you* to the curb. Get out of my house." I head inside, leaving dead silence behind.

CHAPTER 33

Here's to the most awkward lunch ever.

I'm at my table, and everyone's eyes keep shifting from me to Trey and Victoria, who are seated at the opposite end of the table. They aren't exactly respected. Having me back at school has forced everyone to face a new normal.

I bury my nose back in my book, frustrated because Demitri ditched our lunch plans. I have no idea where he is, and I'm rather irritated. I flip the page and hear running feet heading our way. I start to rise, ready for trouble. Turns out that it's Jayla and Demitri. Of course they're together. My irritation skyrockets.

The pair get to us, a little winded. "You're not going to believe this!" bursts from Jayla. "I just got to audition for this HUGE show. I got the lead in a duet, AND I just got signed by MS. ALICE."

"Congratulations, Jayla!" Bear says.

"You're absolutely right," I mutter, completely stunned. "I *don't* believe it."

"Per Adam's warning," Stella hisses in my ear, "I saw her race over here with your man and am admitting it, so I don't get splattered."

"Me too," Dante says, rising to his feet as he glares at Jayla.

Jayla bashfully steps farther away from Demitri.

"Mr. Isley sent us," Demitri attempts to clarify. He puts a hand on my shoulder before mysteriously asking me, "How much are you looking forward to *The Sound of Music*?"

"Being a nun isn't on my bucket list, hence why I didn't audition." I reply through gritted teeth. "Why?"

He winces. "I meant to get here sooner, but Mr. Isley called us into an audition."

"For?"

"The *Jazz Extravaganza* show at the Hollywood Bowl. Mr. Isley's the choreographer." Demitri winces again. "Technically, the audition is finished, but Ms. Alice just insisted on seeing you."

My mouth drops open. "My *agent* is here?"

"Yes. She's demanding to know why you didn't audition. Mr. Isley explained that you can't do the Hollywood Bowl gig because it overlaps with *Sound of Music*. You were cast as Liesl."

I double over in disbelief, before leveling Demitri with furious eyes. "My agency contract states that all agency-sanctioned auditions and paid performances take precedence. I didn't even know there WAS an audition! It sounds like my agent believes I'm in breach of contract."

I zip my backpack and storm to the dance building, but Demitri stops me as we get to the doors in the basement.

"Unfuzz me, please," he murmurs. "I want to fix this before we go in there."

I unfuzz him and send, *"You should have backed me when the audition started!"*

"I was as surprised as you are. I'm sorry."

I take a deep breath to get my head on straight. *"Anything else I need to know before Ms. Alice hands me my ass?"*

"All the advanced dancers who aren't in the musical are in there,"

Demitri sends. *"Only Jav, Jayla, and I got cast at the audition, though."*

"Phenomenal." I rush past the locker rooms.

Demitri sighs as he runs to keep up. *"One more thing. He already had me test run 'Cell Block Tango' with Jayla. You're about to be pissed,"* he sends, just as we step into the dance studio.

My heart nearly explodes. Next to Ms. Alice is Molly Horowitz. She sneers nastily when our eyes meet.

"Melanie Slate," a man says, in awe.

"Sir," I respond politely, while my mind spins. Out of the corner of my eye, I see Jayla come in and stand next to Demitri.

The producer gestures to me, asking Mr. Isley, "You told me your most advanced female dancer is Jayla Bethel, but you have Melanie *Slate* in your back pocket?"

"My apologies," Mr. Isley says. "Because Melanie has a lead in our school musical, I didn't have her audition."

"Do you not understand your agency contract?" Ms. Alice fires off my way, while at least twenty dancers, most of whom hate me, are watching this unfold.

"I perfectly understand it," I respond. "I didn't audition for *The Sound of Music*."

Mr. Isley's eyes widen. "You didn't?"

"No."

Mr. Isley rubs his forehead. "I'll talk to Ms. Ferry. The cast list hasn't been released yet. She must have gone ahead and cast you because you were sick and missed the audition."

I wasn't sick. I was dealing with my divorce, and this complicated relationship with Demitri. Being sick was my cover when I forged a note from my mom because she *certainly* wasn't here to write one.

"I want Melanie to audition for 'Honey Rag,'" the producer insists.

"I REFUSE TO DANCE WITH MELANIE," screeches from Molly.

"Why?" the producer demands.

Ms. Alice grabs his arm and hauls him to Mr. Isley's open office. Mr. Isley follows and shuts the door, while I seethe internally. Molly Horowitz and I have a VERY bad history, but it isn't publicly known. The last thing I want is her dropping that bomb in this roomful of people I go to school with. Luckily, she does little more than glare at me while we wait.

The producer, Ms. Alice, and Mr. Isley come out of the office, and Mr. Isley slides huge eyes my way.

"Per agency contract," Ms. Alice clips, "Melanie is auditioning for this show." She glares at Mr. Isley.

"Understood." Mr. Isley looks to me. "I'm going to have Jayla and Demitri demo a duet section of 'Cell Block' for you. Then I'll teach you anything you need clarification on." I have a history of picking up pieces quickly, in his estimation. The truth is, I review the memory as I dance and can pull off little to no rehearsal that way. While it's been great for my career, the process is incredibly stressful, and I'm spun out.

Demitri is rattling as Mr. Isley calls him and Jayla to the center of the room. He blocks off our soulmate connection as Jayla hesitantly joins him while he sits in a chair.

Mr. Isley starts the music, and Demitri and Jayla begin the sexiest bunch of jazz dancing sleaze I've ever seen. "Cell Block Tango" is a blisteringly vampy piece about a bunch of women who are recalling murdering their men for indiscretions. There are certainly indiscretions on display, but the performance world is built of this. I can't get mad at Demitri over it, even though I'm quaking on the inside.

While they rub and gyrate all over each other, I strip off my skirt and tank top, leaving me in one of my new leotards and little dance shorts. I start to pull my heels off, but decide against it, given the nature of this piece.

The music ends, and Demitri sets Jayla down, stepping back from her.

"Melanie, ask your qu—"

I cut off Mr. Isley with a teeth-clenched, "Got it. Roll the music."

Eyebrows rise from the other auditionees, but no one says anything.

Mr. Isley starts the music right before the monologue for the "pop" character. I step forward, while Demitri slouches in the chair. Unlike Jayla, I know the monologue, and start on cue with all the fire and vindictiveness that it requires. It's about a girl who gets irritated with her husband, Bernie, for popping his gum too loud. She lands in jail for putting two bullets in his head.

I put a hand on Demitri's shoulder and developpé my right leg to a 180-degree tilt. I realize too late that I've never done this in stiletto heels, but the line is perfection. Demitri smirks as he watches me in the mirror. I drop that leg and illusion my other leg up and over while gripping the side of the chair, and whip around to straddle Demitri. He grabs my hips, and I roll through a backbend before he clutches my neck. He yanks me up when he's supposed to and kisses me fast and hard where Mr. Isley put it in the choreography. Jayla and Demitri pretended to kiss when they did their dance, but I'm proving a point.

"Holy shit," Mr. Isley mutters.

I fan kick up and around. Demitri grabs my hand, and I counter-balance while I pretend to shoot him twice in the head. My psyche spins with the reminder of what Trey went through. I haven't even begun to deal with him getting shot.

I let my dark-water side ooze up behind my eyes as Demitri rises for the sexy tango section of the piece. We circle each other, radiating character-needed menace, but I'm truly pissed, so this is easy. He siphons off a layer of my seductive dark-water energy for a boost and winks at me. We get through the run, with all the heat and timing right. Our new soulmate connection has made our dance partnering flawless.

"Wow," the producer says as Mr. Isley stops the music. "I know I was supposed to put Demitri with Molly, but . . ." He gestures to me.

"I agree," Mr. Isley says. He focuses on Demitri. "Will you be upset if we switch you to Melanie?"

"Of course not," Demitri responds professionally.

Ms. Alice smiles at him.

"Melanie is a TWO-BIT HACK!" bellows from Molly. "You can't be SERIOUS."

Mr. Isley's eyes narrow. "I've worked with you for many years, Molly," he reminds her. "What I just heard in my office is repulsive. Don't push me right now."

Her eyes narrow. "*I'm* the star of this joke of a show." She gestures toward me. "I'm being cast with rank amateurs."

"Girrrrlllll," Tanner breathes. He has to turn his back so that he doesn't have one of his trademark blowups.

Finley puts a hand on his arm to silently calm him down.

Unfortunately, no one put their hand on my arm, and I can't contain my temper. "Did you just call me a rank amateur?" I growl.

"Fuck you, Melanie," Molly snarls back.

"No, no," I retort. "Fuck *you*." I slowly pan the other dancers. Most of them hate me, but right now, it's us against Molly. They're all fuming on my behalf, and I smirk. My gaze reaches Demitri, and I send, *"Is there anything in this show that I can challenge Molly for?"*

"She's got a solo to 'There'll Be Some Changes Made,'" he sends back.

I turn and flourish my hands. "I'd like to audition for 'There'll be Some Changes Made.'"

"All right," Mr. Isley says, having to duck his head to cover his little smile.

"You aren't serious?" Molly blisters.

"'Black Cat,'" I say to Mr. Isley, ignoring Molly.

He chuckles evilly while he riffles through his CD cases.

"All of you, join at the breakdown," I request of the other dancers, while I pull off my heels and toss them to the side.

My fellow dancers snicker and exchange knowing looks as I get in place and wait for music. Mr. Isley choreographed "Black Cat" for me, but everyone loved it so much that he added them halfway through the piece. It's going to be the finale for our next dance show, and the piece is damn good.

The Janet Jackson song comes on, and I strut to center before launching into the single best dance performance of my life. I'm so angry that I'm rattling, and I channel the energy into my dance ability. Every double turn becomes a quad. Every leap hits six feet. My extensions and timing are flawless.

We hit the breakdown, and the other dancers join. Mr. Isley is booming praise enthusiastically through the whole thing. At the end of the piece, Demitri presses me into an overhead handstand before I slither onto his shoulders and coil my way down his body. I finish draped on the floor, while the other dancers jazz walk away. The room descends into silence as Demitri helps me stand.

"That was unbelievable," the producer breathes, while Mr. Isley and Ms. Alice smirk. "Melanie, you've got the solo." He surveys the other Hollywood High dancers. "That was young and fun. It's in."

Gasps and strained squeals emit as the dancers try to restrain their reactions to getting cast.

"Do these dancers have another group piece we can add?" the producer asks.

"We've got a great piece to Prince's 'Batdance,'" Mr. Isley says. "It has a musical theater storytelling quality, but it's current, edgy, and fun."

The producer beams. "Perfect. Let's put 'Black Cat' and 'Batdance' in, and nix 'Copacabana' and 'Anything Goes.'"

"I'M the lead in those two pieces!" Molly insists.

"Melanie is now headlining this show with you," the producer says.

"This is *bullshit*," Molly howls before grabbing her dance bag and storming from the studio.

"What about 'Honey Rag?'" Mr. Isley asks the producer. He flicks his eyes to me.

"We'll keep Jayla in 'Honey Rag,'" the producer says.

"Thank you for the opportunity to audition," I say professionally.

"Melanie, it's been a pleasure," the producer says. "I'm going to rush some changes to marketing. I need to add you as a headliner. When does your movie officially release?"

"This weekend," I reply.

The producer shakes my hand, before taking his leave.

"Congratulations," Mr. Isley says. "Nice work. You're all dismissed." He looks to me, Jayla, and Demitri. "You three stick around."

While everyone gathers their stuff, Ms. Alice pulls me aside. "I'm sorry that I assumed. I thought you found out Molly was in this show and ran scared."

"I don't run scared," I reply cooly.

"I know," Ms. Alice says. "This was a matter of a whole lot of miscommunication and assumption. I'm proud of you."

"Thank you."

When Ms. Alice leaves, Mr. Isley pulls the door shut and crosses to us. "Jayla, I need to work you through some of 'Honey Rag,'" he says, sounding very unsure of her being in the piece.

"Of course," Jayla says. "Thank you so much for casting me in it."

"The producer cast you in it," Mr. Isley responds, clueing me in that he had little control of this process. He focuses on me. "Melanie, I'm incredibly sorry for how that mess just went down."

"Thank you for casting me," I respond.

"I thought you two," he gestures to me and Demitri, "had rules about distance because Victoria and Trey get so worked up."

I bark a harsh laugh. "Victoria and Trey were having a two-year-long affair. I divorced him. That's why I was absent for a week."

"Holy shit," Mr. Isley breathes. "I'm so sorry, Melanie."

I hit Mr. Isley with a harsh glare. "Demitri and I are dating, hence why the boundaries have shifted."

"So, you're comfortable with the more seductive movement now?" Mr. Isley ponders.

"Not necessarily," I reply, before sliding angry eyes to Demitri.

"I'm sorry I demoed 'Cell Block' with Jayla," Demitri says. "We were paired together for the audition."

"Oh Lord," Mr. Isley groans. "Please don't have an issue with Demitri dancing with other females."

"I don't," I reply cooly. "That's just more assumption on your, Demitri's, and Jayla's part." I take a slow breath. "My ISSUE is that . . ." I pace the studio for a moment to get it together. I fail. I stop by my dance bag, and tears stream down my cheeks now that the pressure is off. I fitfully throw my stuff in my backpack before putting on my skirt, top, and heels. Dressed, I sling my backpack on my shoulder and survey Mr. Isley. "My issue is that I asked my soulmate, mind-to-mind, what pitfalls were waiting for me in this room." It takes me a moment to find my voice again. "He warned me that the dancers who hate me were in here, which I appreciate." I slide traumatized eyes to Demitri. "My question is, why did you add that I'd be pissed that you did 'Cell Block' with Jayla, instead of telling me that MOLLY HOROWITZ was in this room?"

Demitri puts his hands out to the side, flabbergasted. "What am I missing?"

I look to Jayla. "You also knew, but you were so busy bragging about your big chance to rub all over Demitri that you couldn't warn me either, right?"

Jayla's mouth drops open. "Oh my gosh! Melanie, I totally forgot."

"Sure, you did," I disgust back.

"I swear to you," Jayla whispers, aghast. "I would have never failed to warn you if I had remembered!"

"Somebody fill me in," Demitri breathes dreadfully.

Rage burns through me, halting my tears. "Molly Horowitz is the actress who called Franky Fabulous to film her slopping all *over* Zane on *Splash TV*," I inform. "She's the reason I originally lost *Glamour*. I had to fly to New York to get the role back."

Demitri doubles over, putting his hands on his knees. "Oh my GOD!" He stands and pleads with his gaze.

"I think warning me about Molly takes precedence over telling me that you received a horny 'Cell Block' rubdown from Jayla," I say. "That's clearly what you were focused on, though. It's telling."

Demitri frantically shakes his head. "I was so worried about you blowing up about that. I wasn't gloating, and I CERTAINLY wasn't trying to hide that Molly was in this room so you could be blindsided. Melanie, I'm *so* sorry."

"Wasn't Zane supposed to do this show?" I ask Mr. Isley.

"Yes, but I just found out in my office that Zane quit because Molly was headlining with him," Mr. Isley informs. "He won't dance with her. Demitri replaced Zane."

I give Demitri a pointed look.

"I won't partner Molly either," Demitri says.

"That's a serious problem," Mr. Isley argues.

"Now that I remember what she did to Melanie, I want nothing to do with Molly," Demitri says. "I have to defend my soulmate."

I leave while they're distracted. As the door closes behind me, I hear Mr. Isley ask, "You and Melanie have a soulmate connection?"

I round the corner and stop in the hall across from the locker room. I double over, sobbing again. I just almost lost my agency contract, was told off by Molly at school, and I'm positive Demitri and Jayla have something secretly going on.

"Melanie," Trey says softly. His hand lands on my back, and I cry harder. "Tanner just told me what happened, and I came to find you."

I look up at him, and see that Tanner and Finley are also here. "Demitri didn't warn you, did he?" Tanner asks.

Trey helps me up.

"No," I sob out. "He was too busy worrying about Jayla. I swear to GOD, I'm going to kill her one day! This is a step too far. I can handle being treated like worthless crap by my men, but I can't handle it impacting my professional life."

Demitri rounds the corner with Jayla just as I say that.

"How DARE you!" Trey snarls at Demitri. "You should have warned her."

I take my backpack and tap on our blocked soulmate connection.

Trey drops his side, and I send, *"Would you please handle him? I think I might lose my mind!"*

"Done," Trey says aloud.

I leave to the sound of Demitri rushing my way. I hear Trey say, "If you chase her down, I'll put you through the floor. You and Jayla are scheming, and Melanie DESERVES to walk away."

I stride off campus and quickly walk to Mabel's.

CHAPTER 34

The walk helped clear my head, and I've gutted up to do the unthinkable.

I unlock the suite I need to finish moving out of and stand in the living room, surveying the disaster. I peer into the bedroom and can't believe the mess. My clothes apparently belong to Victoria. Every inch of the floor is covered with my discarded stuff.

I look in the bathroom and wince. It smells like funk. My expression crumples as I see my locket in the sink that's full of dried toothpaste goo. I pick it up and open it. Trey's picture is still inside, with Victoria's picture where mine used to be. I study the engraved *MV* on the outside.

I'm not Melanie Valdez anymore, so I really don't have a use for it, but that's not the point.

I set the locket on the counter as tears stream down my cheeks for a second time today. Trey allowed Victoria to destroy, steal, and violate everything that I own.

I go back into the living room and look around for anything salvageable. Most of my stuff is missing. My copy of *The Road Less Traveled* that my dad got me is still on the bookshelf. I snag it and take one last look at the disaster that now sits in the place that held Trey's and my life.

My hand shakes as I open the door, startling a maintenance man. When I leave the suite, I watch as he finishes unscrewing the name plaque with Trey's and my name and tosses it aside like it's nothing. He delicately unwraps a plaque that says, *Trey Valdez*, and another that says, *Victoria Garcia*. I close my eyes as my heart clenches.

Realizing that I'm leaving with only a book, I feel lost, betrayed, and worthless. I slowly walk down the hall, but stop short at the room I used to share with Trey before we moved to the suite. There's a gold-plated sign that says, *Melanie Slate*, and another below it that reads, *Demitri Cantrell*. I had no idea this was happening. My heart nearly explodes as I turn the key that was left in the lock. I walk in, close the door, and sink to the floor, sobbing as my life falls apart in a room perfectly decorated for me and Demitri.

— —

Demitri is so out of sorts when he enters Mabel's place that I get the warning I was hoping for. I set my pen down on the desk in my office and close my eyes, eavesdropping through the soulmate connection as he surveys the name plaques on our new bedroom door down the hall.

He turns the knob and flips on the light. "Wow," he whispers to himself, feeling as flabbergasted by the surprise as I did.

I didn't really look around before, but now I see through his eyes that the room is transformed into a little piece of us. It hurts knowing I'll be living in the little room again that Trey and I started off in. I'm not ready for any of this, but my life always moves too fast. I don't know how I feel about having a room with Demitri. I had come to terms with losing life at Mabel's. In a lot of ways,

I was relieved. At the same time, Mabel making this special room for us means she cares, and I need that right now.

Demitri studies our colored Laugh-a-Lot Care Bear and Red the Fraggle framed pictures on the wall. There's a fluffy velvet dark-blue bedspread on the bed. He pulls back the bedspread and finds silver satin sheets. *'As often as I was in this room with Melanie and Trey, I never imagined she and I would live here together,'* Demitri thinks. He picks up a framed picture on the dresser of me in a perfect split against his back while he lunges in the Star Shine Grant duet performance last year. He sets it down and crosses to the nightstand that used to be Trey's. He picks up a picture of me in rehearsal, dripping sweat, with my hands on my hips, lost in thought.

I don't remember what rehearsal that was from, but I know that look. I was pondering whether I could do whatever asinine nonsense Mr. Isley had dreamed up for his "Dynamic Duo."

Demitri smiles softly at the picture.

The door opens, and Mabel comes in with a fluffy gray throw blanket that's exactly like my favorite red one. "Hey, kiddo," she says. "Surprise!"

"Hi," he replies quietly. "I'm blown away."

"I'm glad you like it."

"This is amazing," he breathes, looking around. "Thank you."

"You're welcome," Mabel says with compassion. "I figured your other half would be in here surveying the new digs with you."

"I made a big mistake," he admits.

She guides him to sit at the little two-person table, and she takes the other chair. "Fill me in. Maybe I can help."

Demitri spills the Molly drama, and Mabel winces. "Damn."

"I swear I didn't remember about Molly," he insists. "I was such a nervous wreck. I don't want to dance with Jayla. I don't want Melanie to be mad. I certainly didn't want her to miss . . ." He trails off.

"Miss what?" Mabel softly encourages him.

He smiles a little, but it's sad. "Ms. Alice signed me today."

"That's amazing," Mabel breathes. "Oh, Demitri! Congratulations!"

I grimace. I didn't know he was signed.

"It's been my dream since I was four," Demitri says, while he stares at our dance picture on the dresser. "That's what had me so stunned when I ran out to get Melanie. So many things happened so quickly that I couldn't get my head on straight."

"I'm so proud of you," Mabel says.

"Thank you," he says. "I wanted Melanie there so bad. She's the reason I got signed. We've danced together so much that my ability skyrocketed. That's what I told Mr. Isley after Melanie left the studio. He was mortified that he left her out of the audition in the first place."

Mabel blows out a huge breath. "This may get more interesting, I fear."

"Oh God," Demitri groans. "If anything else goes wrong, I really think Melanie might leave me. It's bad enough that she's enlisting Trey's help to corral me so she can run away."

Mabel wobbles her head. "The good news, for you at least, is that Trey's the one she's about to be pissed at."

"Thank God," Demitri groans.

"I went into the suite with the staff, to get Melanie's stuff moved over, and was horrified. Victoria ransacked everything. Melanie's clothes, right down to her underwear, are all dirty and stretched out. I left everything she fouled."

"You have to be kidding!" Demitri squalls.

"The stuff she didn't touch is here," Mabel assures him.

"Everything else has been replaced by me."

I leave my office and make my way down the hall to the room we're apparently sharing now, needing to join them. As I open the door to my new old room, I subtly block Demitri off.

"Hi," Mabel says, aiming for cheerful.

"Hey," I say to Mabel. "This was quite the surprise. Thank you."

"You're welcome," she says with compassion.

I look to Demitri. "Looks like we're sharing an office."

"I thought you two might prefer to be together instead of Demitri continuing to share an office with Victoria," Mabel encourages.

"That works," I reply quietly. "I want as little to do with Victoria as possible."

"I take it you went in the suite?" Mabel asks.

"I did." I look around. "Seems my stuff isn't all missing, after all."

"We packed you up and moved your stuff, so you didn't have to do it." Mabel crosses to my jewelry box, explaining, "We found your black pearl necklace broken. You have a replacement in here." She pulls out a delicate silver locket and smiles as she hands it to me. "I also replaced your locket."

I look at it quizzically. *NB* is engraved on the front. I show Demitri, and his brow furrows.

Mabel grins. "Victoria stole Melanie's engraved locket. So, I made this one. It stands for 'Nobody's Bitch.' That girl can kiss my ass, and yours too."

I crack up and open the locket. Inside is a picture of me on one side and Demitri on the other.

She hugs us and pulls the door closed as she tactfully leaves.

"Today was rough," Demitri says.

"Story of my life," I mutter, while I put the locket in the jewelry box and close the lid.

"This is unreal," Demitri says, looking around.

"Did you know about Mabel making us a room?" I ask.

"No. Did you?"

"No. It was sweet of her, I suppose."

"Melanie, please," he says.

I turn my back to him and open the second drawer. My eyebrows rise when I see the makeup bag, along with bras and underwear, new with tags. I stare at my reflection in the mirror over the dresser. I've stood in this spot, staring in this mirror a million times. I always did my makeup here when I was with Trey.

Demitri drapes his arms over my shoulders and stares into my reflected eyes in the mirror. "After Trey told me off, I went back into the studio and talked with Mr. Isley. He was a panicked mess about how all that went down. I promise that he gets it. He was floored by how you handled that disaster. You were a pro."

"I told Molly to fuck off," I mutter. "I don't think that's very professional."

"She deserved it, and Mr. Isley said as much to me." He squeezes me. "You got away with cussing her out because you backed those words with action. I've been mesmerized by you every time you dance, but 'Black Cat' was otherworldly today!"

"I was pissed."

Demitri laughs. "Maybe, but you harnessed it and did your job. You proved why you got signed by Ms. Alice."

I wait to see if he mentions that he got signed, but he doesn't. I'm going to wait for him to reveal his big news instead of stealing his thunder.

He turns me around and cups my cheeks. "I'm so sorry for how our relationship has started out. I handled NONE of this right. I want to get to a better place with you."

I scoff. "We haven't worked in a week. There's not time for

another discussion right now. I need to get in a few hours before we leave. My dress is at my house. It'll take time to get ready, and I can't be late."

"For what?" Demitri asks, puzzled.

My shoulders drop. "What is WRONG with you? Seriously?"

There's a knock on the door, and Constance comes in and hands me a garment bag. I hang it on the hook my robe used to go on and unzip it. Out cascades a stunning black beaded dress. I gasp.

"Mabel had it custom made for your big night," Constance says. She hands Demitri a garment bag. "One for you too," she says before leaving and closing the door.

He opens the bag to reveal a classic black tuxedo. "Your movie premier . . . ," he says, the formalwear spurring his memory.

"Indeed," I reply as I grab my keys and head back to the office we now share down the hall, because Demitri has been moved in with me. Demitri follows and surveys our office while I get back to my spreadsheets.

CHAPTER 35

We're an hour into work when someone pounds on the door. Demitri glances up from his rental lists. "Apparently they're home."

I look at my calendar, cross-checking my events list. The knocking gets louder, but I do little more than print a fresh spreadsheet.

Demitri taps his pen on his desk to get my attention.

"Were you expecting visitors?" I send. *"I don't have any on my appointment schedule."*

He laughs at my blasé attitude. *"Yup. I'm expecting two. One is going to screech. The other is going to chainsaw through that wall in a minute and drag you back to your previous cave for a discussion about how Victoria was an epic mistake."*

We're doing better now. I requested that we switch gears from the argument, with the promise that we'd deal with it once my premiere is over. I need to get my head on straight for tonight. He agreed and has done a solid job of being the Demitri he used to be—my best friend, instead of my shit-show boyfriend.

"Are you done with your lists?"

He nods. "We need to get ready."

I grin as I grab my keys and iced tea. We head to the door, which Demitri opens to find Trey and Victoria standing there. Victoria tries to shove her way in, but I throw up an invisible energy wall in the doorjamb. She hits it and rubs her forehead before an odd squalling sound builds in her throat.

I look to Demitri as the sound gets louder. "She's either gonna shed her human skin and skitter around like an alien, or she's a teakettle that's done bubbling."

He chokes on his green concoction.

I grimace. "That nasty drink of yours is gonna kill you one day."

Victoria screams, "Why are you in Melanie's office?"

I answer on Demitri's behalf. "We all apparently have new roommates."

"I'm not roommates with Victoria," Trey defends.

I tip my head and chirp, "Really? Her name is on your suite door."

"WHAT?" Trey charges down the hall.

Victoria follows, and I remove the shield from the door. We pass through and stop at the T-junction in the hall, leaning against the wall to spectate.

When he gets to his suite door, Trey bellows, "MABELLLLLL."

Victoria watches Trey lose it before she shoots death daggers my way.

"Why is Victoria being a bitch to me?" I murmur to Demitri.

"Oh well, you see," he conversates back quietly, "Victoria is likely panicking because Trey isn't into her now." He smiles at me sarcastically. "That's your fault, I'm guessing."

"Huh?" I say, as Trey bellows for Mabel. Any comradery I'd built with Trey again is gone. He let Victoria ransack my belongings, and that's inexcusable.

Mabel strides out of her office. She surveys Demitri and me casually lounging against the wall and laughs. She turns and sees Victoria nervously pacing like a cat in labor while Trey storms Mabel's way.

"Why is Victoria's name on my suite door?" Trey demands.

"Because she apparently lives with you now." Mabel's gaze snaps to Victoria. "Explain why Melanie's clothes were all dirty and scattered on the floor."

Victoria gives her a haughty look. "She left them behind. They're my size and were cute."

"You've never thought Melanie looked cute, and you are *not* a size zero, Victoria," Mabel snarls. "No one steals from another in my home. Now that you've been warned, if you ever so much as touch Melanie and Demitri's *doorknob* without permission, I'll launch your ass out."

Victoria gives her a look. "I don't plan to go in their office uninvited."

"I was referring to you never invading their home," Mabel snarls. "I moved them in together."

Trey's mouth drops open. "What do you mean they moved in here together?"

"You didn't think I'd kick out Melanie, did you?" Mabel chuckles. "You may have replaced Melanie with Victoria, but I'm sure not going too."

"I didn't replace . . ." Trey trails off as he realizes that he did exactly that, but it seems he's not pleased with how that's going.

"Why didn't you stop Victoria from stealing Melanie's stuff, Trey?" Mabel spews venomously.

He clears his throat. "It happened when I wasn't home. I'm not pleased."

With no interest in the argument, Demitri and I head to our room. Just as Demitri pulls my black beaded dress and his tuxedo out of the closet, the door flies open and Victoria storms in, followed by Trey and Mabel. Adam leans against the doorjamb. Apparently, he's joined our jamboree.

"Don't do this Victoria," Trey warns, but it's to no avail.

She hits me with a death glare. "I don't want you to live here!"

Mama Mabel stares at Victoria, aghast. "Last I checked, Melanie's lived here for quite some time!"

"Well, now *I* live here," Victoria snips back, "and I don't want to live with Melanie!"

"I *own* HERE!" Mabel says, exasperated. "You don't get to dictate who lives in my home."

"Humph," comes from Victoria before she slides an exaggerated pout to Trey, who rolls his eyes, clearly fed up.

"Well, Demitri," I say, "shall we move out?"

"Absolutely not," Mabel interjects. She turns blistering eyes on Trey, but she's interrupted.

"She's ruining my liiiife!" Victoria screeches, pointing a perfectly manicured finger in my face.

"How?" Mabel demands.

"Before MELANIE started distracting Trey every chance she gets, we were fine," Victoria cats.

I rattle my head about comically.

"*You* were the one doing the distracting. Melanie was MARRIED to Trey!" Mabel says, attempting to defend me.

"Not much of a marriage," Victoria sasses. She smirks my way. "You have no ideaaaaaa how much he hated you." She rolls her eyes. "Now he suddenly loves you?" She shoots her icy gaze to Mabel. "Melanie put a curse on him, or something."

Befuddlement graces Mabel's face. "Or, and hear me out, Trey lost Melanie and suddenly realized how much he loves her." She nods knowingly.

"Ridiculous," Victoria scoffs.

"This is insane," I send to Demitri.

"Is it ever," he replies aloud, before wincing slightly.

Trey's eyes narrow. "Did you just send a message to him mind-to-mind?"

"Here we go," Adam mutters.

"She did." Demitri answers for me with a careful tone.

I hold my breath, wondering how this is going to go.

"Oh my," Mabel murmurs, having not known.

Trey looks like he's going to pass out.

"What's happening?" Victoria asks him.

"They're soulmate bonded," Trey gasps. "Oh my GOD, what have I done?"

"How DARE you steal Demitri from me!" Victoria shrieks. "He's *MY* SOULMATE."

Demitri looks at her like she's insane. "I begged not to be your soulmate. Melanie's spirit guide removed the bond for a reason."

Victoria balls up a fist, glaring death daggers at me. "Demitri's MIIIIINE!"

"Victoria, stop," Trey barks with alarm, but it doesn't stop Victoria from swinging at me. Trey holds her back.

I gather an energy wave. The lights flicker, and any sense of morality dissolves. Victoria's messing with me on the wrong damn day!

Just before I detonate a death load, Demitri wrestles me back, barking, "Melanie, don't!"

Trey grabs Victoria's arms. "You clearly don't get it! Melanie is lethal."

"You used to say she was a pathetic poser," Victoria lobs back.

"Excuse you?" I bark as hurt mixes with rage.

"I said a lot of things I didn't mean." Trey's clearly torn apart. "I'm sorry."

Adam studies my dejected state before he whips back to Trey. "Victoria's *definitely* worth giving up your soulmate for," Adam roars, gesturing up and down at Victoria. "I mean, DAMN! I get it. Fancy cans and a shitty personality make for a real fairy tale, right, TREY?"

Trey's clearly gutted.

"Don't get that look, Trey," Victoria snarls. "We're FINALLY together! We don't have to hide anymore. We have our whole wedding planned, and I want to set a date."

My eyebrows rise. "Victoria got the privilege of planning my wedding, *and* hers?"

"I'm not marrying Victoria." Trey appears destroyed.

"Seriously, Trey?" Victoria snarks. "That's all you've talked about. Wanting to get rid of Melanie and marry me!"

"Please stop," Trey requests pitifully.

"New plan," Adam says with grave weight while he stares daggers into Trey. "I'm going to beat your ass each time Victoria drops some new shit-talking detail."

"Melanie isn't even your soulmate anymore," Victoria snidely lobs at Adam.

Adam menacingly closes the distance on Victoria, and she shrinks a bit from his furious expression. "My GODDAMN soulmate business isn't your CONCERN!" As Trey starts to move in front of Victoria, primal authority pounds from Adam in waves. "If you defend Victoria, you and I are finally going to have it out."

"Trey's gonna beat your ass," Victoria sasses.

"*Please* stop," Trey says. "Victoria, Adam and I have history you don't understand. I don't want things to escalate with him."

"I strongly encourage you to help him," Adam says to Victoria, "because he's dealing with dying from a gunshot wound, losing his soulmate, and getting shackled with *you*."

"Why are you lumping ME into the bad things that have happened?" Victoria says, sounding offended.

"Because Trey is now aligned with you," Adam says. "He went from Melanie's husband, to being your concubine." Adam shakes his head. "Regardless of what your deranged narcissistic tendencies tell you, that's a hell of a slip down the bragging-rights ladder. Now is your chance to be worthwhile, Victoria. Help your guy get through the hardest time in his life. Maybe then, you can both be redeemed."

"The best thing that could EVER happen to Trey is offloading Melanie on someone stupid enough to take her," Victoria growls. She slides contempt-filled eyes to me. "His words, NOT mine." She smiles leeringly.

"Unbelievable," Adam mutters. He gives Trey a look. "You're in the same boat I am. We're both going to be punished for our girls' unhinged behavior. While I welcome a death, because fuck this lifetime four ways from Sunday, you might not want to become Melanie's latest victim."

"Trey doesn't fear death," I inform, blasé because it's all I've got right now. "Let's hit him where it counts." I slide a no-nonsense expression to Victoria. "I'm your boss, you snide, backstabbing, ungrateful bitch. You're fired."

Victoria's eyes snap wide.

I nod. "Rent for half of that suite you're shacked up in is a thousand a month. Dining privileges are another five hundred." I smile at Trey. "Looks like fifteen hundred is coming out of *your* check every month."

"You can't fire me!" Victoria sasses.

"Actually," Mabel interjects, "*Melanie* is the reason you got the job." She gives Victoria a pointed look. "I didn't want to hire you, but Melanie chose to give you a chance."

Victoria makes an uppity, preening face.

Damn, can she switch tactics on a dime.

"I hate working, and besides, *I* shouldn't have to. I've got a man who adores me. Trey doesn't mind paying for me."

The look Trey swings her way is telling.

"Clearly," Adam mutters condescendingly.

"The only things Trey is loyal to are his freedom and his money," I inform. "You now have no job to take up your time, and no way to pay for yourself." I slide a triumphant expression Trey's way. "The good news is that I'm great with Victoria living here, every day, in *your* suite."

Adam chuckles evilly at Trey's desperate expression. "You wanted Victoria," he reminds Trey. "The only thing you forgot in your little 'leave Melanie' scheme is that your soulmate doesn't go away. She works with you, has all the same friends, lives in your home, AND has a connection to your mind." He snaps on a sarcastically elated grin. "What could go wrong?"

"Well, it certainly sounds like we've come to a very agreeable solution," Mabel chirps brightly, clearly approving of me turning the tables on Trey and Victoria.

Adam grins at Demitri. "How does it feel to be the one Trey offloaded Melanie on?"

"Pretty damn good," Demitri says with a hint of hostile arrogance for Trey. He raises an eyebrow. "Now we're both happy guys."

"You'll regret losing me," Victoria venomously tells Demitri, because somehow, she STILL thinks she's valuable.

After Mabel forces Victoria to leave the room, Trey says to me, "I'm so sorry Victoria ran her mouth. I don't want to marry her, and I NEVER should have discussed wedding plans with her."

I just stare at him.

He swallows hard. "You don't understand how big a mistake I've made."

I don't respond. Instead, I take my formal dress from the hanger.

"Good job not killing Victoria, even though she deserves it," Adam says.

I snort. "Whatever." My head drops. "Thank you for helping with that mess, Adam. Why are you here?"

Adam gives me a confused look before glancing to Demitri. "Just thought I'd swing by?" he says.

It comes out a question instead of a statement, but I let it go because I've had enough frustration for one day.

CHAPTER 36

I can't take the first round of pictures because I have no fancy car to get out of. I'm unsure what to do. Out of nowhere, Mabel's burgundy sparkly limo pulls up.

Jayla pops out first in a red satin formal gown, followed by a mad rush of all the Misfits. "I've never been in a limo before," Jayla squeals to Finley.

Everyone from the Hellcats gathers around us, while I say to Mabel, "A limo ride must have been nice."

Mabel's face drops slack. "How did you get here?"

"In Demitri's Jeep that was in the parking garage." I point to the building next to the Egyptian Theater.

"Melanie, I'm so sorry," Mabel says regretfully. "We wanted to surprise you. I scored tickets for everyone."

My gaze lands on Victoria, and I glare at Demitri. "Did you know about this?"

"I thought it would be a nice surprise, but I didn't know Victoria would be invited." Demitri scans the group. "Or Valerie."

Stella surveys Valerie, having heard so much about her.

Mabel's eyes fly into her hairline. "I'm sorry, Melanie. I invited everyone when they came over on Wednesday."

A black Bentley pulls to the curb, and Zane gets out alone. He spots me and smiles. I smile back, and he raises an eyebrow while holding a hand my way.

"If you'll excuse me, I have work to do," I say, while I wall off my connection with Demitri.

"Is that Zane *Drell*?" I hear Stella hiss.

As I strut to Zane, he does nothing to mask the seductive look he slides down my body. "You're gorgeous, Seashell." He wraps an arm around me, and we pose for pictures in front of his Bentley while camera bulbs flash.

He starts to head to the group, but I stop him. He leans in so I can whisper, "There's a lot you don't know." Through my hand on his lapel, I send him a memory pulse I've carefully crafted to just give the bullet points of what's happened since I saw him last.

He closes his eyes and watches. When he finishes, he snorts. "Victoria's cruisin' for a bruisin'."

"You have no idea," I mutter.

"I'm telling you, Melanie, Demitri is up to something with Jayla."

"That's good news for you, I suppose," I whisper.

"The Molly mess is hilarious," he chuckles out. I give him a look, and he rolls his eyes, still amused. "Cast and crew sit together, and I have no date."

"Sounds like a great plan. Demitri can sit with his guests of honor."

Zane makes a happy little huff. "Shall we show Mabel who she left out of the limo?"

"Yes, please," I reply as I lace my arm through his elbow. We strut past my group.

Zane nods politely. "Nice to see you all again." He smirks at

Trey. "Put some clothes on your date. This is a movie premiere, not the annual LA Porn Awards."

Victoria's cheeks burn crimson.

"I love that your celebrity status automatically shuts down her mouth," I murmur to Zane.

He chuckles.

Zane and I work through photos at various red-carpet spots, as photographers clamor. We head into the theater, but Demitri stops me.

"Hey, I thought we'd walk in together," he says, while the Hellcats make a teen ruckus.

"What do you mean there's no snack bar?" Victoria complains loudly behind us.

"Is that Briana Barker?" Jayla squeals, as the meteoric celebrity saunters by.

Zane leans into Demitri and Mabel. "Melanie's reputation in this industry is directly impacted by who she associates with. You people are making an ass out of yourselves, but also out of her." He levels Mabel with a stern look. "We aren't here for fun. Melanie is the lead actress in this film, that had a fifty-three-million-dollar budget. This red-carpet event ran the studio two million. This is a thriving franchise, and your guests need to behave in accordance. If they can't, then trot their tacky asses back to your brothel where they can behave like animals."

Mabel blushes the most vibrant shade of red I've ever seen. She snaps her fingers, hissing, "Every one of you, listen up . . ."

Zane leads me down the aisle to the section cordoned off for cast and crew. We take our seats only to have the Hellcats and Mabel led by an usher to the row behind us.

Mabel winces, stopping to whisper to Zane and me, "When I reserved seats, I knew the concierge who planned the seating chart. She put us here. I'm sorry." She continues down the row.

To add insult to injury, here comes Mr. Isley, Ms. Ferry, and Ms. G.

Mama Mabel looks over her shoulder at us, seeming very unsure. "I invited them as a surprise."

"Holy crap," I yelp to Zane. "Those are my teachers and school counselor."

Mr. Cantrell makes his way down the aisle next. "Mabel got me a ticket," he informs happily. "I rushed to the airport."

My eyes are huge.

Zane whips around and murmurs to Adam, Trey, and Demitri, "I'd like to know if what you see on screen is how Melanie actually is in the sack." He gives an exuberant thumbs-up as my ears burn so hot that they might melt right off my body.

Dante and his bandmates arrive at the end of the row. Jayla flutters a little, glancing to each side. "Hi," she says, flummoxed.

Dante and I glare at Demitri and Jayla. Naturally, they're sitting together. Demitri grimaces hugely, while Jayla dejectedly melts.

"I'm so sorry I didn't save you a seat," she says bashfully.

"I couldn't possibly expect that," Dante snarls.

"Would you switch with me?" Demitri asks Javier.

"Hell no," Javier blusters back. "I don't want to be eradicated by Melanie for being your wingman."

Adam snorts and gives Demitri a look that drips with judgment.

That five-alarm disaster is interrupted as the lights fade, and the opening flyover of New York City starts. It takes no time before the Broadway show sequence ends and my character and Zane's stop at my dressing room door. My character gives him a look, and he smirks, striding into the dressing room and locking the door. Clothes come off, and things get blisteringly hot on the vanity table. I turn to survey the row behind me, and every mouth is dropped wide. Jayla is peeking through her fingers that are over her eyes.

"Holy crap," Demitri breathes.

"That's what she's like, all right," comes from Trey, earning a smack from Victoria.

I glance toward my teachers and counselor. Ms. G is grinning from ear to ear while she watches. Mr. Isley has his hands over his ears with his eyes closed, while Ms. Ferry appears to be analyzing my naughty performance. I wince as I sneak a peek toward Mr. Cantrell. His eyes are the size of satellite dishes.

"I'm going to die of shame," I mutter to Zane while I bury my head in his shoulder.

We get lost in the movie for a while as Zane's character starts his affair and works through his tawdry dealings. I subtly look at Demitri and Trey. Trey has tears in his eyes while Demitri's face is slack. We hear sniffles throughout the theater as my character's husband poorly defends himself.

Knowing that my "Erotica" scene is coming up, I panic internally and lean into Zane, who puts an arm around my shoulders. I swallow hard, and we watch as I follow Zane to the hallway, unzip, and drop the dress.

"Holy crap," Tanner hisses.

I bury my head in Zane's chest, and he rubs my shoulder with his thumb, whispering, "You're okay." When the song ends, I look up at him. He's surveying my people.

"That! That's what she's like," Adam whispers.

Valerie glares daggers at me.

Jayla's staring at me like I'm an exotic animal. I turn back to the screen, lost in thought about Demitri and Jayla, while Zane's and Rachelle's characters continue their romping affair.

When we get to the dramatic drug scene, I nervously perk,

wondering how the work I did will be received. My character breathes, "Finally," before falling in slow motion, and I think, *If only.*

I look at Trey, and he has tears streaming down his cheeks. Demitri is staring at the image of my dead body like he might lose his mind. He inhales sputteringly. Adam's expression is more stoic. He's no stranger to my deaths, but there's sadness in his eyes.

The Jefferson Airplane song "White Rabbit" starts, and Zane tears up next to me as his character runs down the hall and sees my dead body. As he looks down at his wedding ring on the screen, the first tear slides down Zane's cheek in reality. I delicately wipe it away.

Zane offers a sad smile. "Your guys don't know what they have," he whispers as the lights come on.

"Is that what people do?" Jayla blathers while she stares at the blank screen in shock.

Demitri chuckles before offering Jayla a compassionate expression. "That's not for everyone, Jaybird."

Jayla studies Zane before saying to me, "You hang out with millionaires, kill people, get married . . . Is there anything you can't do?"

I nod. "I can't go anywhere without looking over my shoulder. I can't sleep at night without night terrors. I can't hang out with a friend and giggle." I gesture to the screen. "I can't have a private sex life."

"Would you like go to the mall with me?" Jayla unexpectedly asks.

"What?"

"The mall?" Jayla smiles softly. "We could get smoothies while we shop." She looks to Demitri. "Would you and Dante come with us?"

"Done," Demitri says. He smiles at me. "This time, I'll rent a limo."

I raise an eyebrow. "I'm not taking a limo to the mall."

Zane grits his teeth in a compassionate wince Demitri's way. "Missed the boat on that one." He smiles at me. "Cut him some slack. Most seventeen-year-old guys aren't dating an A-lister. I'll buy you a Bentley for events."

I roll my eyes. "You aren't buying me a Bentley. I'm not an A-lister, Zane."

"Uh-huh," he replies.

I give Demitri a catty look. "As we discussed a few days ago, I don't like the mall." I side-eye Jayla before smirking at Demitri. "Jayla does though, so you agreed?"

Demitri rolls his eyes.

"We need to get to the after-party," Zane interrupts. "We have a dance introduction, and then you're singing."

"You are?" Demitri asks, sounding pleasantly surprised.

I nod timidly.

CHAPTER 37

"Introducing Zane Drell and Melanie Slate, stars of *Glamour*."

When I hesitate at the raucous applause, Zane puts a hand on my back. He plasters on a bright smile and guides me through the door. Spotlights hit us and I smile, attempting to work my sequined dress like I've got some clue what I'm doing.

Zane sweeps me around as "Damn I Wish I Was Your Lover" by Sophie B. Hawkins starts. As the end credit song, it summarizes the vibe of the movie. Unfortunately, it also summarizes Zane and me. I give in to the improvised dance piece, knowing we have an audience and don't have actual choreography.

I get so lost in dancing with Zane that I don't realize it's ending until Zane dips me low and whispers, "I love you, girl."

He guides me to my feet as applause rings out. We bow, and Zane escorts me back to my friends. Before anyone can say anything, a man sweeps up.

"Steve, nice to see you," Zane greets him.

"You too. Hell of a movie." Steve smiles my way. "Introduce me to your starlet."

Zane grins. "Melanie Slate, meet Steve LaFron."

"Nice to meet you."

"The pleasure's mine," Steve says with a little too much flirtation. When Zane shifts his hold to subtly pull me closer, Steve nods. "Got it." He smiles at Zane. "I need a dance couple for a commercial. You two appear to be a dance couple."

Zane chuckles. "Negotiate it with Ms. Alice."

"Nice to meet you, Melanie," Steve says before walking away.

"Who was that?" I ask Zane.

"Trust-fund millionaire shithead who owns the LeFron fragrance line. I guarantee it's a commercial for his Electricity perfume and cologne line. He tends to hire celebrities."

"Never heard of the perfume."

"It's what I wear," Victoria says, disgusted.

"Phenomenal," I grunt, looking to Zane.

He chuckles. "I did his commercial for his men's cologne line called Flex. I pulled a hundred thousand just for taking off my shirt and leaning on a pull-up bar after some chick sprayed me down with a water bottle, so I looked sweaty in a gym."

I laugh while the Misfits gape at Zane.

Ms. Alice comes over. "You're each guaranteed a hundred thousand if you'll dance for the pervert."

"What's the wardrobe?" Zane asks, while my friends nearly fall over from shock.

Ms. Alice sighs. "Black boxer briefs for Zane. Black pushup bra and underwear for Melanie."

I grin at Zane. "I get to wear clothes!"

Zane cracks up at my friends' even more aghast expressions. "Underwear and a bra might as well be a trench coat at this phase of her career."

"This *phase* of her career?" Mabel looks baffled. "She just started."

Zane shrugs. "She didn't exactly get eased in."

"This LaFron guy has lost his mind," Victoria sasses, earning exasperated looks from all my friends. "What?" she hacks. "Melanie sucked in that movie."

Tanner rattles his head, but his rebuttal is cut short as the director says over the speaker system, "Your attention, please." We turn toward the stage, and the director is practically hopping with excitement. "*Glamour* has been nominated for best picture for the OSCARS!"

My eyes nearly bug out of my head. I look up at Zane, and he's smirking.

The director flourishes our way, and a spotlight hits us. "Zane Drell has been nominated for BEST ACTOR!"

Deafening applause fills the air.

"AND, in her very first movie, Melanie Slate has been nominated for BEST ACTRESS!"

I'm in such a state of shock that I don't hear everyone cheering, but I see them. The rush of blood clears from my ears just as Zane picks me up and spins me around. He plunks me down and grabs my hand, dragging me to the stage. We join the director, and the place goes wild. I'm in a daze as we take pictures.

The director hugs me. "Hell of a job, girl!" He shakes his head, forlorn. "I'm kicking myself for killing off your character. The third installment of the franchise won't be the same without you, but that death scene is going to win you an Oscar."

I'm so overwhelmed I can't think.

"Melanie, places, please," comes from a production assistant by the side of the stage.

I take a deep breath and slide nervous eyes up to Zane.

"Remember, sing from here." He puts a flat hand on my stomach. "You've got this."

He leaves the stage, and the production assistant rushes the band up the stairs. I grin as the surprise I arranged is revealed.

The producer says into the microphone, "Melanie Slate and the band Diablo."

Dante grins at me, while my group of friends on the other side of the room appear astounded. "I'm so freaking PROUD of you, Melanie," he whispers in my ear.

"An Oscar nomination?" I whisper back.

He nods. "You're the real deal, girl. You ready?"

"Fire it up."

"I wish we had rehearsed," he whispers back.

"Your band is good, and apparently I'm good." I smirk. "It'll be good."

Diablo starts the pounding intro of Joan Jett's "I Hate Myself for Loving You," a song in keeping with the theme of the movie, and my life. The beat kicks, and I clap in front of the microphone while I dance. Dante smiles viciously at my vibe. I start the lyrics, and the audience erupts.

Dante's electric guitar solo hits, and I body roll down his side. He leers, no longer sweet Dante. He's a different person onstage, and I see why girls chase these guys. They're electric. I spin around and snatch the microphone from the stand. I get through the next set of lyrics, and judging from the crowd's reaction, we're killing it.

I hold the microphone between us, and when we get to the vocal breakdown, Dante lets his guitar hang as he leans in to sing with me. He drapes an arm around my waist, and I melt against him while he stands like the rock star he is and gives me a dominant look.

When it's time for my vocals, Dante grabs the neck of his electric guitar and wails. I belt from the gut. We take the song home, and on the last note, I drop my head. As the crowd goes wild, we take a bow.

I put the microphone on the stand, and Dante says into it, "Melanie Slate."

The crowd cheers.

"Diablo, everyone." I gesture to the band and introduce each member, earning raucous applause.

They fire up their version of Ram Jam's "Black Betty." The dance floor fills as I strut back to my group.

Zane hugs me and sweeps me off my feet. "Yes, you did, Melanie fucking Slate."

I grin. "I pulled it off?"

"Girl," Zane says softly, setting me down. "Yes, you pulled it off."

"I didn't know you sing for rock bands," Jayla says, sounding unsure.

"I don't." I shrug. "I sang some in the movie."

Jayla looks to Dante, who's currently proving to be all the things that he is onstage.

I follow her gaze and compliment, "He's a beast." Jayla's huge eyes shift to me, and I murmur, "Your little 'mall-going' act is bullshit." I hit her with blistering eyes. "Screw Demitri again, and I'll do Dante."

"It's really not like that," she murmurs back frantically as huge tears well on her lashes. "Please, Melanie. We're friends!"

"Are we done with Melanie's talent show yet?" Victoria snarls, interrupting.

"Can it, Tori." Trey smiles at me. "You just killed that song. I . . ." He drops his head. "I'm newly impressed."

Demitri's arms drape over my shoulders from behind as Diablo starts Motley Crue's "Home Sweet Home." "If you all don't mind, I'd like to dance with my girl now." He guides me to the dance floor. The song has a slow intensity, and Demitri leads me through an intricate footwork pattern we've done before. "What's up with you and Dante?" he asks.

"Just performing."

"Seems you two vibe."

I laugh. "You're surprised that my vibe vibes with an electric guitar player?" I wobble my head. "Also, Jayla needs to learn to back off. If she comes for you, I go for him."

"Devious," Demitri says.

I shrug. "I'm not stupid."

He gives me a pleading look. "Please give her a chance, Meley. She's so excited about the mall tomorrow, and all starstruck by you. I swear that you don't need to hump Dante to make a point. Jayla knows her place."

"I'm not going to the mall with her."

"It'll be fun," Demitri encourages. "I'm sorry I agreed to it, but I really think it might help you see that Jayla and I are just friends."

"So?" I ask hopefully.

"So, try with her."

I step back.

Demitri reaches for my hand, and I step back again. "What, Melanie?" he asks.

"Sooooo, you were amazing in your movie, Meley," Zane sarcastically coaches Demitri.

Demitri's face drops slack. "Melanie. You really were—"

His compliment is cut off as Zane spins me around before dancing me away from him. "What a douche."

I open my connection with Demitri just enough to eavesdrop as his dad joins him.

"What happened?"

Demitri sighs. "I apparently spent too long talking about Jayla, and it pissed off Melanie."

"Jayla?" Mr. Cantrell says, baffled. "Who gives a damn about Jayla? I mean, don't get me wrong, she's sweet, but . . ." I see through Demitri's eyes as Mr. Cantrell gestures my direction.

"I know. Melanie thinks I've got something going with Jayla."

Mr. Cantrell laughs sardonically. "Based on what I just saw in that movie, you'd be an absolute embarrassment to mankind if you chose Jayla over Melanie." He raises his eyebrow. "Damn!"

"I agree. A lot happened while you were gone."

I close the connection subtly and smile up at Zane. He smiles back before getting me in a firm stance and spinning us rapidly to the right. I squeal happily and he laughs.

The song ends and I slump. "I should get my idiots out of here."

Zane ponders nervously. "Can I drive you home in the Bentley? Proper exit for a movie star."

"That's so thoughtful, but I should take the Jeep route. It'd be shallow if I ditched my date for a fancy car ride."

"It would," Zane says. "You aren't that girl."

"I wish I were." I look up at him. "How's therapy going?"

"Really good," he replies. "I'm getting what I need."

"I'm proud of you."

Zane smiles the sweetest smile. "Thank you, Melanie." He crinkles his nose. "We're winning those Oscars."

"You think?" I ask, unsure.

"I'm positive," he replies. "The producer called me right before I pulled up to tell me about the nominations. I analyzed the movie from that perspective while I just watched it. I think we've got this."

"That would be unreal," I reply. "I'm not getting my hopes up, though." I squeeze his hand. "Good night, Beastie Boy."

"Good night, Seashell," Zane replies sadly. He hates goodbyes.

I head back to my group. Silence greets me. Valerie rolls her eyes, pissed. Victoria is in a rancid mood. My teachers are looking at me with concern. My girlfriends seem to feel awkward, and their boyfriends are keeping quiet.

"Um . . ." I finally settle with, "Thanks for coming." I look up at Demitri. "Think we could head out?"

He nods. I hold my hand his way, but dazed, he just starts walking.

I follow awkwardly. We step out of the building, and I see a photographer from earlier. *I need to fix this.* My fit about Demitri defending Jayla was unfounded. I was just feeling insecure because he hadn't complimented the movie. It's another old bad habit of mine that I need to mindfully work on. "Sir, could I get a picture with my boyfriend?" I ask the photographer.

"Of course, Ms. Slate," he replies.

Demitri smiles the most genuine smile I've ever seen. "Really?"

"Sure! We're all dressed up."

"I'd like that," he says, seeming hopeful with my shift.

I take his arm, guiding him to the red carpet, and we pose for the photographer.

"Who's next?" the photographer asks, and that's when I realize my whole group is watching.

"I'd love a picture with my kids." Mr. Cantrell joins us. We smile and pose.

"Well, hellfire, I didn't even think about getting a picture," Mabel says. "I want one with Melanie. It's not every day that one of my kids is a movie star." She comes to me and poses.

Tanner snaps in a zigzag. "I look too damn good not to have a picture on that red carpet."

He and Finley come to me and pose, and then I get out of the way for them to have a couple's picture. This goes on until all the couples, and so many combinations of people get their shots. Everyone behaves, and it turns into a fun adventure.

"All together," the photographer says, and we all gather up, smiling.

As everyone clears, I ask, "Adam, Demitri, and Trey, think we could take one together?" When they all appear amused, I shrug. "All those lifetimes maybe deserve a photo."

The guys join me, to the irritation of Victoria and Valerie. That added bonus brightens my mood. Adam gets behind me, with Trey and Demitri on either side. I put my hands out to the side and shrug.

The photographer snaps the picture and grins. "That was adorable."

Trey squeezes the blazes out of my hand. He lets go and knocks on our soulmate blockage as he walks with the group toward the street. I open it, and he sends, *"I've never been prouder of you. I was wrong to try to stop you from doing that movie. I'm sorry I dampened the excitement when you got the role."*

"I'm sorry it was so graphic, Trey."

"You're a hell of an actress."

"Thank you. Good night."

Trey sends, *"Good night,"* as he loads into the limo.

It pulls away, and I'm left standing there with Demitri. "Well, there's that."

"An Oscar nomination," Demitri says in awe while he gazes at me. "I don't think anyone even knows what to say. My dad had to hold me up when it was announced. My knees went out on me."

I shrug, unsure. "I certainly didn't expect it." I wince. "Are you mad now that you've seen the movie?"

"Hell to the NO," Demitri exclaims. "Holy shit, Melanie. That death scene!"

"I tried."

Demitri's expression sobers while he strolls with me down the red carpet toward the street. Mabel's limo unexpectedly pulls up to the curb again.

Trey jumps out while the windows roll down and heads pop out. "Keys," he requests.

Demitri appears confused, and Trey says, "Give me your Jeep keys, and tell me where you parked."

"Fourth floor of the garage behind the theater," Demitri informs him, confused.

Trey smiles at me. "Get your ass in that limo."

"Really?" I ask with a hopeful lilt.

Trey nods with a soft expression. "Really."

I look to the limo, unsure. "They all hated the movie, Trey," I murmur.

"No, they didn't. You should have heard them when we got in there." He grins. "Mabel told them to behave, and they were trying not to act like a bunch of high school idiots."

Demitri fist-pounds Trey. "Thank you for this."

Trey snaps twice while gesturing to the open window. "Out, Tori!"

"I'm not riding in Demitri's Jeep when there's a limo," she squawks.

"OUT, HOMEWRECKER!" Tanner screams.

"We should have just gone in the Jeep," I mutter to Demitri, while the squabble escalates.

Finally, everyone in the limo bellows, "GET *OUT*, VICTORIA!"

Victoria flounces out. To my surprise, she's followed by Adam, who guides a fuming Valerie from the limo.

"Mind if we catch a ride back to Mabel's with you?" Adam asks Trey.

Trey fist-pounds Adam, and they drag their pissy girls with them.

Demitri guides me to the limo and shuts the door. When I look at him, confused, he chuckles and opens the door for me again. "I'm not about to have my girl enter Victoria's open door."

I giggle back. "I assure you, I want zero to do with Victoria's open door."

Tanner crows, "Smooth D," before adding, "We all saw your open door in that movie."

The whole limo laughs, while I defend, "You did NOT! There are union rules. No boobs. No open doors. I'm a minor."

"That wasn't minor," Marcus compliments. "That was major."

"Thank you," I shyly say, while Demitri and I take a seat.

"Seriously, Mel," Arch says. "That was a MOVIE movie. That was like, a *movie*."

"An OSCAR?" Bear crows.

I give him a look. "A nomination. I'm not going to win an Oscar."

"Actually," Bear replies with his most serious tone, "I think you might. That death scene deserves an Oscar."

"Thank you."

"Zane DRELL kissed you!" Stella blathers.

I quirk my mouth. "He isn't Zane DRELL. He's Zaney."

Girly squeals emit.

I shake my head, amused. "Just part of the job."

"It's Zane Drell," Deb insists. "He's not like a *guy*." She gestures around to the guys.

"Hey, now," Drake, Deb's fiancé, says, offended.

Deb flops a look his way. "She kissed *Zane* Drell. Come on, Drake."

I roll my eyes. "He's a normal person. So am I."

"I don't know," Darren says. "What we just watched wasn't normal." He grins. "It was phenomenal."

"Hey, Seashell," Zane unexpectedly says.

I whip around, realizing he likely heard all this stupidity. "Hi, Zaney," I reply, as he kneels by the open window next to me.

Zane leans in, cups my cheek, and delicately pecks me on the lips. He pulls back and grins. "Congratulations on the nomination. Love you, Mighty Mouse."

"Love you too, Helicopter Hottie." I giggle at my friends' stunned teen reactions.

Zane levels Demitri with blistering arrogance. "Watch your back, pretty boy." He extricates himself from the window, and belts laughter while we drive off.

"Holy CRAP!" Presley bellows. "You just *kissed* Zane DRELL."

Tanner stares at Demitri slack-jawed. "Zane just threatened you, dude."

Demitri takes a shaky inhale. "Melanie, do you want to explain that kiss?"

"Surely you aren't threatened by Zane Drell. He's just a regular guy."

Eyes widen in the limo. Demitri's jaw tightens.

"A regular GUY?" Tanner bellows. "He's a millionaire hottie!"

"How do you know the most famous young actor in the world so well that you have nicknames for each other?" Stella asks.

"Zane was Pierre's best friend. We met in Hawaii when I filled in for his dance partner, who got injured. Pierre died, and we planned his memorial together. We vibed, and he got me signed as his partner at the Alice Agency."

Stella's mouth plummets open. "When I heard we were going to a movie, I couldn't figure out why we had to dress up. You're a big freaking deal, and I had no idea."

"I'm no one, Stella. We established that the other night."

CHAPTER 38

I look in the mirror and admit that my leather pants, tight black crop top, and high-heeled motorcycle boots look harsh, but I'm faced with my first Saturday living with Trey and Victoria. This group "living together" debacle is going to be a mess. Last night was awkward when we all got home.

Demitri raises an eyebrow but doesn't comment. We head down the hall to the parlor, where we find an irritable Trey. Victoria's already bitchy.

Randall, Mama Mabel's chef, walks out with two plates. He hands one to me and the other to Demitri. I stare down at the scrambled egg-white, spinach, and sliced cherry tomato glop, and make a curiously unsure face.

Demitri raises an eyebrow. "I ordered breakfast for us. Clearly, I chose the wrong thing."

"She eats like a long-haul trucker," Trey gleefully informs.

I make a childish face at Trey, as Demitri asks, "All the time?"

Trey grins. "Her four main food groups are pizza, cake, tequila, and cigarettes."

I can't help but laugh. "I quit smoking, and you know it." I wobble my head. "With the exception of when Adam's around."

"So sorry." Trey turns to Demitri. "Insert burritos in cigarette spot until she gets stressed and lights up again."

I raise my eyebrows. "Burritos *are* good. You can have them for breakfast, lunch, and dinner." I joke to Demitri, "Don't worry, we can put salad and flavorless chicken in one for you and call it a wrap."

Demitri chuckles. "I rarely eat carbs. Now that I think about it, the only time I break that rule is with you. I thought you were breaking the 'no carb rule' also."

"Oh noooooo. You've got me allllllll wrong."

Randall comes back out of the kitchen with two croissant sandwich plates and hands them to Trey.

Trey passes one on to me. "I was in the kitchen when Demitri intercommed in your breakfast order. Knowing that wouldn't work, I had Randall make your favorite egg sandwich."

I glance from one plate to the other and sheepishly hand the egg-white mess back to Randall. I inform Demitri, "It was very thoughtful of you to order me food. Thank you." I roll my head around comically because this is complicated. "Thank you also, Trey."

"How are you going to eat that and manage a two-hour rehearsal with Mr. Isley?" Demitri asks.

"She didn't get an ass like that eating rice cakes," Trey quips.

I glare at Trey, and he smirks.

"Did you order me breakfast?" Victoria asks Trey.

"Nope. I want you out of my suite, Victoria!"

Victoria is rendered speechless.

Trey plunks down on the love seat that was always ours and clicks on the TV. He scrolls, stopping on an episode of *I Love Lucy*.

Victoria plops down with a grimace. "I hate these old shows."

I laugh. "That's his favorite TV show. He watches it all the time."

Appearing frazzled, Arch comes through the door with Javier. "We need you. Now."

I scrunch up my face. "Good morning to you too."

"Good morning. We need you, NOW!"

"What's wrong?" Trey asks.

"Perfect," I mutter. "Trey can deal with this. I want to enjoy my day."

"We have plans," Victoria snarls at me.

"Stella's missing," Javier barks.

"Not anymore you dooooooon't," I singsong at Victoria, before flopping my gaze to Javier. This is the last thing I want to deal with, but that's always how it goes. "When did she go missing?" I ask.

"I talked to George," Javier says. "She didn't make it home from the movie premiere. He's searched everywhere for her."

I turn to Trey. "Get Intel on it. I'll call George and get him over here."

We take off running down the hall. I unlock my office door, grab the cordless phone, and dial George's number while I wrench open the French doors separating Trey's office from mine. George is on the phone. Victoria, Demitri, Arch, and Javier rush through Trey's door as I hang up.

When George doesn't answer, I dial Big Joe's cell, and he picks up right away. "Big Joe, we need you now. Stella's missing. We can't get in touch with George."

"I'll be there in ten minutes. I'll get Mercury and Stealth to meet me there." He hangs up.

"Big Joe, Stealth, and Mercury are on the way," I inform.

Trey nods. "Intel's on this."

"Call Officer Striker," I request.

"No police yet," Trey says. "We don't know what this is about."

My intuition flares, and I unfocus my eyes while I study it. I spin the information bubble.

Demitri hovers in the back of my mind, watching my process. When I'm done, he asks, "It hurts that bad when you get an intuitive pulse?"

I chuckle. "If that bothered you, be ready for a near heart attack when a big one hits. That was just a warning pulse." I ask him, "Will you grab my cell phone? It's on your nightstand."

"Why?"

"Because it's going to ring," I say, exasperated.

He rushes from the office, and Trey shakes his head. "Rookies." He looks at me. "Demitri isn't cut out for this."

"Your blow-up doll is?" I gesture Victoria's way. Victoria starts to chime in, and I bark, "Shut up, Tits-Magee."

Demitri hands me my phone, saying, "Okayyyyy."

Mama Mabel, Big Joe, Stealth, and Mercury all pile in.

"We need to shift to the conference room," I order.

We all file into the conference room, taking seats. Javier puts his head in his hands and looks like he's going to be sick.

"Who would want to take Stella?" Mabel asks.

Big Joe blows out a big breath. "Stella's dad runs the Raptors. They're a rather tame group that fly under the radar. George doesn't have any enemies that I know of."

My cell phone rings, and I answer, putting it on speaker. "Hello," I growl. My intuition tells me this is trouble calling.

The voice on the other end is female. She sounds young as she asks, "Is this La Diabla?"

My jaw clenches. "Yes. Who's this?"

"Chipmunk."

I snort sarcastically. "Give the phone to someone that's not a woodland creature. It's been a long week, and I just can't."

"You listen here, bitch," the girl snaps at me with her squeaky little voice. "You'll talk to *me*!"

I close my eyes and let my dark-water side slide to the surface. When I open my eyes again, they're filled with evil. "No, *you* listen here, BITCH! Where's Stella?"

Chipmunk squeaks. "Holy crap! You talk to her?"

A bunch of voices start arguing about who's willing to talk to me. It's obviously a group of teens. Intel slides through the door and hooks my cell phone up to a handheld machine.

As their argument stretches out, I whisper to Intel, "Do they have to be talking to me for you to get what you need?"

He shakes his head. "No. I just need a solid three minutes of the line open so I can track where they're calling from."

I rattle my head comically as they continue arguing.

Trey checks his watch and mutters, "A minute and a half to go."

I tap my foot and wait, while Intel watches his machine.

"She can't be that tough!" a guy says. His voice is suddenly clearer as he asks, "La Diabla?"

"Where the hell is Stella?"

"You sound hot!"

Intel motions for me to keep talking.

I huff and flirt terribly. "What's your handle?"

"Destroyer," he proudly announces.

"Seriously?" I ask, miffed.

"That's what I'm going to do to you when I get my hands on you!"

Intel gives me a thumbs-up.

"I look forward to draining your life force and watching you *writhe* while you die," I snarl. "Challenge accepted." I hang up.

"Was that necessary?" Demitri asks.

"Yes. I want to enjoy my day. Brevity!"

Trey laughs.

Intel plugs a cable into Trey's security computer and inserts it into the gadget he used to trace the call. He surveys the monitor and pulls up several pages. As he scans down with his finger, his eyebrows rise. "The call came from Northridge."

"They're holding her hostage in the VALLEY?" I baffle. "How menacing."

Intel looks to Big Joe. "The phone line belongs to David Lark."

"Shit," Big Joe mutters. "He was second in command. Looks like we're dealing with a revenge scenario for the death of the Jags."

"Why Stella?" Javier fearfully asks.

"Because she's become friends with the Hellhounds," Trey pieces together.

"She's close with you guys?" Big Joe asks.

I nod. "She started at Hollywood High, and we took her in."

"This is because of her connection with *you*?" Javier asks me accusingly.

"Your girlfriend's FATHER oversees a BIKER CLUB!" I boil back, sick of Javier at this point. "Stella told us the day we met her that she hangs with the biker kids."

Overlooking reason, Javier doubles down on his irrational anger. "I don't want to be a part of this," he bites back, "and I'll be damned if Stella deals with your bullshit."

I nod. "Cool. I'm not involved. You fix it."

Javier's mouth drops open.

"Let's go," Big Joe groans, knowing we must head up the rescue attempt.

When we start to troop out, Victoria struts to the front of the group and gets next to me.

I stop and give her a nasty look. "Where are you going?"

"I'm not letting Trey go into some battle, where he gets to bond with you while he saves your pathetic ass AGAIN!" she barks at me.

I pan my offense to Trey. "Last I checked, I saved *you* from death."

"I'm aware," Trey replies, seeming worn-out already.

Considering that it's only been eighteen hours since I've been back, and Victoria and I have just gotten started, I'm amused.

Trey slides fed-up eyes to Victoria. "You're staying here, Tori."

"I'm not," she insists angrily.

"Just a thought," Arch interjects with light sarcasm. "Bikers don't like overbearing bitches. Perhaps she *should* come with."

"Might get her killed," Demitri adds, grinning at me.

"Fine," I snap. "If nothing else, it'll annoy Trey." Satisfied with that, I start walking again. I get to our room and shove the door open to grab my stuff.

Demitri follows me in. "What are we walking into?" he asks.

I shrug. "Who knows?"

"What's my role in all of this now?"

"Stay out of my line of fire and wait it out no matter how scary it gets," I coach. "You have a direct line to my mind, but you need to learn to decipher the difference between panic and rage. You'll figure it out."

"I don't like this, Meley. I can't stand back and watch you get attacked."

"You have no choice," I inform him, while strutting through the hall into the parlor. I check the time on my pager. "We have rehearsal in two hours. We'll make this quick." I stalk out of Mama Mabel's and hop into Demitri's black Jeep.

Intel runs up and hands us a slip of paper with an address.

I tip my head. "Huh. It's right by Northridge Mall. Wanna

reschedule with Mr. Isley for later this evening and go shopping after? I need to replace a bunch of clothes that Victoria stole."

"You want to rescue a kidnapped teenager, possibly kill people, and then go shopping?" Demitri asks.

"Is that weird?"

He laughs and pulls out of the parking lot behind Intel. "I'll let Jayla and Dante know."

"I don't want them to come shopping."

Demitri gives me a look. "She's so excited about this, Melanie."

"Too bad. I need space from her." I make a childish face while I mimic her saying, "I've never been in a limo before."

Demitri sighs as he dials Mr. Isley to push our rehearsal back.

CHAPTER 39

Intel parks a few blocks away, but I tell Demitri, "Just park in front of the house. I'm not hoofing it."

He continues the few blocks to the house and parks. "Please be careful, Melanie."

I meet his worried gaze. "Whatever we're walking into can't be worse than what I've already faced."

We get out of the Jeep as the rest of our friends' cars pull up. Stealth jogs our way and says sternly, "We never park in front of the place we're headed."

I bobble my head. "Yeah, yeah, I know, but I wasn't up for the trudge. I want to get this over with so I can go shopping."

Stealth cracks up. "You're going shopping after this?"

I shrug.

Our friends have all gathered, and Javier looks panicked. "That's Stella's car!" He points to her little black Geo Metro.

I give him a look. "It's entirely possible that she's just hanging with friends."

Javier shakes his head. "She isn't. Stella ditched all of them when she became friends with us." Now that we're here, some of his bravado has worn off. "I'm sorry I was mean to you, Melanie."

"I'm getting Stella back," I assure him.

Javier's face pinches. "I love her. I'm worried sick."

"I know." I face the house. Pop music is blasting, and a lot of cars seem to be around.

"I'll do recon," Stealth says.

I shake my head. "Anyone over the age of eighteen needs to stay here by the cars. The phone call sounded like a bunch of teenagers, and we'll be less conspicuous." I scan our group. "We slip in, locate her quickly, and sneak her out. If there's trouble, make a run for it. I'll deal with any energy workers who become an issue."

Everyone nods, and we traverse the walkway. I gesture for Victoria, who came despite Trey's objections, to move to the front of the pack. "Sounds like there's a party. Get us in, Jiggle Wiggle Fun."

"Why aren't *you* getting us in?"

I smirk sarcastically. "You insisted on being here. That means you're required to be useful. I've decided you're the trashy cannon fodder. Hop to it."

She rolls her eyes and rings the bell. We all tense, ready for a fight. When the door opens, the guy wanders off without a word.

"Well, all right," Trey mutters.

Cautiously, we slink into the house. The place is overrun with teenagers. It's like an anthill with people coming and going. One kid is throwing up in a big potted houseplant. Another is passed out unceremoniously on the stairs. Apparently, a party from last night is still raging. I step to the front of the group and stride toward the sounds of screaming, sure that's where we'll find Stella. I round the corner and stop short.

A bunch of guys are gathered around a big TV in the living room. Some are sitting in chairs with speakers in them. Two have gaming controllers in their hands, and they yell and scream as the game racket blasts. I survey the room that's covered in crushed beer cans, empty pizza boxes, and filthy pillows that the floor-dwelling miscreants are lounging on. Everyone ignores us, but considering the sheer number of teens milling around the house, I guess they don't care who's around.

I whip around to Demitri, my face awash with snooty mortification. "Ewwwww. What is this?"

Demitri chuckles. "Sweetheart, these are teenage boys."

I glance around at the filthy scene before looking back at Demitri. "You guys are teenage boys." I gesture to Arch, Trey, Javier and Demitri.

Demitri shakes his head. "No, Meley. We're teenage *men*. We work at a brothel. We deal with life-and-death nightmares." He pointedly adds, "We get laid." He turns me around and gestures to the loud ninja-fighting video game. "I can do the things the video game characters are doing because I don't waste time on dumb shit, but those guys," he points to the gamers in the filth, "play these games all day."

I back up a step and squish myself against Demitri as a guy walks by and says flirtatiously to me, "What's uppppppp? Damn, girl!"

I whip around and wrinkle my nose. "WHAT is that *smell*?"

Demitri raises his eyebrows, seemingly thoroughly amused by me. "That smell is those boys. They don't shower."

I look at the gamer guys and gag like a cat yacking up a hairball. "This is what teenagers do?"

Demitri tries not to laugh. "Yes, love. Most teenagers don't get married at sixteen, kill parking lots full of bikers with a thought, or rescue their friend the morning after a red-carpet movie premiere."

I shudder from head to toe. "I'm getting Stella and walking her out the front door. We don't need a plan. This is ridiculous."

On a mission to get this over with as quickly as possible, I take off, striding through the crowd with purpose.

The others follow me, attempting to blend in.

A guy walks up and slides an arm around my shoulders. "What's your name?" he asks flirtatiously.

I shudder from head to toe, wiggling away from him in revulsion. "Ewwwwww!" He appears offended, but I don't care.

Victoria squishes her assets together, purring flirtatiously, "Hi." The miscreant gives her a confused look.

Mortified, Trey stares at the ceiling, while Arch doubles over laughing.

"What's so funny?" Victoria snaps at Arch.

He leans on the wall, chortling at her expense.

I round the corner into the dining room and see Stella tied to a chair. I weave purposefully through the crowd, passing the people sitting around the table. I'm unconcerned. I can level everyone in this house with a run-of-the-mill fistfight. *"This is ridiculous,"* I send to Demitri. *"Waste of my damn time. Just wanted a nice day. I hate my life."*

He's amused, which irritates me even more.

"I'm taking the hostage to the bathroom. Destroyer told me to," I say flippantly.

The girls around the table don't even look up from their hand-held video-game thingies.

Some hostage guards this lot are! I glare over my shoulder at my friends, waving my hands dramatically at the absurdity of all of this.

They're all trying not to laugh.

I untie the simple square knots and smile at Stella. "Time to potty."

She looks thoroughly amused now that she's with us. She glances at her "guards" before flicking her eyes to keys and a purse in the center of the table.

I roll my eyes and grab them. No one notices, and I aggravatedly huff while we join the others. We get her in the middle of the group, and I take point.

As we walk around the corner, a guy strolls by with his dumpy girlfriend. He gapes at me and says in wonder, "Cool! You've got a six-pack!"

His girlfriend throttles him on the arm, and drags him away, shooting a death glare at me.

I toss my hands up. "This place is FULL of every unfortunate in the Valley!"

As if the universe is attempting to prove my point, the front door flies open, revealing two weaselly little guys who strain and heave, but the keg they're attempting to heft goes nowhere.

They're blocking my exit route, and I huff. "For the love of all things HOLY, *MOVE!* I just want to go shopping!" My friends all bust up laughing as I pick up the keg with no issue and ask, "Where do you want your budget beer?"

The weasels stare at me in slack-jawed wonder.

I give a disgusted look to my friends. They're little help, what with their yeehaw good-time laughter.

Aggravated, I look back to the guys. "Yo, broooooo, BEER WHERE?" When there's still no answer, I give up. I heft the beer keg into the disgusting living room and set it down next to a pile of discarded pizza boxes.

The weasels follow, and one of them exclaims, "Damn! Look at that ass!"

More weasels join them, and I send to Trey and Demitri, *"They're multiplyinggggg!"*

Demitri doubles over laughing.

Out of habit I squeal, "Treyyyyyy! Morons incoming!"

Trey grins. "I'm sure Captain America's got this covered." He pats a cackling Demitri on the back.

"I don't have it covered!" Demitri wheezes through hilarity. "I'm definitely useless right now."

"You're shit outta luck," Trey informs behind the ever-growing pack of weasels.

Apparently, none of us are worried about a "daring escape" from this den of slack.

I stomp my foot. "Demitri!" When he looks my way, I ask, "Shall I blast these Decepticons through the wall or are you gonna rescue me?"

Still laughing, he strides my way. He towers over the morons and orders like a drill sergeant, "Weasels! Arms down at your sides!"

The guys all snap to attention.

Demitri grips the arms of the first one and picks him up. Comically, he rotates the stiff guy and sets him down. To the great amusement of our friends, he then proceeds to move each of the scrawny guys in the same manner, until he has a clear path. Seemingly elated with the plan, the weasels ooze hero worship for Demitri. He gets to me and takes my arm, pulling me through the gap.

"He's like the Hulkinator!" one of the little guys says in worship.

I crack up, and Trey flippantly announces, "New nickname achieved."

Regrouped, we start to weave through the milling crowd to the front door, but I'm promptly stopped by another guy who slugs up to me. His face is greasy, and his trucker cap has a ring of dried yellow sweat all around the brim from constant wear. "Woahhhhhhhh!" he says with exaggerated wonder. "AWESOME! I didn't know it was costume day. What kick-ass Comi-Con character are you?"

I look at Demitri, confused. He leans against the wall, laughing again.

"Comic book conventions where douche-turds dress up like trolls and cyborgs," Trey explains.

I look down at my outfit and back at the kid. "This is what I wear."

"You look like this chick named La Diabla, but she's some tall amazon wizard who shoots fire out her ass and stuff."

My eyes nearly bug out of my head, and all my friends are laughing so hard they have tears rolling down their cheeks.

"Oh my God, I'm gonna die," Demitri sends. *"I can't breathe."*

"Wanna come game with us?" greasy guy offers. "You seem cool." He tries to grab my arm.

When I whip into a backbend to avoid the guy's reach, my face lands near Demitri's, who's kneeling on the floor, howling laughter.

Upside down, I hiss, "Help meeeeee! He's going to lock me in his dungeonnnn."

Demitri doubles over harder.

The guy snags my wrist, and I squawk, "No, no, NO! Holy crap, I don't want to be your wizard queen!"

Demitri manages to stand and push the guy's outstretched hand away. A cockroach and his little skittering buddy scamper from a pizza box next to my foot.

"BUGS! BUGSSSSS!" I squeal, as I hightail it for the door, leaving Arch to get our herd of laughing hyenas out of the house. I run to Mabel and shudder from head to toe, wringing my hands and hopping around. "That was horrifying! I'd rather massacre all of Hollywood than ever do that again!"

Javier rushes Stella around the edge of Demitri's Jeep, where Stealth and Mercury are. Demitri, Arch, and Trey are kneeling in the grass, losing it.

Demitri wipes tears of laughter from his cheeks and gasps, "God, I love you, Meley."

I cross to him and jokingly swat his arm. "You didn't even help me!"

"We found La Diabla's kryptonite," Arch crows.

Seeing that Mama Mabel and the Hounds look confused, Demitri calms enough to explain. "Melanie just discovered what actual teenagers are like. The place was full of unwashed gamers and randoms. She did a full backbend trying to get away from a particularly greasy one who wanted her to play video games with them because he thought she looked like a comic book character."

The adults howl with laughter.

I shudder. "That smell!"

Mama Mabel gives me a baffled look.

"The house smelled like cheesy poofs and funk," Demitri explains. "Melanie didn't approve."

"They were just teenagers," Victoria interjects, with a roll of her eyes.

I gag, repulsed. "So gross."

We check on Stella, who informs that she was fed pizza, kept tied up, and got bored because she was largely ignored. Javier takes her to her car, and they leave, with Stealth and Mercury following. Big Joe calls George and lets him know what's happening.

Demitri hugs me, rocking back and forth.

I bury my head in his T-shirt and inhale deeply. The scent of his cologne fills my head, and I murmur, "Thank you for always smelling good. That was repulsive!"

He chuckles. "I love you so much. That was HILARIOUS!"

CHAPTER 40

As Arch finishes regaling the table with our daring kidnap caper, everyone howls with laughter.

I shudder again, and Demitri drapes an arm around me. "She bought three perfumes at the mall to cover the smell she swears is still in her head," he announces.

Jayla ducks her head sadly while Dante squeezes her, murmuring something.

My cell phone rings, and I pull it from my backpack pouch. "Hello." I sound less than enthusiastic.

"La Diabla?"

I set the phone on the table and hit the speaker button. "Speaking."

"Did you steal our hostage?" the voice says with makeshift venom.

"Hello, Destroyer. You lost your hostage? Who does that?" I look Stella's way, and she laughs silently.

"This isn't over."

"How unfortunate for me." I roll my eyes. "I'm terrified."

"Be ready," Destroyer warns.

"You're playing with fire, Destroyer. You and me, we don't specialize in the same games."

"I'm going to bring all the demons of hell down on you!" he gravels, in an over-the-top sci-fi-inspired tone. "Clubbies Pizza parking lot. Saturday. Ten p.m. Be there."

"Can't. I have a show Saturday night."

He seems puzzled. "Ummm . . . okay, what about Friday at nine?"

"I've got rehearsal," I lackadaisically inform.

"Fine, we'll come to you," he says and hangs up.

I look at the phone and scoff. "What a bunch of dingleberries."

The bell rings, and Demitri tosses my phone in my backpack and slings it over his shoulder along with his. We head through the quad. I sigh and crack my back. Because the advanced acting and musical theater classes are rehearsing for the musical during the last two periods, Demitri and I are now rehearsing two hours a day with Mr. Isley. Demitri leaves me at the girls' locker room door, and I quickly change into dance clothes. When I come out, Dante's waiting.

"Hey."

"Hey, Dante. Thank you for taking the gig Friday."

"You killed that song." He gives me a calculated look. "Jayla was destroyed when you didn't want to go shopping together."

"Dante, I'm not buying their bullshit."

"I'm not either. Your threat put Jayla in a fresh tailspin." He smirks. "Well played."

My expression morphs innocently. "I don't know what you're talking about."

Dante chuckles. "You're dangerous, girl."

"Jayla needs to play games with someone else."

He morphs serious. "We have a gig at the Whisky a Go Go in three weeks. I'm hoping you'll front two songs."

"What two?"

He grins. "Tracy Chapman's 'Give Me One Reason' and Janis Joplin's 'Kozmic Blues.'"

"I know them both. Should we practice this time?"

"Yeah. My house after school?"

"I'll be there," I say over my shoulder as I head into the dance room.

Dante follows, and leans against the wall, watching Jayla and Javier's duet.

Mr. Isley gives Jayla and Javier a break after their run and calls up Demitri to work through his solo. They talk through some notes from the last rehearsal, and Mr. Isley turns on the music. I stretch through my splits while I watch Demitri. "The Snake Dance" is a playfully sexy jazz piece. It's character-driven, and I'm not at all surprised that Demitri is incredible.

When it's my turn, I cross the studio, but Demitri stops in front of me. He wraps me up and curls his head around, pressing his face into my neck. We've discovered in our past-life memories that this is how we used to say "I love you" with no words. I curl around the same way, even though I'm full of doubts after my talk with Dante. We inhale slowly and exhale together.

"You know I love you, right?" Demitri whispers.

"You seem to."

Demitri stares in my eyes intensely. "I can feel your doubt. Please—"

"Earth to Melanie!" Mr. Isley's irritable voice breaks in.

"Yes, sir." I step back from Demitri.

"Give me a flawless run of 'Changes Made,' and I'll cut you loose," Mr. Isley offers. "Otherwise, I'm going to drill you like crazy."

Demitri smacks my tush as he walks away. "You better dance your ass off, Meley. I want to go home."

"You need work, Demitri," Mr. Isley says. "I'm keeping you."

"Oh, I'm not going home," I inform. "I have band practice with Dante after rehearsal."

Demitri's eyes snap wide, while Jayla's jaw drops.

I look to Dante. "I'm about to nail this run. Think the band would like to dip out early and get to it?"

Dante chuckles. "The band would love an excuse to ditch."

"I'll need a ride."

Dante nods. "I've got you covered."

"I'm supposed to ride with you to band practice," Jayla pitifully reminds him.

"You can ride with Demitri," Dante says dismissively. "I'm sure he'd love to drive you."

"Are you done socializing?" Mr. Isley says, irritated.

Jayla and Demitri exchange a look as I get in my spot and Mr. Isley starts my music. I pop and sway, strut and kick my way through the piece. It's short, and I'm hardly winded as the song winds to the last few eight-counts. I hit a perfect quad turn and slam into my final pose.

Mr. Isley sweeps his arm to the door. "That's what I'm talking about. You're dismissed."

I grin and grab my backpack. As Dante snags my hand and pulls me to the hall, I squeal happily.

When we're out of sight, he drops my hand and chuckles. "They'll learn."

"At least we're having fun," I huff, and follow him to one of the bungalows.

He makes eye contact through the window, and his bandmates exit one at a time, with backpacks on their shoulders.

"Did she say yes?" Marlo Raine, Diablo's drummer, asks.

Dante nods, and the guys all grin.

CHAPTER 41

Just as we get through our first run of Janis Joplin's "Kozmic Blues," Demitri and Jayla come through the garage door and head to opposite sides of the room.

The band's keyboard player, Clinton Wiles, laces his hands on the top of his head. "I didn't get the keyboard run right. Again?"

Dante smiles at me. "Let loose, Melanie. Janis is unhinged. It's what gave her power."

"Here we go," I reply. The piano intro starts, and I groove with my eyes closed as I begin the lyrics. I let my head roll on Dante's electric guitar pull. A hint of my vanilla pheromone wafts from me unintentionally.

"God, that's intoxicating," Clinton says.

I work through the sultry song about loss, betrayal, and reality, giving it everything I've got, lost in the experience. It draws to a close and silence descends.

"You're unbelievable," Dante finally breathes.

"Thanks for giving me a shot."

Clinton snorts. "I want to hear her do our cover of Heart's 'Alone.'"

"That's the song I sing with you guys," Jayla whimpers.

Clinton rolls his eyes. "You're a soprano. Melanie's an alto. She's better for the song."

"I'm not stealing Jayla's song, but thank you for thinking of me."

Clinton sighs. "Fine. What about 'Bette Davis Eyes'?"

My eyebrows rise. "I've got the raspy voice for a Kim Carnes song, but that one is so," I grimace, "well behaved, stand by your man, good girl."

"It's my favorite song," Jayla bashfully informs.

"That tracks," I mutter. "'Bette Davis Eyes' isn't Diablo's vibe."

"What else you got?" Dante asks.

"We already have two songs rehearsed."

Dante shrugs. "One more, and we can call you when we get a last-minute gig and have choices."

"Nina Simone's 'I Put a Spell on You?'" I suggest.

"You can pull off Nina Simone?" Clinton asks.

I shrug. "I think so."

"We don't have a sax player." Dante sighs. "Damn, though. That would be magic."

I smile as an idea comes to me. "'Black Velvet.' Alannah Myles."

"Hell yes." Dante smirks at me. "That fits our vibe and that gravely tone you hit."

The drummer starts the opening rhythm, and we're off. Demitri and I stare at each other as the lyrics pour from me. The first night we hung out, this song came on, and the air in his Jeep was electric.

Dante hits the guitar riff, and I body roll through my gyrating dance style that I have when I sing.

As I open my eyes, Dante says, "Damn, she's magic."

"Yeah, she is," Clinton crows back. "Let's see if she can hit the high note."

I nail it, and Demitri lets loose a proud, "That's my girl! Yes, you did."

The song ends, and Dante says, "Roll it."

As the band goes straight into "Edge of Seventeen," I grin, and the lyrics belt from me.

"She's like a damn jukebox!" Clinton exclaims.

Dante raises a hand to halt the band after the first few lines. "You can handle that one also. I've seen what I need to."

"I aim to please," I reply, while putting the microphone on the stand. "I should probably scoot out and let Jayla rehearse Heart's 'Alone.'"

"She can't hit the graveled low notes," Clinton says. "Any chance you can help her?"

I shrug. "I'm not actually trained. I just kind of do this."

The band gapes at me.

"You aren't trained?" Clinton asks.

I shake my head. "Until Zane gave me a pointer about singing from my diaphragm, I couldn't really sing at all. I always thought I sucked at it because I can't manage all the fairy princess, breathless stuff."

"The fairy princess soprano crap sucks," Clinton scoffs.

Jayla blushes. That's what she specializes in.

"No offense," Clinton adds for her benefit.

Dante smiles at me with contemplative eyes. "Thanks for spending some time doing this. I'll get you the gig info."

"Thank you for the opportunity. I need to add to my resume." I smile at Dante. "You're doing me a solid."

"Add to your resume?" Marlo says in disbelief. "You just got an Oscar nomination!"

I shrug. "This is a great opportunity."

The band exchanges disbelieving looks, likely because I view working with them as an opportunity.

"Your movie was unreal," Clinton bashfully compliments.

My eyes widen. "Um . . . it's a little . . ."

"Tawdry?" Dante suggests.

I laugh. "Adult."

"It's a little adult in a tawdry way." Dante smiles warmly at me. "But so are you. I was impressed, Melanie. You're no joke. You singing 'White Rabbit' made me cry."

"That means a lot coming from you. Thank you." I survey the band members. "Thank you for not being weird about the naughty movie."

"We get it," Clinton says. "No one in this industry has room to get burned twice. Our people are the ones who keep their shit straight from the start. We won't screw that up with you."

"You'll be the first person we call when we need a female vocalist," Dante says to me.

Jayla swallows hard while I gather up my stuff.

CHAPTER *42*

The soft hum of the Benedictine Monks' hypnotizing voices wafts through my headphones. We had the longest rehearsal for the Hollywood Bowl show ever after school. Considering that the bachelor party I hosted at the brothel last night raged until two in the morning, and I had to be up at six, I'm exhausted. I don't want to sleep, though, because I'm so on edge that I fear a night terror.

Trey's voice breaks into my pondering. "Hey, Mel. Where's D?"

I open my eyes to discover Trey, wearing black slacks and a black dress shirt, unbuttoned halfway. His massive chest scar shows, and my heart hurts a little.

I take off my headphones. "He's spending the night at his dad's."

Victoria prowls dramatically into the parlor, wearing a tiny leopard-print sausage casing. She oozes all over Trey like honey on biscuits. He doesn't touch her. Instead, he just stands there lifelessly. When I make a scrunchy Fraggle face behind Victoria's back, Trey chuckles, but getting a whiff of Victoria's dirty hair as she turns to face me, he cringes.

Victoria looks down at me in snooty disgust. "*What* are you wearing?"

I rally, because I need to give Victoria a chance to coexist. I flip the hood up on my fuzzy onesie jammies. The koala head pops up, and I bobble the fuzzy ears around. "My koala ramble jambles."

"How *fabulous*," Victoria says sarcastically.

Demitri breezes through the door unexpectedly. He surveys Trey and Victoria, before smiling at me softly. He makes a beeline for me and tweaks one of my koala ears, but his greeting is cut off by Victoria.

"What are you doing in that disaster?" She gestures to my whole snuggled situation.

I shrug. "Listening to my new CD and knitting."

Victoria rolls her eyes. "You're pathetic." She smirks snottily, bragging, "My daddy got us on the VIP list at Taint!"

So much for playing nice.

I make a sarcastically impressed face. "Gee whiz. What a *fabulous* opportunity to frolic with self-important Normals."

"A koala suit?" Demitri asks, sounding amused.

I grin. "It's my favorite."

He gestures to my lap. "I didn't know that you knit."

Victoria coughs up a disgusted hairball. "Gross. Who does that? Not even my *grandma* knits."

"Quit being a rancid bitch, Tori," Trey snaps. He looks at me and smiles. "The koala jammies are still the cutest thing I've ever seen you wear." He tells Demitri, "I got them for her for Christmas because she was always hanging on me like a koala bear."

Victoria belts a harsh laugh. "You got toddler pajamas for Melanie and gave me a ruby bracelet?"

I rattle my head. "Wow."

Trey looks like he wants to die.

Demitri carefully picks up my knitting project and changes the subject. "Whatcha making?"

I sigh. "You weren't supposed to come home tonight."

"I know, but I couldn't stand sleeping away from you." He gestures to my knitting. "What does that have to do with what you're working on?"

"I'm working on a throw blanket for you for your birthday. I started it when I was lonely while Trey worked late every night. It's almost finished."

Demitri looks down at the sapphire blue velvet soft blanket. "I love you so much, Meley. That's the sweetest thing anyone has ever done for me."

"I bought you a Rolex for Christmas!" Victoria barks. "What the fuck are you talking about?"

Demitri looks at her like she's nuts. "Melanie is making me a snuggle blanket in my favorite color. Do you know how much time and effort goes into that?"

"Do you know how *expensive* a Rolex is?" Victoria rolls her eyes and says dismissively, "Whatever." She turns to Trey and purrs, "I can't wait to get to the club. I thought we'd get tipsy and sneak into the bathroom to get a little dirty."

I snort.

Victoria looks down at me. "What?"

"Have you seen the bathrooms at Taint?"

"Like *you've* seen them?" Victoria fires back.

"Yeah, Victoria. My stepfather's a Hollywood producer. He's friends with the owner. I saw Hole play there and had backstage access."

Victoria deflates a little. "Oh . . . cool."

I cringe Trey's way. "You might want to dip yourself in acid afterward if you decide to give Backdoor Betty a bathroom bounce there."

Trey looks mortified. "I'm not bouncing Betty, or her backdoor, in a filthy Taint bathroom."

"Trey hates nightclubs," I inform Victoria.

"Like hell he does. He used to screw me regularly in nightclub bathrooms during our affair." Victoria smirks. "While you were home thinking he was working late."

"Wow, again and again." My heart squeezes. I didn't realize he used work as an excuse to sneak out every night. I feel catastrophically naive.

Trey inhales sharply as he feels my dejected humiliation. "Tori, I'm mortified by my behavior. Please stop revealing details."

"It was hot," Victoria purrs.

Trey shakes his head. "It was desperate and shockingly out of line."

Victoria stamps her foot. "I want the daring guy back who was always into me."

"He died, along with our affair," Trey exasperatedly says to Victoria. "I lost my baby. I lost my wife."

"Seems like you got out of a nightmare to me," Victoria snots back. "Who the hell wants to be strapped with a squalling brat at seventeen?"

Rage swells in me so fast that I don't know what's happening. I send out a blistering energy boom. The invisible attack hits Victoria in the chest, and she screams as she flies across the room. She slams into the wall, and I pin her close to the ceiling. All humanity is washed away as I thrum evilly. She whimpers as I skulk her way, releasing the energy line. She hits the ground with a smack. Her breathing ragged, she stares up at me with petrified eyes.

"Melanie, you need to calm down," Demitri implores.

Ignoring Demitri, I snark evilly, "Don't let the koala suit fool you. You forgot who I really am, you rancid, heartless *bitch*. Talk all the shit you want about me. I don't give a fuck. But, if you ever . . .

ever . . . speak of my daughter again, I'll tear your fucking heart out!" I grab Victoria by the front of her sleazy dress and haul her to her feet with one hand. I shake her hard. "Do you hear me?"

She nods frantically and whispers, "I'm sorry."

I hit her with a right hook that snaps her head to the side. She falls to the floor and dissolves into tears, holding her cheek.

I turn slowly, radiating mind-bending rage, and level Trey with a deadly look. "You just stood there while Victoria dismissed our daughter like she was nothing!"

I start to gather a deadly energy load, but Demitri wraps his arms around me tight from behind and sinks me to the ground. "You can't kill him, Melanie."

A breakdown so severe overcomes me that I can't even make sound. My shoulders collapse around my failing lungs. I curl into the fetal position, making an involuntary high-pitched keening sound. Demitri lies on the floor with me and holds me tight while everything in me breaks. Finally, he energetically calms enough of my cataclysmic meltdown that I can take a retching breath.

My screaming lungs fill, laced with fire. "Today was my due date," I lament. "I can't bring her back."

Demitri sits up and pulls me into his lap.

Tears stream down Trey's face. "Victoria, Melanie's and my daughter isn't a weapon in your arsenal."

"I'm truly sorry," Victoria quietly says, seeming to actually get it.

"I can't even look at you right now," Trey says. "Get the fuck out."

"Trey, please," Victoria pleads. "Can we talk about this?"

"Leave," Trey orders, with finality-laced rage.

I hear footsteps and look up at Trey with dead eyes. "She's never going to stop using what you've told her to hurt me." My gaze shifts to Demitri. "I don't think I can live here."

"We'll move into my dad's," Demitri says.

I exhale, and my breathing evens out.

"Melanie, I'm not flippant about losing our daughter," Trey says through tears.

I ignore him, curling my face into Demitri's neck.

My spirit guide rises in my mind. She says to all three of us, in our heads, *"I've made another decision. Trey, you'd lie in bed at night, glaring at Melanie, and wishing with everything in you that Victoria was your soulmate. I'm granting your wish."*

"Please, no!" Trey radiates desperation.

She tips her head. *"That's no longer what you want?"*

"NO! Please don't do this." Trey looks my way. "I've never made a bigger mistake."

"While Melanie was dying in a bathtub full of blood, she sobbed to me that she can't handle any more lifetimes with you. Her dying wish was for me to dissolve your soulmate bond. I'm the reason, Trey, that you felt such a desperate need to get home that night. I needed you to help her. Instead, you didn't even bother to realize she was dying. You were so irritated that you had to leave Victoria at the club that you didn't give a damn about Melanie. I granted her Demitri because he truly loves her. He's who she needs. Victoria is precisely who you need."

"I'm begging you not to do this!" Trey pleads.

We feel my spirit guide ponder. *"You lorded it over Melanie like a dictator. Now, you've got your own dictator, and that interests me. So, let's see how you do being at the mercy of someone who's heartless."* My spirit guide swells with power. *"You have one chance to prove yourself. If another issue arises, Victoria will be yours, forever. Her actions decide your fate."* My spirit guide sinks below the surface of the water that lives in my mind.

Trey doubles over, sick with panic.

"Hooooly crap," Demitri says. "I'd hate to be you, Trey. You're about to be stuck with Victoria, because another issue WILL arise. Being her soulmate is hell. You can feel her shallow, mean vibe all the time. It's why I became such a dismissive dick. She thrums with it."

"Thank you for coming home tonight, Demitri," I say in a wobbling voice, ignoring Trey's plight because I can't even begin to face what he's now dealing with.

Demitri shifts, and his phone materializes from his back jeans pocket. He dials a number. After a moment, he says, "Dad, can Melanie and I head to you?"

"Of course. What's wrong?"

"Victoria made a horrific remark about Trey getting out of having to tolerate the baby they lost. It got bad, but Melanie stopped before she killed Victoria. My girl is lying limp on me. I need to get her to your house where she feels safe."

"Melanie?" his dad says.

"I'm here," I whisper.

"We'll stop time. It's going to be okay."

"Can we play Trivial Pursuit and drink Cactus Coolers?" I whimper.

Mr. Cantrell chuckles. "I always have Cactus Coolers in the fridge for my favorite girl. I'll get the game set up and order pizza."

"We'll be there in twenty minutes." Demitri ends the call.

"Do you need me to take her so that you can get up?" Trey asks, suddenly overly chivalrous.

"No. I need you to leave her alone." Demitri's voice turns steely. "As the person who held your dead child in my hand, I love that baby like she was mine. I love Melanie. You don't need to give a shit, Trey."

Trey's expression is destroyed. "I care so much about losing the baby! It's torn me up."

Demitri stands, and my head droops on his shoulder while he carries me like an exhausted toddler. I feel cold air on my face as we leave through the foyer.

Trey follows. "Demitri, please don't leave! I need to talk to Melanie."

I hear the Jeep door open, and the smell of cologne and leather seats breathes past me. Demitri leans in, and I feel his muscles bunch as he shifts and puts me down.

"Curl up, baby girl."

I bunch my feet up on the passenger seat and rest my head on the center console.

"She doesn't even have on shoes," Trey says. "At least let me get them!"

"She has clothes at my dad's house," Demitri says as he closes the door.

I faintly hear Trey say, "I need to fix this. Melanie and the baby are all that matter to me."

"You want to fix this because being nice to Melanie might save you," Demitri retorts. "I'm not buying it." He starts the Jeep and puts an arm around me as we leave the parking lot.

CHAPTER 43

Despite the longest rehearsal day of my life, I'm still content from staying at Mr. Cantrell's house two nights ago. He did a great job counseling us through. Demitri and I feel like we're on the same team now, so I guess something good came of Trey and Victoria pushing me over the sanity cliff. Demitri and I haven't bickered or had a strained moment in three days, and I like the potential I see in us. Little excited flutters keep drifting up when I think about him now.

There's a timid knock on the door. I glance at the security monitor and wobble my head, not wanting to deal with this. It's better to get it over with, though.

I send to Demitri, *"Trey's at the door."*

"You might as well let him in. I'll throw him out if he becomes an issue."

I unblock my connection with Trey and send, *"Use your master key. I just got all this stuff organized, and I don't want to get up."*

Trey comes in, crossing to my little dining table and taking a seat. "Hey. I figured you'd have rehearsal again."

"Mr. Isley gave us the evening off," I inform him, while I flip through the pictures for one I'm looking for. "We have rehearsal all day tomorrow, and he wanted us to rest up. Thank God."

The bathroom door opens, and steam pours out. Demitri comes into the bedroom. "You still feeling better?" he asks.

"Your show's Saturday," Trey says. "Are you sick?" He sounds concerned.

I shake my head. "Just really sore, but D fixed it when we got home a few minutes ago. This show is brutal."

"We get to miss school tomorrow," Demitri placates while he digs through the dresser.

"True," I reply. "Although, I don't know which is worse. A grueling twelve-hour rehearsal with Mr. Isley yelling and Molly glaring, or school."

Demitri chuckles as he turns to face us, wearing only a towel around his waist. His response is cut off as Trey mutters, "What the fuck has happened to my life?"

I laugh, amused by his pain. "Aw, now, now. Gorgeous Demitri stepping out of what used to be your bathroom, mind-blowingly perfect in a towel, isn't a big deal, Trey. He's covering the most impressive part."

"Don't be catty, Meley. You'll hurt Trey's feelings." Demitri crosses to me, takes my hand, and runs it down his abs.

I look up at him with naughty eyes. "You're killing me."

"I better stop before the impressive part becomes more impressive." Demitri heads back into the bathroom.

"I thought you weren't that guy?" Trey hollers after him. "Arrogant jackass."

Demitri chuckles evilly and closes the door to get dressed.

"Damn," Trey mutters. "He really is perfect."

I nod in agreement.

Demitri comes out of the bathroom, dressed, as Trey asks, "What are you working on?"

"Tanner and Finley's wedding present."

Trey looks alarmed. "Did they set a date, and I wasn't invited? Finley's still furious with me. At least Tanner is talking to me again, though."

"You're still Tanner's best man." I motion to the disaster on the bed. "It's a scrapbook, and it'll take time, so I wanted to get a jump on it."

Trey holds a hand my way, and I give him a stack of pictures from Halloween. Demitri sits in the other dining chair and looks at the pictures as Trey flips through. Trey smiles, but I know his heart is hurting. I send the sentiment that I appreciated that night, even though I now know he wished he was with Victoria. He tried to get out of going to the party. Trey sends back guilt.

Demitri holds out his hand for the stack when Trey is done and shows me a picture. I'm laughing, with one arm around Finley and my other hand snaked around Trey's neck. Tanner's grinning down at Finley from her other side. Trey's expression speaks volumes: love, guilt, fear, and torment, all built into a soft smile. I'm oblivious in the picture.

"I'm the one who took this picture," Demitri says. "I noticed Trey's odd behavior that night." He turns to Trey. "You clearly knew you were making mistakes."

"I did, and I was. That night, I remembered how much I loved Melanie."

"Finley's adorable as Alice in Wonderland," Demitri says to me.

"Tanner killed that Mad Hatter costume," I reply.

Demitri smiles. "You were a really cute Cheshire Cat."

I scrunch my shoulders happily. "It's my favorite Alice character. I love those books."

"Why didn't you didn't dress up?" Demitri asks Trey.

"It's not my thing," Trey mutters.

"It was in Victoria's diary that you two went as the angel and the devil to her parents' Halloween party," Demitri informs. "Clearly, couples costumes don't offend you that much."

Trey blinks rapidly. "The number of reminders that keep popping up of my neglect of Melanie, and catering to Victoria, make me ill." He looks at me. "Please know that I am permanently sorry for everything, known and unknown. You never have to wonder if I feel bad about a new detail that pops up. I feel terrible about all of it."

I don't respond, knowing full well that Trey is panicking about my spirit guide's threat. He's been overly nice to me ever since she made it. It's both manipulative and annoying.

Trey looks to Demitri. "I can't believe you dressed up as a fairy with Melanie."

Demitri slides sweet eyes my way. "It made her happy. You know, Meley, we could wear those costumes for Halloween."

I grin. "Perfect! I'd love that."

Trey awkwardly clears his throat. "Melanie, will you please force your spirit guide up from the evil lake in your head?"

"It doesn't work that way, Trey. I don't control her, and I'm certainly not speaking to her right now. Why?"

Trey hits me with desperate eyes. "I can't be soulmate bonded to Victoria."

I shrug. "Much like what happened to Adam, that's all stemming from what you wanted. It has nothing to do with me."

"You have no idea how upset Adam truly is," Trey says. "He's been talking to me about it. I told him what your spirit guide said, and he was so appalled that he didn't even make a joke about it. Soulmate life with Valerie is a nightmare, and I guarantee it'll be worse with Victoria. Please tell your spirit guide I was dead wrong. You don't understand."

"What don't I understand?"

"Victoria."

I crack up. "I understand Victoria perfectly. *You* were the one who didn't understand her. Again, that's between your past and present *you*."

"I was already furious with myself every time I looked at Victoria. Now I'm terrified."

I grin mischievously. "But Trey! There's a whole wide world full of filthy bathrooms just waiting for the two of you to soil."

He shudders. "I wouldn't touch her with his impressive unit." He juts a thumb Demitri's way.

Demitri gags. "Nope. You sure as hell wouldn't. My unit will never go near that vapid swamp monster again."

Trey cringes. "She hasn't taken a shower since last Thursday."

Demitri winces. "Damn. A whole week?"

We're interrupted by a knock at the door, and Tanner comes in. "There you are. You guys coming to the party?"

"Who's having a party?" I ask.

Tanner rolls his eyes. "Victoria. She's out there acting like she owns the place. Apparently, she didn't even ask Mabel's permission. Mabel seems fine with it, though."

I shoot judgmental eyes Trey's way.

He sighs. "I had no idea about the party, Melanie."

Trey, Demitri, and I follow Tanner into the parlor, where we find our friends hanging out. "Blue Jean Blues" by Jeff Healey thrums through the speakers. It was my favorite song growing up and became Trey's and my song. Someone must have put on one of my mixed CDs.

"I hate this song," I mutter.

Trey sighs.

Victoria slithers up to Trey, seductively purring, "I want to dance."

"There's no way in hell I'm dancing with you to this song," Trey grumbles.

Victoria switches her viper focus to me.

"We discussed this, Tori," Trey barks.

I can't help but smirk. I suspect that Trey's decided to defend me at all costs, to try to stop any incident that might lead to a permanent sentence in Victoria's prison.

Everyone falls silent, watching us.

I catch a spicy whiff of Victoria and grin evilly, deciding to spur her on just to watch Trey jump through hoops. "No, no. I'm going to play her game, her way," I languish to Trey. I gesture in Victoria's direction. "Buckle up, bitch!" I fan my face while I exclaim exuberantly to Adam, "I feel it. It's about to happen."

Adam smiles. "Level her, babe."

Presley bounces. "Here we go! TKO coming."

Stella cocks her chin my way. "I swear, you're my freaking hero. Every damn time I hang with you, I think, 'Did I just find my new best friend?'"

Jayla seems to shrink. Considering that I used to think she was my best friend, and she and Stella spent a lot of time together before things got messy, she's in an odd quandary.

I turn Victoria's way with a flourish. "You stink like a back-alley Vegas hooker that's been rolling around in Corn Nuts and Parmesan cheese. Take care of your lady shit, because there's only so much those leggings can do to contain *that* stench."

Victoria turns fuchsia. "Treeeey," she growls, but he doesn't defend her.

Presley hops up and down, crowing, "Ohhhhhh!"

"BOOOOOOM," Stella bellows. She groans a healthy, "Oooooohhhhhhh. I'd hate to be someone Melanie hates!"

Adam cracks up. "I love you so much, Firebird." He grins at

Victoria. "Welcome to the big leagues."

"I was wondering what that smell was," Tanner says before retching. When he recovers, he turns to Trey. "Seriously, dude, get your girl in check."

Trey raises his hands. "Victoria's hygiene was a shock to all my senses once she got comfortable."

Just to rub it in, Demitri sniffs my neck. "Melanie smells like the strawberry lotion I got her." He kisses my neck.

I shrug my shoulders cheerfully at Victoria. "I smell like a Strawberry Shortcake doll. Sexy boys like pretty scents. You should try it."

Everyone glances at each other, radiating amusement, while Victoria looks like she wants to die.

Demitri lets loose a liberal, "Buhhhhh," and looks at Trey. "Melanie's Corn Nut description is repulsively accurate."

Trey shudders, still not defending Victoria, even though she's glaring at him.

I snap my fingers and clap my hands twice. "Considering how vain you are, Victoria, I don't understand how you don't handle that. What you're marinating could be used as a weapon of mass destruction."

My friends howl with laughter.

I smile cattily at her. "Getting comfortable in a relationship doesn't mean you turn into a ferret. Soap, water, loofah. It's not one of the great mysteries of the world."

Victoria looks like she's going to die of humiliation.

"She's funky, and you had an affair with her while you ignored Mel?" Adam asks Trey.

Trey shakes his head. "The funk started after the affair phase when Victoria was no longer trying to impress me."

"Can we please change the subject?" Victoria sheepishly asks.

"Hell no!" I sound off. "Wasn't it last night that you called my unborn baby a bratty nightmare that Trey got out of?"

Everyone turns vicious eyes Victoria's way.

"You what?" Presley snarls.

I nod. "She got her ass kicked for it."

Presley points at Victoria. "Talk about my niece again, and I'll run you through myself!"

"I'll help," Stella snarls.

"Me too," Susan and Deb add into the mix.

I look to Trey, but he just stares back at me.

"Back to humiliating Victoria." I flourish to Adam.

Adam cackles. "You really do stink. It's like sweaty olives left in the sun too long."

Arch shrugs. "She just smells like dirty girl to me. I never attributed it to food." He sniffs in Victoria's direction. "I can see the comparison now, though." He cringes.

"I'm going to be sick," Finley huffs, while Presley slumps over and laughs so hard that she breaks into a coughing fit.

Stella scrunches her face haughtily. "You smell like caviar and capers." She gags and gives Trey a horrified look. "You must be the STUPIDEST person on the planet. You left MELANIE for *THAT*?" She points rudely at Victoria.

I spurt laughter, because Victoria glares at Trey, who continues not to help. She starts to stride Stella's way aggressively. "Perhaps you don't get it, new girl—"

She's cut off as Stella hits a wide-leg stance and flourishes her arms. "Come at me."

Laughter peels from Adam. "Oh, I like her." He nods enthusiastically. "Stella's daddy is the leader of a biker gang. If you attack her, they declare Retribution Clause against you."

Trey perks up at that news.

Apparently thinking twice about her threat, Victoria stops by Hiram.

He sniffs in her direction and informs Trey, "Damn, that's wafty. It's like anchovies and pepperoni pizza left in a hot city bus all day."

Adam, Presley, and I howl with laughter.

Marcus looks desperately aggrieved. "Please don't ruin food for me."

"Marcus has a weak stomach, so don't do that to him," Bear admonishes.

Victoria walks past Adam, to get away from Stella.

He cringes and snags my arm, pulling me closer. He sniffs my neck seductively before graveling, "I'm good now."

I grin at him flirtatiously, before saying to Victoria, "See! The sexy boy likes pretty smells."

Adam grimaces at Victoria. "It's a hell of a lot better than three-week-old lasagna."

Marcus tosses his hands. "Not *lasagna* too!"

Adam grins at Trey. "I triple dog dare you to run your junk through her. You might get radioactive superpowers."

Trey scrunches up his face and points at Adam. "I triple dog dare *you* too."

"*Hell* no!" Adam looks to Dante. "You're a wild and crazy rock star. Nasty girls aren't new to you, I'm sure."

Dante gives Adam an arrogant look. "Rock stars don't have to grave rob for rotting carcasses, but thanks." He turns to Arch. "You into it?"

"Not for a million dollars. Bear? Wanna take a walk on the wild side?"

Bear busts up and can't even make words. He points at Tanner, trying to pass along the dare.

Tanner cocks a hip and waves his hands flamboyantly by his face. "Leave me out of this! That smell has me sweating gay so hard that I might leave Finley. Lord!"

Adam informs Tanner, "No need to leave Finley, my dude! These three," he points to Finley, Presley, and me, "smell like rainbows."

"Thank you, *Adam*, for the reminder that you've screwed every girl in the room," Tanner disgustedly snarks.

"I've dragged my junk through some dangerous adventures, but DAMN, never anything that daring." Adam gestures to Victoria, who finally tears up.

Tanner flippantly gestures Darren's way, passing on the dare. Darren just shakes his head with such an aggrieved "Darren expression" that everyone howls with laughter.

"Wait, guys. We've been rude." Bear turns to Marcus. "My apologies for leaving you out of the fun." He gestures to Victoria. "Would you like to dive into the corner chicken shack's rotting dumpster?" Marcus puts his hand over his mouth and rushes to the guest bathroom in the hall while everyone snickers.

I snag the air freshener can from the cleaning supply cabinet and cross to Trey. Grinning, I offer him the can. "Maybe if you spray her liberally, you can get through it." I gesture at Demitri. "Demitri can heal any rot that you contract from her science experiment. Give it a shot."

Demitri grins evilly. "Live dangerously. I've got you, bro."

Trey takes the can and informs, "I'll use it to spray down the apartment instead."

"Seriously, dude, your apartment smells like a frat house," Tanner snarks. "Nothing but dirty ass and regret. I've never seen such a disaster."

"That would be Victoria's doing," Trey says, looking dejected.

"Can we please get back to my party?" Victoria haughtily asks.

Tanner slides judgmental eyes her way. "I don't even know why I'm AT your party." He looks to Presley. "Since when is Victoria inner circle enough to warrant us showing up?"

"She's not," Presley snides back. "I showed because I heard from Trey that Mel got a gutful finally, and I figured she'd kill Victoria. I wasn't about to miss this bloodbath."

"Damn was it worth driving all the way over for," Adam crows.

Victoria runs out of the room in tears. Presley cackles.

"Well, on that note, I should go," Arch says.

"Me too," Adam says. "Valerie's going to have a fit if I don't fix the dishwasher."

Chatter starts, and I slide happy eyes to Stella. "I need to speak with you. Biker club business."

"So much biker business to discuss," Stella enthusiastically says and crosses to me.

When Jayla timidly follows, I suggest, "You should head out with Dante."

Presley and Finley link pinkies and cross to me. That's the secret signal, and Susan and Deb join our pack.

"I've also got biker stuff to discuss," Tanner sasses, sashaying to us and leading the way down the hall.

Running feet catch up with us as we round the corner at the T-intersection. "Melanie," Demitri says.

I turn to look at him.

"Would you please include Jayla?" He scrunches his face. "She's crying in the freaking corner with Bear."

Before I can respond, Stella quietly says, "I need a break from her, dude. She's so clingy."

"She's so excited to be friends with you," Demitri defends.

"Okaaaaaay. Back to fun girl time, with no defending Jayla." Tanner gives Demitri a pointed look, who winces grandly in turn.

"Can I come with?" Demitri asks.

"I don't know. Can you convincingly act like one of the girls?" Tanner's question is meant to be a sarcastic brush-off.

Demitri takes a dramatic breath before popping a hip and studying his nails like a girly popular snot. "Yesssss," he flamboyantly oozes.

Giggles erupt, while Tanner nods his amused approval. "Welcome to the real inner circle."

We enter the studio, and Demitri watches, baffled, while we scatter. Tanner snags the CD case from the second shelf above the stereo. Presley and Finley grab armloads of yoga mats from the corner. I grab a grocery bag that's hidden in the back of the closet. Deb and Susan pull six-packs of sodas from a mini-fridge.

"Locked and loaded," Tanner chimes, as we continue our strut out the far door, into the back hallway.

I take out my keys and open the double doors to the banquet hall. On a clandestine mission, we all hurry through.

With my chin, I gesture to the light switches. "D, get the lights."

He flips the switch, and the rainbow lights over the skating rink light up. In no time flat, we've got yoga mats spread out in the center of the skating rink. Cookies and cheese poofs emerge from the bag, and Tanner puts on TLC's "What About Your Friends," through the deejay equipment.

I plop down on my purple yoga mat. "Yessss. Our happy place."

"Girl, I was hoping we'd do this," Tanner says.

"Seriously, I needed a club day so bad," Presley says while she lounges.

Demitri takes a seat next to me on a green mat Finley hands him. "You guys do this a lot?"

Our answer is interrupted as the banquet door swings open and then slams shut. Trey exhales hard, locking the bolt.

Tanner purses his lips. "You know our rule. We don't invite Victoria, or her guy."

"Wait, what?" Demitri says.

"She's crying in the suite," Trey informs, panting like he's run a mile. "I ditched her."

Tanner shrugs apologetically at Demitri. "To answer your question, yes, we do this a lot. You were never invited because you were likely to invite Victoria."

Trey makes his way to us and thumps a box of Fudgesicles into the snack pile. He snags a black yoga mat and spreads it on my other side, where he used to sit before he stopped coming to these little rainbow-lit super-secret fun fests.

As I bop my head to the song, I feel Trey's knee against the middle of my back. He isn't thinking, instead falling back into old habits. He takes a sip of his soda before reaching for another can and popping it open. He absently hands me the can while he chats with Tanner. I sadden at the reminder of how things used to be.

"Hey," Demitri softly says. "I wish you'd invited me. I would have kept it a secret from Victoria. This is fun."

I shrug a little. "Tanner's one of the girls, and Trey and Tanner hang a lot. He started coming with, and then Marcus joined because Pres was here. Then Hiram joined a few times when Susan started coming. Drake tagged along once with Deb."

"What about Arch?" Demitri asks.

I shake my head.

"He's dating Kelsey, who Melanie isn't comfortable around after she lied to Mel about Tiffany," Presley says. "This all started when I came over to hang with Mel as a surprise and found her in here, lying on a yoga mat, watching the rainbow lights. I joined her."

I look Trey's way, knowing it really started off a him-and-me thing.

"What about Dante and Jayla?" Demitri asks.

"They aren't really a part of us," Presley informs. "Inner circle only."

We hear a rhythmic knock on the door, and Tanner jogs to answer it. After Marcus and Hiram slip in, Tanner locks the door again.

"Secret knocks, huh?" Demitri asks.

I laugh a little. "Clubhouse stuff. It's dumb, but we like it."

"Yeahhhh, the gang's all here!" Marcus crows jubilantly as he tosses a bag of chips into the snack pile. "Stole those from the kitchen." He plunks down on Presley's yoga mat.

She shifts to put her head on his leg and joins Finley singing the song coming through the sound system.

Demitri and Hiram wander to the deejay booth. Trey lies down next to me, and we watch the flashing rainbow disco lights together.

"Remember the night we lounged here for hours?" Trey quietly asks.

I nod.

He smiles, but it's downtrodden. "That was my favorite night with you."

"Why?" This news surprises me.

"We had a fresh shot. I wanted you back so much." Trey smiles at me. "I swear, you can make anything funny. We laughed until we cried, about the dumbest stuff that night."

"That might as well have been a million years ago, Trey." The truth is that it was the only time we did that, just us. It was the night before the big earthquake. We had newly hatched our love connection.

I drop the barrier over my soulmate connection with Trey.

"Hey," he softly sends.

"Hi." It takes me a moment to gather the nerve to send, *"Were you conflicted about your affair when we moved in at Mabel's and ended up back together?"*

I see from my peripheral vision as Trey swallows hard while he continues staring at the flashing lights. *"Yes. Moments like that night were really hard because I knew where I belonged."* Trey's mental state falters in our connection. *"How are you two?"* he asks.

"It's strained. I'm having a tough time trusting Demitri."

"Understandable," Trey replies.

"Do you think Demitri's screwing around with Jayla?" I look Trey's way.

He meets my gaze. *"I think he was before you two got together, but broke things off with her because he realized how serious what he had with you was. If it helps, he follows you around like a puppy now."*

"Her cheating on Dante?" I send. *"That's the part that's had me stumped the whole time I've been suspicious."*

Trey nods. *"I think Jayla having a side quest with D is feasible. She's been infatuated with Demitri forever. While out of character for her, I think she couldn't resist."*

"Do you think Demitri's in love with her?" I ask.

Trey snorts. *"No. I think Demitri's a horny godling who enjoys attention. He's a player, but he hides it well. Adam gossiped with me about that back when I was irritated that you and D were so close, while we were dating. Adam says Demitri's got a hell of a conquest list."*

"That tracks with something Demitri alluded to," I interject.

"He used Jayla for sex, most likely," Trey sends. *"He said himself that he wasn't into Victoria in the sack."* Trey winces.

"You certainly didn't mind a nightly club bathroom round with her."

Trey grimaces. *"I was into the taboo kink, not Victoria. She's a dead lay. D was right about that."* When I glare at him, he adds, *"I'm sorry. I'm an idiot. I'm fully aware, if it helps."*

"*Continue your speculative story of doom,*" I send. "*I need help with this.*"

"*D's not into Jayla. I guarantee Jayla's in love with him, though. Or she thinks she is, because she knows shit about shit. Now he's with you, and what's a sweet little simpleton to do? She can't compete with you, and she doesn't have a mean bone in her body, so she hovers and flutters.*"

"*Perceptive,*" I compliment.

"*Purely educated guess, but it all tracks,*" Trey sends.

"*Do you think he screwed her at her house the night I was attacked by the Machetes?*"

Trey snorts. "*No. I think she went nuts when she figured out you two were together at Renn Faire. Her reaction was unhinged, and then he held his breath while he panicked.*"

"*Someone called his cell phone while he and I were discussing my scar tissue,*" I inform. "*He didn't answer, but he got really distant and weird when he checked his phone. He turned off the ringer, but his house phone rang so many times that he left the room to answer it. I didn't know who it was at the time, but he went to her house right after.*"

"*Had to be her,*" Trey sends. "*So, I suspect he went to her house to break things off officially, and she whimpered and simpered like she does. It likely took forever because Mr. Nice Guy couldn't leave her sad, and she needed a million reassurances that 'it's not her' and 'she's so lovely.' Then you nearly died, and they got caught having their little sugary breakup moment. You perceived it as them screwing, and he couldn't tell you otherwise because Jayla was cheating on Dante, and Demitri won't blow her up like that. Now he's sitting in shit stew while it simmers.*" He looks my way. "*You could check his memories.*"

"*I don't want to. I'm so sick of digging around like a sneaky urchin through my guy's dirt. If it was a thing that he broke off right away, then I'm being irrational.*"

Trey wobbles his head. "*I see your point, but it does nothing toward me getting you back, so I'm not a fan of it.*"

I laugh quietly.

"Just the fact that he was with her, without your knowledge, when you were attacked by biker psychos, is grounds for being done with her." Trey scoffs. *"You KNOW she's driving him nuts with all her worrying, because she can't discuss it with anyone else. Her confidants are Tanner, Stella, and Finley. All three would spill her dirt to you out of loyalty. So, Demitri's her sounding board, and LORD can that girl fret. Demitri is likely torn up with guilt, because he used her as a casual conquest. He's an idiot for sleeping with her, because that girl has stage-five-clinger written all over her. He wasn't thinking clearly, but his player game is off because it's all ego-driven, I'm guessing. Long story short, you being pissed at her is likely the worst punishment you could inflict on Demitri. Everyone treats Jayla like shit now. She's getting hers, and in turn, he's getting his. Well played."*

My eyes close. *"I'm so tired of hurtful drama."*

"I know you are," Trey replies. *"If it helps, Demitri was right. "Victoria is a nightmare."*

"I truly just want you to be happy. I'm sorry my spirit guide is playing hardball."

"I'm so sorry I bruised and hurt you." I feel torment tear Trey apart on the inside. His guilt is profound.

"I'll be okay, Trey," I assure him. *"It doesn't hurt like it used to, and things don't pull and twinge when I rotate to the right anymore. Demitri is making progress with the scar tissue healing."*

"It used to hurt all the time?" Trey sends dejectedly.

"It wasn't excruciating," I send. *"More like a nagging ache, but I could ignore it."*

Trey's hands cover his face. I let him work through that reality. He clearly cares, which means a lot.

"I promise I'll talk to my spirit guide," I send, feeling compassionate toward him. *"Thank you for talking to me about this. I've been a confused mess."*

"Thank you, Melanie," Trey sends back, his mental voice choked. *"Please know how sorry I am."*

I sit up as Demitri joins me again. Janet Jackson's "Control" whooms ominously through the speakers. Tanner and I smirk at each other as all the girls slowly rise, while Janet Jackson speaks about control over her life. A dance party breaks out as the beat kicks.

Demitri's phone rings. He answers and scrunches his whole face. "Hey, Jayla . . . No . . . I don't think we're coming back to the parlor."

I give him a look.

"Hang on," he says, before hitting the mute button. "She's asking where we are."

Tanner rolls his eyes.

Trey sighs. "You just broke a coveted rule of the Roller Rink Girl Club."

"What's the rule?" Demitri pensively asks.

"No phones," Trey says. "We're in our own world. The outside doesn't exist until we leave here."

"Think of it as my version of time stopping," I explain.

Demitri unmutes the call. "Sorry, Jayla. I can't talk. Have a good rest of your day." He hangs up and slides puppy dog eyes my way. "I'm sorry I answered the phone."

"All right," Tanner says. "Here are the rules." He's interrupted by a knock on the banquet hall doors. "Bet you money she heard the song through the phone and snooped around Mabel's until she found where it was coming from."

"Shit," Demitri says. "I'm sorry."

"This is why we don't let in outsiders," Presley says. She smiles at Stella. "Present redheaded company excluded."

"I wasn't trying to cause an issue," Demitri insists.

Another knock persists, and Finley groans before heading to the door. She opens it, and in come Dante and Jayla.

"Hey," Dante says. "The others all had to leave." Noticing that there's a festive vibe, he winces a little.

"Hey, guys," Jayla says bashfully.

"Mel, this is your favorite song on this mixed CD," Tanner says when the song switches to New Kids on the Block's "You Got It (The Right Stuff)."

I shake my head and trudge past Jayla and Dante.

Demitri catches up and stops me in the service hall. "Hang on, babe."

I hit him with accusatory eyes. "WHY did you let Jayla crash my club?"

"I wasn't attempting that." Demitri looks beside-himself conflicted. "Being excluded is going to hurt Jayla. *Please*, Melanie."

"I'm SICK of her!"

We're interrupted by Tanner, who comes into the hall and huffs, "Jayla just put on a different CD."

"What's playing?" I ask.

Tanner groans. "Shanice Wilson's 'Saving Forever for You.'"

I laugh, but Demitri says, "It's a good song."

Tanner smirks at him irritably. "Another rule of the club is no sappy songs. Your guest is there two minutes and managed to do the same thing as you: break our rules."

"She isn't my guest!" Demitri reminds him. "Also, you didn't tell me the rules."

Tanner rolls his eyes. "We should have told you when we sat down, but there was a good-ass song on, and we wanted to breathe for a second after Melanie blew Victoria UP." Tanner gives me a sassy look. "Hot DAMN, that was a moment of brilliance!"

"Thank you. That homewrecker deserved it."

"Victoria and Jayla are so freaking annoying. They ruin everything, and none of us want to hang with them." Tanner tosses his hands up. "I suspect our last club meeting just happened."

"No, no, no," Demitri pleads.

I head down the hall while Tanner distracts Demitri. I make it through the winding halls to the garage unhindered and slide into my car. Just as I'm about to pull out, my passenger door opens, and Demitri gets in.

I give him a look. "I need space."

"I know you do, but unresolved conflict drives me insane," he blisters. "*Please* hear me out."

"Fine," I groan. "What?"

"I've screwed up a lot, but I'm in a serious learning curve," Demitri says. "The moment I stepped into Mr. Isley's office, I was essentially married. You've been with me every day since. I'm all in with that deal, but we've made this huge commitment, very quickly. Until now, I've rarely been more than a casual date. Victoria was the most serious relationship I've had, and it clearly wasn't that serious, considering that she was making covert wedding plans with your husband."

I bark a humorless laugh. "Good times."

"I'm unfamiliar with the kind of commitment that you're accustomed to," he says. "I love being your guy, but I've spent so much time just doing what I please that I'm learning through making mistakes. I just need a little time to get this down."

"Perfect," I huff. "We both need time. Go take some."

Demitri smiles softly at me, "I'm not done. I truly get your perspective. You've been hurt, beat, raped, deceived, and almost killed more times than I can keep track of. You've been abandoned by your parents, who are amazing, but still . . . abandoned at a brothel. The brothel madam manipulated you into not moving out. Your ex-husband and his mistress live down the hall. Your cheating-ass, conniving, take-not-a-damn-thing-seriously ex-soulmate, who abandoned you for Valerie, is your voice of reason."

"Ughhhh," I groan.

"That's enough to take anyone to their knees," Demitri commiserates. "Unfortunately, we must add that you were forced into a soulmate connection with me, and I'm a little clueless on a lot of levels. My cluelessness has created a disaster."

"Now we get to what you're really here for," I grumble, suspecting where this is going.

"Please don't shut down," Demitri says. "Yes, this is the part about Jayla, but your suspicions are unfounded."

"I'm positive you're lying."

My tone makes Demitri slide into his most serious version. "Why do you think that?"

"Because I've got all the pieces," I reply.

"Fine," Demitri says. "Put the puzzle together for me."

I succinctly lay out everything Trey helped me piece together.

Demitri doesn't falter while he listens. When I finish, he takes a steady breath. "While that all sounds airtight, it's wrong. I get that it looks bad." He smiles softly at me. "I'd be pissed also if I had all of that rattling around in my head. I'm surprised you haven't forced your way into my memory."

"I refuse to violate you that way," I inform him. "So, that leaves us with the option of you and Jayla not being sneaky cheats. Unfortunately, you both seem to be sneaky cheats. Therefore, I'm pissed."

Demitri squeezes my hand. "There's this thing that's happened to Jayla since we were little."

"Ughhh."

"Hear me out. Jayla approaches life with the sweetest

intentions," he says, "but I can't tell you the number of times Jayla's been in some misunderstanding that seems founded, but has some bizarre set of circumstances that explain everything. This, with you, is an example of the perfect storm she always faces. It always tears her up, but it usually gets resolved after some frustration. This situation is particularly concerning, though. You're on edge, and deadly when you're pushed too far. It's imperative that you understand that Jayla isn't trying to go toe-to-toe with you, steal your guy, or be a problem."

"Explain why she was upset when she found out about us," I request.

"Her reaction was purely because I hadn't told her sooner. She's used to being my confidante and felt like I was abandoning my friendship with her for you. She had a few jealousy-laced worries that we discussed when I went to see her."

"Why did you want to talk to her secretly?" I ask.

"I was feeling not good enough, out of my league, and in over my head. Jayla is good at understanding insecurity because she's VERY insecure. We've known each other since we were little, and she understands me. I figured she also understands you, so I discussed my concerns."

"Rule number one, never tell anyone everything you know, because then they know twice as much as you." I slide heavily weighted eyes to Demitri. "Jayla hovers about collecting intel on everyone. The moment you started secretly feeding her my personal business, she started saying nasty little things like 'Let her go, Demitri.' Same shit Victoria's doing to me. I've learned through the Trey and Victoria mess. I'll be damned if I let a situation get out of control like that again. I'm stopping it before it destroys me this time."

"Melanie . . ." Demitri buries his face in his hands. He takes a sharp breath. "None of that is the case regarding Jayla, but I'm so sorry. I didn't think about that when I was talking to her. She isn't collecting intel to hurt you, and I'm not feeding her info as some 'loyalty to my mistress' mind game. You have my word on that, but I will curb telling her things about you."

I ponder for a moment. "Fine," I reply. "I'll let her secret collecting go, mainly because I can crush her."

Relieved, Demitri exhales.

"I'm surprised you needed to talk to her in the first place. How could you feel not good enough?" I ask, baffled.

Demitri's face scrunches. "I've said before that looking like this is very lonely. I meant it." He morphs with a sweet smile. "Then this tiny girl, that I had a big crush on, walked up, talked to me like I was a person, and I had a best friend. That led to my high school dream. You pulled me into a group of all these cool kids with vibrant personalities. Then, you became friends with Jayla, and I was really happy for her because she had her high school dream also." His expression dips. "Everyone is blaming her because you almost died when the Machetes attacked. It was my fault that I was with Jayla instead of you, but there's no stopping the Roller Rink Girl Club, and her dream world is falling apart. Much like me, she never had many friends before you."

"I never had many friends before high school, hence why I don't treat my friends like shit," I reply. "Her plight isn't my problem. She chose this."

"No," Demitri says, "*I* chose this. We've come full circle. *I'm* the one who went to her house without talking to you, discussed your private business, missed our date, didn't give you a key, and was with her when you got attacked. That's on me, and I apologize wholeheartedly."

I shrug.

"I talked to Adam about this," Demitri says. "He informed that you are capable of extreme forgiveness with your guy, but your punishment for him is the desecration of the other girl in the situation. Jayla doesn't deserve that, isn't built to face it, did nothing wrong, and I need you to understand."

I sigh. "D, I know you see the best in people, but sometimes it's a hindrance. Even though *you* dismiss your looks, everyone else views you as some prize worth destroying the universe for. Women go to unspeakable lengths for a man as rare as you." I give him a pointed look. "Even pretty little sweethearts can be sneaky scoundrels over the shiniest prize. I think you're being shortsighted about this."

Demitri cups my cheek, "You deserve more consideration and forethought from me while you heal from abuse," he replies. "I put you and Jayla in a bad position. Is there a compromise we can make so that both Jayla and I can show you that we can all coexist?"

I ponder before groaning. "Fine. If she oversteps again, she's permanently out of my life."

"Okaaaaay," Demitri draws out thoughtfully. "Now we're getting somewhere." He gives me a soft look. "I guarantee that Jayla won't overstep in some obscene way. You're worried about nothing. I'm going to double down. You can kill her if she goes wild."

My eyebrows rise. "That's a hell of a thing to guarantee to La Diabla."

Demitri tweaks my nose. "I'm that sure of who she is."

"Curb the secret couples' stuff with her," I request.

"I will, but I promise that what you're seeing is friend stuff. I get it though." Demitri exhales, looking relieved. "Thank you, Melanie."

I grin at him. "I look forward to watching you figure out how to tell her our agreement, while not divulging my details, AND not sharing all of this with anyone you enlist to be there while you talk to her, so that you aren't having a secret little lovers' chat." I nod brightly. "That's quite a pickle."

He grins back at me. "One step ahead of you. I don't have to say anything except for, 'Done. Don't screw it up,' because what you offered was PRECISELY what she begged for—another chance, if she never accidently oversteps again."

"Oh ewwwww." I scrunch my face. "You manipulated me right into her hand!"

Demitri cracks up, hugging me. "No, I didn't. You two just landed on the same page, and that's a positive." He kisses me on the forehead. "I think we should go in there and try to salvage Roller Rink Girl Club."

I roll my eyes. "It's stupid."

"I didn't think it's stupid," he says. "I was excited to be one of the cool kids. I love secret knocks, and all that kid stuff I missed out on." He beams. "Thank you for hearing me out."

"Your perspective is irritating," I huff.

Demitri chuckles. "That's because it diffused your justification for being hurt, and you have to learn new patterns now."

"Ugh," I grumble as we head back into Mabel's to create some misfit fun.

CHAPTER 44

"**Y**ou forgot the pivot," Molly cats, and my temper flares. I side-eye the wings, and there stands Ms. Alice, leaving me no room to blow my stack.

"Engage through your abs," Jayla Tinkerbells.

"What?" Molly snips.

"You drop your heel half a turn early every time you attempt a quad," Jayla says. "It's because you release your core a beat early in anticipation when you attempt past a triple, instead of following through." She smiles pleasantly. "Melanie taught me that when she retrained my turns. Thought I'd pass it on."

Molly storms away.

"Thank you," I murmur to Jayla, while we watch Molly attempt a quad turn in the other wing. She holds her core the extra beat and nails it. I smile and nod at Molly, who flounces away in a snit.

"What a bitch," Jayla snarks, and I snap my gaze her way. She never cusses or confronts anyone. "I'm sick and tired of her. She's always rude to you, but today was a step beyond. If she wants to point out you missing one little thing because we're eight hours into this rehearsal from hell, then I'm going to point out what she's done wrong at *every* rehearsal." She squeezes my arm. "I've got your back, Meley Bean."

Demitri smiles as Jayla walks away.

"That was interesting," I murmur.

"She's really trying," he murmurs back.

"You think?"

"I know," he responds.

"I have no idea how Molly gets away with treating me like she does. Mr. Isley, the producer, and Ms. Alice have yet to say anything."

Jayla stomps up to us, with Javier and the other Hollywood High dancers behind her. "Boost me and let's take care of business," she furiously demands.

My eyebrows snap up in response to her pissed order.

She flips a hand toward the stage. "Mr. Isley wants us to run 'Batdance.' Molly just told Ms. Alice that it's an asinine piece, full of a bunch of talentless kids."

I chuckle. "The piece really is a strange addition to this show, but so is my Savage Garden duet with Demitri, and 'Swing the Mood.'"

"The producer and Mr. Isley decided they needed to appeal to a more current audience," Demitri reveals. "There's only so much 'Hello, Dolly' and 'Bye Bye Birdie' we can do."

"Let's nail this, and teach that bitch a lesson," Jayla says.

I snort. "Well, all right." Looks like Jayla has found her inner badass. I touch her arm, sending an energy boost.

"Boost all of us," she requests, gesturing to the Hollywood High dancers.

That surprises me. Most of them don't like me.

"We're with you, Melanie," Jocelyn Sloan says. "I owe you an apology. You've more than proven yourself in these rehearsals. I always thought you got leads in our dance pieces because you have an agent. I now realize that you actually work hard. You also catch more shit than I can believe. I was Victoria's best friend. I backed her for a long time, hence why I was nasty to you. I was obviously wrong. I apologize."

"Me too," Amanda Roberts says. "I told Victoria I was done with her when she talked shit about you yesterday. She stole your man, has no remorse, and I've realized I was doing her shallow dirty work."

"Thank you," breathes from me. I've always thought of Jocelyn and Amanda as just two bitchy dancers, so I appreciate what they just said. "That . . ." Left speechless, I send a bubble of what I'm feeling to Demitri.

"Melanie has been through a lot," he says. "Thank you for this. Your support means a great deal."

Amanda nods. "Jayla told us the nasty stuff Molly has been hissing at Melanie. We weren't aware." She tips her head. "Now we are, and it's about to get live. So, boost us, let's make a point, and then we," she gestures to the three meanest of the female dancers, "are going to handle Molly."

I laugh. "God help Molly. She's certainly met her match. Thank you."

The three rattlesnake mean girls grin at me.

I hold out my arm, and the dancers all latch on. I send an energy boost.

"Places for 'Batdance,'" comes through the speakers, and my fellow Hollywood High dancers and I strut to our spots, off like a shot when Prince's song begins. Being connected to them is new. All I've experienced is disconnection from most of these people.

"Here we go Melanie," Jayla says, as she and I split center stage.

We prep and hit synced turns. I grin. Mr. Isley loves when we hit it right and proves it as he bellows praise through the microphone.

We pull up to our favorite overlook at Mulholland, and I exhale hard as Demitri cuts the engine. We step out into the cool night air, and I take a deep breath to clear my head. It's been a long day, but we're finally through it all. We rehearsed at the Hollywood Bowl for twelve hours.

Demitri pops the back hatch of his Jeep, and my eyebrows rise. "Well, look at you."

He chuckles, flourishing to the yoga mats, grocery sack of snacks, and blanket. He picks me up and plunks me onto my purple yoga mat, then hands me a box of Teddy Grahams and says with authority, "This club meeting shall come to order."

I laugh. "This is really sweet. Thank you."

"Final rehearsal in the books," he says as he settles in the back of the Jeep with me.

I smile as I study him. "This show is going to be really good."

"I'm really excited to be in it." he says.

"Jayla did me a solid today," I say. "Not only did the meanest dancers treat me like a human being, but Molly apologized for treating all of us like crap, two more Hollywood High dancers got agency auditions, and 'Batdance' is FINALLY being performed onstage."

"Thank you for giving Jayla a chance," Demitri murmurs.

"Thank you for changing your behavior with her," I reply.

He looks my way. "I haven't changed anything," he informs. "The difference is that Jayla is comfortable being upfront instead of insecurely whispering."

"I'm sorry I was mean and suspicious." I shake my head. "I feel bad about it."

"I'm sorry I made it seem like it was shady," Demitri replies. "I've done a lot of thinking and realized that a lot of why I was so stunned that you noticed what Jayla and I were doing is that no one ever really paid attention to what I did before. Much like you felt like a ghost, so did I." He looks to me with so much in his gaze.

"What's wrong, D?" I ask.

"No, no, nothing's wrong," he says. "I'm just thinking about all these amazing things. This past month has been a cyclone, but a lot of good has come of it. I love having someone in my life who cares about what I do, wants to be with me, and loves me like you do."

"Soulmate life is hard, but there's good that comes of it," I say softly. My gaze drops. "Adam talked about how the bond can drag you straight to heaven or hell, based on decisions you make before you understand the bond. I think it's also important to be strong enough to be all in once you understand the bond, though. That's where Trey and Adam really failed." I lace my fingers with Demitri's. "I can work through growing pains and mistakes while my soulmate figures things out." I look to him. "Now that you've figured out more about our bond, you're even more committed instead of running scared. That's what sets you apart from my previous soulmates."

He brushes my hair from my forehead. "I didn't put in all this work to run now," he says softly. "Thank you for giving me a chance."

"Thank you for being everything I've wished for," I reply.

Demitri's expression softens almost painfully.

"I'm sorry that I'm broken, because you deserved all the fairy-tale magic. Instead, you're stuck helping me stumble through irrational trauma and fear. I hate that for you."

"I wouldn't have it any other way," Demitri says softly. "You don't trust the easy way, Melanie. It's programmed into you that the only way to earn something worth having is through strife and hardship. I think this was hard because you and I are supposed to stick." He smiles, looking down at his lap. "I have something to reveal."

"Oh, ughhhhhh," I groan. "What?" I'm not in the mood for a revelation. Trey ruined me for secrets.

"Ms. Alice signed me."

That's the last thing I expect him to say, and my surprised reaction is genuine, even though I already knew. "That's amazing!" I bubble over, hugging Demitri.

"Thank you! I was so excited." He gives me a pained look. "That's why I was such a mess when I came to get you during the audition debacle."

I wave a hand. "All in the past."

He chuckles. "Ms. Alice told me that every damn time she turns around, you're pulling in another wad of cash."

I wobble my head. "A girl has to have a hobby, I guess."

"A *hobby*?" he marvels. At my deadpan reaction, he laughs in disbelief. "You've been signed with her less than a year and you've done a blockbuster movie, danced professionally on the surf circuit, booked a commercial, you're about to dance at the Hollywood Bowl, you got an Oscar nomination, AND you just booked a gig at the Whisky a Go Go!"

I shake my head, laughing a little. "We're not talking about me. We're talking about *your* big news."

He laces his fingers with mine. "I'm going somewhere with it. Let me get it out."

We've discovered that Demitri takes the scenic route through thoughts, while I'm on the expressway. We've agreed to try understanding each other's communication styles as part of this relationship building.

"Fair enough. Carry on," I encourage.

"You're a sixteen-year-old triple threat who manages to book stuff simply because you exist," he says. "Ms. Alice just has to answer the phone, sign paperwork, and collect payments." He shakes his head. "She said that she expects that kind of success from me." He winces. "You've set the bar pretty damn high."

I shrug. "Your Broadway gig is looming," I remind of the intuition pulse I got when we were at his dad's house after I nearly killed Victoria in a koala onesie. "She'll be impressed."

"You're sure that's coming?" he asks.

"Positive. That intuition pulse was rock solid."

We stare out at the twinkling city lights. The view from our Mulholland overlook is spectacular. There's only one other car here, and the content quiet is long overdue.

"I couldn't imagine living anywhere else," quietly marvels from me.

Demitri stares at my profile. "I couldn't either, but I heard you when you said you want a quiet mountain house with chirping birds."

I smile at that reminder. The night at his dad's house was the best talk we've ever had. It seems that it clarified a lot for both of us.

An ambulance screams by.

"Maybe we could settle for chirping ambulances." I sigh as it quiets again. "There's nowhere else like Hollywood. We've lived a lot of places over the course of our lifetimes, but this?" I gesture to the gorgeous city below.

"From up here you can't feel the panic and fear down there," Demitri says.

I laugh a little. "It's hard being an empath in a big city."

"It drives me insane," he agrees. "Living at Mabel's is nuts."

"I'm so shuttered there because I don't want to feel it," I quietly say. "It's Trey's dismay that's the hardest to handle."

"He hurts so bad," Demitri says. "I can feel it every time I walk through the door. The only thing that's worse is Victoria's cyclonic jumble of emotions."

A laugh bubbles from me. "We're all bonkers. There's not one person in our group who isn't a complete loon."

"That's why the Misfits have to stick together."

We settle into silence again. After a long stretch of twinkling-light time, he gets out of the back of the Jeep and heads to the driver's door. As our song, Duran Duran's "Come Undone," thrums through the speakers, he comes back and holds out his hand. "May I have this dance?"

I giggle and take his hand, and he breezes me through the song. My breath is taken away as I stare at him by moonlight.

"I can't even breathe around you," he whispers.

"I was just thinking the same thing about you," I whisper back.

"This song is so accurate," he quietly expresses, as he stops dancing. "I always want this with you. We dance together, have a soulmate connection, and my life is almost perfect."

"Almost?" I ask.

"Yeah, almost," he says as he reaches into his back pocket, pulls out a velvet ring box, and drops to one knee. "Melanie, will you marry me?" He pops open the box, revealing a delicate white-gold ring with a round sapphire, surrounded by little black stones in a swirling pattern.

I blink to clear shock from my sputtering brain. I focus on the black stones. "What are those?" I breathe.

"They're black diamonds. Rare, like you. I secretly bought the ring at Renn Faire." Demitri smiles at me. "I saw it and thought, 'That's me and Meley, perfectly embodied in a ring.'"

"It's stunning!" I tear up, suddenly realizing something. I slowly look around. "This is the exact spot," breathes from me.

"What's wrong?" he asks, still on one knee.

"My intuition pulse about being proposed to on Mulholland!" I snap my gaze back to Demitri. "It wasn't originally you, though." I slowly smile. "The paradigm shifted."

"Neat," he says. "Any chance you'd fill a guy in on what your answer was in that intuition pulse?"

I belt laughter, so relieved to have this huge clue about the direction I should head. "YES!" I squeal.

"Yes?" blisters from Demitri.

I nod, caught in a state of excited adoration.

"Holy crap, the girl said YES!" Demitri barks over his shoulder toward the convertible behind him. We hear spurting laughter, and I giggle as the guy gives Demitri a subtle thumbs-up.

I flutter my hands. "Pretty ring, pretty ring," I chirp like a girly nut. "I've never seen such a pretty ring, and I want it on my fing*ggggg*errrrrr."

"Crap, sorry," Demitri says, hopping to his feet. Flustered, he drops the ring box. "Shit!"

The elderly couple in the other car get another case of the giggles. "The boy needs a wingman," we hear the woman mutter to the man.

They get out of their convertible, and the grandfatherly gentleman strides our way. He picks up the box and opens it, standing behind Demitri's shoulder. "I'm not here," he mutters, holding the open box rock steady.

"Thank you!" Demitri boils out, a complete mess, totally out of character for him.

"Take the ring out of the box and put it on her finger," the man mutters comically as Demitri fitfully flaps about.

The man's wife and I try to curb our laughter.

Demitri's hand shakes as he reaches for the ring. The man chuckles and takes it out of the box, waving subtly for my hand. I hold it out, and the stranger slides the ring only as far as the first joint. With the man's encouragement, Demitri pushes the ring the rest of the way onto my finger.

The gentleman claps Demitri on the back. "Good job."

"Thank you for helping me," Demitri gasps.

"Hey, I get it," the man says. He looks adoringly over his shoulder at the woman who's leaning against the convertible. "I proposed to my wife here, fifty-two years ago tonight. We come here every year to celebrate." His eyebrow raises. "The celebrations are a little different these days." He juts a thumb at his wife. "*She* has a bad hip."

We howl laughter while the woman grins, taking the razzing in stride.

"Fifty-two years," Demitri says, in awe.

"It's simpler than people think," the man says. "Be honest, never go to bed angry, if you know you shouldn't do something then don't, tell her you love her every morning and night, and never take the simple moments for granted." He grins. "Also, women are insane. Sometimes you just say, 'Yes, dear,' and go with it."

Demitri smiles and side-eyes me. "I think that might be the kind of help we've needed."

"Me too," I say. "I'm Melanie, and this is Demitri."

"Arthur and Blanche Boemant."

"Now that we're on a first-name basis, can I PLEASE gawk at your ring?" Blanche calls out from her spectating spot.

"Yes, please," I squeal with girly excitement.

She rushes my way, surprisingly spry for a woman likely in her seventies, who supposedly has a bad hip. She delicately takes my hand, and her breath catches. "My dear," she softly says as she looks into my eyes, "That's *truly* gorgeous."

"I really, really, really, really love it," I bubble out. "It's totally different, and not what I had before, and didn't come from the first store that had a sale sign, and he put thought into it, and EVERYTHING." I blather on.

The woman's eyes narrow suspiciously. "You've had a really bad experience previously, I take it?"

"You have NO IDEA!" falls out of my mouth.

"Oh, I do," she says with an air of wisdom. "Arthur is my second husband. I was previously married at sixteen." She rushes to defend herself. "That was common back then."

I scoff. "While not common now, I've been previously hand-fasted twice, and I'm currently sixteen." I wobble my head about. "I'm almost seventeen."

Arthur squints at me. "Oh, my goodness . . ." He looks to his wife. "Don't you DARE get weird. Deep breath." When Blanche takes a deep breath, Arthur says, "You're Melanie Slate."

Blanche makes a strangled sound, and I laugh. "It's okay," I tell Arthur, in response to the horrified look he fires his wife's way. "Yes, I'm Melanie Slate."

"And La Diabla," he says. When I cage up, he rushes to reassure me. "I'm a professor specializing in metaphysics. I've followed your journey through underground tales, because you have incredibly unique abilities. I'm a stodgy, harmless, curious old bookworm. I'm not a threat, but your mention of two previous husbands, in combination with your tiny frame, clued me in that you're *that* Melanie." He squints, seeming to ponder, then snaps his fingers. "Pierre 'Riptide' Strader and Trey Valdez."

"How do you know *that* detail?" I ask nervously.

Arthur tips his head. "You're famous. Your marriages have been in newspaper articles, although most random people don't know that La Diabla is Melanie Slate. I just happened to have all the pieces, because my wife loves smutty movies, and I love metaphysics."

I giggle. "So, you really aren't a threat?"

"Nope," he says, "but I am going to put meeting you, and helping with this special moment, in my top ten life experiences." He surveys me. "You're so tiny, but I know you have an unbelievable ability to use energy as a weapon. You're legendary among the metaphysical crowd as of the past year." He looks to Demitri. "I do believe that you're the healer everyone talks about, although no one has figured out your name."

Demitri takes a slow breath. "I must keep my healing abilities a secret. I've worried incessantly about how exposed I've been the past six months."

Arthur nods. "Your kind is regularly kidnapped and enslaved by people you never want to be trapped by. You have my word that your identity is safe with me."

"Thank you," Demitri replies.

"Enough with all this serious talk," Blanche says. "These two deserve to finish their engagement." She giggles, teasing, "Something tells me that Melanie doesn't have a bad hip."

We all laugh.

"The way my dance career is being pushed lately, I may have a bad hip soon," I joke. An idea comes to me. "Any chance you two are free tomorrow evening?"

"We are," Blanche says, sounding curious.

I cross to my dance bag and pull the tickets that the producer gave me at rehearsal. "I was gifted two comp tickets for my parents, but they're busy jet-setting," I say, as I head back to them and hand over the tickets. I shrug. "I'd like to thank you for helping us, if you're interested in seeing a show."

Blanche's mouth drops open as she surveys the tickets.

Arthur asks, "Two front-row center seats to the *Jazz Extravaganza* show at the Hollywood Bowl?"

I nod enthusiastically, and they stare at each other.

"That was our first date fifty-three years ago," Blanche says in wonder. "We met there by coincidence when we had seats next to each other. We were holding hands by intermission. We've gone every year since but couldn't get tickets this year. It sold out the day that tickets went on sale because Molly Horowitz . . ."

". . . and Melanie Slate were headlining," Arthur says, finishing the statement for her.

Blanche looks down at the tickets. "Are you sure, Melanie? These tickets are worth five hundred each."

"I'm sure. You've helped us a great deal in the past few minutes. Your advice about marriage is what I'd like for Demitri and me to follow, because my previous experiences weren't stellar."

Demitri grins at them. "I appreciate the advice, because this one," he juts a thumb to me, "fights like a wolverine in a bear trap."

Arthur gives Demitri a look. "Believe me, I understand."

Blanche and I spurt laughter that the guys join in on.

"Melanie," Arthur says, "if we helped, when we're really just two bored, old, nosey jackasses who didn't mind our own business when two darling young people were working through a life-changing moment, then I'm glad." He grins. "We were likely to feel bad for interrupting later, but damn did the boy need a hand."

"I wish every interference in my life was so well-timed, kind, and helpful," I inform them.

"Will you be at the show?" Blanche asks Demitri.

"Demitri's my dance partner in the show," I inform them.

"I can't wait to watch you two dance!" she exclaims.

"We're going to cheer louder than anyone else there," Arthur promises, before they take turns hugging us. He squeezes my arm. "Has anyone ever taught you about how metaphysics is directly related to quantum physics?"

Curious, I shake my head.

He raises his eyebrows. "If you gather up your energy working group long enough to sit down with me, I guarantee it'll benefit you."

A giggle bursts from me, and I wave my hand about. "A warning that my former soulmate is hunting up a route to obliterate my spirit guide, and the timing of your offer may not be a coincidence."

Arthur's face morphs with amused shock. "Did your spirit guide do something that warrants obliteration?"

"Did she ever," I reply, while Demitri whistles low.

"Then she gets what she gets." Arthur shrugs good-naturedly. He pulls his wallet from his slacks pocket, takes out a card, and hands it to me. "Call me, and we'll set a time. Please actually do. Your group fascinates me, and meeting with you is the final item on my bucket list."

"You sure you want to scratch that last item off?" I ask, concerned.

"I must," he replies. "The timing is exactly right."

With that, the couple gets back in their little red convertible. Arthur fires up the impressive engine and pops in a cassette tape. Journey's "Don't Stop Believin'" blasts as they speed off into the night. Blanche throws her hands in the air and bellows a vibrant, "WOO-HOO," as they make the turn, driving out of sight.

"Sometimes there are angels on Earth," I murmur.

Demitri pulls me in, hugging me, and whispers in my ear, "We're everything. You're everything. Thank you for saying yes."

I kiss him, and the feeling of fur and satin that's purely Demitri slides up my spine. Contentment fills me as I curl my face into his neck. He curls his to match, and we both breathe in and exhale in unison.

CHAPTER 45

I'm pacing in the wings at the Hollywood Bowl. Half of me is shocked that I'm about to perform on this iconic stage. The other half is terrified.

The stage manager rushes by and announces, "Ten minutes until places."

My heart nearly beats out of my chest, and I turn to the mirror on the wall behind the curtain wings. My hair is slicked back in a high, crisply straightened ponytail. I've got burgundy lips and dark eyeshadow on my eyes. The outfit is a black strappy S and M inspired bustier that I'm hoping I don't fall out of. The bottoms are black Lycra booty shorts. Though the outfit covers everything, I feel naked and vulnerable. Add to it the lace-up knee-high-heeled boots, and I'm suddenly glad my parents aren't here to see this.

The stage manager rushes by again, announcing, "Five minutes."

I unblock my connection with Demitri but carefully fuzz out my nerves so my anxiety doesn't affect him.

"You good?" he sends.

"Nope. I'm dressed like a hooker. I can't remember my choreography. I'm way out of my league. I'm quitting dance after this."

I feel Demitri smile adoringly. *"You look hot. You'll remember the piece the second the music starts. You're right where you belong."* He requests, *"Unfuzz your side so I can fix you."* I do, and he sends surprise. *"You're so cute! I didn't know you get this nervous."* He sends an emotion bubble through our connection that pops in my chest.

Calm capable energy spreads slowly through me, and I exhale. *"Thank you."*

The lights dim, and the stage manager announces that it's time to take our places.

"Here we go, baby girl," Demitri sends.

I head to my spot on the dark stage. All the girls start "Cell Block Tango" behind a long row of jail cell bars. I grab the bars in the dark, and ground and center.

Light slowly builds as the first note of the music starts. My dark-water side oozes just enough to the surface to be helpful but not take over. My heel taps to the rhythm.

Demitri jazz walks out with the guys, and they open the cell doors all down the row. I slither and swirl out with the girls, and we work through a blistering group section downstage.

I turn for our duet section and start my monologue. My voice is laced with my dark-water side, which works for my character. Demitri smirks at me as he slouches in a sexy ooze into the chair. We make it through the monologue and blaze through the slinky body-rolling, dangerous lift-filled tango duet.

Demitri gets an arm under my lower back, and I plunge into the layout at the end of our section. The crowd cheers as he gets my feet under me. I jazz walk through the jail door, and Demitri meets me on the other side of the bars. We're supposed to grip, body roll, and rub all over each other with the bars between us. It quickly gets just heated enough to look right from the audience, but we know there's more simmering under the surface.

We get through the blisteringly sexy routine, and Demitri lifts me for the final pose. As the lights blink out, he lowers me to my feet and kisses me hard in the dark. He sends, *"Dancing with you is everything."*

— —

I take a deep breath in the brief dark silence before "Batdance" starts. The music begins, and I'm off like a shot. My mind blanks in that way that happens when I've got a piece down cellularly. I rejoice in these moments, where I get to thrill in the art of movement, without my usual nagging insecurities.

I hit my turn series and make it all the way to my Vicki Vale section without missing a turning beat. Demitri bites his tongue playfully at me while we flirt, in character. I've intentionally got him shuttered off because I want to enjoy dancing with him without all the soulmate stuff affecting the experience.

I climb the ladder on the side of the set that looks like a building. As I grip the handles on the faux windowsill, a nervous zing shoots up my back. This is the only part of the piece I don't like. It's choreographed with no eye contact with Demitri, who's supposed to catch me as I backflip, leaping from the three-story spot. We've drilled it over and over, though.

The music count hits, and I launch. I hear, "Oh, shit!" and glance, mid-rotation. Demitri is catching Jayla, and panic shoots through me. I just leapt from twenty feet up. There's no time to make some glorious plan, but I'm grabbed. The placement is all wrong, but it stops the momentum some before I hit the stage. I slide through the hard landing, and Javier pulls me up, rushing me offstage. I glare from the wings as Demitri and Jayla make what's supposed to be our trio section into a duet.

"Are you hurt?" Javier asks.

"I don't know yet," I reply, flummoxed. The intense tornado section is coming up, so I tell him, "Get out there." After he rushes away, I assess my state a little closer. My hamstring burns, and my wrist has a sharp pain when I flex it, but it moves.

Mr. Isley rushes to me, looking me over as the piece ends. The dancers rush offstage when the stage goes black.

"Melanie, are you okay?" Demitri panics.

"What the HELL was that?" Mr. Isley snarls at him.

"It was my fault," Jayla whimpers. "I got the count wrong. The music repeats there, and I went when Melanie was supposed to, instead of waiting two eight-counts."

My eyes narrow. "How convenient," I say as Molly's solo music comes on. "You chose the onnnnnnne moment that I have to trust Demitri, because I can't see, and you tried to take me out." My gaze shifts suspiciously to Demitri. "Cute scheme. Break Melanie so that you and Jayla not only get to shove me out of the trio, but I just might land in the hospital. That gets me out of your hair, right?" I smirk. "It certainly worked for Trey, twice. Big Bear with Tiffany and planning my fake wedding with Victoria."

"That was NOT what we were attempting," Demitri insists. "It was an honest mistake."

I shake my head at Mr. Isley. "I'm out. I think I've got a torn hamstring, and I know I've sprained my wrist."

Mr. Isley's eyes widen. "We've got your solo, the duet with Demitri, and 'Swing the Mood' to go." He looks to Demitri. "Can you heal her real quick?"

I glare at Mr. Isley. "I'm not doing the duet or 'Swing the Mood.' Both are full of overhead lifts with Demitri. Until we hash this out, and I check both of their memories to see if they planned that amateur, rookie 'mistake,' I'm out."

"I would never intentionally hurt you like that!" Demitri insists.

"You were supposed to catch ME!" I hiss back. "Why the hell did you shift to catching her instead?"

"She jumped, and I instinctively shifted, thinking I made a mistake. I realized Jayla was the one who got it wrong when you made the jump when you were supposed to. I panicked, but she was already landing."

My focus shifts to Javier. "Thank you for grabbing me."

"I'm sorry I didn't get to you in time to properly catch you," he says. "I ran from the wings as fast as I could, but all I could do is slow you down and slide you to break the momentum."

Demitri cups my wrist. He winces, his forehead beading sweat.

"Survey says?" Mr. Isley asks.

"Broken trapezium," Demitri murmurs.

My wrist feels better a few moments later. He kneels to grab my hamstring, and I glare down at him.

He sighs. "We need to get through the show," he implores.

I begrudgingly relent. While he heals my hamstring, I glare at Jayla.

"I'm so sorry, Melanie," she pleads.

Finished fixing me, Demitri stands. A stagehand delivers my next costume to Mr. Isley, and he hands it to me. This has taken up my time to catch a breather and change.

"Melanie, I'm asking you to finish out the show," Mr. Isley says, before turning his focus to Demitri. "The next time Jayla decides to leap when she's not supposed to, YOU stay with your assigned partner. You don't need to superhero Jayla to safety. That's her error, and Javier could have gotten to her far easier than he made it to Melanie."

"It was just reflex," Demitri explains.

"Why didn't you have that reflex with me?" I ask.

"I did," Demitri says, "hence why I barked, 'Oh, shit.' I couldn't get there in time, and I was a panicked mess." His face falls. "I don't want you to get hurt, Melanie. I certainly didn't want to turn our trio section into a duet. I'm sorry it happened, but I'm not going to drop you in 'Swing the Mood' or our duet. Please."

I roll my eyes and quickly change into my dress for our duet. As Molly's solo winds down, Demitri starts to guide me to the wings, but I shirk away from him. I see his head fall as the lights go out. Our music starts, and we work through the duet to Savage Garden's "To the Moon and Back." Instead of the connection we usually have, the piece is emotionally mechanical.

I grit my teeth as I run his way and prep a leap. He gets under me, executing the lift. We've never had a problem with it, but I don't trust him now.

"Loosen up, Melanie," Demitri murmurs, as I turn around him.

I don't though. I'm relieved when the piece is over.

I finish my solo and rush offstage.

"That's my girl!" Demitri whispers, starting to hug me.

I take a step back, trying to catch my breath. "Thank God that's over," I mutter. My last piece in the show is done, and I'm ready to move on.

Mr. Isley and our agent, Chelsea Alice, rush to us.

"Melanie," Mr. Isley says.

I look from Chelsea to him, taking in their panic. "What's wrong?"

"Jayla's throwing up in the dressing room," Ms. Alice says.

"What?"

Mr. Isley rolls his eyes. "She's terrified to do the closing number. Nerves have her doubled over. Can you do the final piece? I need a Roxie for 'Hot Honey Rag.'"

My mouth falls open. "That piece is *next!*"

"I know," Mr. Isley says. "I never should have cast Jayla. It's our closing number. I can't scrap the piece. Do you know it?"

"I mean . . ." I hesitate, wracking my brain. "I've seen the piece enough in rehearsals. I can fake it, if you'll let me improvise the little solo sections that Jayla never got right. I can do the duet sections if I follow my memory of Molly doing them the right way."

"I'll take anything I can get," Mr. Isley says.

Ms. Alice snags the silver sparkly costume that's draped over his shoulder, and she and Demitri get started quick-changing me, while Mr. Isley crash-courses me on the parts I'm not sure of. Luckily, Jayla's costume fits me.

Ms. Alice hands Jayla's silver character shoes to Demitri, who shakes his head. "Melanie's shoe size is three bigger than Jayla's," he informs.

Mr. Isley has a whispered conversation with the MC, while I look down at the red heels I wear for the "There'll Be Some Changes Made" solo. Applause rings out from the audience as "Life Is Just a Bowl of Cherries" ends. There's no time to figure out shoes. I rush to the wing and nod at Molly in the wing across the stage from me. Her eyes widen, and the look she gives Mr. Isley could melt iron.

"Ladies and gentleman," comes through the speakers as the stage darkens. "To close our *Jazz Extravaganza Evening with the Stars* show, I present to you Molly Horowitz, of *Sometimes in Michigan*," there's raucous applause, "and Melanie Slate, of *Glamour!*"

As the crowd goes wild, my eyes widen. That's the first time my name has been recognized in that way by a huge audience.

"Hot Honey Rag" shimmers through the speakers, and panic overcomes me for a moment as I realize I've never once sung this song aloud. The words come from me as Molly and I sway from the wings and walk toward each other. I nail the opening lines in the song.

We strip off our marabou feathered robes as the ragtime rhythm kicks. Confidence swells, and I laugh with Molly, in character, as we bounce and heel click before we start the Charleston. We giggle and play, pounce and sashay, and it's magic.

She takes my hands, and we circle each other before beginning the synchronized high kicks. Molly's solo section comes up, and she's on fire. What she's truly capable of is on full display.

When she gives me a sassy, challenging look, I nod my agreement, taking her up on the challenge, per the choreography. I take off like a shot, hitting four front handsprings before launching into whatever my body does naturally. I don't know Jayla's solo, but I know the song, and this feeling of complete confidence always offers brilliance when it happens onstage.

The audience roars their approval as I slam into a cute pose at the end of my solo bit. Molly rushes to me with a huge grin, and we take the piece home. The song ends, and we link arms, waving at the audience, all smiles, as the announcer says, "Thank you for coming to our show!"

"That's our GIRLLLLLLLL!" bellows from the audience, and I grin at Arthur and Blanche, who are on their feet in the front row, screaming louder than everyone else in the deafening audience.

Molly and I bow and run offstage as the lights go black.

"Yesssssss!" Ms. Alice bellows as she wraps me in a hug and sways me back and forth.

She lets me go, and Molly grabs me by the arms. "You're incredible, Melanie! You saved that piece." She rounds on Mr. Isley. "What the hell happened?"

"I'm sorry," he placates, clearly embarrassed. "Jayla folded."

"Thank God," Molly hisses. "Jayla's a hack."

I wince internally. Jayla just got signed with Ms. Alice. Her meltdown, and timing mistake earlier, may cannonball her.

"I apologize for all our issues, Melanie," Molly says. "You've got the chops for this business." She squeezes my arm before flouncing to her private dressing room.

"Thank you for saving my ass," Mr. Isley murmurs for only me, Ms. Alice, and Demitri to hear.

"You're welcome," I murmur back, before heading to my private dressing room.

— —

I rush up the steep incline to the outdoor audience area, where I see my friends and run to them. I get to Tanner first.

He picks me up and spins me around. "Super Melanie did it again!" he crows.

I giggle happily as he sets me down.

"What happened in 'Honey Rag'?" Dante asks.

Everyone leans in, clearly curious for the dirt. I glance around, but Jayla isn't out yet.

"Sometimes things shift," I tactfully say. "They needed me to fill in."

"Jayla rehearsed 'Honey Rag' every single spare moment," Dante says dejectedly.

I shrug, not wanting to spill her meltdown business.

"I didn't even know you were her understudy," Dante insists, seeming irritated with me over this.

My expression cages, and Mr. Isley says, "I would never place Melanie in the understudy position for Jayla!"

Dante gives Mr. Isley an aggrieved look. "Then why did you replace my girl?" he demands.

Disgusted, Mr. Isley shakes his head and walks off.

Dante narrows his eyes at me. "You stole her big role?"

"Considering the mistake Jayla made during 'Batdance,'" Tanner sasses, "you should be nicer to Melanie." He rolls his eyes. "We all almost had a heart attack in the wings, but Javier saved the day."

We're interrupted by a group of exuberant women. "Will you sign autographs for us?" one boisterously asks.

I look at them quizzically, but Mama Mabel beams. "You saw *Glamour?*"

They enthusiastically carry on, and I'm nearly bowled over with shock. This has never happened to me before. Mabel chatters brightly with the ladies while she pulls five-by-seven press release headshots of me from her giant purse, along with a black marker.

"I'd love to," I say, as Mabel hands them to me with an encouraging smile. All my friends gape while I sign the pictures and hand them out.

Squeals emit, followed by a chorus of, "Thank-yous."

The women skitter off, and I let my shell-shocked state shine. "Weird."

"Wow." Tanner studies me curiously. "Mel, can I have an autograph?"

Perplexed, I tick my head about. "I've signed birthday cards for you for several years."

"'Love you, fucker,' isn't the same."

Everyone laughs as Mabel holds the stack in front of me. I sign a picture, *Love you, fucker. Melanie Slate* and hand it to Tanner, who wiggles about jubilantly.

"Can I have one?" Jayla, who showed up as the women were carrying on, bashfully asks.

Everyone else asks for one in quick succession.

"Well . . . all right," I baffle while personalizing messages to everyone.

"I want one," Demitri breathes into my ear. I look over my shoulder at him. I don't get a chance to respond.

"Is that what I think it is?" Finley says excitedly.

My left hand is yanked, and squeals emit from all the girls, except for Victoria, as they study my engagement ring.

Mabel pulls me into an exuberant hug. "I'm so happy for you." She shakes her head. "Do we ever have a lot to catch your parents up on when they return in a few months." She lets me go and hugs Demitri.

Arthur and Blanche join our group, Blanche radiating joy. "Melanie, you were phenomenal." Her gaze snaps to Demitri. "And you, young man, could make a dead woman sweat bullets!"

Everyone laughs, and I introduce them. "Blanche and Arthur happened to be at the overlook when Demitri proposed. I invited them."

"I wish I'd known," Mabel says. "I would have invited you to join in our VIP box."

"This little firecracker got us front-row seats," Blanche gushes, squeezing me tight.

"Well, we'd love to host you at my place," Mabel says.

"We'd love that!" Arthur says. "Did you live in the area?"

"Indeed," Mama Mabel says. "On Hollywood Boulevard, as a matter of fact."

Arthur squints at Mabel before his eyes snap wide. He looks to his wife. "Do you remember that bachelor party I was invited to in honor of my godson?"

Blanche cracks up. "At Mama Mabel's brothel . . ."

Arthur nods, ticking his finger at Mabel. "This is the lovely lady who chatted with me at the bar while the boys had their fun."

"Arthur Boemant, as I live and breathe," Mabel gasps. "You're the quantum physics professor who also specializes in metaphysics."

Blanche raises her eyebrows at Mabel. "You either have an airtight memory, or my husband wowed you with his prowess."

Mabel crinkles her nose. "Airtight memory, but now I'm curious."

"Do you have a bad hip?" Arthur jokes at Mabel, earning laughter from Demitri and me.

"Can't say I do," Mabel replies.

"I might have to rectify that," Blanche threatens jokingly.

Mabel laughs. "Not a thing to worry about. We only chatted that night, and Arthur here is a delight. Three of my best girls made creative plays for your guy, and he turned them down with such charm that they were quite disappointed."

Arthur puts an arm around his wife. "I'm stuck in my ways and depend on that bad hip of hers." He leans in like he has a secret, and we all lean in to hear it. "I'm seventy-six. I can keep up with a bad hip. I was scared Mabel's gals would break me."

Blanche smacks him in the arm, but she's laughing good-naturedly.

After Arthur and Blanche say goodbye to my crowd, I walk them to the edge of the audience area. "Thank you so much for being here." I duck my head. "It's going to sound silly, but I needed that so much."

Blanche nods. "We figured that out when you gave us the tickets. Your parents are out of town, and all."

"Any idea when we could have that meeting?" Arthur asks.

"Two o'clock tomorrow?" I suggest. "The energy workers will be at Mabel's for work. They all get off around then." I giggle. "Arthur here already knows where it's at."

"We'll be there," he says. "I want Blanche to see the place."

"We've laughed about that story for ten years," she says.

They leave, and I head back to the group.

Tanner saunters up, and Finley asks, "Where were you?"

"Giving Molly Horowitz nasty looks with a bunch of the Hollywood Hotcakes."

"The what?" Bear asks.

"The Hollywood Hotcakes," Tanner repeats. "They're a vogue house group from the club scene." He cocks a hip. "Five of the most devastating voguers in Southern California, and yours truly, tossed her more sass and frass than she can handle. She's likely crying in her Camaro as we speak." He grins at me. "I've got your back, girl."

"Eh, she and I squashed our beef after 'Honey Rag.'"

"Don't care," Tanner haughtily dismisses. "She deserves what she got."

"Congratulations, Melanie," Trey quietly says, and the mood instantly morphs stoic. He takes a deep breath. "In light of that ring, I think I need to do what you did for Adam."

My stomach free-falls, but I can't tell if it's from relief or panic, as Bear and Darren create a circle with Trey and me. I take Darren's hand, and Bear reaches for Trey's.

Demitri barks, "Wait!" We all look at him, and he asks Bear, "Can you teach me how to take down the blockage you're about to put up?"

"I can, and you're strong enough to remove it, but why?"

Demitri stares at Trey intently. "I refuse to let her die because I'm selfish. I'll do whatever I have to to make sure she's safe." When Trey's eyes narrow, Demitri says, "Please. She might need you to save her again."

Trey nods, and we close our eyes. I watch in my mind while they wall us off. When they finish, I hit the new blockage Bear and Darren erected over Trey and my soulmate connection with the full force I'm capable of.

Bear exhales. "I was wondering if we were strong enough to hold her still. You never know what she can do these days."

Trey tears up and has to walk away. Unfortunately, Victoria follows him, and Mabel follows Victoria.

"Damn," Adam mutters. "That's the last of the connections, destroyed, built, obliterated, and finalized."

I exhale hard, not wanting to deal with that. "What now?" I ask.

"Now we're off to our surprise celebration party," Tanner blusters, earning glares from all the Misfits. He winces.

"We are?" I ask.

Tanner shushes me. "Shit. Act surprised when you arrive or Mabel will kill me!"

We all laugh.

CHAPTER 46

"You still good, Demitri?"

"I am. I didn't expect to have this much fun with Adam and Trey."

Mama Mabel breezes by. "Melanie, why aren't you letting loose?"

I gesture across the room toward Demitri. Amused, I inform, "I need to drive him home."

Mabel chuckles as we watch Adam and Trey play "keep-away" with Demitri's wallet. They're in better shape than Demitri is.

"My limo driver is picking us up, so you don't have to worry about driving. You can pick up your cars tomorrow," Mabel informs. "Everyone's staying at our place. Let loose."

Demitri and I talked on the way to the Swirly Girl Bar Mabel owns on Ventura. We resolved our issue about the mistake during "Batdance," mainly because he was so mad at Jayla when we were finally alone that I was left with no doubt that it wasn't premeditated. The bar is closed tonight for our private party, hence why all the minors are having so much fun. All my drunk friends cheer, and Demitri grins at me while he brings me a startlingly blue cocktail in a giant hurricane glass.

"What is this Tanner-blue drink?" I suspiciously ask.

Everyone laughs at the old inside joke.

Demitri grins. "It's called a Dancing Demon, which seems rather fitting."

As I take a sip, my eyes happily snap wide. I take the drink from Demitri, saying, "Nom, nom, nom," while I down another big gulp.

"Go easy, love. It's solid booze."

I raise a seductive eyebrow.

"Never mind," Demitri says, looking amused. "Guzzle it down."

Adam and Trey are lounging against the bar next to us. Victoria wasn't invited to the after party. Add to it that Valerie also wasn't invited, and the evening has proven quite pleasant.

Adam leans over to Trey and says, "Within three hours, he'll be holding her hair while she prays to the porcelain gods."

Trey checks his watch. "I give it two hours."

I hit them with a glare, but a smile creeps up.

They both grin at me.

"Are you two serious?" Demitri asks.

Adam makes an innocent face. "Nope."

Trey shakes his head. "She'll be fiiiiiine."

I'm halfway through the drink, and my head's already buzzy. I bounce and squeal, "Wheeeeee."

"Oh boy," Demitri mutters.

Adam and Trey high-five, thoroughly enjoying Demitri's inevitable demise.

I squish up my face, but a witty retort is quickly forgotten as a giant plate is delivered to Adam's spot at the bar. I squeal, "Nachossssss," and boing to Adam.

He snakes an arm around my waist and pushes the plate closer to me.

"Nom, nom, nom," I say happily as I stuff my face.

Demitri stares at the nacho mountain with revulsion. "You aren't seriously eating that, are you?"

Adam juts a thumb toward the plate. "She loves these things."

Demitri shudders. "I can't even look at those goopy nachos without feeling sick."

Trey pats Demitri on the shoulder. "You're gonna get to see those nachos again in a few hours."

Adam chuckles while he chomps on a nacho and I polish off the rest of my drink.

Demitri stares at my empty hurricane glass. "That was quick."

Our attention is brought to the other side of the room, as Mama Mabel announces, "I'd like to congratulate Javier, Jayla, Demitri, Tanner, Finley, and Melanie on an amazing professional debut. You just made your mark on the entertainment world. What a way to get your big break!" She smiles at Jayla. "I'm so proud of you, my little meteor. Your star shines brighter than all the stars in the sky."

"Thank you," Jayla preens.

My happy buzz takes a radical dip with that nonsense. "Oh, well, how riveting. Thank *heavens* for my big break. Guess the damn movie I was the lead in doesn't count."

Several wince when they realize I perceived Mabel's pronouncement as a slight.

I offer Demitri a glare. "I get insulted, but Jayla's a little meteor?"

Demitri sighs.

"My apologies," Mabel says, correcting herself. "A big congratulations to my superstars who just made their debut. And congrats to Melanie, who already was a superstar."

I wobble my buzzy head about while I face the bar, muttering, "I'm not a little meteor though."

"You're a supernova, Meley," Demitri says to placate me.

I give him a look. "I want to be an adorable little meteor that everyone marvels at, not a supernova that kills with an explosion."

Behind me, Mabel sighs, and I look over my shoulder at her. "Are you really jealous that I endearingly called Jayla that?" she asks.

I scowl. "She's soooooo enchanting."

"What's the problem?" Mabel asks Demitri, because I'm not very cooperative currently.

"Melanie had to save Jayla's ass in the finale," Demitri informs her. "She was already salty at Jayla for making a mistake that injured Melanie before that."

My expression drops rudely. "Your miraculous little meteor also screwed up half of her duet with Javier. He's pissed that he had to improvise to get through the damn thing."

"Let Jayla be excited," Trey encourages. "We all know she sucks. She can be a dumb meteor."

Mabel gives me a disappointed look. "I wasn't trying to insult you. I'm sorry I discounted your movie. I think everyone knows that a lead in a Zane Drell blockbuster takes top billing over a dance show. The show is a big deal to your castmates, though."

I hit Demitri with a look after Mabel walks away. "Dante already blamed *me* because Jayla's a failure!"

"A *meteoric* failure," Adam interjects, goading me on.

"I know," Demitri says. "I talked to him. Dante's sorry."

I scrunch my face. "You promised Jayla wouldn't be a problem anymore!"

"I promised that with regard to me," Demitri says cautiously. "I didn't promise she wouldn't be Jayla, in general, though."

"You didn't even say anything during Mabel's speech!"

Demitri rapidly blinks. "I wasn't the one making the speech."

"AND?" I prompt.

Trey and Adam give Demitri comically expectant looks, and he rattles his head. "Someone, help me out here," he frustratedly requests.

"That's Melanie's 'Why is the other woman so special?' look," Trey enlightens.

"I didn't say she was," Demitri says, sounding exasperated.

"Oh, that," Trey replies. "Yeah . . . that doesn't matter. You're responsible for what others say about the supposed other flame."

"That's insane," Demitri mutters.

"He's adorable," Adam says to Trey. He grins gleefully at Demitri. "Your little supernova is insanely jealous, irrational, and especially unstable when she drinks. You handed her a glass of liquid-candy-crazy that she pounded back on an empty stomach, just before Mabel shorted Melanie's kudos and called Jayla something so sweet it gave me a toothache. Your job was to yell, 'Jayla's a talentless whore.'"

Demitri's eyes are massive. "Why would I do that?"

Adam shrugs. "To defend Melanie. It's asinine but completely expected."

"Why do you think Adam and I are such cynical dicks?" Trey asks. "Lifetimes of dealing with this unstable squirrel." He juts a thumb at me. "You must tromp all over the little meteor regularly to prove that you love Melanie."

Naturally, Jayla skitters up with Tanner, Finley, and Javier. Why wouldn't she? Adam and Trey slump over, laughing their asses off.

"I made something special for us," Jayla sheepishly sweethearts. She pulls homemade lanyard keychains from her purse. "Demitri told me about Zane's mom and her keychain tradition. I think it's cool and made us these."

Demitri practically collapses against the bar, while Trey and Adam howl louder.

Mama Mabel puts an arm around Jayla's waist, cooing, "That is the sweetest thing." She gives Adam and Trey a scathing look that spurs louder guffaws.

Jayla gives Javier, Demitri, Tanner, Finley, and me keychains in each of our favorite colors, leaving a pink one for herself.

"Thank you," I manage.

"Love you, Meley Bean." Jayla floats away with Mama Mabel, who's still slathering overdramatic keychain praise.

I thump the keychain on the bar. "Really, Demitri! You let her steal the special keychain thing?"

"What tangled webs we weave," Tanner mutters before wandering off with Fin.

Demitri tosses his hands. "We talked during dance class. She said she wanted to do something special, but didn't have money to shop. I told her the story of Zane's mom and the keychains. She's been in Girl Scouts since she was in kindergarten. They make crafty crap. She likely had a whole set of this plastic thread stuff and hopped right to it."

"You're grizzly-bear-in-the-ass screwed, my man," Adam says.

Javier chuckles. "It was thoughtful of her. Can I see the keychain that spurred all of this hoopla?"

I pull my keys from my purse and hand them over. Javier pushes the little button and a snippet of the Beatles' "Here Comes the Sun" plays. I explain the sentiment behind song choices for each movie.

Javier grins. "This is awesome." He shrugs. "So are the very different keychains Jayla made us. They can both exist."

"Now that I think about it," Demitri puzzles together, "I told her about your happy little smile every time you look at the keychain from Cindy. I guarantee she wanted to give a happy little reminder of our show also."

"La Diabla doesn't 'happy little smile,'" I snip.

"You're not La Diabla to us," Demitri insists.

Trey chokes on his beer. "He walked right into that one."

"Lord, did he ever," Adam mutters.

"You and Jayla are an 'us' now?" I demand.

"No?" Demitri hesitantly asks.

Adam and Trey shake their heads.

"No, I'm not an 'us' with Jayla," Demitri corrects. "Wrong word fell out of mouth hole. So sorry."

Dante strides up, interrupting. "Melanie, I'm sorry Mabel slighted you. Jayla's fretting about how you're a big meteor and she's a little meteor. I'm here to inform you that you're the most gargantuan meteor. You take up the whole sky with your hugeness."

I turn to Demitri with a slow, tipsy wobble and hit him with a death glare. "Now I'm gargantuan?"

"Dante said that!" Demitri blusters. "Not me!"

"Told youuuuu," Trey singsongs under his breath at Demitri. "You're responsible for what others say about the supposed other flame."

"Whoa, whoa," Dante rushes to correct. "Your *talent* is gargantuan. Big, fat, gargantuanly talented meteor." He waves his hand frantically at me.

"Stop while you're ahead," Javier chuckles, as he guides a flummoxed Dante away.

Trey and Adam howl with laughter again. "I give Demitri a week before Melanie blows him to smithereens," Adam manages to get out.

Demitri huffs, "Dante says big, fat, gargantuan all the time; it wasn't personal," while he pulls his keys from his pocket. He winds his new keychain prize on the ring.

"Give me that," I snarl, snatching his keys. I struggle to unwind the metal hoop. I stomp my feet rapidly, and Trey chuckles. He holds out his hand, and I thump Demitri's keys into it.

Trey unwinds the keychain and puts Demitri's and my keychains in my purse. "Those," he informs Demitri, "go in the back of Melanie's nightstand drawer, never to be discussed again. She won't throw them away, though, because that would be rude."

"I'll put them in my nightstand," Demitri offers.

I huff and give Trey a look. Trey rolls his eyes. "You just offered to defend Jayla's honor in the oh-so-sacred-nightstand drawer of your love, that Melanie will glare at every time she stomps to the bathroom to take a leak."

Demitri's expression crumples with confusion.

Adam huffs. "If Melanie keeps them in HER drawer, then she's a big, fat, gargantuan barrier between your and Jayla's love."

"I don't think you're fat!" Demitri bellows at me, earning stares as the whole party turns to us in unison. I rub my face hard, while Demitri informs our riveted spectators, "Melanie is a dainty meteor, goddamn it!"

"Shut up, Demitri," I snarl.

The bartender slides our way. "You need anything, Firebird?"

I jingle my glass, and the ice fitfully clinks around. "Hell YES! Another ringy-lingy, please!"

"Let's not," Demitri interjects.

"Excuse you!"

Adam grimaces. "Last time I checked, this is Melanie's party also." He gestures across the room where Jayla is slopping about, more than sloshed. "Or is it just a party for you, Javier, Tanner, Finley, and the little meteor?"

The bartender looks at the guys expectantly. "It was a Dancing Demon," Demitri informs, relenting.

"The one I just made for you? Extra strong because you're a

big guy and could handle it?" Demitri nods and the bartender smirks. "Good luck tonight, to whichever of you is dating this tiny monster. I can never tell."

"Busy, busy girl," Adam says.

"Oh, *I'm* not busy at all. *They* are." I point to Trey and Demitri. Trey just shrugs.

Demitri leans to the bartender. "I'm completely consumed with only *one* crazy-ass woman."

The bartender grins and heads off to make my drink.

Adam chuckles. "Flip the switch, Angel Eyes. You're supposed to be having fun."

I close my eyes and ground out my irritation. When my eyes open, I'm in a better mood. I grab another nacho before I happily scuttle over and snag a fry from Trey's plate. "Nom, nom, nom."

Trey hands me his burger, and I take a bite before handing it back.

He sets it on his plate and pushes it my way. "You need to eat, Mel."

I take another burger bite. "So good!" I happily exclaim.

Demitri rolls his eyes. "We've got to work on your eating habits. This is going to really bug me."

I toss a nasty look his way.

"Danger, danger," Adam admonishes. "Icebergs dead ahead, Captain."

Demitri tries again. "I'm so glad you're enjoying Trey's burger."

Adam nods. "She loves to eat."

New drink in hand, I nod enthusiastically. Tipsy, I squawk, "It's true. Nom noms are the best!"

"Don't try to change the little things about the girl," Adam guides Demitri. "She's got a great ass that's now yours. Let it ride."

I suck down half of my new drink through a straw and wiggle my tush happily.

Arch saunters up and juts his thumb over his shoulder. "Melanie, your presence is being requested. Your gal pals are in a debate on how to execute an overhead handstand lift. I mentioned that we happen to have a couple of experts in the house."

I stumble while I polish off my second drink. I thump my empty glass into Trey's chest, and he takes it, looking amused.

I happily start to skip off, but Demitri grabs my arm. "She's two Dancing Demons in and has a stomach full of that crap." He gestures to the plates on the bar.

Arch grins evilly. "Sounds like she's ready to me."

"Uh-huh," Demitri says. "Great plan. Who, exactly, is going to execute this magical lift with her?"

We all look at the dance floor, and everyone is absolutely wasted.

Arch laughs as Tanner stumbles in his knee-high stiletto boots. "Last I heard, Tanner was gonna give her the old up-and-over."

Demitri rolls his eyes. "I'm not fixing a broken arm tonight. I'll show them how to do it."

"Demitri's the *best* at this," Jayla slops out. "Demitri Cantrell's the best at everything!"

My explosion is cut off as Trey gives Demitri lovey-dovey eyes. "You're my hero Demitri Cantrell," he fawns.

Adam runs the back of his hand down Demitri's cheek. "I *adore* you, Demitri Cantrell."

Trey whips to the bartender. "Have you met Demitri Cantrell? He's ahhhhh-maaaaa-zzzziiiing."

Adam grabs Trey and rattles him about. "Demitri Cantrell hung the moon . . ."

". . . and made it shine," Trey slathers.

"All to light the night sky so we can watch . . . ," Adam says.

". . . the little meteor blaze brighter than all the stars . . . ," Trey heaps on.

". . . IN THE SKY," Adam and Trey crow together with twin arm flourishes.

I crack up, and the meaner of the Misfits laugh with me.

"Stop that," Demitri hisses, slapping at Trey and Adam while they fawn all over him again.

Jayla whimpers dramatically, and Mr. Cantrell guides her to us, with Mabel and Dante in tow. Everyone moves in closer to hear.

"Go ahead, Jayla," Mr. Cantrell prompts. "Tell them what we talked about."

"Meleeeey Beannnnn," Jayla drunkenly slurs.

My eyes wobble about while I struggle to function through two Dancing Demon liquid-candy-crazies.

"Oh, this is *aweeeeeesome*," Adam breathes in anticipation of this drunken discussion.

"It's my *turn*," Jayla snarls at Adam, with a huffy foot stomp.

Adam grins. "It sure is, Jaybird. Tell Melanie *allll* about it."

Trey spurts laughter while Demitri works to stifle a groan.

"Meley . . . Bean." Jayla wobbles and Dante rights her back to something close to standing. "I don't think you're fat." She tap-taps my stomach before looking at her finger. She runs it languishingly down my abs, counting, "One, two, three." She runs it back up the other side, counting, "Four, five, six. Six six-pack, muhahahaha."

"Fucking *Sesame Street*." Adam looks at Trey and chuckles.

Jayla luxuriously runs her whole hand down my abs, and my eyebrows rise as the oddity burns through some of my drunken disaster.

"Damn, you're hot," Jayla purrs.

"This is what you coached her on?" Arch asks doubtfully.

"Not even remotely, but I'm riveted, in rapt horror even, at the shift," Mr. Cantrell says.

Jayla gets distracted as her sloshed gaze slowly tilts to Demitri.

"Hmm," she says. Her eyes narrow. "Yes, *please*."

I turn scathing eyes on Demitri, who just shrugs.

"Ummmmm," Tanner draws out.

"Okaaaaay," Bear says.

"You," Jayla says, booping me on the nose, "are so *hot*. We can ALLLLLL see your abs through that dress."

"Wow," Adam expels.

"Oh my," Mabel mutters.

"You *heard* me," Jayla crows at our flummoxed audience. "You *all* want her. Don't LIE!" She gestures wildly Dante's way, who appears newly mortified. "Say IT," Jayla insists.

"Sure, abs," Dante says.

This seems to satisfy Jayla, who whips back my way. "Melanie Slate, you're the most rock hard, *throbbing* dance talent I have EVER seen. You *rise* to the occasion, *thrust* yourself into every piece, and don't give up until there's *fireworks*!"

Jaws are on the floor.

Adam taps me on the shoulder.

"Don't you dare, Adam," I manage through gritted teeth. "Don't you speak right now."

"I've got this, Adam." Bear grins mischievously at me. "What an *erect* compliment."

Laughter spurts from many.

"I've been described as a lot of things, but a talented dance boner is a new one," I say, and Trey and Adam lose it.

"So, to CONCLUDE," Jayla bellows, "you're the best meteoric bunch of everything." She hugs me tight.

I stand ramrod stiff. "Well, all right . . . ," I say, as Jayla lets me go.

"Ohhhhhh noooooo," Jayla groans.

Presley rolls her eyes. "Come on, Jayla."

"Where are we going?"

"To the bathroom," Presley says. "You'll feel better in a few minutes."

"You're hot too," Jayla purrs.

"Awesome," Presley grunts, before guiding Jayla away to barf.

Tanner emits a spirited, "We need to formally welcome Jayla to the dark side, because that chick is bi and feeling high."

"Cheers," is bellowed, before most of the Misfits wander away.

"Did you let her smoke *pot*?" Dante frustratedly snips.

"Is that bad?" Tanner asks.

"It's NEW," Dante says, sounding exasperated.

Tanner shrugs. "She reached for the joint while you were in the can. She's wound one crank past boing. I figure she needs to let loose."

"I don't know if I can handle this," Dante mutters.

I smirk at Demitri. "Now, your side quest is forging an adventure along MY roadmap."

Demitri's head drops back. "She's not my side quest, Melanie." He glares at Dante. "What in the actual HELL was that about?"

"She's going through a self-discovery phase," Dante informs.

"Christopher fucking Columbus," Adam mutters.

Trey cackles.

"How much did she drink?" Demitri asks Dante.

"One Dancing Demon, because that's what *Meley Bean* had," Dante replies sarcastically.

"For the record, that is NOT what I talked to her about," Mr. Cantrell interjects.

"Do you remember what *we* talked about?" I ask Demitri. At his confused look I smirk. "You promised that if Jayla was an unhinged sleaze toward you, I get to kill her."

"You promised *what*?" Adam barks at Demitri, while Trey sinks to his knees, howling with laughter.

"Shit," Dante mutters.

"Melanie," Demitri cautiously says. "I'm asking you not to. I had ZERO clue Jayla would do this."

"Well, that can't be," I sarcastically retort. "You said that you were so sure of who Jayla is that I could kill her if she proved to be a sleaze."

"She isn't a sleaze," Demitri groans.

Presley emerges from the ladies' room and interrupts. "Dante, you're up. I just got a knocker squeeze while she hurled blue goo."

"Your chick is harboring demons," Adam informs Dante.

"Apparently." Dante looks to me. "Sorry, Mel. She was aiming to say that she's mesmerized by your talent and can't believe she just did a professional show with you."

"That's precisely what we talked about," Mr. Cantrell informs.

"Please don't kill her," Dante pleads. "I'll get her under control."

"Help meeee." We look toward the squeal and see Jayla hanging on Deb, slobbering on her neck.

"She's such a sweet girl," I sarcastically sugar out.

"Look how bright that little meteor shines," Trey jokes.

Jayla barfs on the floor while everyone gapes. She whips right back to sucking on Deb's neck.

Deb winces at the atrocity. "Holy BALLS, help me!" she whimpers.

Dante attempts to extricate Jayla from Deb, but Jayla pushes fitfully at Dante, while saying, "Not you, not you."

Adam claps Demitri on the shoulder. "That's you're cue, Mr. Yes, Please. Jayla certainly didn't push *you* away while she gazed at you like she wanted to eat you."

"Not a shot in hell," Demitri breathes.

Deb's boyfriend, Drake, wades into the mix, and Jayla squalls,

"That'll work," while she attempts to mount him. Jayla tries to punch Dante after he pulls her off Drake. She misses, and splats in her own vomit.

"Your side-ride makes mine look stable," Trey breathes in wonder.

"She is NOT my side-ride," Demitri defends, sounding horrified.

"We're DONE, Jayla," Deb yells. She grabs Drake and hauls him across the room. The bartender supplies her with a wet towel that she rubs all over her neck.

"Holy crap," Mr. Cantrell mutters.

Mama Mabel's eyebrows fly into her hairline. "The limo is here, and there's barf on the floor. Time to close this place up."

"Gee, thanks, Jayla," Presley snips.

"I'm sorry, guys," Dante says, clearly irritable, as he works to steady a flaccid Jayla.

"Yeah . . ." Presley says, plainly irritated. "Mary Poppins can't hang, dude. We're built a little different."

"You'll all take turns making an ass of yourselves," Mabel placates.

As we grab our stuff, the full weight of my Dancing Demons hits overdrive, and everything goes shockingly wobbly. Our exit from the Swirly Girl Bar is hindered by the Misfits, who are all staring out into the parking lot.

All sense of caution thrown to the wind, I snarl, "Fantastical. What now?" I push through the group, pulling Demitri with me because Jayla tries to paw at him. I stop dead in my tracks as I realize the parking lot has a line of people with a bunch of women behind them. They have their greasy gamer kids in tow. I suspect they're the Jags' widows. *I guess we're doing this.* Through my head-spinning fog, I shove Demitri to Trey and Adam. "Keep him safe." I whip around, stumbling dramatically as the world spins, and squawk, "What?"

"We're bringing Retribution Clause against you for the death of our husbands," a woman informs. "They died because of YOU! So, I hired *them*." She indicates the first row of people.

"What did you do, put out an ad in the paper?" I make a dumb face. "Energetic assholes needed who get their rocks off smacking around a sixteen-year-old girl."

"I like smacking around little girls," one of the assholes says.

I send out an energetic whack that thumps the idiot flat on his rear. He looks shell-shocked, and I dismissively shoo him away. "Run along. You got your turn."

Trey cackles behind me.

"Trey, how much fun do I get to have?" I ask.

"There are eleven of them."

I turn to him, and my mouth drops open exuberantly. "You're such a good counter!"

"Six six-pack. Muhahahaha," gurgles from Jayla, who's cradled in Dante's arms.

I turn back to the line of goons and I think for a moment, wobbling a bit. "You know what? I'm not doing this. Screw you guys! I wanna go home and have naughty time with Mr. Bumpy Stomach." I jut my thumb over my shoulder at Demitri.

"Lucky guy!" Arch chortles. "She's gonna barf nachos on you while her dark-water side tries to tear you limb from limb."

"He's so hot." Jayla points a lazy finger to Demitri.

"Okaaaay," Presley says.

Deb puts a hand over Jayla's mouth. "Ewww," Deb squirms. "She's French-kissing my hand." She extricates her hand and rubs it on her pants.

"If she keeps going down this road, I'm hiring Jayla as one of my girls," Mabel sasses.

Demitri puts his forehead on Adam's shoulder while he chuckles.

"Back to Melanie tearing Demitri limb from limb in the sack," Marcus snarks.

"If Melanie doesn't, I will," Finley drunkenly says. She's a sweetheart, but has this wild side when she drinks. "Can I have a crack at him?" she asks me. "I'd totally do it!"

I giggle.

"Yeah, you would, babe!" Tanner belts.

"Do I get a say in this?" Demitri asks, baffled.

Presley snorts. "Triple dog dare you to in the limo on the way home."

"Wouldn't be the first time," Mabel announces.

"Me first!" Jayla insists.

"Shut her uuuup." I wibble-wobble in my heels.

"Trying," Presley announces. "Failing," she adds, while she struggles to extricate Jayla's hand from her top.

"What is happening?" someone from the enemy lineup demands irritably.

I look that way. "Who spoke?"

A man raises his hand while he glares at me. I gather a quaking energy load, making the parking lot lights flicker, and drop a visible bolt down on the man. He face plants, dead and smoking, before he hits the ground.

"One dead, muhahahaha," I drunkenly bark. When the Jags all start to run, I wrap them in an energy casing. "Stand your ground. If you run—"

"YOU *DIEEEEEE*," Jayla gravels out, finishing my sentence.

Trey and Demitri both sink to their knees, laughing.

"This is a circus," Adam mutters.

Jayla vibrantly barfs down the side of Dante's jeans.

"Mel, we should go home," Arch says. He gestures to Jayla.

"Oh, should we?" I retort. "I wasn't aware." I give Arch a fluttery eyelash bat. "You do it." I flip my hand to the enemy lineup and accidently send a few fireballs their way.

They duck and exclaim.

"Prettttttty," Jayla hums out.

"Tipsy Mel has to get through thiiiiis," Tanner singsongs.

"Sorry, Mel," Arch says.

I whip around and stumble. Demitri steadies me.

"I apparently must cater to the saving of Jayla," I squawk. "I'm going to kill all of you in her honor."

"Told you," Jayla says to Dante. "She's the bes . . ."

"Annnnnd, she's out," Adam narrates.

"About damn time," I snarl, before focusing on the enemy lineup. "Who wants the first crack at me?"

"I'm up," Jayla barks.

"She'd like a crack at you," Adam exclaims. "But we already knew that."

"So hottttt," Jayla growls my way.

"Ugh."

"I'll take a crack at you," one of the greasy gamers brazenly says.

"You know what? Yes. All the greasy gamers step forward." I release the shield holding them captive.

As the kids come to me, their moms look nervous.

I glare at the kids. "You guys wanna get laid one day, right?"

They nod enthusiastically.

"Here's the deal. You pigs need to put down your video game controllers, clean up your funk nests that you wallow around in, take a shower EVERY DAY, and get your crap together. This whole cheesy poof ninja game vibe of yours is tirrrrrred."

"THANK YOU!" one of the moms exclaims. "I tell that one that every day." She points to the one who thought I looked like a comic book character when I infiltrated their party to rescue Stella.

I stride up to him, yank the sweat-stained baseball cap off his head. and fling it away like a Frisbee. "Look at you! You don't have a shot with ANYTHING that has a pulse! Except maybe *Jayla*." I snap my fingers over my shoulder. "Tanner, fix this mess."

Tanner struts forward, a little unsteady in his stiletto boots, and surveys the boy. "I don't think Jesus and all the disciples could fix this train wreck, but I'll take a stab at it." He starts giving the boy orders like a drill sergeant. "Unbutton the top three buttons of your dress shirt . . . Roll your pant legs that are dragging the ground . . . Roll up your shirt sleeves twice . . . Run your fingers through that slimy hair of yours!" He surveys the boy. "Damn, I *am* good!" He gestures at the boy, addressing the rest of the gamers. "See! Much better. Now, imagine if he took a shower!" He hits the boy with a death glare. "WITH SOAP." Tanner takes a flourishing bow.

Our friends cackle again. I shoo the kids away and focus on the line of enemies. "Which one of you has the balls to get down to the big finish?"

A wiry-looking middle-aged guy at the far end of the line smirks. "I'll give you a big finish REAL good!"

My dark-water side surges to full power, and I'm suddenly radiating blasting waves of brutal seduction. My chest rises and falls dramatically.

"Here we go," Trey says.

"Let's get ready to RUMBBBBLLLLLE!" Tanner bellows.

I saunter to the man who offered to finish me "real good" and run my hands down his chest, unleashing everything that makes my dark-water side tick.

He shudders and tries to take a step back.

"Huh, uh-uh," I cajole. "This was your idea, remember?" I grab the front of his shirt and yank him out of the line, hurling him to the pavement at Demitri's feet.

As Mr. Big Finish starts to get up, Trey raises an eyebrow my way.

"Stay!" I snap at the guy. My gaze shifts to Trey. "He's mine. Don't even think about it." I get to the guy, who visibly shakes on the ground. "Showtime," I purr at the man. "You need to know what I like, after all." I turn to Demitri. "Shirt off."

He smirks and takes it off. I raise my hand that sparks with a flame. Demitri's head drops back, knowing what's coming. He moans as I run my fire-coated hand from his chest to his abs.

"Whoa," comes from Jayla.

I look her way with a challenging gaze. "Welcome to the play-room." I raise my eyebrows. "You sure about that seduction you leveled my way?"

Jayla seems to sober a bit while she hunkers closer to Dante.

"She lights you guys on fire?" Adam asks Trey.

"News to me," Trey admits.

Demitri smolders at me. "Kill these motherfuckers so we can go the hell home."

"I'd like to formally rescind—"

I look at the enemy lineup. "The next person who speaks DIES."

Fear radiates from the enemy crowd.

As I start to slink down, Mr. Finish Me Off begs, "Please, no!"

I grin maliciously. "Oh, honey. If you think begging's gonna slow this ride, you don't know me very well."

"Melanie, please," Jayla Tinkerbells.

I look up at her, mid-crouch. "Please, what?"

"Don't cheat on Demitri with him!"

I blink befuddlement at Jayla.

"Melanie's planning to kill the man, not hump him," Dante explains to Jayla.

The man starts begging and thrashing. I hold him tight with an energy line.

"You can't doooooo that," Jayla whines.

I straddle the guy. "If she doesn't shut up, you die!" I snarl.

"Please shut up, stupid girl," the man begs frantically.

"Please keep talking, Jayla." I smile menacingly.

Presley rolls her eyes and clamps her hand over Jayla's mouth.

"That's no fun," I huff. "Back to that Redemption threat you made."

"It wasn't me," the man insists.

I tip my head. "Then why are you here?" At his apparent confusion, my expression snaps evil. "Ever wonder what tantric death might feel like? Because I'm your girl."

The guy makes a terrified keening sound.

Trey grins. "She broke one of my ribs once, and I thanked her."

Demitri points to his washboard stomach with a giant hand-shaped burn on it from a little too much energy play last night.

I wince. "Sorry, love."

He shakes his head. "I'm gooood with it."

Trey surveys the burn mark. "That's going to scar."

"Perfect," Demitri gravels.

Jayla looks like she's going to pass out from fear as she surveys the handprint.

"If you let me go, I swear you'll never see me again!" the man screeches.

I survey the line. "If I let him go, will I never see the rest of you again?"

Heads nod desperately.

"Good. That's settled then." I hop up off the guy, and he makes two false starts before he manages to get up and scuttle back to his spot in the lineup.

I expand an energy bubble, trapping the enemy horde. A quick energy flex shrinks the shield, and they all skid to the center of the group until they're comically balled up like a bunch of toys in a claw machine.

"Squeezy!" Tanner drunkenly proclaims.

I send the bubble bouncing through the parking lot like a rubber ball. My friends howl with laughter. I stop the squishy bundle by their cars and burst the bubble. They're all left panting in a pile.

I wave my hand, shooing the Jags away. "Go home and have nightmares now. Have a lovely evening." I turn to my friends, who applaud, and take a moment for a ladylike curtsy.

We load into the limousine with Jayla on the floor. She barfs in a garbage bag the whole way, while the rest of us hang out the windows to avoid the spectacle.

CHAPTER 47

I open my eyes. It's a terrible plan. I squeeze them shut, and my head spins like a Tilt-a-Whirl.

"La Diabla lives again!" I hear Arch announce exuberantly.

"Demitri!" Trey crows. "Your Dancing Demon could use some assistance."

Laughter peels, and I throw an arm over my head, moaning, "Too loud. Shhhhh." My head spins worse, and I scrunch up in a ball.

"You ran the gauntlet again, Melanie," Adam taunts.

I manage to open my eyes again, this time revealing Demitri across the way with a hand on the stomach of a moaning Jayla.

"Shhh," Mabel coos. "You're okay, Jayla. Just give him a second."

My dark side rises rapidly, burning through my hangover. "*I ran the GUANTLET? Are you SHITTING me?*"

"No, no, no!" Mr. Cantrell barks.

Hands land on me, and I'm mentally rolled while I plunge. I energetically flex hard and hear a scream. I stand up, opening my eyes as my psyche clears.

Demitri rushes to his dad, who's out cold on the floor. "Melanie!" he admonishes, while he puts his hands on his dad to heal him.

"Is there a reason you were just groping Jayla?" I demand.

"He wasn't," Dante rushes to explain. "She's terribly hungover, and he was fixing it."

"Why don't YOU fix your sloppy girlfriend?" I retort.

"I believe the idea was for Demitri to cure the hangover, so she didn't suffer all day," Bear rationalizes.

I shift my glare to Mr. Cantrell as he sits up. "Why did you roll me?"

"I thought you were going to attack Jayla!" Mr. Cantrell barks.

"Mind rape me again, and you're dead," I threaten.

Mouths fall open as everyone realizes my take on the indiscretion.

"What?" Demitri gasps.

"Melanie, Mr. Cantrell was trying to keep you from irrationally attacking Jayla while you were out of it," Bear chastises.

I blink befuddled eyes at Bear. "It's fine for *Jayla* to attack us when *she's* out of it, though?" At Bear's confusion, I clarify, "Last night, she threw herself at me, Demitri, Presley, Deb, and Drake. That's acceptable, but I deserve to be rolled against my will for being pissed that Demitri and Jayla are at it AGAIN?"

"What?" Jayla says.

"Things got a little wild at the party," Dante vaguely explains.

"I don't remember anything," she whimpers.

I gather the memory and hurl it into Jayla's mind. The memory hits her so hard that she careens off the cot and lands on her back on the wood floor.

"Melanie!" Mabel scolds.

I shrug. "Uninvited mind shit is acceptable." I gesture to Mr. Cantrell. "You didn't scold HIM."

Everyone's mood shifts with deeper cautious alarm.

Jayla's eyes close, and she burns red as she witnesses her indiscretions in the memory.

Mabel starts to speak, and I give her a warning-laced look. I cross my arms over my chest and wait. Everyone exchanges worried glances, but no one speaks.

"I'm so sorry, everyone," Jayla whimpers once she's through the memory.

"You're good, Jayla," Drake says compassionately. "We all have our moments."

Jayla slides big sad eyes to Demitri. "I'm so sorry for what I did at the party."

"It's okay," Demitri says.

"It absolutely IS NOT okay!" I bellow, thoroughly fed up.

"Melanie!" Mama Mabel scolds again.

"WHAT?" I scream. "Why does everyone tell these overstepping bimbos that it's okay? It's NOT okay for Victoria to decorate my wedding while she's having an affair with Trey! It's NOT okay for Valerie to attack me in my home! And, let me be ABUNDANTLY clear that it's NOT okay for Jayla to overstep repeatedly with Demitri!" I toss my hands up. "Stop excusing the inexcusable, all while you CHASTIZE ME."

"Melanie," Dante says, "they were just trying to curb an awkward situation for Jayla."

My frustration mounts. "Maybe if you'd nurse your fragile little troublemaker's hangover, we wouldn't be having this PROBLEM!" I flip a hand Jayla's way. "Her coy sluttery affects you the same as it does me, but you'd rather hide behind me, because you could never hurt little Miss Perfect, right?"

Dante levels me with serious eyes. "I'm furious with her and Demitri, but I've chosen not to escalate the situation. I apologize that it came across like I was hiding behind you while you did the dirty work. I'd be happy to deal with this." He pans the room. "What I'm witnessing is disturbing on many levels, but *we're* all to blame, not Melanie."

"*Excuse* you?" Victoria sasses haughtily.

"Shut up," Dante says dismissively of her.

He's rarely rude or harsh, and everyone is clearly surprised.

Dante levels Demitri with challenging eyes. "Your savior complex is your worst quality. You strut around like you know everything, but you don't. Jayla has every marker of a future addict. She's insecure, desperate for acceptance, miserable most of the time, and has deeply rooted daddy issues. You harmed her by helping her instead of allowing her to face the consequences of her actions. Then, everyone excused her flagrantly inappropriate drunken molestation of half of this group, instead of making her take accountability, further reinforcing that being an out-of-control party girl is acceptable."

"That's beyond harsh," Finley says, defending Jayla.

"I'm not judging Jayla!" Dante roars angrily. "I'm speaking from experience. I had a serious cocaine and alcohol problem that I kicked."

"What?" Arch asks.

"You heard me!" Dante barks. "My partying was out of control, and I got sick of being a sloppy mess. It was affecting the quality of my music, and my health. I found a nice girl, who didn't expect me to be all the rock-star shit. Now, she's acting like the girls that I became a junkie with, while you all dismiss it like it's nothing." Dante raises his eyebrows as he surveys the room. "Now that you know, will you make fun of me and tear me down?"

The Misfits appear stunned.

"We would never do that," Adam insists.

Dante appears surprised. "Really? That's what you do to Melanie!" He flips a hand my way. "After everything she's been through, Melanie was finally happy at a party in her *starshine* honor, and Trey and Adam made sure to throttle her with their tacky teasing and heartless comments." Dante glares at everyone in the group. "She doesn't deserve to be excited, or relaxed, or proud, right?"

Regret streams from Adam and Trey.

"You offer everyone else grace, though," Dante says. "It's fine that I'm a reformed junkie, Adam is a womanizer, Demitri fawns all over Jayla, and Trey cheated on Melanie with Victoria. *That* is SO fine that Victoria is welcome to LIVE HERE and torture Melanie daily." Dante tosses his hands up. "She can't even eat nachos without catching shit from her judgmental fiancé!"

Demitri appears stunned.

"Six six-pack muhahahaha," Dante harshly jokes. Everyone laughs bashfully, and Dante scolds, "Your girl can afford to eat nachos, Demitri. You never once defended Melanie when Trey and Adam were launching attack after hilarious attack her way."

Demitri slides a mortified expression my way. "I'm so sorry I didn't stand up for you last night." He starts to tear up.

"Well, you have more to be sorry for, Demitri, so don't *melt down* yet," Dante lobs cynically. "You should have seen this coming. I've realized for a long time that Melanie is sick of being treated like shit. Her reaction this morning is a warning you need to consider, because your fiancée reached a boiling point long ago, and when she erupts, people are going to get hurt. Then she'll get blamed, yet again, because no one in this group takes accountability for pushing Melanie over the edge." He levels Demitri with a weighted stare. "Jayla slopped all over you last night with her, 'Yes, please' and 'Demitri Cantrell's the *best* at everything.' You just stood there!"

"I had NO IDEA what to say!" Demitri barks.

"How about, 'Stop it, Jayla,' because CLEARLY you were the only one she was likely to listen to," Dante bellows.

"I didn't want to overstep you," Demitri insists.

"Overstep me?" Dante barks in disbelief. "You've put yourself on a pedestal with Jayla our entire relationship!" He gestures to Trey. "You did the same damn thing to Trey with Melanie. You strung Melanie along so brazenly that we were all STUNNED Trey didn't kill you! Now we know Trey didn't give a damn because he was treasure hunting in the town dump," he gestures to Victoria, "but that's no excuse for *your* behavior!"

When Victoria starts to rage, Dante snaps a furious look her way. "What part of 'Shut the fuck up,' and 'You're irrelevant' do you *not* understand?" Victoria is stunned silent, and Dante glares at Demitri again. "You might be the prettiest shithead in this room, but I'm not impressed. I'm not some no one who you get to overlook because you think you're God's gift to my girl. I'm not okay with you healing her, but you didn't ask. Since social decency doesn't seem to matter to you, let's try intimidating your professional dancing ass with *my* credentials."

"Credentials?" Demitri squawks. "I don't need to compare credentials! You're my *friend*."

"I promise I'm not!" Dante snarls.

I clear my throat. "I happen to know your latest credentials," I inform. Dante looks to me, and I smile a little. "Congratulations, Dante. I almost popped with joy when Ms. Alice informed me at the show last night."

"Why did she tell you?" he asks, seeming surprised, but not angry.

I quirk my mouth. "I took the demo tape to Ms. Alice the morning after you gave it to me to check out. She listened to it and nominated you."

"You got us the *Glamour* after-party gig, and now THIS?" Dante asks in disbelief.

"Hell yes! I think Diablo is stellar," I reply. "Any chance Ms. Alice mentioned anything else?" I ask mischievously.

Dante nods. "She's meeting with the band tomorrow at four. You know what it's about?"

I nod.

Demitri knocks on my blocked connection. He's like a little kid about secrets, and despite this mess, I find it charming. I drop the blockage.

"What's the secret?" Demitri sends.

"Ms. Alice is signing Diablo. She got them a recording deal. I had a phone meeting with her after she saw them play at the Glamour *party. I vouched for them."*

"NO WAY!" Demitri bellows aloud excitedly.

"Shhhhhhh," I scold.

"Did she just tell you what my meeting is about?" Dante asks.

Demitri nods excitedly.

"Tell me," Dante insists.

"I thought you hated Demitri and wanted to kill his know-it-all ass?" Adam snarks.

"Oh yeah," Dante says, trying and failing to wrestle his expression back to pissed.

Demitri sags. "I'm so freaking sorry, Dante. I never meant to make you feel like that. Now that I know, I'll try my best to be more mindful." He glances to me and then back to Dante. "Melanie and I had a heart-to-heart about how I was around Jayla and came to an understanding. That's why I didn't interject last night."

"Ohhhhhh," Dante says. "I'm sorry that I assumed you had devious motives."

Demitri ducks his head. "I rarely have devious motives."

"Do you see my point, though?" Dante asks.

"Definitely," Demitri replies.

"Then I'd like to try to be friends still," Dante offers.

"That would mean a lot," Demitri replies gratefully.

"Yeah, yeah, yeah," Tanner blathers. "Woo-hoo! You're friends. Can we please get back to the big mystery?"

"What?" Dante asks.

"Nomination?" Tanner says, sounding exasperated. "WHAT is happening?"

"My band just got nominated for a Grammy for a song that I wrote about Jayla," Dante informs.

"What!" Adam barks.

"Is it 'Mist'?" Jayla asks, bowled over by this news that she apparently didn't know.

Dante nods. "We rented studio time and recorded it. It's our first released single."

"We've never heard it," Finley softly says.

"Yes, you have. It played when we had the KROQ station on last month. Presley said, 'I love this song,' and you all agreed." I sing a line from the chorus, and mouths thump open.

"That's YOUR song?" Presley breathes.

Dante nods.

"Why didn't you tell us about the nomination when you found out?" Finley asks.

"Because I got the call from Ms. Alice yesterday morning," Dante informs. "It was a big day for my girl, and I didn't want to steal her thunder."

"Had we known, I would have included you in our party honors last night," Mabel insists.

Dante glares at her. "I didn't want to be included in your drunken teenage party honors. Every damn time I'm at some party you host, all everyone does is drink, smoke pot, hump each other, and treat Melanie like shit. I'm trying to stay sober! Maybe you should encourage your charges to do the same." He flips a judgmental hand her way. "You pass out booze and weed to this group like an ice cream man at an elementary school on a hundred-degree day!"

"Dante!" Mabel gasps.

He doubles down. "I'm dead serious. The teenage corruption around here is UNREAL! We all work at a damn BROTHEL."

"It's an event center," Victoria cats in Mabel's defense.

"Oh, please," Dante says, sounding exasperated. "We're all so desensitized to the moaning and carrying on that the TEENAGE GUYS in this group don't even notice when one of the porn stars on Mabel's hooker roster struts by naked in the hall."

Mabel's chin shakes with looming tears while she surveys all of us.

"Sorry to put a damper on the fun," Dante says, "but I've had a lot of barely contained frustration for a long time."

I glance at the clock on the wall and huff. "Well, on that note, I need to set up for an orgy."

Laughter spurts from Presley, who ducks her head. "Sorry, but it's ironic, given the final topic in Dante's fit."

"Orgies are the worst," Trey groans.

"You know what this means," I joke sarcastically.

"Cleanup on aisle nine," Tanner spouts.

"What does an orgy party entail?" Mr. Cantrell asks, bewildered.

"Four sex swings, and shelves with whips, and other handy-dandy tools," I reply.

Mr. Cantrell looks at Mabel, caught between anger and amused disbelief. "You have teenagers doing this?"

Mabel shakes her head, distraught. "You're all so mature for your age that I forget. I lost sight of the nature of this place." Her head drops. "I wasn't trying to corrupt a bunch of kids. I'm so sorry."

"Hey, hey, hey," Adam placatingly interjects. "I've learned a whole lot working here."

"Oh God," Tanner mutters.

Adam gives him a look. "What I learned was that I used to be a pervert around women. I viewed a hot set of cans like they were put on this Earth for my pleasure. *Now*, I don't even notice hot cans because I see them pushed up, spread out, propped on the bar, and jiggled around so often that I've become a better *guy* for it."

Arch spurts laughter. "Me too."

"Same," comes from Tanner, Marcus, Javier, and Demitri.

"I concur," Trey mutters. Everyone gives him a judgmental look, and he winces. "I recognize the irony of me saying that, given my affairs, but it's true."

"I'll set up for orgy," Mabel says.

Trey sighs heavily. "We're handling the setup. We take our jobs seriously. Unless Melanie starts booking Girl Scout meetings, we're likely to prep naughty stuff."

"Booked any Scout meetings lately?" Bear sends an amused look my way.

"Fresh out of those," I reply. "We do have a random children's birthday party next weekend though."

"We could make an indoor playground with the sex swings," Adam ponders.

We all crack up, the remaining tension dissolving.

"I'll help you hang the swings, Melanie," Adam offers.

"Me too," Trey says.

"I know you want to help Melanie to make up for razzing her last night," Demitri says, "but I need to hang the sex swings for her to make up for dropping her while I rescued Jayla in 'Batdance,' and for healing Jayla, all while I had an agreement not to cater to Jayla."

Tanner winces. "That's a lot of catering."

"It is," Demitri says. "Dante, I agree with you. You need to handle Jayla, while I handle Melanie. The next time Jayla launches herself off a three-story set during a dance piece, with intricate timing and danger, you need to rescue her."

"In that instance, I'm grateful you helped," Dante assures.

"Melanie got hurt because of Jayla's oblivious mistake," Demitri says. "I tried to send a mind-to-mind message to Melanie not to jump, because she couldn't see what was happening, but she had me blocked off so she could focus. Then, this morning, my dad got hurt because of a chain reaction that started off with Jayla getting piss drunk. My family is being harmed by Jayla's habit of having mishap after mishap, and I have no choice but to do as Melanie asked and recognize that Jayla causes issues for us." He gestures to Dante. "I appreciate this discussion, and I agree that I've overstepped, to the detriment of everyone. I won't do it again."

"That creates a safety hazard in the studio and onstage," Adam says. "That means Melanie and Demitri can't dance in pieces Jayla's in."

I shrug. "I guess we let Mr. Isley and Ms. Alice know, and they can decide who gets auditions."

Dante groans while Jayla tears up. "Ms. Alice is going to send Melanie to every audition, and she's Mr. Isley's lead in everything," he defends. "Please don't do this. That'll tank Jayla's career right when it starts."

"Jayla's poorly timed mistake in 'Batdance' has likely already tanked her career," Tanner interjects. "Javier threw out his back trying to save Melanie, and Melanie broke a bone in her wrist and tore her hamstring. Demitri healed them both, but Jayla can't be in shows if that could happen. It's not normal to have a friend who can heal you in the wings, and I heard Ms. Alice tell Mr. Isley exactly that. He agreed."

"I promise it won't happen again," Jayla tearfully says.

"Just like you swore you and Demitri wouldn't have private little lovers' moments, yet he had his hand on your stomach while he healed you today?" I rattle my head. "I'm not okay with that. You weren't dying. I can't figure out why Demitri had to grope you." I look to him. "Couldn't touch her arm instead?"

"Her stomach and head were the problem," Demitri explains. "I fixed her headache first. You woke just as I shifted to her stomach."

"She'll sprain her snap trap next," Presley mutters sarcastically to Tanner, who spurts tacky laughter.

Trey glares at Demitri, who drops his head back. D had to heal MY snap trap while I was with Trey.

"I don't mean to overstep when I heal," Demitri says. "I'm sorry that it seems that way."

"We've come to a solution that works for us, and fits the parameters of what Dante requests," I say. "I'm willing to let the healing of Jayla issue go."

Mr. Cantrell focuses on me. "I'm sorry that I used my abilities against your will. I knew there was tension, but I'm much clearer about the layers now."

"I appreciate that," I quietly reply. Considering how amazing he's been to me, I feel terrible that I threatened and harmed him.

Mr. Cantrell's face scrunches. "Orgies?" he asks Mabel, pivoting the topic back because he's still befuddled. "You taught Demitri how to hang a sex swing?"

Demitri flinches a little behind his dad's back, and Mabel's eyes widen with fake brightness. "Sure did. That's where he learned to hang one. Purely for work."

I fight to quell my urge to giggle. I taught him, but that's a different matter.

"Holy crap," Mr. Cantrell mutters.

"The faster we hang those contraptions, the faster we can get showers," Trey grumbles.

"I don't know about you guys, but I smell like yesterday," Tanner says with a wince.

"Yesterday needs to be washed down the *drain*," Demitri insists.

"Oh, and Dante?" Adam says teasingly now that the pressure has released.

"Yeah?"

"You ain't shit! Don't let that Grammy nomination go to your head." Adam grins at Dante, who grins back.

"Shut up, gearhead," Dante lobs.

CHAPTER 48

The dream shifts with the feel of the start of one of my night terrors. I'm unable to wake up, but aware of what's happening. I brace emotionally, wondering what direction this is headed.

"Melanie."

I look behind me in the dream, and Demitri is there.

"I need to talk to you," he admits. *"You've been asleep for hours, and I'm a nervous wreck."*

"What do you want to discuss?" I ask.

"I'm eaten up with guilt. I would never allow you to get hurt intentionally, and it's tearing me up that you leaped and I wasn't there to catch you. I know you don't trust me, and I can't handle that. I love you and need you to understand."

He crosses to me and places his hand over my heart, sending an emotion pulse so monumental that I fight to inhale around it. The power of the love sentiment is soul bending.

"That is how I feel about you," Demitri sends.

The deepest love for Demitri settles in me, taking my breath away, because THAT emotion is the one I've searched for without knowing it. My eyes still closed, I tip my head back and let my spiritual weight go, draping backward over Demitri's arm. His hand gently runs from my heart to my forehead, and I sigh contently.

I feel a burst from his hand, and everything spirals. I have no idea what's happening, as my dark-water energy and his healing energy pour torrentially. The mixture closes over our heads, thrumming with an intensity that's going to burn me up. I'm powerless to stop it.

There's a blinding blast, and blistering pain stuns me awake. My eyes snap open, and I'm lying on the wood floor in my room, in a heap. A fist pounds on the door while I hear chaotic screaming. I hear, "MOVE," and then the door opens. Trey rushes to me and kneels by my side. Adam drops to my other side.

Trey rolls me over, and his eyes are huge with panic. "Someone, talk to me!" he yelps. "Why is she charred?"

I can't do more than blink in a daze.

"Ugh, what now?" disgusts from someone.

"LEAVE, TORI!" Trey screams.

"Move," I hear Bear order.

"Close the door." Mabel's voice becomes clearer as the ringing in my head dies out. "Talk to me. What's happening?"

"Something is very wrong," Trey says.

"Unblock Trey's soulmate connection," Mabel orders.

Darren and Bear come into my spotted view. I feel something blast open in my psyche.

Trey's eyes close. After an intense stretch of silence, his body seems to collapse on itself. "Her energy isn't the same. It's . . ." His eyes open, and he slowly pans his gaze to Bear and Darren. "Her energy feels like a mega version of her and Demitri."

"That's impossible," Bear replies.

Mabel kneels, wrapping her hands around my head. She inhales sharply. "No, it's not. The blast that rocked the building was their energy fusing. They're Twin Flames now."

"What . . ." I squeeze my eyes closed tight. I can't get my head together. *What does that mean?* I send to Trey.

Trey passes on my inquiry with a sense of dread.

"Twin Flames are a step beyond a soulmate bond," Mabel marvels.

Jayla rushes in, a panicked mess. "Demitri collapsed!"

"He's supposed to be the security for the orgy," Trey says.

"I was in the hall with him and his dad," Jayla explains. "Demitri felt weird being in the room with . . ." She swallows hard. "It sounds really icky in there."

"Is he unconscious?" Bear asks.

Jayla nods frantically. "Mr. Cantrell was going to talk to us, but he and Demitri stared at each other instead."

"They can speak mind-to-mind with each other," Darren informs.

"What happened then?" Bear asks.

"Mr. Cantrell put his hands around Demitri's head, and Demitri closed his eyes," Jayla says. "They both just stood there for a while, and I kept an eye out because they were TOTALLY zoned out. There was this CRAZY blast that shook the ground. It came from Demitri, I swear. Then, Demitri just fell over, out cold, and Mr. Cantrell yelled for me to get help."

"Let's go!" Bear insists of Darren. They run out of the room.

"I'll report back and tell you what happens." Jayla speeds out the door.

I squeeze the daylights out of Trey's and Adam's hands before closing my eyes to explore the changes. What I find is cataclysmic. My energy and Demitri's energy have become one combined entity, but it's at the source that it's mixed.

"What were you doing when this happened?" Adam asks.

I fight to breathe through panic. "I . . . was . . ." I manage a breath. "I was asleep, and Demitri invaded my dream."

"Send us the memory," Adam requests.

I try, and my brow pinches. "I can't."

"Send *me* the memory, Melanie," Trey guides. I send it through our soulmate connection, and he closes his eyes. His eyes open when the memory ends. "Oh my God," he warbles out. "Demitri invaded Melanie's psyche and forced this on her, but his invasion had some trapping element."

"What!" Adam barks.

"The trapping was Mr. Cantrell's trancing ability," I croak out.

"Demitri violated her while she was in that deep-sleep state she hardly ever reaches," Trey whispers in shock.

Adam gazes down at me, broken. "In all of our lifetimes together, that deep-sleep state was when I'd stay up, determined to protect her with my life if I had too." His tragic gaze meets Trey's.

Trey chokes out, "She hardly ever trusts enough to really sleep."

I curl up tighter, reduced to nothing, because I never in a million years thought one of my soulmates would do this to me. I'm already plagued by so many night terrors about all the atrocious things I've experienced over my lifetimes. I fear sleep like nothing else in my evil-ridden life.

"She's so scared," Trey gasps, affected by the emotions I can't block in our soulmate connection right now.

"I trusted Demitri," Adam breathes in disbelief.

"Why the hell are you holding Melanie?" Victoria snarls ferociously.

"Get OUUUUUUUTTTTTT," Trey screams so loud that I cover my ears and cower smaller.

I hear the door close before a hand touches my arm lightly. "Hey, Melanie." I open my eyes, and Dante is kneeling next to me, with Tanner standing right behind him.

"What happened?" Tanner asks.

Mabel fills them in, and Dante asks, "What does this mean?"

"A Twin Flame bond is eternal," Adam chokes out.

"Why is this bad?" Dante asks. "Melanie and Demitri love each other."

"Energy workers have a standing rule," Trey explains. "We don't use our abilities against our loved ones. Demitri and Mr. Cantrell invaded Melanie's mind and rendered her helpless while Demitri manipulated their connection."

"It's permanent," Adam breathes tragically.

Tears torrentially pour down my cheeks. "I'll never trust Demitri again."

Trey blinks rapidly. "Does that mean that what Demitri has with her trumps her and my soulmate connection?"

"What they have now beats the dog shit out of my two hundred and three lifetimes, *original* soulmate bond with her," Adam replies.

The gravity of that sinks heavily into the room.

"I gave up my soulmate connection with Melanie," keens from Adam, high-pitched and desperate. It's so unlike him, and my heart clenches tight. He doubles over, gripping his stomach, and Dante hugs him.

I watch Tanner crack open the door. "Arch, I need you in here."

Arch comes in, closing the door, as Trey pants, "Tanner, take her." I look up at Trey, and he's pale. Tanner rushes around Adam and Dante, scooping me up from Trey's lap, as Mabel plunks down a well-placed wastebasket just in time. Trey vomits violently.

Dante helps Adam up. His legs don't work quite right, and Dante manhandles him around the bed and into the bathroom. We hear Adam retch through sobs.

Tanner lays me down on the bed while Mabel helps Trey to the spot next to me. He drapes himself on me, holding me tight, crying like his world is ending.

"Holy shit," Tanner whispers.

Adam stumbles from the bathroom, a cataclysmically emotional wreck. He crawls onto the bed, putting his leg and other arm over me and Trey. He covers as much of us as he can with his mammoth size. Adam's a beast, and I've never been more grateful.

"I thought I'd seen them lose it, but this is different," Arch says.

Dante gestures to our pile of doom. "I've been waiting for the big breakdown, because Melanie and Adam haven't come to terms with losing their soulmate bond. Trey also needs to process that he left Melanie for Victoria."

"Dante, hit the panic-room button in the panel," Tanner says. We hear the locks slide into place.

"We're in lockdown protocol," Tanner authoritatively orders. My lungs rattle with a wheeze.

I feel Trey fumble by my hip, the one his pocket is pressed against. "I've got it," Tanner says.

A hand snakes through the guys' bodies, and my inhaler lands in my mouth. Tanner presses the button twice, and I fight to inhale the medicine that I hate. I know it's successful as I get the jitters.

"Trey had her inhaler in his pocket?" Dante asks.

"He still keeps it on him just in case," Tanner dejectedly replies.

"What do we do?" Dante asks.

"I need to go check on Demitri," Mabel says.

"No one opens that door until those three get through this breakdown," Tanner says with authority. "Trey, I've got this. I know what to do while you're in this condition."

"I still don't understand why this issue is causing the biggest meltdown I've ever seen from them," Dante says. "They weren't this upset when Trey was shot, and Melanie had to energetically murder an entire biker gang."

"The level of manipulation it took for Demitri to fuse a soul-mate bond is unimaginable," Mabel explains. "A Twin Flame bond is built of a shared love so great that the bond gently fuses. It's supposed to be the most beautiful energy fusion that a spirit ever experiences. It's built of ultimate respect and love that is truly unbreakable. That kind of bond is the rarest among energy workers. It doesn't just fuse in life," she explains. "A Twin Flame bond carries into the next step. Once a soul reaches the end of its learning lifetimes, the soul becomes a spirit guide. Soulmates have a choice once they reach spirit guide status. They can either dissolve their connection or become Twin Flames. A Twin Flame bond is eternal, but Demitri forced it on Melanie. She got no say, and this has altered her soul path irrefutably, forever."

"Sounds like rape," Arch gravels out, weighted with understanding.

Mabel stoically nods. "Accurate. This indiscretion is unimaginable. The violence of that fusion rocked the entire building. My ears are still faintly ringing from the energy detonation. All the energy workers in this building are likely experiencing the same thing still."

"I can't believe Demitri would do that to Melanie," Dante says, aghast.

"Now you're getting it," Mabel snarls. "This is the most sinister thing Demitri could have done. It's also terrifying, because the volume of power it took overwhelmed Melanie."

Trey completely craters. I have no idea how there's another layer of dejected loss in him, but he finds it. "I'm so sorry that I sacrificed us for Victoria," he sobs. "It opened the door for Demitri. He's now done the most sinister harm to you, Melanie."

There's a knock at the door, and Tanner orders, "Don't open it."

"It might be Jayla," Mabel says. "She was going to report back with an update on Demitri."

"We don't need an update right now," Tanner says. "We need to focus on these three. I need intel."

Mabel fills Arch, Dante, and Tanner in on what Jayla reported when she rushed in about Demitri passing out.

My room phone rings, and Tanner unplugs it, because the sound makes Trey quake. "Take the guys' cell phones out of their pockets and silence them," Tanner orders.

A few moments later, I hear little clinks from the bathroom.

"They're on the counter," Arch quietly says.

"We must assume that Mr. Cantrell and Demitri plotted this," Tanner insists.

"Demitri and *Jayla* plotted this," rumbles from me.

Adam and Trey move off me, pulling it together now that there's war room chatter to engage in. I sit up and stare at my reflection in the big mirror attached to the dresser across from the bed. I have a wicked charred burn on my chest from the Twin Flame blast, but I ignore it.

I methodically inhale and exhale, out of sorts in that distantly shocked way. "Mr. Cantrell tried to incapacitate me in the banquet hall this morning," I say, my gaze slowly sliding to Adam. "What happened before I woke up?"

"Me and Trey were up all night talking while we guarded the group," Adam says. "Everyone woke up about an hour before you. You and Jayla were the last to wake, and Mr. Cantrell kept checking on you."

"Checking on us how?" I ask.

"Not both of you," Trey corrects. "Just you. He'd cross to you and put his hand on your forehead." His eyes narrow calculatedly. "We should have scanned to see what he was up to."

"Then Jayla woke up and caused quite the fuss with her moaning and crying," Tanner says.

"That's when Demitri went over to heal her," Dante adds.

My gaze snaps to Dante, and alarm bells go off in my mind. *"We're making a rookie mistake,"* I send to Trey. *"He keeps asking questions, and Mabel has given him energy worker intel that flat isn't discussed with Normals. He's got ulterior motives."*

"He has to go," he sends back.

I feel a forced smile slide up. I'm still remotely detached from shock, and I'm certain my expression is creepy instead of friendly. "Thank you so much for helping us."

Trey and Adam steer twin expressions to Dante. I know those looks, but generally only see them on the battlefield during former lifetimes. They radiate survival instinct animalistically. My arms goose-bump, but it's the wary slide of Dante's expression that clues me in that the Normals in the room can also feel it.

I watch Tanner and Arch make eye contact. Without being told to, Tanner crosses to the panel on the wall, while Arch makes his way to the door.

"You should go check on Jayla," I say kindly, but it sounds more like a warning.

Dante slowly shakes his head. "I'd like to help you."

"We've already taken up so much of your time," I reply, emotionlessly dismissive.

Trey looks to Mabel. "Go check on Demitri."

Mabel's mouth drops open.

"I'm sorry," Trey says, "but you're so split into every camp."

"I'm not," Mabel says.

"You are, and it's okay that you're everyone's mama around here," Trey says.

Mabel swallows hard. She and Dante walk to the door and stop by Arch. Tanner pushes the panic-room button, and Arch turns the knob the moment we hear the locks slide away. Dante steps out, followed by Mabel. Arch shuts the door right on her heels. Tanner pushes the button, and the panic locks engage again.

"It sounds like it's the three of you versus Demitri and his dad," Arch says cautiously.

Trey nods. "That's what I'm scared of."

"Let's hash this out," Tanner says.

CHAPTER 49

I try again and shake my head. "I can't spark a flame."

"Why don't any of her abilities work?" Tanner asks.

Adam rubs his face hard. "I can't check her metaphysical center because our soulmate connection is gone."

"Guide me," Trey says.

— —

"What does this mean?" Arch asks.

"Her abilities are gone," Adam answers for me, while my mind spins into the ether.

Tanner's mouth drops open. "*Gone* gone?"

"Yes," Trey says.

"Do you think Mr. Cantrell channeled through Demitri and took them?" Adam asks Trey.

Trey shakes his head. "Mr. Cantrell channeled into Demitri to use his mind-flipping trick to crash Melanie's final shield down to allow Demitri into her mind. Demitri's the one who somehow managed to neutralize her abilities."

"But he fused a Twin Flame connection while he was in there," Arch rationalizes. "If weakening Melanie to kill her was the objective, why would he deepen the bond first?"

"Good point," Trey says. "He likely wasn't trying to kill her then. Besides, he did all that show-and-tell about how he loves her when he got in there. So, what else could the goal be?"

"To make Melanie his slave?" Tanner ponders.

"What's the point of having a metaphysically dormant slave?" Arch says. "Without those abilities, Melanie's just a girl who's funny, bitchy, and likes to dance." He looks to me. "No offense."

I shrug, exhausted. "Whatever."

"Demitri and Mr. Cantrell have done the bachelor thing D's whole life," Trey says. "They don't need an enslaved wife to do their cooking and cleaning. This makes zero sense!"

"If Trey can't figure it out, then we're thoroughly screwed," Adam groans.

"Why?" Arch asks.

"Because Trey has been a military general more times over our lives than I can count," Adam informs. "I was usually his first in command on the battlefield, but it was Trey who masterminded war strategy that my troops followed."

"I never knew that," Tanner says.

"I know why," slips from me.

"Fill us in," Trey says.

"Gauntlet," I reply, but it means something different than when Adam was joking this morning.

Adam groans.

"What the hell does that mean?" Tanner asks.

Trey shakes his head, apparently not liking the direction this is going. "It's an old code for the three of us. We've been through this in past lives."

"Oh God," Tanner huffs. "We've slipped into the code-word level of bad?"

"I need Trey's bodyguards mixed into the enemy ranks when this goes down," I inform.

"Covertly give Marcus, Bear, and Darren the following message," Trey says. "Torrent."

Tanner and Arch exchange looks. "Shit," Tanner breathes.

"You can't be serious?" Arch says.

"Yup," Trey replies.

"What about Javier?" Arch asks. "He's one of our trained bodyguards."

"He's on Demitri's side," Adam reminds. "That's his boy."

"What's the goal?" Arch asks.

"I'm aiming to sneak Melanie out. If that doesn't work, then we're in a war and the objective is to neutralize the threat."

"You're asking us to fight DEMITRI to the death?" Tanner gasps. "I've never viewed Demitri as scary."

"You should have," Adam informs. "Demitri's a beast, but I've always counted on his morality and 'nice guy' nonsense to keep him in check. He neutralized Melanie's power base while she was asleep. He isn't a nice guy now, and naively assuming he is will likely get Melanie killed."

"Are we front lines, or do we fall in line behind Melanie?" Tanner asks.

"Melanie is now a Normal," Trey responds. The gravity of losing me as the source of never-ending destruction and protection descends on all of us.

"You still have two hundred and three lifetimes' worth of deadly warrior training," Arch reminds me.

"Melanie has a standing rule," Adam informs. "She won't kill one of her soulmates."

Trey looks to me. "If we don't get you out of this alive, please know how much I love you."

I nod. "I love you too, Trey. No matter what went on, that hasn't changed."

Adam steers my gaze his way with a finger on my jaw. "I love you, Angel Eyes. I'm so sorry that our soulmate connection is gone, but I'm going to fight to get you out of here."

"I love you too, Adam." I smile softly. "Thank you for helping me."

"You guys are talking like this is endgame," Arch says.

"It may be," Adam says. "Melanie was the most powerful energy worker I've ever known. The second most powerful is Demitri Cantrell."

"He's taken top spot," Trey says. "The only hope we have is that while we were decimating entire armies, Demitri was wasting time in libraries translating ancient Egyptian into Latin, and other such nonsense. He's a part of our original group from our first lifetime together, but he doesn't know our warrior sides."

"Who else was a part of the original group?" Tanner asks.

"Bear and Darren," Trey says. "They'll know what to do."

"Can the original group metaphysically incapacitate Demitri so we don't have to resort to killing him?" Arch asks Trey and Adam.

"Not a shot," Trey replies. "He's got us beat by a mile in that arena."

"This is really bad," Tanner whispers.

"You two need to leave," Trey says. "Act casual. Get the word to our key guys. Don't answer questions. Get me a clear path to a door to the outside. No one gets hurt that way."

"What direction do you prefer?" Arch asks.

"Escape route A is the quickest," Trey says. The bodyguards are all trained on prepared emergency scenarios. "Get us out that way, and we keep Melanie alive. She doesn't leave with Demitri or Mr. Cantrell. She only leaves this building with me or Adam."

Adam shakes his head. "I can't skip town. I've got two babies at home. *You* need to get Melanie out of here."

"Where will you go?" Arch asks.

Trey doesn't answer, and Tanner says, "You two will disappear, won't you?"

My head drops. I've been backed into a corner where Trey is my only hope. I worked my ass off to escape the prison of life with him. Being in a soulmate alliance, in hiding, with Trey is devastating.

"Melanie," Trey sends. I look his way, and he smiles the slightest bit. *"I promise I'll do right by you."*

I nod, but refuse to respond, because I know this man. He can't handle monogamy, especially with me. I can't worry about it now, though. We've got bigger problems.

Arch and Tanner hug the three of us before leaving. Adam hits the panic-room button again as the door closes, and Adam, Trey, and I get down to the business of my escape.

— —

Adam shakes his head, clearly worn out. "I wish we had slept last night," he says to Trey.

Trey snorts. "The end of a war is always like this," he reminds. "The big hoorah hits when we're sleep-deprived, at our wits end, and somehow we pull it together and level the playing field."

"I'm so sorry, Melanie," Adam says dejectedly. "I can't believe Demitri manipulated you like this, but I think you're right about his motive."

When I finally figured out what I think is behind Demitri neutralizing me, it went over like a bomb detonation in a circus tent.

Chaos, planning, and focused panic prevailed for the past fifteen minutes. The guys are in overdrive, hatching a plan for my and Trey's covert escape. The stakes are higher than ever.

"I'd rather leave than have to kill Demitri and Jayla," I say. "I'm sorry you have to bail with me, though, Trey."

"I'm not," he replies softly.

I wince as I peel off the charred sports bra that's adhered to the destroyed skin on my chest. Adam and Trey survey the damage now that I'm topless.

"Sorry I can't prop them on the bar or jiggle for you," I joke to Adam.

He chuckles, but it's laced with extreme concern. "That burn is bad, Melanie. We need to clean it up."

"We can't spare the time," Trey says.

I put on a tank top, wincing at the pain.

Adam puts the travel first aid kit in my backpack and zips it. "What about cash?"

"I've got a thousand in my wallet," Trey says. "I'll get us out of here and figure it out." He puts my backpack on.

"Swear to me that you won't destroy her again, Trey," Adam says past an emotionally choked throat.

"I promise," Trey says. It's his most sincere version, but I know better. No one goes back on his word like Trey. He's at his best in life-and-death moments, but it's the boredom of daily life that renders Trey a destructive, scheming, cheating liar.

Resigned to this, I take the flannel that Trey hands me. I tie it around my waist and slide on my tennis shoes. I study my pretty engagement ring before sliding it off and leaving it on top of my jewelry box. Adam hands Trey and me our phones, but Trey sets them on the bed.

"We can't take those," Trey says. "Demitri could trace us."

"That means you can't use the bank account either," Adam warns.

"Shit," Trey mutters. "I've got ten thousand in cash in the safe in my office."

"That's several doors down this hall," Adam warns. "I don't think we can chance it." He takes his wallet from his back pocket and pulls out cash, giving it to Trey. "I've only got a hundred on me."

"Thank you," Trey gravely responds. "Does everyone understand plans A, B, C, and D?"

Adam nods while he takes his Harley key from his pocket and gives it to Trey. I give him the key to my car.

Trey puts each key in a different pocket of his jeans, so they don't get mixed up when we get to an escape vehicle. We may have people on our tail, and seconds count. He looks to me. "The moment we get out of here, we're driving as fast and hard as we can. I need you to suffer through it because our easiest route is Adam's Harley in the parking lot. Our cars are in the garage, and I don't think we can get all the way through the parlor, dining room, and kitchen without being noticed. The Harley ride is going to be rough on that chest injury you're sporting. I know what route out of town I plan to take. There's a bank that we'll hit just as they open, if we ride through the night. We'll empty our account there, and there are four different directions out of that town. I'll take the one Demitri would least expect, and we're gone."

"*Our* account?" I ask.

Trey winces. "I've always thought of it as our account."

"I didn't even have a debit card for that account," I remind him dejectedly.

"You should have," Trey apologetically says.

"Well, now you never get to have a bank account again, so it doesn't matter," Adam jokes darkly.

"Do you have any idea how hard it's going to be to disappear in today's society?" I marvel.

"We'll figure it out," Trey assures.

"Where do you plan to take her?" Adam asks. Trey swallows hard, and Adam's expression falls. "Trey, I won't tell anyone, but I need to know."

"I can't chance it," Trey replies. "You know that. We've had to do this in past lives."

Adam hugs me, careful not to hurt my mangled chest. When he releases me, he chuckles sardonically, gesturing between me and Trey. "You two are going to have matching chest scars."

Trey and I laugh pensively.

Adam stares deeply at Trey. "Those chest scars are your reminder of your and Melanie's commitment to each other. Once this is done, you've both saved the other. Anytime the soulmate bond becomes too much for you, look at those scars and get your head on straight. Cut those cheating tendencies off right when they start to creep up, and you've got a shot."

Trey nods. "Thank you. I will."

"I'm proud of you, brother."

They clap hands, and Trey says, "See you on the flipside."

Adam crosses to the panel on the wall, while Trey and I head to the door. "Maintain contact while we get you out of here," Trey coaches me. "We're in enemy territory. You know the drill."

I nod.

Trey cups the back of my neck with his hand.

"Here we go," Adam says, and Trey nods. Adam pushes the button and races across the room, getting to us before the locks finish sliding away.

Trey's hand tightens on the back of my neck as he opens the

door, and we walk out in unison. He glances to the right and swings us to the left.

Adam falls into step on my other side. This was our least preferred direction choice. We were hoping to head through the parlor and out the foyer door.

"Melanie," sounds behind us. Mr. Cantrell was in the parlor, visible from the hall, hence why Trey turned left.

Trey picks up the pace, and we match his speed. Being back in sync with Trey and Adam is a perfect ending to this chapter of my life. I've always loved being a warrior with my soulmates. It's who we truly are at our core.

We get to the T-intersection, and Trey immediately swings to the left again. I internally groan because the exit past the suite we used to briefly share was our plan B. I didn't see who was down the T-intersection hall, but it must have been someone that would be a hindrance to us leaving that direction. I don't dare send Trey another mental message to find out, because it occurred to us too late that Demitri may be able to listen in on my mental chatter with Trey, now that Demitri is my Twin Flame. We have little insider intel about a Twin Flame connection, and now isn't the time to take chances.

"Melanie," is barked behind us by Javier.

We hear running feet, and Trey covers the back of my head with his hand and picks up the pace while Adam whips around, facing off with Javier.

"Go, go, go," Adam barks, and Trey and I hit a dead run.

Trey kicks open the closed door to the dance studio, and we careen into the middle of the orgy that I totally forgot was happening for another thirty minutes. Lucky for us, the revelers are so committed to their activities that only Mabel's working girls notice us rush through.

"Left! Banquet hall," Adam orders, taking over the decision-making while Trey focuses solely on keeping me moving.

"Talk to me, Adam," Trey barks.

"They're organized," Adam says.

"Guys, wait!" Bear cries out behind us.

"We've lost Bear and Darren," Adam informs.

"Shit," Trey hisses, while he grabs the banquet hall doorknob and opens it. We fly through the door, only to be met by the Misfits, who close in around us as the ones who follow join, tightening the circle and forcing us into the middle of the room. Marcus, Tanner, and Arch are mixed in the crowd. Knowing that Bear and Darren are compromised means we can't count on the other bodyguards.

The three of us seamlessly shift gears as Adam steps in front of me, and Trey steps behind as we're surrounded. With both of their backs to me, I put a hand on Adam's left hip in front of me and Trey's hip behind me, maintaining contact because neither of them can see me. Adam defensively crouches into a lunge, and I feel Trey shift to match. I swallow hard, knowing this is the plan D we hoped to avoid. Surrounded by the enemy, we're going to have to fight our way out. We didn't bring weapons because none of us were positive we could take a blade to someone we love. Luckily, we're all skilled at hand-to-hand combat.

"We've talked," Bear says. He glances toward Tanner.

That simple actions tells us what we need to know. We're on our own.

"Traitor," Adam snarls.

Tanner shakes his head. "We had it all wrong. That's why I told them. I had to stop this."

Trey inches back, pressing me tighter against Adam's tush. Adam feels the shift, and his muscles bunch taut. Trey's communicating with Adam through methods that are silent but very telling. It's a bad sign.

Hearing a knock on the door from the parking lot, we all freeze. When we don't answer, the knock becomes more persistent. Finally, Tanner says, "Well, hellfire," and opens the door that's behind him.

Adam, Trey, and I move as a unit, rotating to put our backs against the wall. Arthur and Blanche come in, and everyone stares at them, the air heavy with uncertainty.

"You must be here for the orgy," Tanner puzzles out.

"Well, what a lovely offer!"

"Arthur," Blanche admonishes, smacking him on the arm.

"I don't want to be RUDE," Arthur says. "Besides this is our year that we agreed to truly live life. I've never been in an orgy. The universe provides!"

Laughter spurts from several, as I groan.

"Who the fuck are they?" Adam mutters.

"You remember," I say. "Arthur and Blanche Boemant from the show last night." I have no clue what to do now that Arthur and Blanche are in this deadly situation.

"Welcome?" Mabel says, but it comes out as a very unsure question.

"Why are you here?" Tanner says, sounding exasperated.

"We're here to meet with the energy workers," Arthur cautiously replies as he surveys the standoff they interrupted.

"Yesssss!" Marcus says. "Help has arrived."

"How nice!" Mabel enthusiastically agrees.

"Well then, by all means, get your asses in here," Tanner barks. He points to us. "We've got a big problem."

"You'd be better off joining the orgy," Adam snarks.

Arthur's eyes narrow a bit. "This interests me more."

"Than an *orgy*?" Bear asks.

Arthur nods. "I'm a quantum physicist who moonlights as a metaphysical historian."

"Ohhhhhh," Adam says. "Nerd. Got it."

Mr. Cantrell politely nods to Arthur. "Birds of a feather, you and me."

"The best viewing spot is likely by that skate counter," Adam informs, pointing across the room.

"Seriously?" Trey hisses.

Adam shrugs. "The man likes to document metaphysical stories, and this one's about to be a whopper."

"You have a point," Trey grumbles. He waggles his hand toward the skate racks.

Arthur and Blanche make their way past the circle of Misfits and hop up to sit on the counter.

"Back to the nightmare," Tanner sasses.

Trey grabs my hip, guiding, and I steer Adam to the spot we were in previously.

"Why would you shift back there?" Bear asks. "You had a better defensive spot with your back against the wall."

"Right here is a better position to murder everyone in this room," Adam says.

"Oh, makes sense," Bear says like that's totally normal.

"Maybe we should have chosen the orgy," Blanche says to Arthur.

"Hell no," Arthur says intensely, leaning forward in rapt fascination.

"No one hurts my friends Arthur and Blanche," I order, earning agreement.

"Well, how sweet," Blanche murmurs.

"Trey," Adam prompts as he lunges back down, his muscles bunching.

I grab Trey's and Adam's hips again.

"I need everyone in my view to slowly move to the other side of the banquet hall," Trey orders, his tone leaving no room for argument. I hear people start to move and Trey barks, "Halt." The sounds of movement stop, and he says, "Move together clockwise."

"Why?" I hear Victoria sass.

"DO IT!" Trey bellows.

I hear them all move around together, and Trey silently communicates with me with his right foot that pivots against my ankle in time with their movement. Victoria, Mabel, Arch, Presley, Tanner, and Dante come into my peripheral view on my left.

"Stand with the others," Trey orders as he shifts in front of me, clueing me and Adam in that there's no one at our backs now.

Adam and Trey shift shoulder to shoulder in front of me, blocking my view. I put a hand on each of their outside hips, and the three of us back up, until my rear meets the push bar to the door headed into the parking lot. I squeeze my hands, indicating to stop.

"Look at that squadron training in action," Arthur murmurs.

"Debrief," Trey orders, now that we have a clear escape route. He and Adam part enough for me to see the group.

Tanner nods frantically, seeming elated with the opportunity. "Demitri wasn't trying to harm Melanie. He's as confused by how the Twin Flame connection fused as she is."

"I've checked his mind about that," Mr. Cantrell rushes to assure. "It's true."

I hear Arthur gasp and side-eye him. When he meets my gaze, I mouth, "Yes," and tick my finger once. I mouth, "No," and tick my finger twice.

He nods subtly.

My attention is drawn back to the debrief as Darren says, "You three can ease down."

"You're out of order," Trey deeply gravels.

"I'm not trying to override your authority," Darren says placatingly. "I'm telling you that you don't need this heightened battle readiness. That's why we're all trying to stop your plan to leave."

"Demitri has been sobbing in his office this whole time," Bear explains.

"The last thing we need is Trey and Melanie hauling ass out of here and disappearing forever over a misunderstanding," Dante assures. "There's no danger."

My shoulders start to relax, but Adam's and Trey's tension escalate.

"No one was scheming," Jayla says softly. "You guys need to take a breath."

"They can't," Mr. Cantrell says. "I speak from experience because my soulmate was a Normal, like Melanie is now. The guys feel a newly heightened sense of deadly responsibility to protect her."

I flick my eyes to Arthur and then back again, warning him that I need intel.

"Who told everyone that Melanie is a Normal?" Adam demands. Arch raises his hand, and Adam nods. "You and I have a serious problem."

"After hearing Demitri's side of the story, I had to tell everyone because you three have this all wrong," Arch explains. "We stationed the people we knew you would avoid so that we could block your route to every exit, and funnel you in here so we could fill you in. I wouldn't have told them if I thought there was a threat."

"Telling them creates a new threat," Trey informs. "When this information gets out, and it will because Victoria knows and Jayla spills all of Melanie's dirt, every asshole who Melanie's beat in a battle is going to come for her."

"Shit," Arch mutters.

"You sure you trained your bodyguards?" Adam sarcastically asks Trey.

"I clearly suck at this job," Trey replies. "Good thing that I'm leaving, huh?"

"No one needs to leave," Mabel says.

"He wasn't trying to steal your abilities," Bear says. "Demitri's abilities are also gone."

I look to Arthur. He flicks his finger twice, giving me the intel I need.

The hall door opens, and Javier rushes through with Demitri.

"Here we go," Arthur murmurs.

I brace, thinking he's warning me.

"Melanie," Demitri barks.

We make eye contact, and a huge energy detonation rocks the room. People lose their footing, falling to the polished wood floor. Adam, Trey, and I maintain our legs. My guys shift, their shoulders coming together in front of me, blocking my view. The entirety of my metaphysical ability booms back into place in my psyche, my body reacting like a struck tuning fork.

"Think," Arthur says, his statement blending into the general cacophony everyone's kicking up, but I know the message is for me.

I survey a new, and certainly monumental, oddity. I search the Twin Flame connection and discover that there's no new method of overhearing his thoughts, so Demitri likely can't hear mine. I reinforce my blockage with Demitri. I snap my hand onto Trey's and Adam's backs and send the memory of what just happened.

"What's the game plan?" Trey sends, now that he's sure Demitri can't hear us.

The Misfits are all squawking about what could have caused that boom, giving us time to hash this out.

"Order Adam to stand down, but don't tell anyone that my abilities are back. I'm running a loyalty check."

"Why did your abilities come back?" Trey sends.

"I suspect it's because Demitri and I were apart when the Twin Flame bond fused," I send back. *"The moment he and I made eye contact, the metaphysical alignment hit. Arthur gave me an answer."*

"Send the memory of our chat to Adam." I do, through my hand on Adam's back.

After waiting a moment for Adam to review the memory, Trey says, "Fall back."

Adam and Trey part, and I step through the middle, careful to appear scared and helpless.

"It's okay, Melanie," Jayla encourages.

"Demitri's been so upset," Mr. Cantrell gloms on. "You're safe, I promise."

"I can vouch for that," Bear says.

I glance to Arthur, who flicks his finger twice. That's a no, I'm not safe. I make eye contact with Demitri.

"You need to come to terms with this," Demitri says with an air of indignant authority, earning surprised looks from most of his allies. His eyes narrow while he sneers. "We wanted back our spirit guide eternity. It's back now." My mouth plunges open, and Demitri rolls his eyes dramatically.

"Why are you being such an ass, Demitri?" Adam demands.

Laughter, laced evil, bubbles from Demitri.

"Shit," Trey sends. *"Looks like he intended to render you helpless."*

"Yup," I send back. *"The question is, are the rest of them in on it with him?"*

"Keep up the helpless act and let's see," Trey sends.

A slow smile builds as Demitri luxuriously raises a hand, and a fireball blasts. It spirals before extinguishing as it gets to the lofty ceiling. Everyone stares in awe at the ceiling where the fireball was. Adam's hands twitch. It's a battle quirk that I recognize from many lifetimes of him being a warrior.

"Nice trick," Trey says, milking the moment so I can internally study the abilities I've gained from Demitri.

Demitri's head tips, and I recognize the gesture on a cellular level. My head tips to match as a deeply resounding calm spreads through me. I feel Trey studying the shift in me.

"Go ahead," I encourage. "Fill us in. Fireballs are new, Dragon Warrior."

"When the Twin Flame bond fused, I gained your abilities," Demitri informs.

"Whaaaat?" Bear murmurs.

"It seems you also got some of my less charitable personality quirks," I reply, breathing methodically as the calm in my core deepens. I study it at rapid-fire pace, unsure how it works.

"You hid in a room with Trey and Adam instead of working with *me* through this new Twin Flame bond," Demitri furiously accuses.

"I didn't ask for this new Twin Flame bond," I reply. "You forced it on me."

The air becomes stiflingly heavy with what Demitri's leaking. Considering the magnitude, he has enough rage to power a nuclear bomb gathered in his five massive reserves. I send out a clandestine energy scan and discover that he's fighting to control his desire to detonate the load.

"Stand down, Melanie," Trey warns. "You can't go up against that." He sends to me, *"Figure this out quick."*

"Keep distracting him," I send back, needing more time.

"Someone is FINALLY putting that fucking wannabe show-boating bitch in her place," belts from Victoria.

"Never mind," I scoff. *"Victoria's doing it."*

Demitri slides ice-cold eyes Victoria's way.

She smirks seductively at Demitri. "Sounds like you stole Melanie's power base." She gives me an arrogant look over. "How does it feel to be a lowly Normal like the rest of us?"

Demitri studies me, realizing that Victoria might be right.

Fear of that "reality" blasts from everyone.

"If he checks your soulmate blockage, he'll realize what you've gained," Trey sends.

"He won't," I send back.

"How do you know?"

"Because my arrogantly confident habit of attacking first and asking questions later is at the helm in his psyche right now," I send back. *"It seems that we gained each other's personality staples, along with the metaphysical abilities."*

Victoria strides my way, draws back a fist, and punches me in the cheek. I hit the ground and smirk behind my hair that covers my face. I let her hit me intentionally as part of the ruse that I'm helpless. I can't out that my abilities are back until I figure out the direction Demitri plans to head with his newly gained abilities. He's on the edge of annihilation-level disaster. Now that my abilities have returned, and I don't need to run away, I must stay and handle him.

Rage blasts through the room from Demitri. A scream blisters, and there's a rush of hot wind. Victoria smacks into the wall above the door, before hitting the floor behind us. Adam and Trey haul me to my feet, and we pivot to the left as a unit.

Demitri's thrumming with power as he mentally booms the audible words, *"That's my Twin Flame you attacked, BITCH!"* He starts to stalk across the room. When Jayla rushes to block his path, he stops and stares down at her.

"You aren't evil, Demitri!" Jayla implores. "Melanie's evil was what held you back from giving a relationship with her a chance."

Demitri's focus shifts from Jayla to Victoria, and unchecked rage blasts from him. Victoria soars to the ceiling in the middle of the room above Demitri. He pins her there with an unseen force.

"Unbelievable," Arthur breathes, mesmerized.

"HOLD!" Stella bellows. She strides to Jayla and says, "Back off, Jaybird." As Jayla scuttles to Dante, Stella takes her place facing Demitri.

"What?" Demitri snarls.

Stella glances up at a suspended Victoria before settling her focus on Demitri again. "Adam told us about Melanie liquifying her daughter and destroying that entire village when she was wronged in a past life."

Demitri tips his head. "Intrigued. Continue."

Stella nods encouragingly. "You and I talked after that. You said that Melanie's irrationally pragmatic rage was something you wanted to help her with."

"Now I understand that rage better," Demitri retorts.

"Do you respect Victoria that much?" Stella gestures flippantly to a petrified Victoria on the ceiling.

"Interesting," Adam and Arthur murmur simultaneously about Stella's tactic shift.

Demitri scrunches his face arrogantly. "How does me attacking her mean I respect her?"

"You care so much about Victoria that you're willing to sacrifice your morals for her?" Stella lobs back.

The Misfits collectively suck breeze, while Adam smiles the slightest bit.

Demitri cocks his head contemplatively.

"What does this mean?" Jayla interrupts to ask Bear. "The

whole stealing Melanie's abilities thing, I mean."

"It means that Demitri is now the most powerful energy worker in the world, without question," Bear informs with gravity.

"Um," Arthur murmurs.

Blanche puts a hand on his arm to silence him.

Demitri glowers up at Victoria. "You're an abomination," he bellows.

When he releases his energetic hold on her, Bear and Darren run at full bore and catch her just before she hits the floor.

Bear sets down a shaking lump of Victoria before rounding to face Demitri. "You need to remember who you are—at your core!"

The look Demitri gives Bear sends ice down my spine. "Fuck you, Bear, with all your condescending know-it-all bullshit!" He scans the room, and his gaze lands on Trey. "You're NOT kidnapping Melanie. I'll kill you before you make it out that door. Melanie's mine now."

I fight with everything in me to mask my surge of dark-water energy from detection by the energy workers in the room as I shift in front of Trey to confront Demitri. "Did you just say I'm yours?"

Adam chuckles. "You're in deep shit now, King Ding-a-Ling."

"How are you not mine?" Demitri demands. "You're my Twin Flame."

I snort and gesture to Adam.

He gleefully says, "Melanie has a lot of rule number ones. Today's rule number one is, she is her own autonomous being. Melanie Slate belongs to no one, you arrogant waste of air."

I feel Demitri's mammoth reserves overflow. He gathers an energy attack and launches it at Adam. I throw up an invisible shield and absorb the death blow. My head tips back, and an odd hum vibrates from me as the power Demitri is capable of thrums through my body.

"Unbelievable," Arthur says in awe.

"Well, you can't hide that your abilities are back now," Trey sends. *"They're all oblivious traitors who trusted Demitri and got snowed. Loyalty check is done. Demitri is deadly and unhinged. Might as well thump him hard and establish dominance now."*

I sight on Demitri and send the blast energy I absorbed from his attack on Adam back his way. It hits him in the chest, and he soars across the room, smacking into the wall before ricocheting to the floor.

"You forgot to shield," I condescend, as his body audibly splinters, bones breaking with the impact.

Demitri moans as everyone screams. They start to rush to him.

"STAND DOWN!" I order.

Everyone freezes except Jayla. She plunges to her knees by him, with tears pouring down her face. I tip my head, feeling the maniacal desire to kill her blister through me.

"Don't, Melanie!" Dante screams.

I take a deep breath and draw Demitri's trademark calm from my core, allowing it to coat my rage. My eyes narrow as I fumble with the balance. Finally, I wrap Jayla in a shield and toss her across the room to Dante.

"Control that girl," I snarl, as he catches her.

"I thought Melanie was a NORMAL!" Jayla screeches.

"You'd love that wouldn't you?" I growl.

Demitri stares at me with pain-filled eyes from his spot on the floor. I glare at him while I survey the energy he contains, discovering that it's being generated by his own body. Not even the slightest bit is from an outside source, which is odd. Even when I don't try to, I still draw in minute amounts of energy from sources all around me.

I siphon off the overwhelming energy load he's quaking with.

Once my tanks are refilled, I continue pulling energy and ground it down into the earth. Knowing that he can't generate another maniacal, personality-warping load in his current state, I wrap Demitri in an energy net so powerful that it's visible to the eye, before dragging him across the room to me. He moans, in excruciating pain from his injuries. I stare down at him with the grace I'd give a chihuahua who humped my leg. "Look at me."

When he doesn't, I send out an energy pop that flips him over. He screams in pain. Our spectators gasp.

"You can't kill him, Melanie!" Mabel insists.

"Melanie, PLEASE!" Mr. Cantrell screams.

"Remember who you are!" Bear begs.

I pan an arrogant look around the room. "I'm reminding *every-one* who I am." I point to Victoria. "NONE of you stepped in when she not only dismissed me like I was no one but also punched me!"

"Demitri suddenly becoming evil shocked all of us stiff," Mabel defends.

"You all assured me that I was safe." I gesture to Demitri, who's a pathetic broken heap. "You call the behavior he just exhibited *safe*?"

"He was nothing like that when you were locked in your room," Mr. Cantrell rushes to explain. "He was an emotional WRECK."

I nod, slow and steady. "When did that change?"

"When he got in here," Mr. Cantrell says.

I smirk. "Yeah . . . So, when Demitri and I landed in the same space, what happened?" I ask, like I'm prompting a room full of kindergartners in a lesson.

"That big boom," Bear says, seeming to put pieces together.

"Very good," I say, condescendingly. "Now, what do you think the big boom was?" Bear starts to respond, but I shake my head at him. "Let's let someone else in the class answer."

"Twin Flames share abilities," Arthur says. "Your abilities disappeared because they had to mix with Demitri's, but you two had to make eye contact for that infusion to settle in each of you. Someone mentioned that you were in different spaces when the Twin Flame process ignited, hence why you thought he metaphysically incapacitated you."

"Correct. He didn't steal my abilities. They were dormant until we were together and gained each other's. I used his little mantrum, and Victoria's vapid fit, to study Demitri's calm that now lives in me. I learned to harness it while this spiritual disaster," I point to Demitri, "got lost in my rage."

"Oh shit," Tanner breathes.

I smirk at him. "I now harness my rage, energy control, killing abilities, and allllll that Demitri is." I look down at Demitri, wanting to test my suspicion. "Pull an energy load. Black out Hollywood. Let's test the extent of what you gained."

"I can't," he barely gets out through chattering teeth caused by horrific pain.

I narrow my eyes. "Then you have a serious problem, because you aren't the most powerful energy worker in the room. I am." I snort. "There go your grand plans! You're as stupid as your previous soulmate is." I look Victoria's way. "Speaking of which, it's time that you're punished for punching me."

Her eyes widen as I flick a wrist and she drops, screaming as she writhes on the floor.

"What are you doing to her?" Mabel gasps.

"Putting her in her place, because none of you did."

I flick a wrist again and she stills, but her trepidatious panting persists. She grips her head and moans.

"Next issue," I say as I kneel next to Demitri.

"Please don't hurt him," Jayla begs.

I slide a judgmental expression her way. "That would make you sad, wouldn't it?"

"Yes," Jayla whimpers. "This is terrifying."

"I agree," I reply. "I found being trapped here by all of you positively petrifying. We got through that. There's a good chance Demitri will make it through what I'm about to do to him." I put my hands flat on his chest.

"Stop, Melanie!" Bear barks, but I ignore him.

I close my eyes and pull up the collection of memories I pilfered from Warlock, who was an incredibly powerful healer. I find one of repairing broken bones and play it at rapid-fire pace.

Confident I understand it, I gather an energy load that I cool off with the new calming ability I've gained. I send the energy into Demitri. Sweat instantly pours from my forehead, and soaks through my clothes. A moan escapes me as I experience the incredible capacity of this healing gift. I'm a killer at my core, and this ability wars with the essence of who I am, but I wrestle the conflict into submission.

My eyes open, and my vision warbles before coming back into focus. I stand and watch as Demitri sits up and stares at me in wonder.

"You healed me."

Mr. Cantrell kneels by his son and looks him over frantically. "Oh my God," he whimpers. "I've been terrified because you could heal everyone, but there was no one to heal you."

"She handled all of it," Demitri says, in awe. He rotates his shoulder that's been giving him trouble in dance rehearsals.

"A muscle in your shoulder was torn," I quietly inform. "I fixed it also."

"I thought you were going to kill him," Mabel says, seemingly in disbelief at the turn this has taken.

I shake my head, hurt but not surprised. "You always assume I'm the villain. My psyche was broken into, you trapped me, Demitri went rogue the moment he thought he was more powerful than me, *and* Victoria punched me, but the worst is still assumed of me."

"You attacked him, though!" Jayla blathers.

"I attacked him because someone needed to disarm him before he killed everyone in this room," I inform. "He's calm now because I got him to the floor and syphoned off his energy overload. He didn't know how to handle it because he's full of MY deadly instincts!"

Everyone appears thunderstruck by the layers of what just went on.

"I swear to you that Demitri showed every sign of being distraught," Bear says. "I never would put the three of you at risk on purpose. That shift in him was a layer I didn't anticipate."

Adam points to Bear. "You've lost your fucking edge! Melanie had ZERO abilities except for mind-to-mind soulmate speech with Trey. She was INCAPACITATED in her sleep. We had to get her out of here."

"I still need to get her out of here," Trey insists.

"The threat is neutralized," I say.

The wave of dismay that streams down the connection from Trey seizes my heart. He blocks me off on his side, but it's too late. I study the sentiment and realize Trey is heartbroken to lose this chance with me. He planned to hide with me and work his ass off to rectify his wrongs for the rest of this lifetime.

"Will you please heal Victoria?" Mabel requests of Demitri, albeit timidly.

Victoria is still panting dramatically on the floor.

"There's nothing wrong with Victoria," I inform. "All I did was wrap her in an energy casing and send a gong-like whoom into the shield."

"Why didn't you hurt her?" Mabel asks.

"Because all of you needed to see what's at her core. She's a coward, like most bullies. All that huff and puff she spouts is nothing but a cover she hides behind, so no one discovers how pathetic she really is. She was merely scared of a little noise." I smirk. "She's allowed to beat the shit out of me when you think my abilities are gone, though?"

"Why didn't you defend Melanie?" Tanner asks Trey. "You were right there, and you're with Victoria."

"Because," Trey quietly replies, "I was in Melanie's head studying what was actually happening. I knew that she was milking the distraction Victoria provided so she could get a handle on the new abilities she'd gained from Demitri."

"I want you to know how much it means to me that you were willing to leave everything behind and disappear with me," I tell Trey.

"WHAT?" Victoria blisters.

"You're welcome," Trey says, ignoring Victoria.

"With that said, you learn the hard way." I smile softly at Trey. "You're in deep shit, with zero intuition, and baddddd judgment, where your love life is concerned. It's time for me step aside so that you can truly commit to the woman you chose." I gesture to Victoria.

"Thank GOD!" Victoria barks.

"You promised you'd talk to your spirit guide!" Trey yelps.

"I did," I reply. "I conferred with her the day after you asked me to. She and I agreed to precisely what I'm about to do. Bear and Darren, please do the honors."

I grab one of Bear's hands and one of Darren's, and they place their other hands on Trey's shoulders. I exhale hard as they wall off the connection. Trey hyperventilates as Bear and Darren let go of him.

"I apologize on behalf of all of us for trapping you in this house when we thought you were running from a misunderstanding," Mabel says. "It was clearly shortsighted, and we have a lot to consider, because today has been a real eye-opener in many ways. With that said, I'm not losing you, Melanie." She looks to Victoria. "I'm sorry, but you need to move out."

Trey blasts the room with relief.

"Excuse the hell out of you!" I bark at Mabel, while Adam cracks up. "You're going to let Trey off the hook the MOMENT he's finally learning?"

"I believe this is another example of 'suffering is what's best for someone,'" Dante schools.

Mabel huffs. "I apologize." She looks at Victoria again, seeming exhausted. "You must continue to live in the suite."

Victoria appears immensely relieved while Trey visibly panics.

"Does that suffice?" Mabel asks me.

"Looks like you're finally learning," I reply.

"Talk about learning the hard way," Tanner mutters.

I slide a challenging look Jayla's way. "It's your turn to face consequences. Not only did you think your relationship was so deep with my man that you stepped into conflict to stop him ON VICTORIA'S BEHALF, but you also revealed that he thinks I'm evil. I didn't know that, but he shared it with *you*."

"We discussed that before the two of you were together," Jayla defends. "Not after!"

"How do you explain defying my order to stand down, and rushing to Demitri when he hit the floor?" I demand.

"He was broken," Jayla gasps.

"He needed to be broken," I retort. "It fixed this little tiff, didn't it?"

"Little *tiff*?" Tanner mutters.

"Demitri decided to not only infiltrate my mind, but he also forced this Twin Flame connection, all before enlisting all of you to trap me when I was helpless, and THEN he attacked me." I look to Dante. "Isn't that EXACTLY what you discussed this morning? Don't kick Melanie when she's down? Don't trap her? She's a worthwhile person who deserves discussion and consideration?"

"Yes," Dante replies. "Then he did precisely those things hours after promising he wouldn't do it again."

I nod. "Indeed. Just like Jayla promised not to interfere with Demitri and me again, and Mr. Cantrell promised not to use his abilities on me without permission. We have quite a few liars in our ranks."

"Melanie, I wasn't trying to use my abilities on you in a harmful way," Mr. Cantrell rushes to say. "Jayla came to me and asked if I would guide her and Demitri into a better communication routine because Dante so clearly brought the issues into focus. Unfortunately, when we got to Demitri, he was an emotional wreck. I had a mental chat with him, and he was desperate to clear the air with you. I agreed to rolling your mind solely for the purpose of Demitri reaching you in your dream state because you were shielded off."

"How did that work out?" I ask cynically.

"Pretty damn horribly," Mr. Cantrell admits.

"What does that tell you?" I ask.

"That I shouldn't have done it."

"Do you want to know what it tells *me*?" I ask.

"Probably not," Mr. Cantrell says, earning laughter spurts from Adam and Trey.

"What it tells me is that you got snowed."

"How?" Mr. Cantrell suspiciously asks.

"Jayla and Demitri had a plan." I give Mr. Cantrell a knowing look. "You were fetched to offer *supposed* guidance, but the moment you arrived, your son changed focus to you breaking into my mind so that he could get in." My maniacal gaze shifts to Jayla. "I don't know why the two of you thought you could get away with this, but you can bet your ass that you're both fucked."

"What are you talking about, Melanie?" Demitri asks dreadfully.

"Here we gooooo," Adam singsongs to Trey. They huddle together, excited for the big unveiling.

"You and Jayla planned this in hopes of stealing my abilities, rendering me helpless, and killing me so that I'd no longer be in the way of your true love," I inform.

Arthur's and Blanche's gasps give voice to everyone's stunned shock.

Demitri's eyes nearly pop out of his head. "Holy SHIT! *That's* what you think?"

I nod calculatedly. "I was rendered helpless and had to get out of here before either of you killed me. Unfortunately for both of you, my abilities are back." I slide challenging eyes to Jayla. "I wish you'd still try though."

"Oh my God," whispers from Dante as he realizes this new threat to Jayla.

Demitri's expression drops compassionately. "I didn't plan any of this. A Twin Flame bond fused because we both felt whole, and completely loved, at the same time. I didn't cause that. *We* did."

"You formed an army of our people against me!"

"Now that I understand your perspective, I think I can clear this up," Demitri says.

"I highly doubt it," Adam mutters.

Demitri gives him a look before focusing on me again. "For the record, I wasn't attempting a Twin Flame bond. I just wanted to show you how I felt."

"Fine," I reply. "What did you and Jayla discuss before she got your dad?"

"She wanted to talk to me, but you requested that I not have what you call 'sneaky little chats,'" Demitri explains. "To be on the up and up, I requested that she grab my dad because I couldn't abandon my security post."

"Uh-huh," I grunt. "Why didn't you have a little chat once your dad was there to be a sneaky conspirator?"

Mr. Cantrell slumps.

"My dad sent an inquiry mind-to-mind, because he wasn't sure what Jayla wanted him for," Demitri says. "I was so emotionally screwed up that I immediately started begging him to help me with the issue I had with you. I couldn't focus on Jayla's need to talk."

"We still haven't had the chat with Jayla," Mr. Cantrell says. "I think it's best if you join that discussion, and I mediate, Melanie."

"That's an excellent idea," Mabel interjects.

"Not happening," I deadpan her way.

Demitri's head drops. "I truly was a wreck in the office. My behavior after that boom, when I saw you, was the direct result of me having no CLUE how to handle your metaphysical abilities that roared into me." He gives me a mesmerized look. "Holy Satan, woman! Your metaphysical abilities are straight from hell! I didn't stand a shot."

"Sweet talker," I joke, bitingly.

Demitri chuckles, before requesting, "Check my memory."

I pull up his memory of the conversation he and Jayla had right before she got his dad. It went down exactly how he described. I speed through it as he sobs in the office, while Bear plans to stop us after Arch and Tanner explained the gauntlet plan.

"There's no plot to kill me," I announce. "Just a whole lot of people with a death wish, making asinine choices."

Everyone collectively exhales, the tension diminishing a bit.

"I have no clue how to make it up to you, but I'm so sorry," Demitri says.

"There's a way, right here and right now," I say. "Do you plan to return the favor? Because DAMN, am I hurting."

"I know how emotionally painful today has been for you," he says. "Would you like to sit and have that conversation to set parameters with Jayla now?"

"JAYLA is what you're concerned about?" I ask in disbelief.

"Holy smokes," Arthur mutters. "I've got my work cut out for me in more than one way."

Blanche sighs.

Demitri appears stunned. "What were you referring to?"

"Don't blow up, Mel," Dante interjects, grinning at me. "Let's try something new to get through to him." He crosses to a wall with all the cots from the sleepover last night stacked against it. He takes one out and carries it over, places it in front of me, and gestures to it, giving me an amused look. "Time for a dramatic recreation."

I lie down on it, dramatically flourish a hand to my forehead, and let loose a squall. "Ohhhhhh, ouchieeeeeee!" I add a few whimpers and thrash about pathetically, in an overexaggerated imitation of Jayla this morning.

"On today's episode of *Is Her Twin Flame a Totally Oblivious Douche?* I present to you, Melanie and Demitri," Adam says, like a game show announcer, unable to resist being a jackass.

I give up on my Jayla imitation to watch his performance.

Adam comically crosses to Demitri. "This fine contestant lives in a state of oblivion, except when he's catering to pitiful simpletons." He gestures to Jayla before smoldering at Demitri again. "Unfortunately for this gorgeous moron, he's engaged to a woman who wants what she wants but never gets what she needs."

Everyone cracks up.

Adam struts to me and flourishes. "I present to you, Melanie Last Name Unknown because she's had forty-seven of them."

I give him a disgusted look.

He hits me with a million-dollar game show smile. "Melanie was just in a battle for her life, soul, and sanity. In said battle . . ." He waves for me to sit up, then hooks the front of my tank top and pulls it out to take a gander. "Damn," he murmurs, ogling me.

"Don't drop character," Presley scolds.

"So sorry." Adam smolders again, getting back to his dumb skit. "In said battle, her chest was scorched like a Thanksgiving turkey prepared by a newlywed eighteen-year-old." He leans in to the spectators. "Let's see if the oblivious moron figures it out." Adam snaps at me, hissing, "Do the 'poor me Jayla thing' again."

I flop down and moan and "ouchie" dramatically.

Demitri stares at my charred chest that's partially visible in my tank top. "Oh my God, Melanie," he gasps, rushing to me.

"We've got a winnnnnnerrrrrr," Adam crows, earning applause from the spectators.

"What happened?" Demitri asks.

"Spoke too soooooon," Adam crows again, and everyone spurts laughter. He gives Demitri a deadpan look. "Your little Twin Flame scheme scorched your girl, numbnuts."

Demitri looks like he's going to cry. He pulls my tank top over my head. Realizing too late that I'm not wearing a bra, he winces. "Sorry."

"Whatever," I groan, lying down.

"We're all *winnnnnners*," Adam belts, while Demitri starts healing me.

"Put on your SHIRT!" Victoria snarls.

"Put on a *muzzlllllle*," Adam crows, keeping up his dumb show announcer ruse.

"I hate you, Adam," Victoria snarls.

"Trey, your girlfriend's sweet-talking me!" Adam tattles, while I put my shirt back on now that I'm healed.

"I couldn't care less," Trey grumbles, while offering me a hand up.

"Hey, wait a minute!" Adam says, rounding on Trey. "I gave you a hundred bucks and my HARLEY key to escape with my little Angel Eyes. Give them back."

Trey smirks challengingly. "Come and get them."

Laughter spurts from our spectators.

Adam glares at Demitri. "You started this mess. If I have to fight Trey for my Harley key, I'm going to give Arthur over there a REAL metaphysical spectacular!"

"No more fighting," Jayla pleads, butting in. "Trey, please give them back!"

"Oh no," Victoria snarls. "You aren't getting your claws into *my* man."

"That could be interesting," I mutter to Adam and Trey.

"She flirts with me, *secretly*," Trey belts, lying to Victoria.

Adam struggles not to laugh. Victoria grits her teeth while Jayla rapidly shakes her head with hugely terrified eyes.

Trey shrugs. "Those two might kill each other. It'd solve a lot of problems."

"Stop it," Mabel scolds Trey. She shakes her head at Victoria. "They're just trying to get you to fight with Jayla because it amuses them."

"I hate you," Victoria barks at me.

I toss my hands up. "More blaming me for the actions of others. I swear, you people are impossible."

"No, we're not," Demitri says. "Change starts right here and right now. Name your boundaries, Melanie."

"So much room for new rules and fuck*ery*," Adam singsongs to me.

"True," I groan, before pondering a moment. "I think I need to set boundaries that are actually productive instead of screwing with them, though."

"Good girl," Blanche murmurs.

"Please do," Demitri says.

"I'm respectfully asking that Jayla and your dad no longer be in my life."

"Oh heavens." Blanche sighs.

"What?" Demitri and Mr. Cantrell say in unison.

I nod. "Your father broke into my mind and held me prisoner. Jayla was your confidante while you mind-raped me while I was asleep."

"Melanie," Demitri chokes out. "I would never mind-rape you!"

"That's precisely what you did," Adam informs. "Just like Trey had his partner in crime," he gestures to Victoria, "who he schemed with while he destroyed and raped Melanie, you had *your* partner in crime." He gestures to Jayla and smirks. "You also had your dad hold Melanie down while you had your way with her."

"Damn, that sounds bad!" Tanner yelps.

Adam nods vibrantly. "You *all* helped THEM!" He gestures from Demitri, to Jayla, to Mr. Cantrell.

"Melanie," Demitri whispers, aghast, while Jayla whimpers pitifully.

"Oh my God," Mr. Cantrell gasps. "No, Melanie! We *must* discuss this."

"We are!"

Mr. Cantrell frantically shakes his head. "We need to talk privately!"

I snort. "I'll never be at your mercy again," I inform him. "I plan to shield off so hard from you that you can't bust in, but in case you decide to do Jayla and Demitri's dirty work again, be warned that I *will* kill you for it." I survey the entire group. "If that day comes, I want zero pushback. He's been warned. I have the right to invoke Redemption Clause against most of you, based on what you all did to me. I've chosen compassion by not doing that, but you're pushing my limits.

Mouths thud open, while Jayla instantly turns on the waterworks.

"Please sit down with us," Bear desperately requests.

Staring at Bear makes me so sad, but I maintain my composure. "No thank you. I've had enough."

I start to head to the door to leave, and Tanner rattles, "Stop, stop, stop. Who, exactly, are you likely to be perma-done with once the emotional smoke clears? There's a lot of us."

I survey the crowd. "All right . . . Let's see . . ." After careful contemplation, I inform, "Once I'm no longer irate, I'm likely to be wary of Mr. Cantrell, but I'll decide to feign respect out of obligation. I'll hate Victoria forever, but that's not new." I smirk to myself. "I need a voodoo doll with jet-black hair and a fat ass."

Laughter spurts from the spectators, while Blanche gives me an admonishing look that I ignore.

"Jayla has irritated me into hatred, and I formally request that she crawls in a hole and whimpers with someone else, who isn't me or Demitri," I snark. I look around and wobble my head. "The rest of you will earn a pass back into my good graces."

"Even Demitri?" Stella asks, her tone hopeful.

I roll my eyes. "I'm going to my parents' house to get my head together."

"You can't be there alone!" Demitri panics.

"What it boils down to is, I've been alone every time things go bad," I reply stoically. "You all show up like spectators watching a prisoner being attacked by gladiators at the coliseum. Your presence doesn't stop evil; it just gives me something else to worry about while I do the unthinkable. I don't need a cheering squad or people to plot against me, and I sure as hell don't need anyone to kick me when I'm down. What I need is peace, quiet, and time to breathe."

I start to leave, and Adam says, "Well, Trey, looks like we're getting in a swim before we finally get to pass out cold."

I look his way, amused. "Did you not hear me?"

"Hell yes, I heard you," Adam says. A slow grin builds. "We did a great job telling off these asshats!"

I roll my eyes. "What part of 'I want peace and quiet' do you not understand?"

Adam chuckles. "Girl, you've wanted that for two hundred and three lifetimes. Give up."

I belt laughter, and it feels pretty good after what we've gone through.

Trey drapes his arm over Adam's shoulders, and they grin at me like jackasses. "We're heroes," Trey says.

"Heroes who deserve to swim," Adam lilts.

"Swim, swim, swim, swim," they chant.

I relent because they were amazing today. "Heroes *do* deserve a swim."

Trey and Adam high-five.

Adam holds up a finger to Trey before looking my way. "Heroes deserve sex?"

"Oooooh," Trey says. "I've heard that's the grand prize for heroes."

"TREY!" Victoria bellows, but she's ignored.

"Greek historyyyyy," Adam lilts at me. "You love history. It could be research!"

"Unfortunately, I've already done that research," I retort with an eyebrow raise. "I've read Homer's *Iliad*."

"A play, perhaps," Adam says. "We could act out the *Iliad*."

I giggle. "You get to swim. That's it." Trey and Adam grumble, and I quirk my mouth. "I've got four boxes of Pop Tarts at the house."

"Cinnamon?" Trey asks.

I nod, and the guys strut to me. Trey snags my backpack from the floor and gives Adam back his Harley key.

"I want my hundred bucks back," Adam says.

"Not a shot," Trey replies, earning laughter from Adam.

Adam raises an eyebrow. "You coming, loser?" he asks as he turns to face the Misfits.

"Which loser are you referring to?" Bear asks.

"Peter Pan," Adam says.

Demitri perks. "Really?"

"Yeah, dumbass," Adam says. "I promised I'd help you with the pitfalls of being Melanie's guy."

Trey snorts. "You *need* help," he lobs at Demitri. He scrunches his face. "You're *terrible* at this, and that's coming from ME!"

Laughter spurts from several of the Misfits.

Demitri hesitates but clearly wants to come with us.

"Do I need to *beg*, Demitri?" Adam languishes out melodramatically. "You always make me beeeeeeg!"

"I bet you wouldn't make JAYLA *beg*," Trey piles on.

"Didn't you just plot to murder Demitri?" Stella asks.

Adam shrugs. "Yup. Welcome to the Misfits."

Demitri jogs to us, and holds his hand my way.

Adam slaps it away. "*We're* escorting her out of this prison, thank you VERY much!"

"We're *heroes*," Trey haughtily says. "*You* have to carry this." He thuds my backpack against Demitri's chest, and Demitri chuckles.

"We don't get sex though," Adam obnoxiously schools Demitri.

"Only Pop Tarts," Trey says.

"And a swim," Adam adds.

"And you get to fight with me," I chirp.

"Best night ever," Demitri lovingly adores while he puts my backpack on his shoulder.

"Well, my dear," Arthur says as he guides Blanche to us, "it looks like we're swimming."

I turn a mortified red. "I'm so sorry you witnessed that!"

Arthur grins. "I just had front-row seats at the metaphysics Olympics." He shakes his head. "You people are incredibly powerful. You're also in need of a lot of intel. I'd like to talk to the four of you. We can set an appointment with the other energy workers later."

"We'd love that," Demitri says, before looking to me, unsure because he took over.

"I live in the Valley," I warn. "It'll be a thirty-minute drive."

Arthur shrugs. "We've got gas in our sportster, and nothing but time today."

"Let's roll," I say.

"Trey, you're staying here, and we're talking about you plotting to leave forever with MELANIE," Victoria bellows.

Adam, Demitri, and I crack up at Trey's expense.

"Ugggghhhhhhh," Trey groans. "Please rescue me!"

"Grip the back of his neck and keep moving!" Adam hisses to Demitri. "I'm the last line of defense. Our objective is to get him out the door."

"Ready," Demitri dramatically replies, and grabs the back of

Trey's neck. "She's watching," he adds as the guys all chance an overly dramatic look toward a fuming Victoria.

Everyone tries not to crack up because it'll further irritate Victoria, who they're about to be stuck with.

"Nice and subtle," Adam coaches. "Head for the door like you're anticipating Pop Tarts and a swim, instead of the *Iliad*!"

The guys stride for the door, while I saunter after them, laughing with Arthur and Blanche.

"Don't you dare eat Melanie's Pop Tart!" Victoria screams.

Well, that does it. The spectators howl with laughter.

"Hey, Trey," I bellow, "we should snag one of those swings on our way out the door. That orgy should be finished."

"That's certainly the easiest way to eat a Pop Tart," Trey bellows back.

Blanche and Arthur crack up with me.

"We can't divert from our mission!" Adam barks.

Demitri looks over his shoulder as Presley, Stella, and Deb block Victoria from following. "The A-squad bodyguards are covering," he announces. "Make a break for it!"

"You should hire *them*, Trey, because your guys SUCK!" Adam fires off.

The door slams behind us as Victoria throws a raging fit.

So . . . How did it go? Well . . .

I'm exhausted . . . I'll fill you in later. I need a damn nap. Just suffice it to say, there was counseling, a whole lot of quantum physics connections made, swimming, and they ate all the Pop Tarts. Their *Iliad* hero prize dreams were unrealized, but Pop Tarts really are a nifty runner-up.

Special thanks to the incredible team of models that keep pulling through for me over and over. Thank you to Deidre Michelle for her endless ability to find the right people to depict these characters. Thank you to Tino Duvick, Anna Hall, Kyle Fager, and Stephen Knezovich for making this series magic. Thank you to Bear and Carol for their endless conceptual support.

MELISSA VELASCO is a true explorer of the arts. With a well-rounded background as a choreographer, professor, dance teacher, stage manager, author, and Crystal Grid teacher, she thrives in creation. At her core, she believes that the arts save lives and provide a route for passion and connection. The artistic ride makes life a whole lot brighter.

With a quick wit, often edgy mouth, and loud laugh, Melissa exuberantly embraces life. To find balance from the mental cacophony in her head, she enjoys expansive views in her mountain home. Her ideal day involves a mug of hot tea, music playing, and a whole day to write. Her greatest loves are her three children and husband. The four pillars of her ultimate happiness include her family, friends, dance, and laughter.

www.ingramcontent.com/pod-product-compliance
Lightning Source LLC
Chambersburg PA
CBHW021328310726
48971CB00001B/31